RUSSIAN KEYS

BOOK ONE

G. A. Ross

RUSSIAN KEYS

BOOK ONE

Vanguard Press

VANGUARD PAPERBACK

© Copyright 2019
G. A. Ross

A CIP catalogue record for this title is
available from the British Library.

ISBN 978 1 784655 27 3

Vanguard Press is an imprint of
Pegasus Elliot MacKenzie Publishers Ltd.
www.pegasuspublishers.com

First Published in 2019

Vanguard Press
Sheraton House Castle Park
Cambridge England

Printed & Bound in Great Britain

Dedication

To the six-man crew of the fishing vessel, Premier Ins. 121
lost with all hands, 12th January 1990

CHAPTER ONE

Major James Anderson, retired, scanned the company around his yard. Smoke from the barbecue had long gone but before departure it had arranged people up-wind beside the shearing shed against which his old motorbike was parked. The bike was harnessed between the shafts of a rickety leaf-gathering buggy.

People were milling around eating and drinking, occasional laughter becoming more frequent with consumption. The Leper, as he was known locally, watched and waited from the shade of the veranda. It was not a party; it was a wake and he had a promise to keep.

He took a deep breath and strode from his comfort zone. People he could live without but sometimes he had to tolerate them. This was such an occasion. His recluse standing he could shake off at will, but the smell of eucalyptus concentrate was impossible to remove; it was engrained into him, being his main source of income for the last fifty years. Tall, upright and with a spring in his step which depicted his military connection, his eighty years of age was well concealed.

Leper! Major! Jock! He was greeted with all three and acknowledged all three as was his way. The dog followed close behind the swishing plaids of his kilt. He socialised and traded small talk about his health, the weather and what was below his kilt. Nothing changed and he had answers for all but his focus was on one person and eventually he managed to get him isolated.

"Thanks for putting this on. You're looking well," Ian complimented him.

The Leper acknowledged with a grunt.

"Laddie! When they leave, you stay here! Alone! That's an order." He turned away and joined the others, throwing the remains of his hamburger to the sheep dog.

Ian looked curiously after him and decided not to question why. He followed him, beer in hand, and joined his brother and sister, both engrossed in conversation about abalone and the dangers of white sharks. His mother, Maria, was close by engaged with neighbours she hadn't seen in many years.

Ian took it all in. "Changed days," he muttered. Mobile phones and internet; the Leper even had a TV but his eyes were drawn south across the home paddock. In the distance, he could see the roof of his father's shearing shed, rusted iron with a smoke haze hanging over it. With mixed feelings, he joined the conversation with Joe and Debbie; he was glad to see them but he wasn't happy to be here. The Leper had demanded he attend.

The funeral was in Kingscote some twenty miles away; there were more in attendance than expected but the island was sparsely populated. Obligation or sympathy for the family must have played a part. Certainly not love for the deceased.

"Rub some of the Leper's brew on you, that will keep the bloody sharks away," Ian announced, joining his twin and younger sister.

"Would kill a brown dog that shit. Or pickle it like the Leper," Joe returned.

"Embalmed!" Debbie added glancing sideways, "Here's trouble," she whispered.

Mr Young, the banker, approached courteously.

"Debbie, you have grown into something special. Boys! Glad to see you in attendance. May I take a moment to put you all at ease?" Young smiled.

Joe frowned; *at ease* was the last thing he expected from this man.

"There is nothing owed to the bank from the estate. All debts have been cleared," he said, looking at each stunned face.

They, in turn, looked at each other in disbelief but, before they could speak, Young added, "Mr Talbot will explain all to you tomorrow when you have your meeting; eleven a.m., I believe?" he queried.

"At his office," Joe confirmed.

Young excused himself and returned to the largest group which included Maria and Talbot.

A small, squealing pig rounded the shearing shed closely followed by the sheepdog, laughter filling the air as the pig sought refuge on top of the motorbike, slid off, and scattered the onlookers with the collie hard behind.

"Away with you, hound! Sheep have wool, you bloody idiot!" the Leper screamed at the dog.

Between the pig and the beer the ice was broken. They began to relax and moved back to the veranda, all ushered by the Leper who demanded they remove themselves from the battlefield before the next attack.

Ian locked eyes with the Leper who held his finger to his mouth. He got the message and mingled with the others, exchanging banter courteously; they were all very friendly, which surprised him considering his father's reputation. Sympathy was endemic; for the first time he was glad he had come and Maria had melted also. That in itself was a victory considering the circumstances of her and the children's departure.

At length, people started to excuse themselves and head away in various directions, mostly to neighbouring farms but some back to Kingscote, Young and Talbot the latter. Ian tried to think up an excuse to stay back and eventually settled on his hire car. Going round to where it was parked to drain the dragon, as he put it, he let down the rear driver's tyre and re-joined what were now only family and the Leper.

He got little sympathy from them when he informed them about the flat tyre.

"OK!" he insisted. "You go on ahead, I'll fix this and be in Kingscote before you," he said, holding one finger up to Joe.

"Like hell you will, I'll drive," was the reply from Joe, who hurriedly ushered Maria and Debbie into Debbie's car.

"Clever!" commented the Leper.

"Got a pump?" asked Ian before Joe's car cleared the cattle ramp.

"Better than that I have a compressor, but talk first. Come into the house," came the reply.

Ian had stayed in the house many times when he was young, and when he had attempted to help his father. After leaving university he had started visiting Korena. Only once had Russell spoken to him and that was only to ask who he was. Total rejection was hard to accept but it made Ian determined and he came back many times each accomplishing the same result.

"He's no right in the head, laddie," the Leper had insisted.

Ian looked at the bayonets he played with by the fire, the dress sword still above the fireplace, a Gordon tartan plaid with a bearskin busby adorned one corner; the place was clean and tidy as it always had been.

"When are you *scheduled* to go back to Vietnam?" the Leper cut into his memories.

"In a week," Ian replied, wondering about the emphasis on 'scheduled'.

"That's no going tae happen. Let's go and get the compressor running," the Leper beckoned; taking a ring of keys from behind the door, he headed out of the house and Ian followed.

"You respect my judgement, laddie?" the Leper threw at him over his shoulder.

"Yep!" Ian replied.

They entered the shearing shed, which was anything but a shearing shed, with large vats at the far wall and stacks of eucalyptus leaves wherever they could be stored. The place reeked of eucalyptus; the concentrate the Leper produced was very strong and in demand. The compressor was attached to some kind of press and it was disconnected quickly. It fired up first time and was very noisy. The Leper grabbed Ian's shoulder.

"Now we talk – sit down," he commanded.

"What? With all that bloody noise?" Ian shouted.

"Aye it's what we need – Noise! Now! Listen to me and don't say a word till I'm done," the Leper instructed, shaking his finger in warning, his lips close to Ian's ear.

Ian gave him a 'whatever' shrug and relaxed on a bundle of leaves; he had many lectures from the Leper when he was growing up, another one wouldn't make any difference.

"This is gonna take two minutes, that's all. I'll get straight to the point. Your old man came here two weeks ago and spilled his guts. He was sober for the first time since Maria left. I listened to what he had to say and, believe me, that was a hard decision. I *decided* your father was not such a selfish bastard as he led everybody to believe. That's my judgement, and that's final! No argument!" He glared at Ian.

Ian stared at him; the Leper had hated his father. The Leper had even threatened to kill him if he ever beat up his wife again. For the Leper to be siding with his father was unheard of. For his father to come here was also unheard of, they detested one another.

The Leper reached into the silver edged sporran hanging around his waist and pulled out a USB memory stick. Ian eyed it and was even more puzzled; no way, neither his father nor the Leper could use a computer as far as he was aware. He had hung his old computer and a book called the idiot's guide to computers on the door at Korena two years ago but had concluded Russell had probably dumped it. Unlike Joe, who had given up, Ian was determined he would help Russell whether he wanted help or not, but he could never even speak to the bastard. The time lapse between his first attempt to make contact and when Maria had ran away with the three children was ten years. In that time things had gone downhill badly. He looked at the leathery face of the Leper curiously.

"Take this! Whatever it is! According to your father, everything you need to know is on there." He thrust the stick into Ian's hand.

"Quiet! I'm not done," the Leper barked before Ian could speak.

"I said you respect my judgement. This judgement is not for discussion. I have been an honourable man all my life. Here! The damage was done long ago and you're the victims. Compensation is an honourable thing. You must do as I ask and trust me more than you have ever done in your life!" the Leper barked sternly.

Ian remained silent and stared at him, bewildered.

"You must go back to Vietnam within the next forty-eight hours. Guard this thing with your life! Three numbers you must remember: eighty, seventy, thirty-five – my age, your father's age, and your age – ya got that?" the Leper barked.

"Yeh! eighty, seventy and thirty-five, what the hell are they for?" Ian asked but was ignored.

"Remember this! Count number seven from the bottom as number one. That's my duty done. That's the message from your father. Don't speak to anybody about this. I'm only the messenger. That's the instructions he gave me, but only if you came to the funeral. If you didn't come I had to burn the thing!" the Leper stressed.

"Hang on a minute. You trying to tell me he knew he was going to die! How the hell did he know that?" Ian queried, his voice laced with scepticism.

"No questions! Everything you need ta know is on the thing I gave ya." The Leper handed Ian an envelope he took from inside his shirt.

"Here! It's a ticket for tomorrow's flight to Adelaide. Go and blow that bloody tyre up and get the hell out of here," the Leper ordered.

"Tomorrow afternoon flight? Bugger off!" Ian retorted.

"Believe me, laddie, this is deadly serious, you must go!" the Leper ordered.

Ian stared at the envelope and the USB; *what the hell is this all about?* he thought, as with his other hand he dragged the compressor to the car.

"Sure your name's Anderson and not bloody Bond?" he threw at the Leper.

"Move your arse! An alcoholic, stinking of drink in a ditch with a broken neck. An achievement for a man who hadn't had a drink for over a month. They didn't test his blood, there was no need, and I said nothing, not very honourable," the Leper whispered into his ear as he connected the air hose. Kneeling beside him he grabbed Ian's arm in his strong, bony fingers.

"Don't fuck around, boy. Blow the bloody tyre up and get the hell out of here. One dead and you could be next. Get the hell off this island," the Leper hissed into his ear. The curse had the desired effect. Ian had never heard the Leper use that swear word before. He realised how serious this was to make him swear.

"He was murdered? That's what you're saying. So, why the hell didn't you go to the cops? Bullshit!" Ian stated.

"Aye, it crossed my mind, laddie. But your father couldn't go to the cops, and after you find out what's on that thing you'll understand why. He never lost his fingers in a car accident. He never caused the fire that burnt the house down. And he didn't go to the cops. It's his wish you make your own judgement. It's *my* wish *you* finish what your father started," the Leper snarled.

15

"I need time to think," Ian heard himself say.

"Don't think! Follow orders! You can do all the thinking you like when you reach Vietnam. Now bugger off!" The Leper turned and walked away pulling the compressor behind him.

Had it been anyone other than the Leper who had dished out the orders as if it was his god given right to do so, Ian would have told him to go to hell. The Leper! That was different; there had to be a genuine reason for him to be acting the way he was. He didn't take any prisoners when dealing with people – especially Ian's father, whom he hated with a vengeance. Ian drove the car out of the station track, kicking up dust and rattling the cattle grid with speed. He soon reached the site where his father was killed. The car had been recovered from the ditch and there was little sign that anything had happened here. He didn't even slow down as he headed for Kingscote, hot on the heels of his family, his mind in a whirl.

He had to be drunk to go off the road there, he had to be, there was little damage to the car, he wasn't wearing a seat belt but wasn't speeding, no sign of skid marks, no potholes, nothing to force him into the ditch. He was drunk, stinking of drink and had probably fallen asleep at the wheel. That was what everybody had been told and that was no surprise to anybody. Now, the Leper comes away with this shit.

"We're not gonna dig the bugger up now to find out. Eighty, seventy, thirty-five and number one is number seven: what the hell's that about?" He spoke to himself feeling the USB in his pocket. He was more than tired, he was exhausted and he had learned long ago that his judgement was seriously impaired when in this state. The flight from Vietnam via Singapore and Adelaide was long and tedious. He only had two hours sleep before coming to the island and it had caught up with him.

Joe was leaning on his car when Ian pulled up behind him. Rivalry was not dead and he immediately started to wind him up. Ian let him ramble on.

"You look buggered," Joe finished with.

"You got that right. Stuff you! I would have beaten you if the bloody Leper hadn't insisted the tyre was nipped on the cattle grid and pumped it up to make sure. Bloody foot pump took forever but he was right! So now I don't have to screw around with a puncture repair, but I need to sleep," Ian responded.

He ignored the remarks Joe fired at him about stamina, lasting the pace and being a wimp.

He made for his room with his case and threw himself on the bed. The Leper could go to hell if he thought he was leaving on the afternoon flight to Adelaide. He fell asleep wondering how the car went into the ditch.

Talbot's office was a short walk from the hotel as was everything in Kingscote. They went there after breakfast and a little early. He greeted them and immediately ushered them into a back room for privacy.

"Everything is ready and we are all here, so we might as well get on with it, be seated. I'm so glad he came in only last month and made a will. Makes everything much simpler," he began.

"Was he sober?" blurted Ian, louder than he had intended, and Maria shot him a look.

"I believe he was," came the tactical reply from Talbot who also cast Ian a stare over his glasses as he raised the will aloft. "Of sound body and mind!" he reminded all of them.

"Before we go any further do you want all the jargon that accompanies such documents or can I get straight to the point?" He looked to Maria who nodded.

"Right, I mention documents because there are two and one is relevant to the other. One is your grandfather's will, the other your father's," he addressed Ian, Joe and Debbie.

"I will read the extract from your grandfather's will which is dated June, 1960.

"The area of land four thousand acres known as Huntly Station will remain in the custody of Major James Anderson for his lifetime." Talbot looked up.

"That is the relevant fact from your grandfather's will and it goes on considerably to cover all eventualities. Major Anderson has comprehensive protection for life."

The family looked at one another in disbelief. At length, Debbie spoke, "Are you trying to tell us that my father owned Huntly?" she asked in astonishment.

"You mean you didn't know! Maria, you must have known?" Talbot said quietly.

"Only that it belonged to Grandfather's brother before Major Anderson," she replied.

"Yes. I have made some enquiries – a bit before my time but I believe he was killed in Korea and Major Anderson's regiment, the Gordon Highlanders, relieved the Australians just in time or they would all have died, your grandfather included. After the war the Major was invited here and he has been here ever since. They were mates, the major and your grandfather." Talbot gave a big sigh and continued, "Thus the restraint on the present will. Do you understand?"

They all muttered they understood and Talbot picked up another document from the table. He read:

"I, Russell John Ingles, being of sound mind and body bequeath all my worldly possessions to my wife, Maria Tottemanti, to dispose of as she sees fit." Talbot put the document down.

"That's it folks; he left everything to you Maria. That's why I insisted you attend. Mr Young has informed you all that there is no longer any debt on the property; however, I have something to add to that. Major Anderson insists the property, Korena Station, remains in the family until his death. In the event Korena Station is sold prior to his death, the debt, which runs to eighty thousand dollars, Australian, will be subtracted from the purchase price as per agreement with the bank. To all effect, the station is viable and must be worked! These are his conditions. There are no time frames attached to these conditions, so take your time. When you leave here, you're under no pressure to make decisions. As your lawyer, I strongly advise you to comply with the major's wishes. He is eighty years old, God bless him, but he can't live forever despite being pickled. Consider all the facts before reaching a decision," Talbot advised.

Ian leapt to his feet.

"Unbelievable! I expected debts that only the sale of the station could cover, now, the debts are clear and we have two stations not one. Bloody brilliant I reckon!" Ian beamed.

Talbot smiled. "*Maria* has two stations," he pointed out.

"*We* have two stations," Maria corrected him.

She stood up, embracing each of her family in celebration. Debbie was ecstatic and could barely contain her enthusiasm. Joe had a furrow of perception along his brow as he eyed Ian who nodded his understanding. What would this mean to their way of life? Who was going to run the station? An avalanche of problems still existed.

"As I said there is no time frame attached to this agreement. However, I fear the longer you delay in getting Korena Station up and running, the more expensive it will become. If you require to borrow money, I have Mr Young's assurance that money is available," Talbot said, holding out his hand to Maria.

They left a lot more relieved than when they had arrived on the ferry from Adelaide. They ambled back to the hotel; they were out of the funeral garb and out of the shit. They were in high spirits and rightly so. All had feared total forfeit of the station and probable liability, if its sale couldn't cover the debts. A catalogue of disasters had befallen Korena Station after Maria had removed the children and herself. A car accident had turned Russel to drink and everything went downhill from there. The fire which destroyed the house and machinery had forced the station into debt. Assets had slowly siphoned away over the bar and despite Ian's attempts to help him, Russel had rejected every offer of help. Ian even had to stay with the Leper as he wasn't welcome in Korena.

Plenty of tourists were walking around Kingscote and many were in the hotel and around the jetty a short distance away. For some reason, Ian found himself searching faces as if somebody was watching him. He excused himself from the offer of coffee and headed for his room. How the hell he was supposed to leave here within a day was a challenge. How he was going to tell the others he was leaving was an even bigger challenge and why the Leper wanted him to leave, especially now, was beyond him. He fumbled the USB which he had slept with in his pocket, and remembered the envelope the Leper had given him. He opened it and the flight ticket was there, but immediately he saw it was made out in Joe's name.

"Stupid old bugger," Ian muttered.

What the hell's this? A mistake or is the old bastard trying to tell me something? He sat on the edge of the bed staring at the ticket and the reason he had it. Suddenly he twigged. "Leper! you cunning bastard," he mumbled.

Identical twins, easy swap. Same clothes and nobody would know who the hell was who. He had to shave. Joe didn't have a beard. This was going to hurt; he always had a beard but the orders he had been given by the Leper and his belief that Ian's life was in danger spurred him into action.

He joined the others five minutes later clean shaven and with denim on top and bottom just like Joe.

"Wow! You look ten years younger," Debbie complimented.

"Yeh! Ya old bastard, you look the same age as me," added Joe.

"I've got bad news people. That was Vietnam on the phone, I've to go back immediately. My back to back is in a hell of a state offshore, and he wants me there ASAP," Ian announced with a serious air.

"You've gotta be jokin? You just got here!" exclaimed Debbie, her disappointment very evident.

"Yeh, it's a bastard but hopefully it's not a big problem, but could be. As soon as we've got everything under control I'll come back," Ian assured her.

"What's happened?" Maria exclaimed.

"Excessive gas pressure; they might have to drill a relief well, worst scenario, but the pressure might reduce. Two days to decide one way or the other," Ian declared.

"How long to drill a relief well?" asked Joe.

"Three months, ninety days at least – but that would be the last resort. I think it'll reduce with other measures. Keep the chin up! Debbs, I might be back next week." He laughed, and ruffled her short blonde hair.

"When can you leave? The ferry doesn't come back for two days?" Maria pointed out.

"I'll see what I can arrange flight wise if you can drop off the car in Adelaide, Joe? What about Dan the man, Debbs, you reckon he could help out over here?" Ian asked.

"Dan the drone," Joe added; Ian gave him a questioning look.

"He's into drones now! Takes photographs of places hard to reach." Joe grinned.

"Don't bloody start!" Debbie threw Joe a warning look.

"That could be sore!" Ian jibed and got a kick in the shin for his effort.

Maria was more serious. "That's a good idea, it's about time he had a job, and there's plenty to be done at Korena. See if you can get him here as soon as you can," she half suggested, half ordered Debbie.

A group of tourists came and sat close to them and Ian gave Joe the nod to follow him.

"You have a rucksack?" Ian asked.

"Yep! Travel light," replied Joe.

"Go get it, I'll leave most of my gear here. No point in lugging it to Vietnam and back here again." He handed Joe his room key and headed towards the reception.

After skirting the contents of a tourist brochure, Ian headed back to his room. Joe was already inside with the rucksack.

"That'll do, everything taken care of. Flight at 1400 and checked out already," he said, putting on a baseball cap.

"Where's mine?" Joe enquired. Ian ignored him.

"I can stay for a while, no problem. Our Abalone quota is nearly full and the season's nearly finished. Anyway, there is too much teeth knocking about over there. Them do-good bastards want to go down under with their pets, they'd shit themselves, bloody conservation." Joe groaned.

"You still have a power head?" Ian asked.

"You're damned right I do. They come within range of the Sling, and that's the end of them, fuck the conservationists." It was Joe's favourite subject as it was with most Abalone divers.

"See if you can make up a list of everything that needs to be done at Korena. The Leper should know what livestock still exists. I think he's been looking after the animals for a while by the look of things. The house!" Ian shook his head. "God knows what state that's in, but bad enough they didn't want us to see it till its dunged out, as Talbot put it. If Debbs can get Dan to fix that up we can pay him. Don't take Maria near there till the cleaners are finished," he warned Joe.

"OK, you only have two hours to get to the airport." Joe looked at his watch. "Piss off when all the work has to be done, eh," he jibed.

"Little choice. Here, take this back to your room, that's all I need to take with me and the laptop." He handed Joe his suitcase and slung the backpack onto one shoulder. He checked the side pocket of the laptop bag for his passport as Joe disappeared. Going out the back door he put both bags onto the back seat of his hire car, locked it and went back inside to re-join the others. Formalities over and promising to get back as soon as possible the two brothers left for the airport.

"I drive!" Ian insisted. "You get back and sort out what you can," Ian instructed Joe as he took his place at the wheel. "I'll go straight through, no point in you coming in. Here! You can have this cap," Ian offered.

He clapped his baseball cap onto Joe's head and gave it a thump with his palm. A driver with a cap to the airport. A driver with a cap back from the airport. Joe's bag, Joe's name on the ticket, what the hell! Ian thought, cursing the Leper.

"Arsehole! Don't screw around up there. Get your arse back here as soon as you can," Joe pleaded.

Security was, as most semi-bush airports are, a flutter with reality. Through check-in, through security and into the waiting room in two minutes without any identification being asked for, nor provided. It used to be called civilisation before these bastards started blowing planes up; however, it was highly unlikely anybody would want to blow up the plane from Kangaroo Island to Adelaide.

Ian had to go to Melbourne to catch the only flight available to Ho Chi Minh City (Saigon), as most people now called it. Another long-haul flight left him in the same state as the last one. He took the hydrofoil to Vung Tau, a ninety-minute hell raiser journey down the Saigon River at over sixty kilometres an hour; even exhausted he loved this journey. He took a taxi to Truong Gong Dinh Street and the maid let him into his house.

"Mr Ian, you back! Very good, you want eat?" she asked, smiling broadly, a gaggle of voices coming from behind her.

When the cat's away, the mice will play. Even when he went offshore half her family moved in, it was normal. He just smiled as they hurriedly packed and skittered around before leaving, all ten of them.

Vui arrived with noodles and chicken; he ate most of it and fell asleep on the settee, out for the count. The return journey was a nightmare. Waiting in Melbourne and Bangkok had meant taking twenty-four hours for him to reach Saigon, and another four to get home. All his electronics had died long ago which he concluded was probably for the best in his state of irritation.

CHAPTER TWO

Debbie had gone to see Talbot first thing in the morning. He informed her that the cleaners were still at Korena, and it was their choice whether they wanted to visit the house or wait. Maria wasn't keen, she would have preferred to wait, however, she resigned herself to the inevitable. They arrived at noon; heavy smoke was hanging over the buildings and Maria had to be prompted to get out of the car. Reluctantly, she resigned herself to facing her demons. It had been twenty years since she left in the middle of the night with the children, fearing for their lives. The twins were ten and Debbie a babe in arms. She could hear the screams and threats now and her heart sunk. Despite the fact this wasn't the same house, it looked similar and it was in the same place.

"Come on, Mum, it's over," Debbie encouraged, taking Maria's hand.

"What a bloody mess. Fifteen years old, looks more like a hundred and fifteen," commented Joe, looking at the house. Several broken windows were boarded up and faded paint was flaking everywhere. Smoke hung in the air, adding the smell of a garbage dump to the scene. A figure appeared around the side of the house and looked at the visitors. Hooded with a dust mask on and gloves, a sense of filth was projected by the protective clothing and they stopped dead when they saw him.

"I'm not going inside. Wait until the cleaners are finished," Maria stated and pulled back on Debbie's hand.

The figure lifted his arm in greeting but didn't approach. Another figure could be seen by the smouldering fire. He was dressed like the first and looked at them from a distance.

"Joe! It's not the time," Debbie announced, feeling her mother shaking.

Joe stopped in mid step and looked at them, then the house.

"OK. We can go and see the Leper; we need a list of livestock and machinery." He lifted his arm to the onlooker, turned and went back to the car with Debbie and Maria. There were more important issues they had to take care of and the cleaners were taking care of this. He drove towards Huntly Station to see the Leper.

IN VUNG TAU

Ian woke to a most hellish thirst and he was covered in sweat. The sun was belching in through the sliding doors that opened into the garden and it was bloody hot. His clothes were stinking and after a drink of water he headed into the shower. The sleep cascaded from him along with the cold water and he had only one thing on his mind. What the hell was this all about? Half dry, he set up the laptop and inserted the USB.

COPY COORDINATES AND DESTROY.

"More orders," he mumbled and read on.

"You're reading this, they did what they said they would and you're next. Make no mistake, boy, you have two choices. Go to the cops with this or go and find Lacey. If you go and find Lacey, there's a chance they'll kill you. If you go to the cops, you can live with the consequences. YOUR CHOICE!

In 1975 I got discharged from the army and went a bit wild after Vietnam, me and my mate, Lacey. Eventually, we ended up in the Opal Fields at Andamooka. We spent a year and a half there but didn't find much. We decided to rob the opal dealers who came from Japan regularly.

Took six months to plan. There's three ways to get out. North, east or south. No way to get far before they find you by road or overland.

Nobody would go west, it's salt lake and desert. Tracks would be easy to follow and Woomera Radar would detect anything in the air. So we went west under the radar with a microlight at night.

That's the major detail you need to know. The rest is well documented. We had three stops with fuel. Lacey reached the first and second stops to re-fuel. He didn't reach the third. I was waiting at the third stop with transport but he never came. I went searching for a week until I ran out of water but I couldn't find him. He had no food or water with him, so I reckoned he must be dead.

The cop at Andamooka was called Fletcher, a hard bastard. He was escorting the dealers. Shortly after I got back to Adelaide he pulled me in for questioning. They were tracking everybody who had been in Andamooka; they couldn't find Lacey and I couldn't account for the week after the robbery. That was when I was looking for him. The cops couldn't prove anything and let me go but Fletcher nailed me the next night when I left the bar and beat me up. I thought he was going to kill me, he was like a maniac. He knew that I knew what had happened to Lacey. We were mates, we went to war together, we did everything together and we were Fletcher's suspects for the robbery.

I reckoned they were watching me day and night, so I headed back to Korena. This robbery was hit or miss. At best, we reckoned on ten to fifteen thousand dollars, no more, and it would all blow over quickly. Were we wrong! Cooper Pedy had a big strike and black opals among them. That, with what the dealers picked up in Andamooka, put the value up to over half a million. Then the shit hit the fan. Looked like the whole bloody world was looking for what is now known as the mookas and some are still looking, but looking in the wrong place. God knows what the value is now.

Things went quiet for the next three years. Your mother and I got married and the two of you were around. I got my first taste of what was to come. Your mother was told I had been hit by a car. It was an axe that took off my two fingers and broke my leg. That was my big mistake, because I didn't tell the cops what happened. I suspect Fletcher had me done over.

Now he knew I was involved and it got worse. In the end, when Debbie was born I had to get you all away from me before their patience ran out. NOW IT HAS! Seems there's new players involved. My only shield was to live as I did. I was the only one who might have the information they wanted and the bastards knew they couldn't break me. They tried, even fired the house, and a hell of a lot more.

Our family has paid the price and I have done the time. Choice is, tell them what I know or tell you and telling you puts you in the same position as I was but at least you have the choice of going to the cops. Had I gone to them you would never have been born, I would have got life. My biggest guilt is not finding Lacey: he was my best mate and I might have left him to die. For that I would have landed twelve years, and likely the same again for the robbery. I wished it was possible that Lacey pissed off with all the loot. I know he didn't, that was impossible, if he had he would have gone east, he went west as planned.

There's a cairn of stones on a ledge beside the first coordinate with an old penny under it. We had no GPS in those days but I managed to get a GPS map and I remember exactly where the fuel stops were. The coordinates are as close as dammit. Likewise, at the second and third, at each, fifty paces ninety degrees to the ledges you will find the fuel and water cans and some lamps. Lacey only had a compass and a full moon for the first and second legs but we reckoned it could be timed for daylight to reach the third. He made the second which took him clear of the lake but didn't make the third.

There are a hundred coordinates, but only three that matter. He had a range of one hundred and fifty miles max with the extra fuel tank we fitted. Where he is, I don't know but where he was heading to and coming from was number two fuel dump to number three. That narrows things down to about ten thousand square miles of desert; he's in there somewhere.

The best trackers in Australia worked on this, hundreds of searches; they found nothing because they were searching in the wrong place. The media speculated it was an inside job planned for a large shipment and so on. They also concluded the best place to hide opals is in the Opal Field which was fine by me. It was about three years after they cut my fingers off Fletcher disappeared. Then the pilot of the plane disappeared. The media made a big deal of that. I've no idea what happened to the Japanese but it was then they started on me again. Fletcher was on my case. He had a private vendetta, but then, HE disappeared.

I had to give the impression I had cracked and hit the bottle. I had to run up debts and I had to get all of you away from me in a way that was permanent, before focus shifted from me to all of you. I had to become the selfish bastard you remember and probably hated. That was my objective: to keep you all safe and believe me it wasn't easy

That was it! Every birthday, Easter, Xmas a card would arrive with where is Lacey? on it; (This is your last invitation our patience has expired and you will soon) that was the last card on my birthday and if you're reading this you tell me what happened. There's some money in the roof of the dog's kennel (inside) I didn't drink the lot.

Whatever way you want to go is OK by me. The only request I have is bury my mate, Lacey, with me if you find him.

Father."

The next pages contained all the coordinates. Ian immediately cut and pasted them into his file. He checked they were there, only the coordinates, and printed them out. Three copies. Deleted the memory stick and removed it. Going into the kitchen he took the cleaver Vui used and smashed the stick to pieces. He was shaking. He sat down stunned; no words could describe his feelings and he ran out of profanities trying.

"The stupid, old bastard!" being his last.

His head was in a spin and he couldn't think straight. He was in shock and just stared at the wall, he couldn't believe what he had just read. He couldn't accept it. It was crazy, but everything fitted the mould. He read it over and over in disbelief and shook his head accordingly but the Leper's words kept ringing in his ears.

"You trust my judgement, laddie?" He did, and this was his judgement. If the Leper believed him after years of bad blood he had to believe it. But he couldn't.

Ian grabbed the house phone. His mobile was still flat, he forgot to charge it; he called Joe's mobile.

"About bloody time you phoned, I've called you heaps of times and no answer," Joe yelled.

"Where are you?" Ian asked.

"Huntly! The house is being cleaned out and most of the rubbish cleared. Maria didn't want to go inside."

"Who cleaned out the house, Joe?" Ian asked.

"Buggered if I know them, they came across from Adelaide. They clean out dead people's houses," came the reply.

"Don't let anybody see you doing this and KYBMS – Keep Your big mouth shut," Ian ordered him.

"Fire away," Joe answered.

"Find a kennel and see if there's anything hidden inside the roof. Phone me back yes or no and KYBMS." Ian rung off and waited.

A good business if you can get into it or a good way to ransack a house and get paid for it. Ian thought. He recovered the sheets of print and stuck them into his computer case.

IN HUNTLY

The Leper was showing Maria and Debbie the finer points of distilling concentrate. They were in the shearing shed and Korena was close. Joe decided to head back alone. As he approached the station, he saw a camper van pulling out onto the road and heading for Kingscote. He didn't see anybody around the station when he pulled up at the house, and reckoned they must have gone to eat or whatever. He went out back and looked for a doghouse, and he hoped there wasn't a dog in it. He found one tucked in beside the wood shed. *In the roof look inside,* Ian had instructed. There was no dog and he stuck his head through the entrance and looked up. It was dark but he made out the outline of something stuck to the roof, material of

30

some kind. He ripped it off and came out holding a piece of denim with something inside the folds.

His pulse raced as he felt the unmistakable feel of banknotes. He gasped as he looked at the bills and quickly shoved them into his pocket, looking around to see if anyone was watching. He saw nobody and wiped his hands on the denim.

How the hell did he know that was there? Joe pondered as he returned to Huntly.

KYBMS – A long time since they had used their twin talk. A long time.

IN VUNG TAU

Ian paced the small garden for an hour; it was as hot as hell in the sun, but he barely noticed. How his father had lived with this for twenty-five years was beyond understanding. Not being able to speak about it to anybody and living the life of an alcoholic as cover, broken and missing limbs, would break most people. Not to mention losing his family and friends. Ian was desperate to speak to somebody, he needed a confidant he could trust and he was in Huntly Station. He had only the information for an hour and he hated it.

Vui broke his concentration shouting to him to come and eat. He wasn't hungry but went through with it. Even his taste buds had rebelled and nothing tasted of anything. He cursed the fact he had told Joe anything over the phone, anybody could be listening but he had no choice. If there was nothing there, the rest of the information was a load of garbage; if there was money there it was confirmation that it wasn't garbage. He resigned himself to wait.

IN HUNTLY

Maria came out of the shed with Debbie and the Leper who was scolding her mother for smoking. Maria lit up and blew smoke at him in reply. They were both a lot more up-beat than when they had arrived. They saw Joe coming and went to meet him.

"Where the hell have you been?" Debbie asked.

"Get into the car we're going back to Korena. There's nobody there, they must have gone to eat somewhere. We can look around outside, we don't have to go into the house," Joe fired at Maria.

"Go! the three of you. I'll follow shortly on the bike," the Leper ordered.

"Thank God for that!" Debbie muttered.

Surprisingly, Maria agreed and they headed back. The Leper followed several minutes later in the settling dust with buggy and his dog.

"Let's have a look around!" Debbie shouted excitedly and headed for the large shearing shed.

It wasn't as bad inside as it looked from the outside. Daylight shafted through some small holes in the roof but the pens and the four stands looked in good enough nick. Shears were rusted but not badly, the lanolin had protected the metal as it had on all the hinges and latches. The wool press was filthy and smelled. Everything in there was rundown, but not beyond restoration.

"How many sheep and cattle have survived?" Debbie spoke aloud.

"We'll have to ask the Leper that, they must be in the outside paddocks; nothing here, only chickens, and the eggs haven't been picked up for a hundred years. There's eggs everywhere," Joe stated with his hand in his pocket trying to count notes.

"Stop playing with your nuts!" Debbie ordered.

He burst out laughing. No nuts. No smoke. God help Dan the drone. She was back to normal, Joe noted with satisfaction.

The Leper handed Maria a sheet of paper. "That's what belongs to Korena," he said.

"You're a mind reader," commented Joe, straining to see what was listed.

"Thirty-two beef cattle," Maria read but was cut short by the Leper.

"Aye, there was six bulls amongst them, five half grown. Too big for the calf cradle but he gave them a tranquiliser and we managed the rest! That quietened things down a bit. They were not happy beasts when they came to. That's what's left," he gruffed.

"I wonder why? Only twenty sheep from two hundred," she read on and read out, "One tractor, wake rake, culti-packer, mulesing cradle, seed drill. Ogre. And a lot of things I don't know what they are," Maria finished and handed the paper to Joe.

"That's a hell of a lot more stuff than I had expected," Debbie commented.

"The Kanga has been shearing your sheep the last few years, I'm too old for that caper and I told him to keep the wool as payment but he gave some money to Russell," the Leper added.

"What state is the livestock in?" Joe asked, concern in his voice.

"They're OK, the vet had a look when I moved them and he wasn't concerned – only about the bulls that weren't supposed to be bulls. And one sheep or pig dog, it's jumpin' oot its skin, that hound, rounds up anything that moves," the Leper confirmed as an afterthought, pointing to the collie waiting with his tongue hanging out in expectation.

Debbie looked at Joe whose hand was back in his pocket. He quickly withdrew it.

"The Leper has a fine way of dealing with those things," she warned.

"I have a flea. Piss off," he replied.

Joe was breaking his neck to call Ian and eventually managed to get far enough away from the company to do so.

Ian ran inside and grabbed his mobile, the charging cable attached.

"Yes!" was all he heard and he terminated the call instantly.

"Prick!" Joe shouted loud enough for all to hear.

"Clinker, won't answer a bloody phone," he explained; Clinker was the Sheller on his abalone boat.

"There's a thing, can't we get him here if you are finished for the season?" Maria asked.

"Yeh! That's what I was going to ask him but he won't pick up the phone. I'll call him later," answered Joe.

IN VUNG TAU

Ian sat down heavily on the garden seat. He had been unsure whether he wanted to hear *yes* or *no* but, in his heart of hearts, *yes* was what he wanted to hear. His heart was racing.

"Now what?" he asked himself and noticed the wires hanging from his phone. That jerked him into action and he fired up his motorbike; he needed the phone. He got a new charger from the phone shop in the corner of Lea Hong Fung just down the road and headed for the Rex Hotel. He didn't go into the hotel but parked at the bar built between the road and the swimming pool and went in. He was greeted like a long-lost bank account but managed to convey the message to plug in his phone before ordering a beer. He needed one.

IN KORENA

Joe had been ushered out of hearing distance of Maria and Debbie by the Leper and into the shed to see the state of the roof.

"Have ye spoken to Ian yet?" the Leper asked him quietly.

"Yep! Weird bastard hung up on me," Joe replied.

"Aye, he will do that. Now, I am giving you an order. Don't question anything Ian asks you to do, just do it. No matter how weird you think it is. All will be revealed when the time is right, but you must trust him and me until the time is right. Or I'll cut your balls off OK? Now listen to me. Try and find out who, exactly, the people who are dunging out the house are? Names, who is paying them, and so forth. Anything you can learn about them and don't arouse suspicion. Look after your nuts." The Leper slapped him on the back; he hadn't missed Debbie's jibe about the bulls.

"The plot thickens. Two bloody weirdos. Why? I take it is out of the question?" commented Joe

"It is! Now go! Let's see what the females are doing, never mind that." The Leper pointed to the roof. Joe followed, shaking his head.

The collie thought it was Xmas getting petted by Debbie. Maria, on the other hand, had great reservations about dogs and fleas. Floss was her name, so the Leper informed them, and she tagged on behind them as they walked around. They didn't go near the house for fear of upsetting Maria who kept glancing at it and looking away. The barn and other outhouses were in a shambles and stank of rotten vegetation and chicken shit. The hens had taken over the yard and were wild, scattering in all directions and making a hell of a noise. Surprisingly, the collie made no attempt to chase them or round them up and the hens weren't afraid of her, Debbie noted.

"I shot six for the barbecue… ya can't catch them," the Leper declared.

IN VUNG TAU

Ian was on his second beer before he slowed down. It was hot even with the fan on him and the pool was getting more inviting but he had no trunks with him. He looked at his watch; it was still morning and the wrong time to be guzzling beer. Adelaide was three and a half hours ahead. He reckoned the family would be heading back to Kingscote within the next few hours. He sipped the second can and recovered his phone; there were signs of life in it so he hadn't been sold a dud charger. That was a first.

He went out with the bike and onto the boulevard, intending to follow it to the start of Chong Cong Dinh Street and head home, but the breeze was just what he needed and he continued past the fishing fleet and ferry terminal gunning the small Honda on around the headland under the statue of Christ, which looked like the one in Rio and was nearly as big. The statue in Vung Tau allowed people to walk out on the arms and there were people out on the arms. Around the headland, the expanse of Back Beach opened up before him and, to his surprise, hundreds of people were out on the sand and in the water. Hotels had sprung up everywhere along this stretch, most catering for Korean and Taiwanese tourists. It looked good.

He hauled in by the big whale statue and had a moment looking at the beach close up. He was impressed instantly; no rubbish, food, bottles and debris of all kind used to litter this beach and it was a haven for beggars who pestered the hell out of everybody. He could see no beggars and the beach reminded him of Italian beaches around Rimini. They are swept clean and the people are very proud of their beach and rightly so; it was their livelihood. Maria had come from Rimini and he had taken her back to visit her mother before she died.

They're learning, he thought as he headed back via the huge memorial round-about and onto Le Hong Fung, turned at the phone shop and reached the house. He felt better having done something besides thinking; you couldn't think amongst the turmoil of traffic, you would be wiped out quickly.

He ate and lay on the bed, with the fan whirring at his feet; he dozed off and fell into a deep sleep.

It was dark when he woke up. Vui had gone home but left food for him in the fridge so her note said. He made coffee and switched the air conditioning on. He took the coordinates from the printer and glanced at them. He had to memorise the three relative to instructions just in case they disappeared. Without the numbers they were a shambles of positions which would make no sense to anybody. He couldn't separate them; they had to remain in the collective list or that would defeat the objective. He couldn't even highlight them and found even finding them a pain in the arse. He resorted to using chopsticks to point each one out and cursed his father for the hundredth time throwing several curses at the Leper as well. This was going to take a jar of coffee but it had to be done.

There was an easy way and he had contemplated that from the moment he realised that if these people are willing to kill for this information and he was the only one who had it, his life was now in danger. He could go straight to the cops and tell them all he knew and that would be the end of that.

He stared at the coordinates in front of him for a long time. Possibly the key to a fortune in opals was at his fingertips. He might have been rather abrupt in destroying the USB, he thought; but there again the only critical info there was the coordinates and the fact a microlight had been used. Once he had memorised the coordinates he had all the info required and he could go to the cops or not; it was a decision that could only be made after speaking with the family. This had to be their decision not just his. He resigned himself to a long night.

IN KINGSCOTE

Debbie had taken deliverance of a present from Floss and it had bitten her in a very private location. She was squirming to scratch the spot but was paranoid that Joe would see her. She tried the hand in pocket method, and it worked but Joe spotted her.

"Yep! Are you playing with your balls or have you got my flea?" Joe shouted.

She blushed deep red. "Shut up, you prick, everybody can hear you," she hissed.

They headed into the hotel, Debbie heading straight for her room. Joe and Maria went into the lounge. It was getting dark and several rod fishermen were heading for the jetty to fish for Snook. The jetty at Kingscote was very productive at night and it was lit, so many people who came for Pacific Salmon during daylight on the numerous beaches also fished the jetty at night. Joe nearly started with 'do you remember' but bit his tongue. It had not been unusual for them to get back to Korena with fifty pounds or more of Snook for a night's fishing. His father smoked them and they were delicious.

"Those cleaners, Mother. How come they were so quick on the job?" he asked Maria.

"So as the bank could sell the property. Then unknown to anybody the Leper paid off the debts and it is, what it is. Why?" she replied.

"So the bank will be paying for them?" Joe suggested.

"That's a good question. They won't be cheap: those people charge a lot of money. They clean out houses nobody else wants to go into, especially if somebody has died in the house," she trailed off.

"That's what I was thinking; nobody died in the house. It's just a clean out so they better not charge top dollar for that," Joe insisted.

"We can go and see Mr Young in the morning and find out," Maria replied.

Debbie soon joined them, she was flustered and starving. Joe looked at her.

"You look like a baked bean," he commented, observing the effect of very hot water on her already tanned skin.

"I got the flea! And the Leper gave me some of his eucalyptus oil. The old bastard never told me it would burn me alive. I was going round the shower like the wall of death before I got the water onto it. You try it on your balls." She flung the small vial at Joe.

"Stop it you two." Maria paused. "No! Getting back to normal is what we should be doing. We should be happy that things have turned out the way they have. We need to eat. I'm starving," she exclaimed.

They ate and chatted for a while, then Joe went for a shower. "Ten minutes," he informed Debbie, and he would be back for a beer.

"Good luck with your flea bite," she teased.

He got back to his room and pulled out the money. He counted it rapidly; just short of four thousand dollars.

"Bloody hell," he said to himself, stuffing the money into Ian's suitcase. He headed for the shower.

Maria had gone to her room but Debbie was sitting on the hotel veranda when he returned. It was a beautiful night, warm and no wind. They sipped several beers and observed a few of the Orientals who were in the dining room making their way, rods in hand, to the jetty. At length, Joe's curiosity got the better of him.

"Come on, let's go and see if these drongoes are catching anything," he instructed Debbie.

"No problem, I wondered how long it would take you," she replied.

They seemed to be all together, the Orientals. Clustered around a jetty light, staring at their rod tips, and gibbering.

"Any fish?" Joe enquired.

"No feesh," they replied as one.

Along the jetty, some young boys were using a squid jig, obviously locals.

"You got any snook hooks and split shot?" Joe asked.

"Yeh plenty, ready ganged, a dollar each," was the reply.

"Entrepreneurs, ripping off the tourists, you little shits. OK! Here's a dollar, give me one ganged and one split shot. And one white-bait, free."

The boy grabbed the dollar and handed Joe the tackle along with two white-bait.

"We have plenty," the boy informed him.

"I bet you have. I'll tell them where to get them." Joe smiled and headed back to the Orientals.

They got the message and wound in one of their lines. Joe bit off the tackle and tied on the hooks which were ganged, one point going through the eye of the other and both points facing the same direction. The Chinese, as they turned out to be, looked on with great concentration. About eighteen inches above the hooks Joe bit on the split shot. One hook through the eye and the other through the body of the white-bait; he used sign language to get the message across that the white-bait had to be perfectly straight and not wobble. They seemed to understand. He checked the tide. You had to fish on the lee side and close to the shadow or the line would hook-up on the jetty.

He cast out a short distance, pulled some slack line with his left hand, jammed the rod under his right elbow, and lowered the tip. He started walking slowly along the jetty keeping the rod perfectly straight. It was the feel of a feather he waited for and he didn't wait long. Instantly, he let go of the slack line and thrashed the rod with all his might. A small snook flew out of the water and landed a rod length ahead of him.

"Shit, it's an egg," he commented and handed the rod to its owner, who was ecstatic.

They left after the fish was landed and Joe suggested they throw it back and go for much bigger ones.

The entrepreneurs were quickly on the scene and he even got a 'thanks, mate' from one as he and Debbie headed back to the veranda.

"That's our contribution to the tourist industry over. Local knowledge, if you want to catch fish do it the way the locals do it," Joe boasted.

"Yeh, and if they want to catch fleas we can teach them that at well." Debbie laughed.

They were in good spirits and added a few more before going to bed. Joe was desperate to tell her about the money but Ian had told him to keep his bloody mouth shut. It could wait.

CHAPTER THREE

With the coordinates engrained in his head, Ian decided to test his memory. It was five a.m. and time he went for a run. He didn't jog if it was avoidable. He went hell for leather from beginning to end; he didn't see the point of wasting time. There were many runners out on the street and not so much traffic so he headed at a good pace for the Memorial roundabout. He knew his limitations, he had done this hundreds of times. Like driving a motorbike here, pedestrians also had to concentrate. Traffic lights were often disregarded, especially early in the morning and late at night. The bikes also were travelling faster and some had no lights. He had to concentrate or get hit, it was as simple as that.

He knew most of his fellow participants, it was pretty much the same mob every morning at the same time. He passed the 'Pile Driver' struggling on as usual; her bum wasn't getting any smaller, he observed, and many others who either waved or hissed 'Hi!' in passing. On reaching Back Beach he immediately turned and headed back the way he had come. He reached the house and looked at his watch. It wasn't his best time but good enough. He was drenched in sweat and gulped some water, not too much but enough. After a shower, he seated himself on the end of his bed and tried to remember the coordinates again.

With some satisfaction, he made some coffee. "Not bad," he congratulated himself but wondered if he would still remember in a week. He lay down.

He slept until noon and again set about testing his memory but only at the hesitant spots. Over and over again until he was sick of it.

To hell with it, they are only part of the bloody problem, he thought, eating heartily the dinner which Vui had planted in front of him with her usual advice, 'No eat! you die!' He needed to see Wilson. He was the only one around who could give advice that was worth a shit. He lived only a short distance away and snatching up a paperback he had recently read he headed there.

"Aww, not you! What you want?" was the usual greeting.

"A blow job," Ian pleaded.

"Pervert! Go and buy some balloons," Wilson responded.

"What shit you watching?" enquired Ian, looking at the TV.

"Rawhide! It's in Vietnamese you know. Subtitles in English. I have seen it plenty of times but I never read it before. You want coffee?" he quipped.

"Right! How about the Viagra?" Ian replied.

"Doesn't work, I gave it to her last night and nothing happened," Wilson said dejected.

Ian threw the two books he had brought onto the settee and picked up one already there.

"You read this, any good?" he enquired.

"Got half way. Takes ten minutes to describe a tree and a bush. If I wanted a gardening book I would have bought one. Cow juice and two sugars?"

"God, you have a good memory for a fossil," Ian remarked.

Wilson waddled away to the kitchen, smiling.

"The runt returns," he said to nobody in particular."

"Was that a C or R you used then?" Ian shouted after him.

Ian was tall and lean, Wilson was short and fat and he always called Ian 'the runt' to wind him up. Ian was glad he had come here for the crack. He looked at the large painting of a square-rigged sailing ship on Wilson's living room wall. He had always insisted that ship was Wilson's last command. Humility was

Wilson's greatest asset. From appearances, it was difficult to believe that he was an extra master and had captained some of the largest passenger liners in the world. He returned with the coffee and switched off the TV.

"Now, young man, how did things go?" he asked, genuinely concerned.

"A lot better than I feared; we don't have to sell the station and we got another one into the bargain," Ian began, and went on to tell Wilson all about what had happened, keeping to the relevant subjects he had aired as his concerns to Wilson before he went to Australia.

"Tremendous! Congratulations! Where did you say this gentleman came from – the major?" Wilson sucked hard on his pipe.

"Huntly! Wherever that is," replied Ian.

"It's just north of Aberdeen. A small farming community – you do know where Aberdeen is?" Wilson jibed.

"Piss off. That's where it is then. How you do know, being a Pom?"

"Well, if Glasgow is in England then I am truly a Pom." Wilson billowed smoke.

"I read an article on the plane about some Great Train Robbery, you know anything about that?" Ian enquired.

"Don't tell me that news has reached Australia already," guffawed Wilson.

"Some dickhead found a mailbag full of money in a phone box and handed it to the cops. Is that true?" Ian asked.

"I believe so, the day after the robbery, a mailbag with thousands of untraceable notes. Early morning, nobody around and he phoned the police to tell them. Bloody fool!" Wilson scorned.

"So, you would have nicked the lot, would you?" Ian threw at him.

Wilson bit his pipe in thought. At length he concluded, "That is a difficult question. What you do in the spur of the moment may be different than what you would do if you had time to think. This guy acted on impulse, was a hero for five minutes and lost the opportunity of a lifetime, in my book. I bet he regretted doing things the way he did more than once. I don't even know if he was rewarded. I'll have to check that one up!" Wilson loved investigating.

"That's not an answer, you still haven't told me what you would have done?" Ian insisted.

"This is not a new dilemma for me you know, or thousands of people who have asked themselves the same question. Stealing by finding isn't a major crime. And it would have been easy to prove he had nothing to do with the robbery. I would have taken the chance," Wilson concluded.

"You would have *stolen* the money?" Ian pressed the 'stolen' home.

"Don't be facetious, I would have borrowed it from HMG to invest in a good cause," Wilson elaborated.

"What good cause?" Ian enquired.

"ME! Being an officer and a gentleman," Wilson replied.

Ian was thinking. A once in a lifetime opportunity and he might regret his decision for the rest of his life but that applied to both scenarios. He had to find out about a reward also.

"Now I know why God made you so low to the ground," Ian slung at him.

"When there is money like that laying around, young man, you crawl under a snake's belly with a bowler hat on to get it. Take the chance and take the consequences I say, if there are any consequences. Better than a lifetime of wondering 'what if', don't you think?" He eyed Ian over his glasses.

"Yeh, I guess you're right, I think money going to be destroyed anyhow could have been put to better use."

"Any word from Linh?" Wilson changed the subject.

Ian sighed and shook his head; he slapped both hands on his thighs and stood up.

"Nothing! Not a cheap. That's three months since she buggered off, and she can keep going as far as I am concerned. She didn't take anything from me but it's all about money, Wilson, all about money. The writing was on the wall months ago, job wise; I made a mistake but I won't make another one, that's for sure. I need a piss," Ian announced.

"What about work then, anything happening?" Wilson enquired on Ian's return.

"Still slow, this bloody drop in oil price is hellish. We were outsourcing from Abu Dhabi and Oman but that has dried up considerably; the seismic ships are expensive and they're not getting the work. We'll be lucky to survive for a few more months, sooner if nothing comes in locally," Ian answered.

"Then what? You going to open a bar like the rest of the idiots?" Wilson teased.

"Not as long as my arse is pointing to the ground. Become one of them? A couple have lasted but most go under eventually and they won't be told," he declared

"That's because they're Australians," Wilson put in quickly.

"They're not all bloody Aussies," insisted Ian.

"Well, they are either Aussies or Yanks; all the intelligent people got out before the development started. Exploration was the time to make money. There were six thousand ex-patriots here, now there are two hundred and a heap of Asians who don't go to bars, they only chase chicken girls. And the Russians left have their homes and families here except for a few and they don't spend much. The tourists are mainly Korean or Taiwanese and they don't go to western bars which leaves the paedophiles and they are mostly Aussies."

"Go to hell, Wilson; you're not going to wind me up, you old bastard," Ian said calmly.

"Let me tell you, young man, the transition from a young Runt with a C to an old bastard is quite painless," Wilson informed him quite categorically.

"I'll take your word for it," Ian agreed.

"Have you heard about your friend, Captain Dick?" Wilson asked.

"Dick, I haven't seen him for a month, what's up?" Ian asked.

"Retirement!" Wilson spoke one word.

"Never! He's not going to retire, is he?" Ian asked, his voice laced with disbelief.

"Told to. Has no choice, it's either that or gets fired. The Vietnamese have introduced a minimum age limit to work here, like some other countries trying to get their nationals employed, and Dick is too old. Didn't you know that was in the wind?" Wilson asked.

"In the pipeline, but not decided; it was inevitable, I suppose. What the hell will he do now?" Ian was greatly concerned.

"Not a lot a captain without a ship can do. He won't go into an office like I did, knowing him. So, he will just have to adapt to life on the beach. He comes from your neck of the woods, doesn't he?" Wilson stated.

"Adelaide, but, hells bells, there isn't work anywhere for supply boat captains, even the North Sea, they're cutting back everywhere," Ian said.

"He might start a bar?" suggested Wilson.

"Now, that would be a disaster, he would have every chicken full of eggs, and you would have to go next door to get a beer within a month." Ian laughed.

"Very true. You had better see him before he goes. The ship is due in in the next couple of days I believe," Wilson informed him.

"Where the hell do you get all the information from?" Ian wanted to know.

"Bush telegraph, you go to the wrong bar. You have to mix again, not listen to professors gibbering on about how great they are. Get back to the human race before you start picking up English."

"Wilson, bugger off, and read your Rawhide, I'm off to find some good company," Ian said, rising to leave.

"Fare thee well, young man, come back the next time they let you out of the nut house for a day. Or I might see you in the bar on Tuesday."

"I'll think about it. Hope your next shits a hedgehog, Wilson," said Ian, starting the bike up.

"I love you too!" shouted Wilson.

Ian stopped to get some fresh sugar cane juice from a vender at the old market on his way home. He still marvelled at how much juice could be removed from what looked like a stick. The machine rollers were powerful and noisy but the juice was delicious and ice cold. He felt good, he knew what he was going to do; his enthusiasm was only dampened by the news that Dick would be leaving. Ian was as attached to Dick as he was to Wilson; both were his mates despite the age gap. He loved the conversations with them and the banter. They were a different species from his generation and they didn't give a shit for anybody. They were the closest he had to the Leper.

The AIS Live vessel tracking would show where Dick's ship was in seconds. The MV *Alesia* was at anchor in Vung Tau it revealed. Ian was desperate to meet with Dick before he left Vietnam and he knew from experience that Dick wouldn't get much time. His flight would be booked for the earliest departure time to keep accommodation and expenses to the minimum. Would the crew change at anchor or wait until the ship was alongside? Ian headed for the pilot station; they would know if there was a crew change at anchor as the pilot boat was used for that.

On the off chance and because he went past the door, he decided to stick his head into Rosie's Bar; Dick had no scruples about drinking times. He wasn't only there, he was half pissed. He looked more like a bush ranger than a captain perched on a bar stool. Ian came up behind him; he was deeply engrossed in the laws of physics which according to Dick were all screwed up by Viagra and another black hole. His audience of chicken girls were seemingly spellbound. They hadn't a clue what he was talking about but kept him going, he was spending money.

"You speaking shit again?" Ian whispered into his ear.

"Fuck my old boots. The Bucko! Where the hell have you been?" Dick exclaimed, without turning round.

"Where's your bags?" Ian asked, tipping his bar stool forward.

"Through the back, asshole," grunted Dick, fighting gravity that won.

"How long you been here? You didn't phone me, trying to escape without buying a round?" Ian said.

"Bullshit! *you* were in Aussie, when did you get back?" Dick turned to face Ian and burst out laughing.

"What an ugly bastard, where's your beard?" he yelled.

"Go and sit down before you fall down," Ian instructed.

"Drowning my sorrows, you know I've been dumped? Bastards!" Dick cursed.

"About time they cleared out you old buggers anyway," Ian baited him.

"This is serious, you young shit. What the hell am I supposed to do now?" Dick queried, running his fingers through his beard and looking at Ian with Labrador eyes.

"Open a bar!" Ian suggested.

"Have you been told today?" Dick asked.

"Told what?" Ian asked.

"To go and fuck yourself?" Dick retorted.

"Not a good idea then. But your only experience is in bars, massage parlours and ships, so that leaves only a massage parlour," Ian deduced.

"Your opinion of me is commendable; I wonder what company runs floating brothels? I will pursue this line of enquiry forthwith," Dick announced. Taking a slug of beer, he added "Out of the blue. No warning, No consultation, No redundancy. Bugger all. You're finished on arrival. That's all I got. I was gobsmacked. What a kick in the balls. I've been with them for twenty years and they drop you like a piece of shit. They wouldn't get away with this on an Aussie ship, the bastards. The union would go on strike like Linda's fanny, it's in the union. It's been on strike for years."

Chickens tried to mosey in beside Dick, but he slapped one on the rump and they skittled back to the bar giggling and strutting their plastic bits. They never attempted to get near Ian; this he noted with satisfaction.

Ian knew Linda, she was Dick's wife and he grinned.

"You need to get a hobby," Ian threw at him.

"That's exactly what I need to get. I don't give a shit about the money, we're OK. This has been a good milk cow, the last twenty years. Kids are grown, we have a big house in West Lakes, a boat, cars, everything you could want, but I can't catch fish every day, or sit looking at the bloody wall every day; it'll drive me nuts, and Linda mental."

"I read somewhere there were people looking for… What the hell did they call them? Yeh, the mookas," Ian hung out for him to bite.

"You got it, boy, that's exactly what I'm looking for. Positive thinking that will take up my entire bloody lifetime, and several other lifetimes. After I find them, I can search for the Loch Ness monster and that should take another few lifetimes.

Brilliant! I'll be a thousand years old before I solve that lot. Any other bright ideas?" asked Dick.

At least he knew about them, Ian thought and wanted more.

"They reckon in the article I read, there was a robbery, and everything disappeared," he added.

"Yep! I remember it well. There was a robbery, a bloody big one. The papers were full of it for months till everybody got sick of it. It went from a straightforward robbery to speculation and went mental."

"What you mean?" asked Ian.

They reckoned the only ones who knew the value of the shipment were the miners, bankers, cops and couriers. It was impossible for anybody else to have known the value. Nothing escaped from Andamooka, nothing! The entire place and surrounding area was in lock-down within hours. A bloody snake couldn't move around there without being spotted. If there was another party responsible, they were bloody good, and bloody lucky," said Dick.

"Well, at least you know something about them! You know anything about Loch Ness?" Ian enquired.

"Bugger off! The papers, they reckoned the miners from Cooper Pedy did it, but that doesn't hold water; they'd already been paid, so had the mooka miners. It had to be an inside job. Insurance fraud or the like. Whatever, the insurance paid up in the end and the gems were never found, probably re-sold over time to the same dealers they were stolen from. Where better to hide opals than in the opal fields. Some stupid bastards are still looking for them yet, bloody idiots! And you want me to be another. I reckon the monster is easier, at least they know where the damned thing is," Dick scolded.

"Only trying to help. You want another beer?" he queried.

"Is the Pope a Catholic?" Dick snapped.

"You staying here for the night or what?" Ian asked, handing Dick a cold one.

51

"Don't fuss, you're worse than my mother. Taxi's ordered, flight at eleven Ho Chi Minh. I've done this before you know. Sit on your arse," Dick instructed him.

"Keep your hair on, or what you have left of it, you know at your age you can forget things," Ian said, dodging a flying beer mat. It was going to be a fine session and he was in the mood. Pace yourself, Pace yourself, Wilson had drummed into him until it was now second nature.

ON KANGAROO ISLAND

Debbie had a good bucket full the night before and didn't show up for breakfast. Joe and Maria decided to leave her sleeping; there was nothing for her to do anyhow. They went to the bank at ten a.m. to see Young and were greeted warmly.

"How can I help you, Maria, is everything all right?" he asked.

"The cleaners at the house—" Maria started to say, but was cut short by Young who held up his hands in surrender.

"I'm sorry we acted so fast, but I asked Mr Talbot to explain to you over the phone. He informed me that you only wanted a few items kept, and as they had already started it was all right to carry on." Young was eating humble pie.

"I'm not concerned about that. I'm wondering who has to pay them, you or us," Maria corrected him.

"Well, I guess the bank will be liable since we organised them. Luckily, this team are not too expensive. I have had dealings with these teams before and they can be very expensive, depending on circumstance of course. We were lucky two of them were already here taking a break, and they have their own camper van which is a great saving in itself. Are they nearly finished yet?" Young asked.

Maria and Joe looked at one another and shrugged.

"We have no idea. They don't speak very much and I didn't like to ask," said Maria.

"Our agreement is cash and low cost or invoice and standard rate. Ask Miss Fletcher, she was the only one I asked for ID, her driving licence, and I surmise she is in charge, she appeared to be. Ask her when you go out there again. Are you heading out today, Joe?" Young enquired

"Reckon we will, after we get Debbie up. OK. Thanks for that, Mr Young, we will get out of your way," Joe answered.

"What was that all about?" Joe asked once they were outside.

"Well, it seems the bank jumped the gun by the look of things; their first move was repossession the day after your father died, but the next day, the Leper moved in and paid the debt off. By that time the cleaners had started. Talbot phoned me and insisted that I attend. He asked me if there was anything in the house we wanted to keep and I told him, nothing is to be kept except documents belonging to your grandfather and his medals. That's about all that was saved from the fire. 'That's as well,' he said, 'as the cleaners have orders from the bank to clear the house'," Maria tailed off.

"Jesus Christ! So much for kind hearted Young, the day after he died, that's a bit rich," Joe stressed.

"As he said, the opportunity was there to get it done cheaply. It had to be done, nobody would buy the place as it is. He was within his rights, a bit callous but that's business I guess. At least he is going to pay for his mistake and we get it done for nothing," Maria said.

"You look like you've been on the piss! Had to put you to bed last night – strip you as well – your flea bite's a bit close to the mark, isn't it?" Joe dodged a slap as he finished.

"In your dreams, mate, you and those Taiwanese were still catching snook when I left – big, bloody snook. And you were speaking your best Chinese, king prawn chow mein! Chop suey! Very impressive, shit head," Debbie retaliated.

"Right! Are we going out or what?" Joe changed the subject.

"We'll go and get some stores first; the Leper can't have anything left, and we'll have to eat there again," Maria pointed out.

"I'll drive!" Debbie insisted, pushing Joe away from the car door.

"That's a bit over the top," Joe said, holding up a can of flea spray at the checkout; Debbie threw him daggers with her eyes and he said no more, just smiled.

They called in by Korena to ask about progress but couldn't find anybody there and the doors were locked. They concluded the cleaners were away for lunch and headed for Huntly. The Leper greeted them with his usual enthusiasm and was delighted with the food they had brought. The dog wasn't too happy once Debbie was finished with her but she didn't go far; there was plenty of grass to roll in and get rid of the stinking intrusion to her coat.

"Sheep dip, throw her in with the sheep, lassie," the Leper had insisted but Debbie was stubborn.

Maria was busy preparing food, much to the Leper's delight. He took the time to show Joe around the farm machinery from Korena.

"Looks like shit!" Joe commented.

"Aye it does, laddie, but it still works. You wouldn't get a lot for it if it was sold but to replace it would cost a fortune," the Leper pointed out.

Joe had to agree with that, but all this machinery had to be refurbished before anybody could use it. Some of it was seized, some broken in places. Hydraulics and engines, everything had to be done. This was another big job.

"How the hell did it end up here?" Joe asked.

"I didn't object. Have you heard from Ian?" was the reply.

"Yeh! He arrived OK, didn't say much," Joe replied.

The Leper didn't comment. He looked at Joe, taking in the scale of work which confronted him.

"Start with the tractor, when the time comes," he advised, and thought, the right choice, brawn or brains, and Ian had the brains. They started back to the house, the smell of food getting stronger as they approached. Debbie and the dog joined them. Maria had set the table on the veranda, it being the only table she could find.

They ate, exchanged banter and the Leper insisted that after such a sublime feed he would wash up. Nobody objected to that and the three of them headed back to Korena.

The bloody place is still locked," Joe called back to Maria who was standing at the gate. He looked through the front window but could see nothing but curtains. At the back the result was the same. They returned to Debbie who was still in the car speaking to Dan. She looked at them quizzically.

"What's up?" she asked.

"Nobody here, mate, the place is still locked. Buggered if I know? We might as well go back to Kingscote. See if we can find out what's going on. A wasted bloody day," Joe assessed.

"Dan's crashed his thing at Tailem Bend, went into the river as well and he can't find it. Shit!" said Debbie.

"What was he doing in Tailem Bend?" Maria wanted to know.

"E.W.S Pipeline survey, they wanted to try out his thing to look for leaks and things. They reckon people are tapping into the pipe and growing all sorts of stuff in the scrub. They had been using a helicopter but that was too expensive. Bugger it! He worked hard to get his chance to prove the thing would work," Debbie seethed.

"Well, he can see how many fish are in the Murray now," Joe jibed.

"That's not bloody funny, that thing cost a lot of money and it wasn't insured. He's really pissed off." Debbie gunned the car as a sign to Joe to shut up.

Young met them at the door of his office, he was holding the keys aloft.

"I'm sorry, I was busy and I forgot to call you. They finished and left on the ferry a couple of hours ago. Here are the keys."

Debbie took the keys and threw Young a disgusted look.

"Did anybody check they had done a proper job? We haven't even been inside yet," she declared.

"There is a list of what was done and a box of items they believed were to be kept; the list I have here, the box is in the house," Young said, unperturbed; after all, *they* weren't paying for anything. He was!

"Can I have the list?" Maria asked.

"Certainly," replied Young and retrieved a document from his desk. He handed it to Maria.

"I hope we continue to service the accounts for Korena. And rest assured, if you require any finance to get things going I will be only too glad to assist."

Maria thanked him and they left.

It was too late in the day to return to the station so they headed back to the hotel at Joe's request, to take stock of the situation.

"We need to get some other accommodation sorted out. I reckon I should get the Clinker here with the camper. I think you two should head back to Adelaide on the next ferry. What do you think?" Joe kicked off with.

"This hotel will cost a fortune if we stay here much longer. And there's Ian's hire car, it has to go back," Maria added.

"Well, we need to decide before the next ferry. What about the rest of your season?" she fired at Joe.

"There's only a couple of weeks left so stuff it. We did all right so far and there's a hell of a lot of things to be done at

Korena. Clinker can bring the tools and the camper and we can get stuck into the machinery first," Joe suggested.

"OK, but I need to make a list of everything needed for the house and get it," Maria said, motivated.

"Well, we can't get much here. We need to get everything in Adelaide."

"OK, we have a couple of days to sort out the list and get the Clinker on the road; he has to drive from Lincoln, so he better get cracking as soon as he can. I'll give him a shout!" Joe said.

Maria was searching through the list of work and was impressed. "I don't believe this; they stripped wallpaper from the living room, and painted it. Tiles from the kitchen and re-tiled it. All floor coverings, and all furniture with the exception of one welsh dresser incinerated along with all clothes and miscellaneous material. Curtains salvaged and washed – It goes on – Brilliant!" Maria exclaimed.

"Well done, Young, you arsehole!" Joe added.

Debbie would have liked to go through the contents of the house and decide herself if there was anything she wanted to keep, however, she knew Maria's feelings. If they had told Maria they were burning the house down she wouldn't have raised any objection at the time. Not now though, she was coming round and her dread of the place was being replaced with a vengeance.

"OK. Tomorrow we make up a comprehensive list of requirements. The next day, Clinker arrives on the ferry and we catch it back to Adelaide. Check out of the hotel. You and Clinker head for Korena once you get everything you need and start on the machinery," Debbie said.

"No! We need to fix the fences first and get the livestock back onto our own land. They're eating all the Leper's fodder and he ain't got much. Quicker we get them back the better. Then we can start on the machinery," Joe corrected.

"Open every window and door every day. Get rid of any smell in that house," Maria ordered.

"Easy, just spread some Leper juice around," suggested Debbie to the others' disgust.

IN VUNG TAU

The session grew arms and legs; there was a fine selection of other body parts thrown in as well. The night shift had wind of a party and descended on Rosie's with haste. She was making sure the atmosphere was such that nobody would want to leave. Many of Dick's friends got wind of the situation. Aussies, Scots, English, Russian and Vietnamese seamen had come up from the docks to say farewell. Dick was popular with everybody and he thought it was Xmas, drinks were flowing freely from all directions and chickens were roosting on knees; the cream of them, seldom seen in Rosie's but all Dick's babies. Very few of them didn't come and say hello to Wilson or Dick. It was a sublime send-off.

Ian was conscious of the fact he had a motorbike outside and had to drive it home; however, Rosie had that under control and delegated two chickens to take his bike home. His protests were futile and he gave them the keys to his gate. That out of the way he sent a taxi to get Wilson. It wasn't Tuesday but worth a shot.

"How dare you change the days of the week, Dick? Give me one of them don't be so greedy. *Not* a plastic one, a beer please, I don't drink during daylight but one has to adjust to barbarian habits," Wilson announced.

"Don't bloody start, Wilson, Pommy bastard." Dick was saying hello.

The night descended quickly, and with it, even more revellers. This was going to be a party Dick would never forget but could he stand the pace? Being at sea without a drink for nearly a month doesn't prepare the body for such a binge.

They sang and danced into the night, and Dick was holding his own. Unlike Jeff, who staggered away and caused a great commotion across the street.

Ian went to look and came back laughing.

"Jeff's head's up his arse again. He's in his Jeep cursing and swearing and calling the Vietnamese all the bastards under the sun. I asked him what's wrong. 'The wheel, the wheel, Ian, they've stolen the bloody wheel.' He's slapping his hands on the dashboard, bastards, bastards. 'Jeff, you're sitting in the passenger's side, the wheel's over there.' 'Bloody hell!' he screams, 'the bastards have shifted it.' The Vietnamese were pissing themselves laughing I thought there was a murder going on. Bloody idiot."

"A bloody Pommy! What do you expect?" came a voice from the bush.

"One to you! So far," Wilson conceded.

Rosie must have been busy on the phone; no way was she going to lose this windfall not even to eat. Food of all descriptions arrived and the chickens, under her direction, set up several tables along the back wall, clear of the dance floor but on the toilet track which was unavoidable.

The free food was like a magnet and the place was packed quickly. More food arrived and they revelled under the disco din. Dick's crew were the first to hit the ground slithering off their seats or tumbling backwards; the one hundred percent knock-backs, which was their culture, didn't work with Black Label Scotch.

"And another one bites the dust!" everybody sang out as each fell by the wayside.

There was a crash at the back wall; Clint, a mud engineer from Melbourne took a stagger, sending the contents of a table crashing to the floor. Empty vessels make a hell of a noise.

Assisted to his feet by chicken power he disappeared into the toilet.

Without turning round, Wilson declared to Ian, who was looking at the direction of the commotion.

"One suspects that was a barbarian trying to defy gravity. Was it not?" He smiled.

"One each, good job the grub was finished," Ian confirmed.

"He's next!" Wilson pointed across his chest to Dick, who was desperately trying to connect a glass with his hand and failing.

"Phone me drunk I'm a taxi," Dick slavered, struggling to keep his eyes open.

He was a mumbling heap when Ian took him through the back and dumped him on Rosie's bed. He went out like a light. Rosie was unperturbed.

"As long as he pays the bill in the morning," thought Ian, "he'll be well looked after."

"This, 'pace yourself' works, Wilson, I feel bloody brilliant," he shouted over the music, slapping Wilson's back as he spoke.

He spotted a large uniformed figure making his way towards them through the dancers and smoke.

"Here comes Alexi," he informed Wilson.

"I wondered if one of them would appear. Good evening, Captain," Wilson replied, standing up and shaking hands with the newcomer.

"Captain! Where is Dick?" the huge Russian asked.

"Fucked!" Ian replied.

"Slightly intoxicated: will you join us Alexi?" Wilson corrected.

"I am thinking fucked may be correct. No! I have to sail shortly. We are not happy about this. Here, give this to Dick. Make sure he gets it. It's from all the Russian captains. And wish him luck from all of us, he is a gentleman. I must go back to my ship!" he shouted, looked at his watch and handed Wilson a small package. Alexi hurried away.

"You see, Dick was a gentleman!" Ian threw at Wilson, who was weighing up the small package.

"One is not a gentleman if complimenting the size of a woman's breasts is… I would sit below that with a wee stool and a bucket for a fortnight and never say boo to a goose… I am so glad one of them appeared; we need to make sure he gets this, it will be important to him. Looks like you're getting up early in the morning, boyo." But Ian was staring across the room. Wilson followed his gaze.

"Put your eyes back into your head, you look like a predator," he ordered.

"A night in Silicon Valley is tempting, Wilson," Ian declared, pulling his eyes from the valley.

"They may not be silicon," Wilson replied with authority.

"One way to find out, dirty old man. You and Dick! Five years and I've never seen either of you go with any of them, and they hang around you like you're their fathers," Ian pointed out.

"Which we are. My wife used to call me a dirty old man as well. And you know something, she was right." Wilson lit his pipe and surveyed the scene.

"Every night, in every bar in town was like this when I first came here and there was no closing time all night if you wanted. As long as there were customers the bars stayed open. Not like now. Still, it's a good thing, stops temptation at eleven p.m. and it's getting close. I'll drop you off with my taxi. Here, you had better keep hold of this and give it to Dick in the morning," Wilson said, handing Ian the small package.

Ian was tempted to suggest they simply stick it into Dick's bag, but that was not a good idea, its presence being observed by who knows who. Even Rosie had things disappear.

Singles started leaving and doubles shortly afterwards. Chickens snared the unsuspecting and the downright randy with ease. Most of them were beautiful, they had to be to stand a chance of work; however, going down that track had repercussions for the resident population which could be dangerous, as many had found out.

They left after saying thanks to Rosie and reminding her to get Dick up in the morning. Wilson's regular driver was waiting and they took the short trip to Ian's. Straight down the same street Rosie's bar was on, but two kilometres away. Vui let him in the gate much to his surprise. Thank God he didn't bring anything back with him, he would be right in the shit.

"Why you let Chicken Girls bring your motorbike back? I nearly die I think it is robbers," she let fly, "You with Wilson and Dick? No Chickens? That's good – you eat yet?" Vui demanded.

"Yeh! We ate plenty food," Ian answered, but thought, *why do I pay somebody to give me hell?*

She gave a grunt of satisfaction and locked the gate then, headed to her room muttering something in Vietnamese. Ian picked up the familiar Com Ding (Crazy) and grinned.

He wasn't grinning in the morning, he was cursing. Dick was well on his way to Ho Chi Minh City before Ian crawled out of his bed at seven thirty a.m. It was lashing rain and he was soaked through by the time he reached Rosie's. As he feared, Dick had left early, fearing the inevitable congestion getting to the airport. He returned home and took a shower. There was nothing he could do about it so he just accepted it. As Dick had said on many occasions, worry about things you can do something about. If you can't do anything about it, to hell with it.

He had a snack and waited for the rain to clear. He was feeling OK. He was also quite chuffed with himself as he recited the coordinates flawlessly. That subject jerked him back to reality with a surge of dread. He was out of his depth and he knew it. He stared at the wall for a long time, his thoughts tearing through the information he had and his own position, which he had concluded was untenable. He wasn't going to rush into decisions regarding his work. He was still on contract and obliged to give three months' notice reciprocal. Unlike Dick, he was still covered by Australian terms and conditions but things were not good and the company had started voluntary redundancy elsewhere. Not yet in Vietnam but already in Thailand and Singapore. It was just a matter of time unless the oil prices started to recover and there were no indications that would happen any time soon.

Ian had some serious decisions to make. After his long-term girlfriend buggered off with her rich, Russian toy boy to Sakhalin he had been hurt like he never imagined. He never thought he would ever lose her but, as they say, it's all about the money. Events since then had taken his mind off her but she wasn't far below the surface. However, there was nothing to keep him here now, except his job, and that was the bottom line, whether he liked it or not.

He phoned Joe, holding the phone at a distance until the verbal abuse finished, yet monitoring everything he was saying; he had no reason for concern and at last, he got a chance to speak.

"How's it going, mate, what have you decided?" Ian asked calmly.

Joe's enthusiasm was infectious. He explained the plan of attack: what Debbie and Maria were going to do and Clinker getting the camper van across from Port Lincoln; what had been done to the house and what had to be done to the equipment at Huntly; the plan he had to get the livestock back into their own paddocks and lastly, insisted Ian take down the new telephone number for Korena.

"I'm impressed and we didn't have to pay for Young being a prick. That's brilliant, I didn't expect the place to be painted. Right; get as much done as you can, it looks like this job's going to take the full ninety days, there is no alternative. They tried everything else and it's a relief well. No choice," Ian lied.

"Bugger! Oh, I forgot, Dan the drone has fucked up again, crashed the thing into the Murray, he's a bloody disaster," Joe yelled in pain.

"Don't listen to that dickhead," Debbie butted in and went on to explain the incident at Tailem Bend.

She was really upset that Dan had lost his investment before he could prove it in the field. However, Ian didn't know him well enough to make a comment so sided with Debbie.

"The bait ball in a wet suit should buy him another one. He's got plenty money," Ian suggested.

"You! You bastard, you have to buy Dan a new thing!" Debbie shouted.

"Bloody hell! Three months! OK, we'll manage without you anyway. As soon as that other shark bait arrives we can get something done. I might get Dan here as well, he's pissed off. You want to speak to the bait ball?" Debbie asked.

"No! Tell him I'll update him as soon as I get some info. Be good," Ian replied.

"Don't be stupid, see ya," Debbie giggled.

Ian felt invigorated after his call; everything there was in hand. It was only his dilemma which concerned him and only he could sort that out. He put Dick's present into his wardrobe and locked the glass door. Snatching up one sheet of coordinates he underlined three with pencil and rubbed out the pencil marks; they were relevant to the Flinders Ranges to the east of Andamooka. Satisfied the pencil marks could be seen with the aid of a magnifying glass, he put them together into his writing desk. Recited the memorised ones quietly, and slammed the top shut.

He pulled up at the office of Geological Survey and put the bike on the stand. The secretary was surprised to see him and he headed through to the operations room where he had sighted his boss through the window, extending his hand in greeting.

"I knew you were back but I didn't expect you till Monday," Fred announced.

"Yeh, things are a little bit screwed up at home. How's the job security looking?" Ian got straight to the point.

Fred gave a big sigh, and held both hands out palm upwards.

"Same as when you left I guess," he answered, stooping over the reel of seismic data he was studying.

"I'm thinking of asking for redundancy. Should take some pressure off the rest of you. We managed to hang onto the station but there's a mountain of work needed and quickly. What do you think?" he fired at Fred.

Fred peered at him over the top of his glasses with an 'are you for real' look.

"That's a bit drastic, isn't it?" he said.

"Yeh! Drastic just about covers it. Fred, I know we're not being asked to take redundancy *yet*! But I reckon it's only a question of time. Any chance you could put out the feelers and see what they come back with?" Ian asked.

"No problem, I'll see what the reaction is in Sydney. You sure you want to do this? There's no work around, I would advise you ride it out and see what happens. Look at this, there's plenty of targets to go for; it's as good as you get!" he gestured at the graph.

"If the price of oil doesn't rebound they'll just leave it where it is, until it does." Ian stated the obvious.

"Ian, you wouldn't be asked to take redundancy. There's a lot of older people who would be first, including me," Fred explained.

"Yes, I know, but the reality is this. I have something to go to, albeit a bit of a gamble, but, as you said, there is no work available anywhere in this profession. What would others turn to?"

"True. OK I'll put out the feelers and see what transpires," agreed Fred, somewhat reluctantly.

"See you on Monday. Thanks for that, Fred." Ian left with a wave to the secretary.

He breathed deeply when he came outside. He hated what he had just done. Fred was a brilliant manager and his colleagues were also his friends; they had been together for a long time. Ian had been with them since he had left university and they were literally his teachers in operations. Eleven years he had been with them. He would await developments; he could always change his mind. He headed home then to the Rex Hotel pool; he had some serious thinking to do in the sun.

He took the plunge into the deep end and headed for the shallows. I don't go in the ocean, they don't come into the bar was a good arrangement with the sharks. He always thought about Joe when he went swimming. The deck chair was bliss and he ordered sugar cane. The sun was hot and he lay back to contemplate his situation. His mind was made up. They were going for the mookas and to hell with the consequences.

ON KANGAROO ISLAND

Joe and Clinker entered Huntly with a resounding rattle of the cattle grid, ringing it like a bell. The Leper rushed out of the shed in response.

"I thocht it was a bloody tank!" he shouted at Joe.

"I surrender; Leper, this is Clinker, he's come to help. We have our camper but I think it would be better to stay in Huntly till the machinery is fixed. What you reckon?"

The Leper leaned on a stick he was carrying and weighed up the camper.

"Aye, a fine shed," he concluded. "What's the rules of engagement then?"

"Eh!" said Joe. "Fences first, Major, then move the livestock."

The Leper eyed Clinker closely and nodded. He was military despite his appearance. He would find out where he served later.

"Aye, before you start thinking about fences you better get rid of your tenants," the Leper barked, pointing out to the back paddocks.

Joe and Clinker followed his pointing finger but could see nothing. The Leper went into the house and came out with a set of field binoculars. He handed them to Joe.

"Jesus Christ, what the hell is all that?" Joe exclaimed, still holding the binoculars to his eyes.

"Wallabies and goats," the Leper stated. Joe handed the glasses to Clinker.

"Take a shifty at that," he said.

"Before you start putting fences up you better get rid of the ones who knocked them down in the first place." He went on to explain, "They dug under the cyclone (sheep fence) as normal but the holes got bigger till the posts started falling over. The cattle did the rest, without the top barbed wire they walked the fence to the ground. The five bulls were in the scrub along with about thirty sheep. They were going in and out in both directions; your father lost interest a long time ago, this didn't happen overnight. That's why we took them here."

Joe looked at the Leper and he read his mind.

"Follow me and grab that dog," he commanded, heading for the shed.

"As soon as she sees the guns you won't catch her. Chain her up; if she corners one she is likely to get gutted with the big toe," the Leper instructed Joe, handing him a three-o-three rifle and one to Clinker also. Flossy went crazy when she saw the guns.

"Go and scare the hell out of them and don't kill any, it's one live wallaby against a thousand blowflies. You see that daft dog would round them up and bring them back. Here! Twenty rounds, that's all your getting, now go, see what you can do," he instructed, handing them a box of bullets.

"Brilliant! You reckon firing in the air and howling at them will do it! They'll die laughing." Joe was heading for the fence as he commented, Clinker hard behind.

The Leper grinned; they wouldn't be so fit by the time they came back. He went for a mosey into the camper van.

Sporadic rifle shots rang out over the next two hours, getting more distant each time. The Leper grinned and the dog barked and whined in frustration. They had no water with them and it was hot. No hats on and no way of keeping the chisellers off (small bush flies that chisel into the corners of eyes to drink); they would be in a fine state by the time they came back. They would learn the hard way, he chuckled, and returned to his vats.

He had greatly underestimated both of them and was indeed impressed to see them striding back to the house, guns over their shoulders and laughing. Open shirted but full of beans.

"Hundreds of them in the back paddock," Joe informed him.

"Any goats?" enquired the Leper.

"Never saw any but plenty wallabies and there's still sheep in the scrub. We didn't see them but we heard them. Might be cattle in there, too – you think?" he asked the Leper.

"Could be! Go and clean those guns and put them back with the rest." The Leper looked at them again. "You two not thirsty? I hope you didn't quench your thirst at a trough. You'll get the shits," he advised.

"Naw! We're used to no water for hours. Bloody difficult to drink with a face mask on underwater, you know. I'll clean the rifles," Clinker volunteered.

"I'll make a brew," the Leper decided.

"What's with the goats?" Joe asked, following him into the house.

"Wallabies mean blowflies, wild goats, on grass and not in the scrub, mean meat. It's the same as mutton and they should be in the reserve anyway," the Leper chuckled.

"Right! I see what we are up against; there is serious damage along the boundary fence but I think we can salvage most of the wire; we just need to dig it out of the sand. They have a bloody highway into the bush not a roo run. The posts, some need replaced and some are OK. Jesus, they've knocked the hell out of the pasture all along the boundary fence. In places into the middle of the paddock," Joe elaborated.

"Get the tractor up and running first and a trailer. There's wire stretchers, posts and wire at Korena in the Dutch barn under all that old hay. You'll just have to fossick about, and see what you can find – like I did," the Leper put in and landed the kettle on top of the wood stove with a hiss.

"You got that lot insured, Major?" Clinker asked on joining them.

"Aye, there's a pound or two in that cabinet right enough. And which regiment were you with?" the Leper asked.

"Three RAR Woodside," Clinker answered, somewhat taken aback by the question.

"And did you see any action?" the Leper enquired.

"Rwanda!" came the reply.

"Well, laddie, you'll have seen things you don't want to remember there. Did you put the lock back on?" the Leper changed the subject. He was well aware what the Australian troops had encountered in the Rwanda genocide.

"Yep, the armoury is secure," Clinker answered, grateful that he had been understood without question.

"I must be the odd man out here, what the hell are you speaking about?" Joe queried.

"I'll let the dog loose," was Clinker's response, heading for the door.

"You heard from Ian?" the Leper asked.

That jolted Joe out of his ignorance.

"That bastard! You know what he did? He buggered off and never checked out of the bloody hotel. Told me he had, but I got his bill, the sneaky prick. Wait till he phones next time," Joe exploded.

"Like I told you, whatever he does don't question it. Whatever he asks, or does, go along with it. All will be revealed when the time is right," the Leper said, very calmly.

"What the hell are you two up to?" Joe insisted.

The Leper held his finger to his mouth as Flossy raced into the room followed by Clinker. It was a long time since the Leper had company. He conceded, too long.

IN VUNG TAU

Ian had drifted into sleep on the sunbed. He came to bursting for a piss and he had a chocolate frog on. Luckily, he was lying face down and the bulge in his trunks remained out of sight. He glanced sideways and spotted a blonde two chairs distant. She was also lying on her face and her face was turned away from him. He craned his neck and there was another one on the far side; both were tanned. He grabbed his towel, wrapped it around his waist and headed for the toilets, stooping slightly forward.

Relieved in more ways than one he waited for the frog to melt and headed back to the pool. *Where the hell did they appear from?* he thought, as he tried to act uninterested. He knew from experience not to get too excited. Russian beauties were usually accompanied by Russian men, but that didn't stop him looking. He ogled the nearest one from head to toe. Her hair was so long it hung over the sunbed onto the tiles. He found himself staring at both of them; they looked like models from the back. God knows what they looked like from the front. The frog stirred again and he hastily headed for the cool water.

He suddenly became aware of the thick stubble growing around his chin; it was an interim between clean and bearded, not a favourable presentation. He heard them speaking in Russian and viewed the far away one getting up and putting on a white robe over her bikini. She smiled in his direction and he smiled back more in shock than courtesy. She was stunning and Ian was disappointed they were leaving. However, only the darker haired one left, the long haired one still lay face down on her sunbed.

She'll burn to death if she doesn't turn soon… He cast his eyes to the sun cream by his chair which he never went without. There was no sign of any Russian men anywhere and he wondered if the girl who left would come back.

Suddenly, the long blonde hair stirred and he dived underwater to avoid staring at her. Next thing, she plunged head first into the pool and swam over him. She could move like an athlete. He surfaced and headed for the shallow end; she did another length and stopped beside him sitting on the bottom, shoulders lapping.

Intense pain, intense heat, intense cold he had encountered but intense beauty never before. She smiled and that made her more unapproachable. No way was he going to attempt to chat up this girl, she was in a different league. Unbelievable, the type that can be seen only from a distance, the reserve of film stars and millionaires. She was a keeper, not a one-night stand, and she scared the hell out of Ian. He was speechless.

"Hello, I'm Lada," she said quietly.

"Hi Lada, I'm Ian. You speak English?" he choked.

"Yes, I teach English," she answered, to Ian's surprise.

"Where do you come from?" was all he could think of asking.

"Vladivostok in Russia. Do you know where that is?" she asked.

"In the Sea of Japan, where all the most beautiful girls come from," he answered and blushed; he couldn't believe he had just made that remark.

"Thank you, where are you from?" she asked.

"Australia," he replied, meekly.

"Where all the handsome men come from." She laughed and launched herself down the pool.

"Race!" he shouted and went hell for leather after her.

The ice was broken and they played without touching until they were exhausted, like two children.

"You better put some sun cream on," Ian suggested as they left the water.

Without a word, she moved her things to the chair next to his and laid full length on her face.

"When I dry you can put it on," she instructed.

He couldn't wait for the sun to dry her and rubbed her back down with a towel as she wriggled.

God! am I going to wake up soon, he thought, as he applied the lotion. His heart was racing and he was shaking. Her long, blonde hair hung down to the ground as she reached behind her and unfastened the straps of her bikini. Ian took a deep breath and spread the cream where she exposed. Legs next, he had reservations about hitting too close to target but decided to be reckless; she didn't object. He wiped his hands on his chest and lay down on his own chair; he couldn't trust himself to lay on his back, that could have been embarrassing.

He saw the waitress looking from the hotel and waved for her to come.

"Would you like something to drink?" he asked.

"Not alcohol, I never drink during daylight," she answered.

"Me neither – as a rule," he lied.

"I thought a Lada was a car?" Ian teased and wished he hadn't.

"Yes!" she replied simply.

He couldn't take his eyes off her, he was spellbound.

"Mr Ian," the waitress spoke.

"Sorry! Eh, two sugar cane please with ice," he ordered.

"Sugar is not good for you. Is sugar cane any different?" she asked, turning her head to face him.

Those blue eyes and high cheekbones were magnetic. His mind was in turmoil, scared to death he would screw up.

"When you taste it, I think you will like it. Do you live in the compound?" he asked.

"No! I live here in the hotel, you cannot live in the compound unless you have a job and I don't have a job yet! So I must stay here until I get one," she explained.

This took him by surprise but it was obvious she hadn't been in Vietnam very long.

"How long have you been here?" he enquired.

"Only two days. My friend, Hanna, the one who was here, she arranged the hotel because she says the English teachers all drink here and they would know who to contact to get some work. Was she correct?" Lada asked.

"Yeh! I guess they drink here, the professors, but they won't be exactly helpful getting you a job." Ian was downbeat. She sensed it, lifting to her elbow, and holding the bikini with her one hand.

"They won't help me, why?" she pleaded.

Ian swallowed hard. In the name of god, how could he look at her and answer questions about the professors? It wasn't easy.

"They're rather, er... strange people. They take care of themselves. I've never known them to help anybody. But, there's always a first time," he pondered.

She lay down again until the sugar cane arrived, then she asked him to fasten her bikini. There wasn't any hint of silicon, Ian found himself thinking, and the frog was stirring again. He covered it with his towel and sat up, taking the drinks from the waitress.

"Beautiful! I like it," she expressed after the first mouthful and smacked her lips.

Ian rested the cold glass on his towel and hoped the ice would kill the frog. It worked.

"The professors, where do they drink? I stayed in the hotel bar last night and I never heard anybody speaking English."

"Lada, the professors are only my name for them they are not proper professors, they're not highly qualified. They're just a bunch of people who like it here and want to stay here. To do that, they teach English. It's hard for them to find work that pays enough, they're always moaning about not being paid on time, or not being paid the right amount. They drink over there." Ian pointed across to the far side of the pool.

"Will you be coming here tonight?" she asked.

"I will, I come here for a few hours every night. Mostly to wind them up, but they're OK, only one a Scotsman, he is something else. You'll see..." Ian tailed off.

"How do you mean, 'something else'?" she asked.

"Well, if you have a black cat he has a Panther. If you have a Honda Dream he has a Harley Davidson. If you can swim the length of the pool underwater, he can swim across the Sea of Japan underwater. You understand?" Ian asked.

"If you have a girlfriend he has a more beautiful one. Is that right?" she enquired.

"About right, he just has to be better than anybody else. The rest, they're a mix of Americans, English, Australians; they're OK. You judge for yourself but be careful not to alarm them. As I say, they might see you as a threat to their own positions, just be careful."

"What time do you come here?" Lada asked.

"Around six, that's when everybody meets. We don't stay long, usually only an hour or two. Have a few drinks. They teach on Saturday, as well as during the week. Tonight should be no different. Just listen to them. Don't ask any questions. They'll be speaking about their jobs, and you'll be able to get a clear picture of an English teacher's life in Vung Tau without them knowing they're giving you one," Ian explained.

"OK, I understand. If I don't get a job as a teacher I might get a job as a taxi being a Lada." She laughed.

They spent another hour on the sunbeds and her skin was becoming a concern to Ian. The frog was a concern on numerous occasions too. She was stunning, funny and gorgeous. He couldn't find the right words to describe her. Irresistible, he settled on.

"I think you'd better get dressed. Even with the cream on, you're starting to burn," he suggested.

"Thank you. You are very kind. Will you take me over there tonight? We might be able to silence the man who has everything." She smiled.

"That would be my pleasure and I don't care if we shut him up or not." Ian stared into her eyes.

She leaned across and kissed him full on the mouth and his heart nearly came out through his chest. She raked her fingernail through the hairs on his chest and smiled.

"I will come over there at six tonight. Thank you again, Ian. I hope we see each other in the future." Lada strolled away with the robe over her shoulder, her long hair touching her hips and swinging with her body movement.

Ian was ecstatic. He lay on the sunbed staring at the sky wondering how the hell he had managed to pull that! It was impossible. He had to check the two empty glasses to reassure himself he wasn't dreaming. He jumped up and got dressed, paid the bill and headed home. He was so bewitched he forgot to turn left. He went around the roundabout instead and did that again before getting his bearings on the hospital. He was like a dog with two cocks. But he had to concentrate in this traffic or he would be a dead dog very quickly.

He showered and headed into the lounge, Vui watching him with suspicion.

"What's wrong with you?" he asked.

"You are in love again or you have won money," she stated quite categorically.

"I knew you were a witch," he fired back, switching on the computer.

"Lada… what the hell is a lada?" he murmured to himself. "It must be something?" He typed in the name and stared at the result.

Lada – ancient Slavic goddess of beauty, love and marriage.

"Goddess! That's the word I've been searching for all day. Shit! They got this one right," he said out loud.

Vui eyed him through the kitchen door, thinking he had gone mad, and she wasn't far wrong; she knew something was up and she liked to know what.

He settled down but the words of wisdom, 'if something looks too good to be true, it usually is', he couldn't push aside. A reality check was called for. He had just had his love life torn apart by Linh leaving him. That still hurt – getting less but still painful. This bloody crap his father had landed on him. His job?

Bugger it! 'We are stronger than that'. The words of Maria ending his quest for self-pity, he switched to the positive aspects. Thank Christ Dick's not here, he would be hovering around her with his wee stool and a bucket. Linh can go to hell. It's redundancy or hand in my notice. Sort out Father's mess. Try my hardest to win the goddess. Sounds like a plan to me. He slammed the laptop shut.

Time took forever but finally he set out for the Rex. He grabbed Vui's crash helmet before he left as he only had one, and she was not amused. "I have to stay here tonight I can't go home."

"Tough shit! You wouldn't go home anyway," was the parting banter.

It didn't have to be Friday night at this time. Every night, at this time, was pandemonium, known as going around, and it would last until about eight thirty or nine o'clock. Thousands of families on bikes sometimes four or even five to a bike, going around the sea front in the cool of the evening. It was a way of life, and the children loved that and the numerous funfairs dotted everywhere.

Two of the American teachers were already seated, backs to the swimming pool wall looking out to the funfair across the road. They raised their hands in greeting and Ian got a beer.

"G'day, Cobber," Garry greeted him with.

"Not bad, you're learning." Ian sat down beside them.

"Where's the rest of the brains trust?" Ian asked.

"They have a seminar till six then they'll be along," drawled Jimmy the Texan.

"You get everything sorted out?" Garry asked.

"Yeh! a good result. Better than I expected. Willie at the seminar too?" Ian answered; he had confided in them before he left for Australia and they were aware of the situation as it had been.

Garry laughed. "Don't start. He didn't get invited and his nose is out of joint. He'll be here in a minute." He was about to add something else but a fit of coughing stopped him.

"Brilliant! You need to lay off the smokes," Ian advised.

"Speak of the devil," said Jimmy.

"Willie! How's it goin', mate?" Ian shouted at the figure coming through the entrance.

"William! You're here again," he snapped. "My private bottle, a glass, and some iced water," he ordered and strode to the table.

"Thought you were at a seminar, Willie," Ian started winding him up. He had been content to be called Willie until Ian had pointed out it was another word for a penis but in his case a prick.

"Below my level," he answered, puffing himself out like a blowfish.

Water off a duck's back this one, you couldn't get the better of him. You couldn't even offend him; he slithered out of everything.

"I saw a goddess today. I reckon she was the most beautiful chick in the world. Man, you should have seen her. Long, blonde hair, beautiful eyes and a body you would die for. She was something else," Ian threw into the fire and waited. The two Americans said nothing, they were waiting for a response also.

"I remember when I was in China – Dalian to be precise," Willie began. "The Swiss Hotel at the top of the hill. You wouldn't know. There was a girl working there – I was dumbstruck when I saw her. Beautiful doesn't even begin to describe her. She was gorgeous. Out of this world – Valarie her name was – I don't suppose this thing you saw had a name?" he fired at Ian.

"Lada!" Ian replied.

"I didn't ask what she was driving but if it was a Lada that says it all for who was inside, don't you think?" He chuckled and dismissed the subject.

"No! Her name is Lada. Surely a man of your intellect knows the definition of Lada?" Ian queried.

Willie sighed and took a sip of whiskey. "I am not really interested but I would imagine it is an eastern European description of a heap of scrap metal with an engine on it," he concluded.

"No! Lada is, and I quote: 'The ancient Slavic Goddess of Beauty' and she is standing behind you."

Willie spun around, spilling half the contents of his glass when his eyes saw what was standing behind him. He made a fumbled attempt to stand up but made it only half way. From a bent position he issued an apology and extended his dry left hand meekly.

Garry and Jimmy were on their feet also and if Willie had bothered to take notice neither of them had heard a word he had said, they were both transfixed by what had come through the entrance.

Ian gave her a cuddle and introduced her. She smiled and shook hands with all. He returned with a beer for her and they settled into the company. Willie pointed an unsteady finger at Ian and blurted, "you win, *this time,* Heathen."

"Well, that's a first." Ian smiled in satisfaction.

Soon afterwards, the seminar mob arrived and were equally dumbstruck by what was in their midst, Ian throwing down the gauntlet from the start as he and Garry waited to be served.

"Yeh! We're long-time friends. I went to Vladivostok to get her here, and God help the bastard who tries to steal this one," he confided in him, knowing full well he would soon spread that shit amongst the others, 'lay off' being the message.

Ian could scarcely believe she was real. The sun had reddened her face a little and it only added to her beauty. Dressed in a body hugging, bottle green, low cut top and jeans, matching gold necklace and earrings shrouded by glistening blonde hair that cascaded across her left eye and shoulder. His heart was thumping again and she slid her hand into his making him jump.

"She better take them off," Garry advised, pointing to his neck and ear.

Ian got his drift.

"Take off your jewellery and give it to me. It's dangerous to wear jewellery out in the street. Somebody will grab it off your neck and you might get hurt. You're beautiful without it anyhow," he added, squeezing her hand. She smiled and squeezed his in return.

She was doing as Ian had advised. Taking in the conversation and getting an overview of the situation without revealing her interest in teaching English. Apart from not being able to keep their eyes off her for more than a few seconds, the professors were engrossed in their usual post mortem of the day's events and being Friday, pay day, they had more than a little complaining to do. Ian had to time this right before they extinguished their gripes and started firing questions at her. He noted she was the focal point of another audience at the entrance. Mostly girls and small children fascinated by her hair. She attracted them more than the fun park across the road.

"Finish your beer and we'll go around," Ian suggested.

"OK! I see what you mean." Lada smiled and scooped up, they started to leave. Much to the disappointment of all but Ian was adamant.

"No more drink, we're going around. You know what that's like. You want me to kill her?" he insisted. "Willie! The floor is yours." Ian bowed in victory.

The onlookers at the entrance were buzzing as Lada neared them. She looked at Ian.

"They're fascinated with your hair," he explained.

She waded into the crowd and rubbed a few heads playfully and much to their glee. They wanted to touch her hair but she kept it draped over her breasts and managed to avoid the groping fingers cordially. One little girl she picked up and let her feel her hair. The child was ecstatic and shouted to the others. The effect was instant and they calmed down. Ian could only surmise they were having bets as to whether Lada's hair was real or not.

It took some adjustment of Vui's helmet to get all her head into it, but eventually he succeeded. Thank God she was wearing jeans; at least she could sit secure on the bike, unlike the Vietnamese girls who sat side-saddle with dresses on. They left the bar and turned right along the boulevard into the throng of 'going around' people. Hundreds of bikes were on the move. She squeezed her breasts against his back and put her arms around his waist, rested her chin on his shoulder and gazed at the amazing spectacle all around. Vung Tau came to life in the dark. They turned at the Cable Car and stopped for a look at the brightly lit cars going up and down the mountain. She wanted to go up but Ian persuaded her that was for another day.

Next, they headed along the beach front past all the restaurants and bars along the seafront, the ferry terminal and everything all the way to the dragons at the headland. The statue of Christ was lit up also and around the bend the spectacle of back beach opened up to the horizon, hotels, bars, massage parlours and shopping malls stretching to Paradise Park. Lada was delighted. Ian did a U-turn at Paradise and headed back. He turned right at the bottom of the statue mountain and followed the road all the way back to the front beach. Going a few hundred yards up on the wrong side of the road he started to climb the road leading to the lighthouse. It was the only road all the way to the top of the ridge, and it was steep. Slowly they crawled their way to the lighthouse perched above the city; the view was spectacular. They kissed long and hard and he never wanted this moment to end. He was indeed in love with this girl.

CHAPTER FOUR

Debbie stared at Dan, she was getting really pissed off with his self-pity and defeatist attitude. She knew he had a bad experience when he was a paramedic but it was what he had trained to do and there was nothing more he could have done to save a young boy's life. The boy had died in his arms and he had cracked up. She had to tread carefully as he was in denial and, being a nurse herself, she knew he needed time to heal.

"Shit happens, unlucky or whatever, you have to get on with it. I'm calling Joe; will you go and help them on the island if I ask him?" she said soothingly.

He said nothing. His silence more than anything was getting to her. She grabbed her phone.

"Hi Joe, how's it going? Dan is coming over to help. Is there anything you want him to bring with him? You can get stuffed – a sleeping bag, that's it? OK, he'll be over on the first flight he can get."

"What else did he want?" Dan asked curiously.

"A rubber doll – pervert!" she replied.

Dan smiled for the first time in days.

"I reckon you're right, I need something to do, before you drive me mad," he said grabbing her arm. "Fancy a quick one before I fly away?" he suggested.

"OK," she blurted, amazed and surprised. 'How can anybody snap out of depression like that? The bastard, he is having me on,' she thought, as she got undressed.

"Disastrous Dan is coming on the next flight," Joe announced to Clinker and the Leper, both busy at the tractor's engine.

"Is that good or bad?" asked the Leper.

"He's like Errol Flynn, fucks everything he touches," replied Joe, oblivious to Dan's present activity.

"If you're away to pick him up, take my jars to the ship and drop them off with Donny. That'll save the Kanga a trip into town. And if ye want any more whiskey, buy your bloody own," the Leper ordered.

Clinker reckoned the adjustments he had made to the carburettor were enough and he slammed the cover down.

"Try again!" he shouted at Joe, sitting in the driver's seat.

The fiat jumped into life and roared soot out of the exhaust for a few seconds before it settled down and the smoke decreased.

"Jesus Christ – what the hell has he been putting into that thing?" Clinker sputtered, running from the cloud of smoke.

Joe backed the tractor away, then took it for a quick run out over the cattle ramp and back. By the time he returned the machine was running well.

"One down! What next?" he shouted to the Leper, who pointed to the bogey.

"I'll leave her running," Joe declared, parking the tractor away from their working area, and they started on the trailer, or bogey, as the Leper called it. It wasn't a big job, mainly freeing the brakes and tow hitch. Clinker had brought the gas axe and the heat soon made an impression.

Debbie called to confirm Dan's flight time. Joe loaded the camper for the trip to Kingscote under the Leper's direction; two five-gallon jars of eucalyptus concentrate, in two wooden boxes lined with straw.

"Don't break them!" the Leper barked.

"If I break them I'll have to sell the bloody camper, and nobody will buy it with the bloody smell," Joe retorted.

"Away with you!" the Leper waved him gone.

Maria had a list as long as her arm of furniture and everything else for the house. There were four bedrooms, living room and kitchen to furnish and equip. Luckily, there were plenty of second-hand warehouses in Adelaide and she found the bulk of what she wanted very quickly in one. It was also good quality and cheap. She had haggled seriously with the owner and even managed to get delivery to the island arranged directly from the warehouse. She was cock-a-hoop by the time she started on electronics and kitchen utensils. And even more pleased when Debbie phoned her and told her Dan was going to Korena. Like Debbie, Maria was worried about him, she had been the victim of manic depression, which the doctors had eventually diagnosed Russell with.

After what she called *her escape from hell with three children and little else,* she had turned to what she knew best: cooking, Italian style, and soon she was in demand in restaurants around Adelaide. So much in demand that she was offered a partnership in one just to keep her there. Eventually, her partner died and she took over the restaurant. That had allowed her to send Ian to university. Joe couldn't make the grade and wasn't interested in anything except diving. Debbie also went to university but dropped out to go nursing. Maria was a fighter, and her spirit was engrained in her children. There were things she could not forgive or forget. She never divorced, it was against her religion, and now things had come full circle. She wasn't going to let her own misfortune impact on the opportunity her children now had, no matter what her personal feelings were regarding Korena.

The Leper was in good fettle. He had more company in the last few days than in the past few years. He liked this Clinker, he knew what he was doing. He was a good engineer and, unlike

Joe, more military. He had been disciplined properly and had faced death. That changes a man's perception of life like nothing else.

Clinker reversed the tractor to the tow ball hitch and lifted the hydraulics. The trailer responded and he drove away slowly, the Leper peering at all four wheels in turn to make sure they were turning freely. They were, and Clinker decided something to eat and a drink would be in order. The Leper scuttled off and put the kettle on the stove. Clinker left the fiat running; this wasn't an old machine, it looked old and run down but under the shit it looked brand new.

They ate and drank tea but didn't wait long before heading to Korena, Clinker towing the trailer and the Leper following behind with the buggy. Flossy didn't know which one to choose, so ran alongside all the way. The Leper had explained access to Korcan's paddocks was easier from Korena. That made sense and they arrived at the Dutch barn.

The sight inside was not good. Bales of rotten hay and straw were collapsed along the back wall. Where the Leper had been looking for fencing equipment along that wall was going to be a nightmare to clear. Baling string had rotted away and the bales were loose. The place stunk of decomposing material.

Clinker looked at him and laughed. "Looks like we got the short stick!" he said.

"Aye that you did, laddie," the Leper replied and wandered away towards the house.

He hadn't been in there since the house was built. He wouldn't be in there now, if Russell hadn't come and spilled his guts. Still, he got the shivers on approach remembering the old house and those long gone. He entered; the rooms were bare, nothing was left not a stick of furniture or anything which could be identified. The floors were bare, the walls had been painted. Kitchen stripped and the place was like a hospital it was so clean. He gave the place the third degree inspecting every inch of each room. He could see nothing out of order and concluded his suspicion about a good way to ransack the place might have been ill-founded. They had done a good job in a short time. He stared around the barren room and tried to envisage the torment that had ended in this. 'Lacey was your mate, all right, that's for sure, and you paid the price.' Striding outside he looked forward to the future. Maria would soon bring the place back to life. He returned to the barn to find Clinker scattering rotten hay with a pitchfork like a dung spreader. He was fit.

Eventually, Clinker uncovered a tarpaulin; it had rotted away at the top and he could see rolls of fencing underneath.

"Bingo! Looks like were in business, Major!" he shouted.

Strainers, posts, and cyclone were all here and not in bad condition either considering how long they had been abandoned. They started loading the trailer. They were well into it when Joe arrived back from Kingscote. He introduced Dan and in the next breath yelled, "Let's get this show on the road. Get your arse into gear, Danny Boy, there's work to be done. This bastard will need a pair of gloves," he jibed.

Between the four of them they had the trailer stacked high with what the Leper suggested they would need and they called it a day. It was getting dark and they would hit the paddocks at first light. That was the plan, however, Joe had bought several bottles of whiskey and a couple of cases of beer so the plan could change. He also had the sense to get a takeaway for everybody and they were starving. Leaving the tractor and trailer they headed back to Huntly, satisfied with a good day's work.

IN VUNG TAU

Ian and Lada made their way towards the fishing village around the boulevard under the cable cars and straight on. They had spent Friday night going round until close to midnight. She loved seafood and they had plenty to choose from. He hated leaving her at the hotel. However, starting early Saturday morning, they had run together for miles. She appeared wearing a restrainer. He knew immediately when her chest was flat she was an athlete, only they would have such a garment. He wasn't wrong and found it tough going to keep up with her. However, the view of her from behind with a ponytail swishing along her bum was quite enjoyable. All day they spent together and he took her up the mountain in the cable car, to the small zoo on top and the restaurant. They went to a pagoda and gave some money to the monk for the poor, walked for miles along back beach and watched the fishermen catching fish, wading neck-deep out with one end of a net then pulling both ends in together. Lada joined in pulling the net, much to the fishermen's delight when she was bent over, and she didn't seem to care.

They didn't swim on the beach. Her being dressed was attraction enough and they scarpered back to the swimming pool before she was groped to pieces. It wasn't her hair the men wanted to touch. Saturday night he took her to places he had stayed away from for months. He was showing her off and was proud to do so. Some Russians tried to speak to her in Russian but she answered in perfect English, 'Sorry, I don't understand' and they backed off. They both paced themselves and enjoyed the night-life but again he felt sick when he dropped her back at the hotel. Ian had bought her a phone as she had no service on the one she had which looked like a brick, but she could get Russian music on it and clung to it. At least he could call her now or she could call him but Ian was far from happy with the situation.

They came to the start of the fishing village and on both sides of the road frantic activity was going on as catches were sorted out. Crabs, fish, crayfish, and prawns were all being put into air supplied tubs to be kept alive. They stopped at one and Lada jumped right into the middle of things getting splashed, giggling and poking at things in excitement which was infectious.

He left her playing and went to the manager to get crabs to cook, blue swimmers – the same as crabs as he could buy in Australia. The price was extortionate but he got him down a few dollars starting at two then five then ten. "OK, ten good ones," Ian instructed him and watched as they were selected. He ordered two iced coffees and handed one to Lada, who had found an octopus and was fascinated by it.

The crabs were cooked on the premises; it only took ten minutes and they headed in the same direction past large racks of drying squid and small fish until they reached the end of the village a mile away. Ian turned up Truong Cong Dinah and headed for his house.

"You bought a lot of crabs," Lada observed.

"Yep, a peace offering," Ian replied and opened the gate. He was apprehensive of the reception he would receive.

Vui came rushing out and took the bags from him before he had time to speak.

"Hello! You must be Lada! Welcome, I am pleased to meet you, come inside, come inside," she insisted.

Ian was gobsmacked then twigged – Rosie, she must have phoned Vui – brilliant. But Ian knew the past, and Vui's family were South Vietnamese, some didn't take kindly to Russians.

Lada had a good look around and Ian took her upstairs to view the surrounding gardens. Palm trees and mango, jack-fruit, banana, star fruit, and papaya were all growing next door. He pointed out and named each one.

"You have a very lovely house," Lada said.

"Let's go and have some crab," Ian insisted.

Vui had already set the table and the crabs were in the middle.

"You take six home with you," Ian told her.

"Six! You sure? Thank you, Ian." She busied herself putting the crabs back in the bag. "I will take them home now!" she announced and looked at Lada across the table. "Why you stay in the hotel? Why you not come and stay here?" She waited for an answer.

"Because I haven't been asked to come and stay here," came the reply.

Vui threw Ian a look and turned away saying, "You are very beautiful, and I want you to come and stay here before *he* goes Com Dinghy," she pleaded, and left.

Ian couldn't believe she had just done that. He turned to Lada who was busy breaking off a crab claw.

"Are you serious, you would come and stay here if I asked you to?" he queried.

"Why don't you ask me and find out?" she replied.

"Well! Will you come and stay here?" he asked, his heart in his mouth.

"Yes! These crabs are brilliant, you should try one," she teased and threw her arm around his neck.

"The hotel won't be pleased if you leave early," he said and kissed her.

"No! It's OK, I didn't know what I was going to do so I have just been paying one day at a time. I can leave whenever you want because I know what I am doing now, I am staying with you!" She straddled her legs across his lap and kissed him hard.

"We can eat crabs later." Ian picked her up and headed for the bedroom; she didn't object.

Despite the fan, the heat drove them apart drenched in sweat and body fluids. They had a shower together, cold and refreshing. Ian could scarcely believe what had just happened. He could scarcely believe what he was looking at. A body you would die for, an artistic form of doom, he couldn't take his eyes off her and his hands began to caress her again.

"Come! We must go and get my things from the hotel," she said, running her fingernail through the hairs on his chest and lifting a towel.

She was right but Ian wanted more of her. He took the towel from her and crushed her into his chest, kissing her tenderly. She returned the gesture and they stood embraced until she stared into his eyes with a meaningful look.

"Come! We have plenty of time," she whispered and scarpered off to get dressed.

She was cracking crab claws when Ian joined her and he suddenly became aware of another hunger. They ate and had tea, hers with a slice of lemon, no sugar. He suggested they get a taxi and bring her luggage back to the house. That wasn't hard to arrange as hundreds of taxis went up and down Trong Cong Dinah.

The reception was as he had feared but not so bad. He was known in the hotel, he was a regular customer, so they accepted the loss of their guest, knowing she would be back. Lada paid for that night also and that made them happy. At length they escaped and returned to the house. Vui had not reappeared but her crash helmet was still hanging on his bike. He decided they would go around while daylight lasted; there were many things she still had to see and he wanted to display her, especially along the bars beside the palace where the good time guys hung out on a Sunday afternoon. The paedophiles, as Wilson called them.

Lada knew instinctively what he was doing when she saw the stunned effect she had on her admirers. She poked him hard in the ribs. "You are a bad man! Go! Go!" she insisted.

Ian grinned from ear to ear and turned right onto the boulevard. Ahead, there was a school set back from the road. In the playground at the front were several hundred kids in martial arts dress. The heat was out of the day and this was their training time.

"Stop! Stop! I want to stop here," Lada insisted.

Ian drove up onto the pavement beside the school gates and stopped.

Lada jumped off the bike, threw him her helmet and before he had time to question her she shot through the gates. He watched as she approached an instructor, who looked at her very strangely. She bowed and the instructor bowed in response. He had about twenty children lined up in single file and Ian watched bewitched as Lada joined the end of the line. She smiled at him and suddenly took up a stance with her left arm outstretched and fist clenched. Right arm elbow to her hip and palm open. Instantly, all the children took up the same stance. Ian was intrigued. He hadn't a clue what they were shouting after that but it was a synchronised display of rapid movement of body and limbs. The last command was accompanied by a thunderous roar of hand clapping as both arms outstretched and feet together they finished. He suddenly realised all the children watching were clapping madly and shouting the commands.

Instant silence ensued. Lada bowed to the line and they bowed back. Then, she was rushed by hundreds of smiling faces. She managed to escape with the help of several instructors. They passed her safely through the gate, bowed and turned yelling at their pupils.

She jumped onto the back of the bike.

"That was good!" she exclaimed, a little breathless.

Ian was breathless as well. *Bloody hell,* he thought. *Have I just been in bed with that? She could have killed me.*

"You OK? You didn't hurt yourself?" he asked, concern in his voice.

"I have a black Belt in Tae Kwan Do. No problem. Can you help me put this thing on again?" she asked.

He fastened her up and drove back onto the road, the children waving as they left. Lada waved frantically back.

"Do you do any martial arts?" she asked over the bike's engine.

"Wilson reckons I have a black belt in the Kama Sutra," Ian replied.

He couldn't see her face but from the reply he concluded she hadn't a clue what the Kama Sutra was, which might be just as well.

"This Wilson, you always speak about him. When am I going to meet him?" she asked.

"How about now! We'll go and pick up some food and go see him now – OK?"

"OK!" she shouted.

"Aw, not you again, is this for me?" Wilson greeted them, brushing Ian aside and taking Lada's hand.

"Come in, my dear. Just ignore the company – it might go away." He beckoned her to be seated.

"You must be Lada!" He glanced at Ian who gave him a quizzical look in return. "The bush telegraph, it was wrong; she is much more beautiful than I was told. Welcome, my dear." He planted a kiss on her cheek and she blushed.

"If he offers you Viagra don't take it," Ian advised Lada to add to her confusion.

"Now, tell me all about yourself while the maid prepares our food." He dismissed Ian with a wave of his hand.

He wanted to say, 'And fuck you too, Wilson' but had been keeping the swearing under control since he had met Lada. He gave a grunt and went to get plates and chop sticks. She was amused.

Wilson had more out of her in two minutes than Ian had in three days and they were having a jolly good time when the maid interrupted them with food.

"No cowboys today, Wilson, or your TV's broken," Ian stirred.

Lada excused herself and they pointed the way.

"Bloody hell. How did an unshaven, uncouth barbarian win that?" Wilson asked to nobody in particular.

"Charm, Wilson, pure Aussie charm. Have a noodle," Ian responded.

The crack was good and Lada relaxed; even more she seemed to relish the banter and quickly latched on to the young and old relationship as though it was something she was used to. She cleaned the dishes and put everything away under Wilson's gaze of approval.

"Let me show you I got a new thing from my daughter in England yesterday. It's complicated but a lot of fun." He scarpered into his office and returned with an iPad.

"Games, hundreds of them in here, let me show you!" he said excitedly.

"This the reason the floor isn't covered in bullets?" Ian asked.

"Don't be facetious," he replied and activated the iPad.

Lada looked at Ian, she didn't know what to make of this. She actually felt a little sad that he had to resort to computer games. However, she prompted Wilson to show what he had learned and was impressed.

"When did you get this?" she asked.

"Yesterday DHL," he answered, clicking away.

"You are very good, have you played this before?" she asked.

"Never seen one before. Right! Enough of that, now tell me what's happening with you two?" Wilson closed the iPad and put it onto the table, conscious he had guests.

"Lada's moved in with me!" Ian informed him.

"You have my sympathy, dear; I wouldn't move in with him, too hairy for me." He laughed.

They spent several hours with Wilson then returned to the house. Vui still hadn't returned and they decided to have an early night and run in the morning before Ian went to work. Lada changed into some house clothes as she called it and Ian's pulse started to race again as he caught glimpses of what showed through the silk. The night wasn't going to be long enough.

Only Fred was at the geological building when Ian arrived. He immediately asked Ian to join him in his office.

"I contacted John on Friday and this is his reply." Fred passed a sheet of paper across the desk and Ian read:

Dear Fred. Ref your Email regarding Ian Ingles. His proposal to take the pressure off the rest of your team is very noble and has been noted. However, at this stage we are not contemplating any redundancies in Vietnam in the near future. The consolidation of resources if the worst comes to the worst, at a later date, will envelop your entire team as they are young and will be of great value to the company going forward after this recession.

We are aware of Ian's recent loss and I have discussed this issue with the board. They all agree that if he requires time to sort out affairs relating to that loss we are prepared to allow him to take garden leave for as long as he requires. This measure is entirely at your discretion as will be his placement after taking such leave. I hope this compromise is satisfactory to his needs and between you an understanding can be arranged.

Yours sincerely,

J Crombie C E O.'

Ian looked at Fred and shrugged. "What do I make of that?" he asked, slightly confused.

Fred smiled. "It's what I suggested myself but it has to go through the proper channels. I need you to stay here for the next three weeks. After Albert gets back from offshore you can return to Oz. However, you'll not be on wages but your job will remain open until you sort everything out. There's one other thing, when Albert returns he has to move into your house, I can't justify paying for an empty house and his is more expensive than yours. We will rearrange accommodation when you get back and take it from there."

"What about the maid?" Ian asked.

"Vui will stay. She's the best there is. Albert's maid came with the house and she will go back with the house, that was the agreement."

"Brilliant!" Ian expressed.

"Right, we have work to do so let's get on with it," Frank concluded.

The day passed so quickly Ian had to be told to stop work at four thirty. There was a mountain of graphs to study and he had to concentrate on his job; it wasn't a job which allowed concentration to either lapse or deviate. It was hard not to at first but his professionalism kicked in and he got on with it. Lada met him at the gate, excited as hell. Vui had taken her to the market and to meet her family. She had a good day and met a lot of people; she wished she spoke Vietnamese and she had cooked fish Russian style, delighting Vui who could cook whatever she was shown exactly as she was shown. Something new was like a present to her. He was glad they were getting on together; it had worried him that they might not and it was a load off his mind.

He tried to call Joe but the phone signal was gone so Vui informed him, which wasn't unusual. He hoped it would come back before it was too late in Australia; it was ten p.m. there now.

He went on to his computer and wrote things down. They were doing the dishes and giggling in the kitchen. He waited, watching CNN news. More gloom and doom, but the signal never came back. They showered together after Vui left for home and came close to another session in bed but she held off and got dressed, insisting they could do that later: they had all night. He couldn't argue with that and got dressed also.

"I'm going to see Wilson for a couple of minutes. Do you want to come?" he asked, putting the paper he had written on into his shirt pocket.

"Yes! I don't want you to leave me for a whole minute. Somebody might hurt me." She laughed.

Little bloody chance of that, he thought, *more the reverse.*

"Go away – but leave the beautiful one," was Wilson's greeting.

Lada gave him a big hug full frontal and he swooned.

"My God, I'm glad Dick's not here; take a pew," he invited them.

"No! We're only passing by. A quick one, Wilson," Ian said. Taking the paper from his pocket he read aloud:

"Parallel tracking, creeping line, expanding square, sector, barrier, track line." He looked at Wilson.

"And what might you be searching *for*?" Wilson asked.

"Just checking you know what they are," replied Ian.

"Don't be a buffoon. Do you know what a core sample is?" Wilson fired back at him.

"Yeh! they take them at the clinic to see if you have the clap. You ever been in the desert? Apart from when you're in *Rawhide*?" Ian enquired.

"I have been in many deserts and they were all blue," Wilson snorted.

"You better pack your flip flops, you may be going to another one and it's not blue," Ian responded, guiding Lada towards the door.

"Elaborate! Why are you interested in search patterns, young man – tell me!" Wilson demanded.

"I will when I'm ready," Ian answered, leaving Wilson muttering about upside down illogical riddles.

"And don't come back!" he yelled after him.

Lada looked at him curiously.

"You and your father get on very well," she commented.

"He isn't my father. I told you my father had died—" He was silenced by her finger across his mouth.

"He is! You just don't know it," she said sternly.

"OK, I will adopt the little shit if it makes you happy," he agreed.

"It *will* make me happy. Can we go around?" She squeezed into his back, digging her fingernails into his chest.

CHAPTER FIVE

Every option available to him had been thrown around in Ian's head but there were so many variables he concluded there was nothing he could achieve from Vietnam. Now, Fred had given him the opportunity to go back and his job remained open, which was something he couldn't have dreamed about a week ago. He would be crazy not to take advantage of the opportunity. He was worried about Lada. There was no way he was going to leave her here. There was no way he was going to leave her anywhere. Either she went to Australia with him or they stayed here, but both options had complications. He thought for a long time and could see no alternative. It might backfire but he would never know unless he tried.

He stopped at Kim Hang the jewellers and looked at the engagement rings glistening in the soft light. One thing was for sure 24 carat meant 24 carat in Vietnam, no cheap rubbish here. The Vietnamese viewed jewellery as an investment, not as a sentimental decoration, and they didn't take kindly to being cheated. The prices were the local prices. Not inflated tourist prices, so anyone could get a fair deal. His heart was pounding when he selected a ring. What kind of ring does a goddess wear? Certainly not a small one he decided, and went for the most expensive one on display. A ruby and diamond cluster set in 24 carat gold. It was six hundred US dollars but would have cost twice that anywhere else.

She was busy with Vui in the kitchen when he arrived at the house. He showered and they ate together. She insisted on clearing up and Vui left.

It was time to do some explaining.

"Lada, you know my father died a short time ago. Sit there and I will explain something to you." She sat opposite him and waited.

"There are things which need sorting out in Australia that're impossible to sort out from here. My boss has given me permission to go and my job is OK when I get back. But I might be away for quite a while and I don't want to leave you. I would like you to come back to Australia with me until I sort everything out."

She blinked a few times and nodded her head.

"To get an Australian visa for you in Vietnam is not easy, you are Russian not Vietnamese. I spoke with the Australian consulate in Ho Chi Minh today and they are prepared to give you a visa. Except there's a catch." He looked at her sitting silently with wider than usual eyes. He went on, "I told them you were my fiancée and that we were going to Australia to get married." She stared at him wide eyed and waited.

He pulled the box out of his pocket and took the ring out. She gasped at the beauty of it.

"You need to wear this when you go to the consulate. That's if you will come to Australia?" He handed her the ring.

"You had better ask me first," she said.

Ian frowned. "I just did," he answered.

"Not to wear that ring you didn't," she insisted.

The penny dropped and from what was supposed to be a convenience he found himself asking on one knee, "Will you marry me?"

She pushed him and he fell over backwards. She jumped on top of his belly and smothered him in kisses. He was overwhelmed with confusion and pleasure. At last he managed to reverse the posture and stared down into moist eyes.

"Was that a yes or no?" he laughed.

She held out her hand. It was shaking uncontrollably and he slipped the ring onto her finger, his own hand shaking just as much.

"Yes," she whispered and drew him down on her. Time was not on his side. Ian knew as soon as Albert returned he would be expected to move. A visa without complications took a standard five working days to be issued and he needed her to go to the consulate in Saigon first thing on Monday morning but first, he had another task to perform.

"Ow, not you again, don't you have a home to go to?" Wilson queried, landing a kiss on Lada's cheek.

"Never let a chance go by, pervert!" Ian threw at him.

Wilson spotted the ring on Lada and peered over his glasses at Ian with a questioning stare.

"You're going to Australia," Ian announced.

Wilson's eyes enlarged and he looked at Lada then back at Ian.

"Am I to assume congratulations are in order?" he asked.

"You are! And never mind the pep talk we are going to get married." He smiled as Wilson stole another kiss from the beauty.

"You have my sympathy, dear. Be Seated!" he shouted at the top of his voice and they obeyed.

"Now, young man, elaborate!" Wilson demanded.

"You know the Australian consulate, Wilson?" Ian asked.

"I do, the zookeeper is a friend of mine as you know," he answered, very coy.

"Can you take Lada up there on Monday and get a visa organised for her and you? Just a tourist visa, ninety days. I know you are very busy playing games and shooting Indians, but can you tear yourself away for a while?" His voice was laced with sarcasm.

"One will have to think about this!" Wilson snapped and sucked on his unlit pipe. "OK, I've thought about it and what part will I play in this endeavour?" he enquired.

"Bridesmaid!" Ian replied.

"Let me see your ring," Wilson demanded, taking Lada's hand.

"Vui will arrange transport for Monday and pick you up here. As soon as we get the visas organised I'll get flights arranged. *And paid for,*" Ian announced.

"You are a very lucky scoundrel," Wilson answered.

As arranged they left for Saigon, ninety kilometres away through traffic which had its own way of life, and arrived at the consulate at opening time. Wilson asked to see the Consul General and was invited to do so.

"Captain Wilson, it's been a long time, I'm glad to see you. You are looking well." He hadn't taken his eyes off Lada as he spoke.

"Clive! Good to see you also. May I introduce Lada. She is Russian and she is about to marry one of your countrymen *in* Australia," Wilson announced.

"I am delighted to meet you, Lada. Congratulations; that's a beautiful ring, it suits you. And how can I help, Captain?" he asked, tearing his eyes away from Lada.

"Visas, Clive. We need visas so Ian can arrange dates – I believe I am to be the bridesmaid." Wilson dismissed the formality in one statement.

"Ian?" Clive picked up on it immediately.

"Ian Ingles in Vung Tau, the geologist," Wilson enlightened him.

"Ah! Yes, we have met, I believe. But you can get a visa on arrival, Captain," he pointed out.

"Yes, Clive, I know, but she can't, so it makes sense to get both visas here and everything in order before we leave. These two have been corresponding for years and he eventually managed to get her here. However, he wants to get married with his family around – you know the situation, Clive; can you streamline things a little? Ian has to arrange leave as well so it's imperative we have some specific date to aim for," Wilson lied.

"I will certainly see what I can do. Lada, as long as your passport is in order I can't see there being any problem. It will still take five working days, I'm afraid, that's the law." Clive summarised, "I will take you to reception, Captain, and you can fill out the documents required. Do you speak much English, Lada?" Clive enquired.

She laughed and took Clive's hand, much to Wilson's amusement.

"I teach English, thank you very much for helping me." She kissed the back of his hand softly and Clive blushed. "We will be forever grateful to you." She smiled and he melted.

Clive cleared his throat and Wilson winked at her as they made their way to the reception.

Ho Chi Minh City (Saigon), a city of turmoil to the unwary. Organised chaos, and some not so diplomatic descriptions. It was still fascinating and had many attractions. They spent several hours going places even Wilson had never visited and had lunch on the roof garden of the Rex Hotel overlooking the statue of the man himself, Ho Chi Minh, his arms enveloping the children on the square below.

They hit the road, Wilson insisting they leave before the rush hour or they would never get out of the city. They stopped again at Baria and bought some cold drinks before finally arriving back at Ian's house at four p.m., exhausted. It was a long day.

Lada was spread-eagled on the bed when Ian came home and she was fast asleep. He decided to go and see Wilson alone.

"Aw not you again, can't you give me some peace?" Wilson greeted him.

"Any problems?" Ian asked anxiously.

"None whatsoever, that girl could walk into the White House if she put her mind to it," Wilson replied.

"Right! Wilson, I need to speak to you seriously. I need your help in Oz. I can't tell you why; you just have to trust me, it's important. I'll tell you what it's all about when we get there and *you* can decide if you want to get involved when I put you in the picture."

"I strongly suspect ulterior motives are afoot. You hurt that girl and my foot will go right up your rectum, got it?" Wilson snapped.

"Don't worry about that, there is no way I will hurt her. I didn't expect to marry her but now I can't think about anything else. But, first things first, Wilson, we have something to do that won't wait and I need your help."

"The search patterns?" Wilson said, raising an eyebrow.

"Don't bloody start. I'm not going to tell you until we have a team together and that's that. So piss off," Ian hissed.

"I didn't see a dress that fitted me in Saigon," Wilson replied.

"You should have gone to the shipyard, they would have welded something up for you," Ian quipped, heading for the door. He was closely followed by a hurtling paperback.

"Be gone, you goat," echoed through the wood.

His love for her was getting stronger by the day and they were joined at the hip whenever they were together. He found himself looking at his watch longing for work to finish, something he had never experienced. Lada didn't speak much which was unlike Linh who never stopped. He was intrigued to find out she had been educated in Japan of all places, in the international school in Tokyo. They had a lot in common; a broken marriage had resulted in her grandfather taking her under his wing. He had worked in the Russian Embassy in Tokyo and had her educated according to what he decided was her ticket to independence: English and chemical engineering. Lada had a degree in both which made him curious until she explained she had to get one to get the other as both were in English.

She just laughed off his suggestion she could have been a model, saying, 'tell my grandfather that and he will kill you.' This explained her martial arts achievements; where better to learn than Japan?

Ian had talked to Joe, Debbie and Maria over the course of the week and everything was going ahead at Korena. Joe reckoned Dan thought manual labour was a Spanish immigrant and had dispatched him and the dog to find sheep in the scrub as he was good for fuck all else, Joe decided. One shipment of furniture had arrived at Korena and they had people from Kingscote laying carpet.

"Give the dog money to Maria," Ian had ordered Joe and waited for a response. It was delayed action but eventually he said OK and changed the subject.

On the Friday, both Lada and Wilson went to pick up their visas personally from Clive, who was all over Lada like a rash, according to Wilson.

"One can misjudge people, I always thought he was queer. As well as being Australian," he informed Ian.

"Bent as a cowboy's hat, you got it right the first time."

As Ian had suspected, Albert came back early, a week early. However, thanks to Clive they had everything needed to book flights. Vietnam Airlines to Adelaide – nothing else! Wilson had insisted.

"Cattle class, I take it!" he moaned when Ian gave him his ticket.

"They wouldn't give *you* any other class," was the reply.

"Ninety, sodding, days," Wilson blurted out.

"Yeh! That's your visa time, isn't it?" Ian teased him.

"Aw! Now, look here you wretched individual. What in the name of god is to take three months?" Wilson spluttered.

"Culture, Wilson, I reckon it will take three months to educate you in the finer art of Aussie etiquette," Ian said.

"You'll need longer than that. You'll have to find some first!" he shouted.

"Exactly that's what the search patterns were for, you happy now?" Ian laughed.

"Go to hell!" being the reply.

Ian had dreaded telling Vui they were leaving and that Albert would be moving into the house and, as predicted, she started crying. Lada comforted her and assured her they wouldn't be away for long. She came around quickly.

"I won't miss him, I will miss you," she said, clinging to Lada.

"Thank you very much. See what you've done, woman, stolen my mother." Lada pouted her lips at him in response.

"I will come to the airport with you!" Vui announced. Ian didn't object.

He had the flights booked for the seventh of June. Gone were the days of formal dress for travel. Jeans and T-shirts were standard especially in cattle class. Security was a nightmare as usual.

"We should come undressed and get dressed inside. That should hurry things up a bit," Wilson grumbled.

"Not if she was in front of you it wouldn't." Ian pointed at Lada.

"True! It would take a week to get through. That's if they ever let her go! Osama Bin Layabout, this is all his fault you know?" Wilson pointed out.

They made it to their seats eventually, Lada headed straight for the window one. She was bubbling with excitement and kept squeezing Ian's hand and anything else she came in contact with.

"Thank God that's the worst bit over," Ian declared, sitting in the middle next to her. Wilson took the aisle, so he could stretch his legs. Ian reckoned he would have to stretch his legs to reach the floor.

"I only like landings and take-offs, the bit in the middle they can keep. My bottom's sore already thinking about it," said Wilson.

"Sure you're not thinking about Clive?" Ian asked.

"Uncouth savage," Wilson grunted.

"We will drink three little vodkas and eat. Then we will sleep until we wake up!" Lada turned to Ian, who looked at her curiously. "That's what my grandfather recommends for long flights. OK?" she asked.

"Sounds like a good idea to me." Ian spoke to the back of her head, she wouldn't stop looking out the window and shouted 'Go! Go! Go!' as the jet taxied for take-off.

He laughed at her antics. She obviously hadn't much experience in the air, it would wear off.

She went wild when the plane lifted off, such was her joy she threw her arm behind his neck and pulled him to her, smothering him in kisses and tears.

"Keep your knickers on, girl, you'll do yourself an injury," Ian soothed, stroking her hair. She laughed and again the window became irresistible.

It was a seven-hour flight; not exactly long haul but long enough They would touch down in Adelaide at seven fifteen a.m. and Ian reckoned they would be clear of the airport by eight thirty. The seatbelt sign went off and Wilson bounded into a four-seat middle row which was empty much to the annoyance of a young Vietnamese man who looked pissed off.

Wilson put his thumb up to Ian. Experience! Now they all had leg-room. Three little vodkas and some food later, Lada and Wilson slept nearly all the way to Adelaide.

"West Lakes," Ian instructed the taxi driver, and they headed off.

Lada and Wilson sat in the back chatting and taking in the surroundings. Ian was tired; unlike them, he hadn't slept. The effect she had on the waiting crowd at arrivals, who were mostly Vietnamese, was a repetition of her reception in Vung Tau, except they didn't try and touch her. Just smiled and stared.

Wilson whinged like hell because nobody met them at the airport. Nobody knew they were coming. "I didn't want to alarm the people you were here, Wilson," Ian declared.

"I'm amused the sun comes up in the east. Upside down it should be back to front." Wilson rambled on, trying to wind Ian up.

Ian had been here before but couldn't remember the number. The taxi followed his directions until told to stop.

"OK, we're here. Let's go!" He paid the driver and they got their luggage.

The house was large, no fence just lawn both sides of the path. A sleek Jaguar was sitting in the drive and Lada stared at it. It was indeed cold and all three of them shivered in their tropical attire. Ian had misjudged the weather.

He rang the doorbell and waited. And waited. He rang it again and heard a commotion inside.

Dick threw the door open and his mouth followed suit,

"Linda! Phone the nuthouse and book me a room, the world has ended. What the hell are you doing here?" he shouted.

"Good morning, sir, we are from the Salvation Army. We have come to *save you*," Ian announced.

"Get bloody inside before you freeze to death," Dick ordered, grabbing Lada's bag.

Linda came hurrying from the kitchen, concern etched on her face then she screamed out, "Ian, it's been a long time, have you come to take him away? Please, he's driving me nuts," she pleaded.

She landed a kiss on Ian and addressed the other two. "And who have you brought with you?" she exclaimed.

"This is Lada and Wilson. Kindly meet Linda," he introduced them.

Linda hugged Lada and, still hanging on to her, asked, "You are the famous, Captain Wilson, at last and in the flesh?"

"Just Wilson, dear; I'm a Wilson and he's a Dick!" Wilson replied.

"Yes! You got that right." Linda laughed.

"Come on, girl, go and get some clothes on, for God's sake. You idiot, didn't you know it was bloody freezing here?" she fired at Ian as she led Lada into a bedroom with her case.

"I don't bloody believe this!" Dick said, shaking his head. "What the hell are you two doing here? And where the hell did you get *that*?" he thumbed towards the bedroom.

Ian grinned and said nothing.

"Come on, into the kitchen, it's warmer in there. A waste of time putting the fire on, it'll be thirty degrees by ten a.m.," Dick gruffed.

"If you see any buckets or wee stools in here Wilson, throw them into the lake," Ian suggested.

Dick fired up the jug; the kitchen was spacious and modern: there was a veranda overlooking the lake and a small speedboat was tied up at his private pier. Wilson took it all in. It was impressive. He had known Dick for twenty years but had no idea this was what he was coming home to.

"How did an old goat manage to get such a young, good looking wife?" he said out loud.

"Sit down, you old fart," Dick instructed.

"I'm not sitting with my back to *that*! Crocodiles," Wilson muttered, pointing to the lake.

"No problem, Wilson, the sharks have eaten them all. Coffee! Help yourself," said Dick, straddling a chair at the head of the table. He shook his head silently as they obliged.

There was great hilarity through the house and Linda came dancing into the kitchen, grabbed something and danced out singing to herself.

"That's what she does when I leave," Dick said.

"We all do that when you leave," Ian added.

"I was Shanghaied you know, I was supposed to be going to Australia and I ended up in the South Pole," Wilson announced to nobody in particular.

"Well, shit-head, where did *she* come from?" Dick demanded of Ian.

"From Russia with Love!" Ian replied.

"Wilson! Kick him in the nuts. How the hell did you manage to woo her? She's far too bloody good for you, little shit," Dick insisted. Ian grinned.

A blast of sunlight spread across the lake, lighting up the kitchen as Lada and Linda came in, holding hands.

Linda thrust the engagement ring under Dick's nose. "See! Love still exists," she announced.

Dick pointed to her own hand, "Woman, you have more rings than a racing pigeon and you don't home-in on anything. They don't work." Dick dismissed the claim, throwing Ian a questioning look.

"I see you're not booked in anywhere. Where are you going to stay, and for how long?" Dick went on.

"They're staying here for as long as they like. Come on, Lada, let's get things sorted out," Linda declared and the two of them flirted out of the kitchen, laughing.

"Fuck me drunk, don't tell me I have to put up with you bloody pair *day and night*? I'm doomed." Dick sighed.

"It's your lucky day. Where's your car?" Ian asked.

"In the drive!" Dick replied.

"That's Linda's, where's yours?" Ian insisted.

"In the bloody garage, I suppose," Dick replied.

"So you've been back for a month and never even took the car out of the bloody garage. What the hell have you been doing for a month? Sitting here feeling sorry for yourself. Well, you'd better move your arse now, we have a big job on. Ask Wilson." Ian scurried away to see Lada.

Dick looked expectantly at Wilson and waited.

"I think it's mission impossible. Dick, we are searching for etiquette, Australian etiquette, the baboon knows more than I," Wilson said.

"Nothing changes, you two are still *mad*! Thank God you're here, Wilson; I'm nearly round the bloody bend!" Dick confessed.

"Curiosity, Dick, it's all about curiosity. I have no idea what he's up to. But *we* are going to be as curious as hell and find out. Keep curious about things, it's the only way we can survive ashore," Wilson advised.

"I'm curious as hell about Mrs Baboon; that's a good start, Wilson," Dick agreed.

Linda met Ian at the bedroom door and ushered him in.

"You two get a few hours' sleep. I'm going to the galley, to make some dinner. Don't argue," she warned.

Lada embraced him, smiling, and looked into his eyes. "You have two fathers," she whispered.

"Yeh! And it looks like you have one mother so far and one to come." He kissed her; they undressed and dived below the blankets.

CHAPTER SIX

The next two days were frantic, emotional and complicated. Ian didn't want to phone Joe, Debbie, or Maria, yet he had to get the men off the island. Debbie and Maria he contacted directly and emotions ran wild when they were introduced to Lada. She, in turn, was overcome with emotion.

The three at Korena had to be herded by the Leper. They protested all the way to the airport. Debbie picked them up and delivered them to Dick's.

The four females were in the bedroom and Debbie was worse than the other two with her new sister. She'd never had a sister and to get one like Lada sent her into seventh heaven. A life size Barbie doll on steroids, as she described Lada, and whacked Ian every time he touched her. This action amused and delighted Lada. She was loved every minute.

"Come on then!" Dick yelled at him. "Get them bloody parrots in here, and put us all out of our misery," he yelled at Ian.

Lada came out first and the three from the island froze, speechless.

"This thing here is your future brother-in law, Joe. The other one is Clinker, his friend. And the other one is mine and if he doesn't stop staring at you his balls will be removed. Dan!" Debbie shouted.

"Sit down, everybody, this won't take long," Ian started but stopped as Lada went to each of them and kissed them on the cheek; she put her tongue out to Ian.

"Sit down before you fall down," he ordered.

"As I was saying, this won't take long. I'm going to tell you most of what I know but not everything. When we get to where we are going I'll tell you then! So don't question me, because you won't get an answer – understood?" Ian stared at them defiantly. They looked back in silence.

"To those of you who have never heard of the mookas and those of you who have, I have one thing to say. My father – our father – was one of the robbers."

Total shocked silence prevailed until Ian spoke again.

"There is only one man alive who has a lead on where the gems are and that's me. You all have to trust me on this. Dick said in Vietnam that the robbers were either very lucky or very good. The truth is they were very good but very unlucky." He looked at Maria who was stunned.

"My father and a man called Lacey, his mate, carried out the robbery at Andamooka Opal Field. They got away with half a million dollars' worth of opals.

"Lacey disappeared and my father gave up trying to find him. A cop pulled my father in for questioning, then he was released, but they never found Lacey. Lacey has never been found, neither have the opals."

Ian let this information sink in before continuing.

"I know what you're thinking, but that was impossible according to my father. Lacey could not have double crossed him. Don't ask me to explain why, that's one of the questions I will answer when we get there. You have to trust me that I'm satisfied he didn't double cross my father.

"So, put yourself in my father's position. The two of them planned and executed the robbery. Lacey is missing. My father can't find him and he can't contact anybody for help. He looks for Lacey for a week until he runs out of fuel and water by which time he is sure Lacey must be dead as Lacey had no water with him. The cops pick him up for questioning as he and Lacey were last seen in Andamooka only two weeks before the robbery. They were best mates and the cops knew he had to know where Lacey was but they couldn't hold him and they let him go. One cop suspected he was involved and he became a marked man.

"He went back to Korena and met Maria. Everything went well until we were about ten, then, he had an accident. Lost two fingers and broke his leg. His leg was broken and his fingers were cut off with an axe, not in a car crash. The reason my mother is hearing this *here* is so she can verify what I'm saying from this point on.

"After the so-called accident he started hitting the bottle. Became paranoid about small things, even taking mail from the mailbox. He was diagnosed with manic depression and one thing led to another to the point where Maria had to run for her life and take us with her; I remember that night, so does Joe!

"Apparently he had to get rid of us for our own protection. That's what he claimed. There was pressure on him constantly, through the mail, to reveal where Lacey was. That's why he wouldn't let anybody near the mailbox. If he had gone to the cops when they cut his fingers off he would have been OK but he didn't and they knew for sure he knew where Lacey was but he was a hard nut to crack so they concentrated on breaking him mentally. That lasted until recently as he said new players were involved and they were in a hurry. They told him his time was up, they had had enough of him. What did they have to lose? He had three options. Tell them what they wanted to know. Die taking everything with him. Or pass the information on."

Ian looked around; everybody was glued to what he was saying and a tear was running down Maria's face.

"The Leper is of the opinion my father was killed. He came to him and spilled his guts a month before and insisted on making a will. The Leper claims he had sobered himself up enough to do that. Then the accident that killed him happened – coincidence? The Leper doesn't think so. My father gave the Leper the information to pass to me to make a decision whether to go to the cops with it or find the mookas and then decide what to do. In a nutshell, what I'm trying to tell you is that somebody suspects this information has been passed on, and they will be watching every move we make."

Ian had a captive audience. Nobody spoke.

"These are dangerous people but we don't need to worry about anybody until we find what we are looking for. The present value is over two million dollars. The reward is two hundred thousand and still active. I had a month to sit on this. My father did the time and paid with his life. We paid with a good part of our lives and my mother's life was ruined because of the robbery. We have a good claim on these gems, more than anybody else.

"Maria, can you verify everything I have said, apart from the robbery which you didn't know anything about until now?"

Maria was holding Debbie's hand and she put on a brave face but tears were welling.

"I'm sorry!" she said at length. "What Ian has told you is true…" She fell silent.

Ian wanted to console her. What she had just heard should have been in private, however, her verification was essential. He took a deep breath and continued, "Right we can speak about this all day and get nowhere. Remember, my father couldn't find Lacey, his best mate. There is no X marks the spot. We have to find Lacey and all we have is some information to go on but it's the information nobody else has and nobody knows how they carried out the robbery except me. I know what we'll be looking for."

He turned to Dick.

"You ready for a monster hunt?" he asked.

"You're bloody right I am!" Dick replied.

Wilson chuckled as a response but said nothing.

"Who the hell are the people you spoke about, have you any idea?" Joe asked.

"To be honest, no! But the Leper thinks the people who cleaned out the house might be connected He reckoned it was an excuse to ransack the place. They certainly did that, even tore off the wallpaper to check behind it according to him, and they connected the phone line. He reckons the house phone is tapped and your mobiles may be getting listened to. That's why all the secrecy. We just don't know. It was very convenient that their team was already on the island and they moved in before anybody else got a chance. Your guess is as good as mine."

"So, what do we do now?" Joe wanted to know.

"Like Wilson said, we are at the planning stage. Go and digest what I have told you and we can speak again once you've had time to think."

"Bloody good idea," Linda piped up. "I'll put the jug on." She disappeared into the kitchen and the rest of the females followed.

"Suck a rat's arse. The old man was a *robber*. I'll be buggered. You know them bastards over there? Now that you mention it, they never showed their face. Every time you saw them, they were suited up with fumigation masks on, and Tyvek suits. One of them was a Sheila or a bloke with tits. Fuck me. Couldn't you have let us know what you suspected, and, the bloody Leper he never said anything," Joe fired at Ian when the kitchen door closed.

Ian looked at him coldly.

"I have no idea what he told the Leper, but it was enough to convince him he was telling the truth. The conformation of something I was told was when you found the money in the kennel. The rest is speculation; they might have been legitimate, who knows, and there was no way of letting anybody know about anything, except over the phone or internet. exactly what anybody listening would have wanted. Then, they would know for sure the information had been passed on. You're not going back to Korena. And from now on everything will be word of mouth between us unless it's nothing to do with this business – OK?" Ian left them with that, and went to the kitchen.

Maria was sitting out in the sun looking across the lake on her own.

"I'm sorry about that. You OK?" he asked, expecting a backlash.

"I'm better than OK, Ian, I've got closure. What did I do wrong? *That's* haunted me for years. and now I know the truth. I didn't do anything wrong." She looked up at him. "Do you have any idea what that feels like just to know it wasn't *me*." She trailed off, and he squeezed her shoulder.

There was nothing he could say. Debbie poked his ribs and cocked her head towards the kitchen.

"Nick off! Your coffee's inside." She handed Maria her tea. Ian did as she indicated.

Lada and Linda had served the others and were in the living room. Wilson had gone to the front door to smoke his pipe, deep in thought as they all were.

Wilson came back inside and it seemed to mark a resumption. Maria and Debbie joined them and Ian continued.

"Right! I know you haven't had much time, but it's like this! We either go for it or hand over the information to the cops. If *they* recover the gems using the information I have, the reward is one hundred thousand. If *we* find them and hand them over it will be two hundred thousand. It's information leading to the recovery. Or the recovery, but it will cost a lot of money to go and look. I have been in the bush on field trips a lot of times but only for a few days, a week at most, and we're looking at a month or months. This reward was a lot of money *then*; it isn't now. Only the family would get the reward if I hand over the information. The family is in no position to negotiate in any way. That could open a can of worms we might regret. If the papers got hold of it, which would be very likely, we will pay the cost and we have paid enough." He looked around. "You get my drift?" he asked.

They muttered their understanding and he continued.

"Right, this is going to cost a lot of money to…" Joe interrupted him,

"How much you reckon?" he asked.

"However much it takes," Dick cut in.

Ian looked at him. "And then we go for the Loch Ness Monster once we've sorted this shit out," he replied to Dick.

"Get on with it!" Dick commanded.

"OK. That's about it; we have little choice, in my view other than to go and find them. Can we get each individual view starting with you, Dick?"

"Go for it."

"Wilson?"

"Go for it."

"Linda?"

"Me too."

"Lada?"

"I am very confused because you are speaking about gems then moo cows?"

There was an outburst of laughter and she blushed. Debbie threw her arms around her.

"OK with me, Maria and Lada." She chuckled. "And bloody Dan," she added. "That leaves you two!" Debbie stared at Joe and Clinker.

"Bloody hell, mate, we're with you all the way!" Clinker yelled.

"We're all in this because if anybody wants out the answer is *no*! That was before I asked you in the first place," Ian declared, taking a piece of paper from his pocket. "Maria and

Lada will put together a list of food required for one month. Debbie – calculate water and medical supplies. Joe and Clinker – source vehicles either to rent or buy. Dick you and Wilson – concentrate on strategy: maps, GPS, search patterns and the like. Dan and I have some business to attend to that's critical and you'll know what that is in due course. We will need a reasonably comprehensive list prepared for tomorrow. Joe you can start now and track down four-wheel drive vehicles. And costs."

"Thank God, I thought you were never going to stop speaking," Wilson grumbled.

"You lot, bugger off and do whatever you have to do we are away to... Where are we going? Arsehole!" Dick yelled at Ian.

"There!" he said, throwing a sheet of coordinates to Dick.

"Bloody hell, Wilson, we've signed on for a ten-year trip!" he said, and handed the coordinates to Wilson.

Wilson agreed and looked at Ian curiously.

"At the centre is Andamooka. The coordinates cover a three-hundred-mile radius around Andamooka. You'll need all the maps to cover all the coordinates. And they must have Lat and Long. We can't have only the one we need, we need to carry all of them." He awaited the response.

"You know what! You could fuck up the Lord's Prayer if you put your mind to it. Complicated bastard," Dick concluded.

"Get your car out, *if* you can still drive, and bugger off to the port." Ian dismissed them.

"A splendid idea; we can stop by the Globe and have a pint," Wilson suggested. Dick threw a look at Ian.

"What did you say?" Ian asked.

"The Globe for a pint!" Wilson repeated, grinning.

"That bastard's been here before, Dick... Dan come with me before we get fossilised." Ian grabbed Dan by the arm and marched him to the bedroom.

"Remember and wear a condom!" Dick shouted after them.

Ian closed the door and turned to the confused Dan.

"The drone you lost; did you get it back?" he asked Dan.

"Nope, it's at the bottom of the Murray," Dan confirmed.

"Pity! OK, I want you to find out the cost of a replacement and it has to have GPS, a recording capability for film as well as transmission to the controller. We need not less than a mile range and more if it's available. Price for one, see what we are up against then, we will price for two. And keep your mouth shut," Ian ordered him.

Dan smiled broadly. "You bloody beauty!" he shouted and scampered out the door.

"Forget the baby oil?" Dick shouted after him.

Joe and Clinker hit gold within minutes of searching Linda's computer ads and left in Debbie's car to check it out. Semaphore Park was only a stone's throw from West Lakes and the advert had only been placed that morning.

An elderly woman answered the door and looked questioningly at them.

"We're here about the Bush Ranger," Joe informed her.

A broad smile lit up her face momentarily, but was erased by a shout from somewhere inside. A man wearing black glasses felt his way along the lobby towards them.

"Hi! I'm Mike, you lookin' to buy a vehicle or rent?" his voice was deep and powerful.

"We don't know yet? Depends. If the Ranger is still available can we take a look?" Joe asked.

"Yeh! It's available but it's not here. Go and phone Dinky, get the dog out and they'll be there soon," he instructed his wife. "Had an accident Xmas time, bloody battery blew up in my face. Got my eyes and I can't see much. This is her idea and I want to keep the Ranger until my sight returns. It's getting better, it'll take a long time they tell me. Where you from?" he asked.

"Port Lincoln but we're in Adelaide for a while," Clinker answered.

By the time Mike had explained all the customised details on the Rover they were both shifting from foot to foot impatiently.

"You know the way to outer harbour?" They nodded. "OK, follow that road all the way past the refinery. You'll see my garage on the left – Mike's! Have a look and come back here, we can discuss terms after you see the vehicle. The gate will be open. Make sure it's me you make arrangements with, *she* wants to sell it," he said quietly.

"Thank Christ, I never thought he would stop bloody speakin'," Joe grumbled.

The garage they found easily, not a large business but not so small either. There was a worker leaning against the fence by the gate, a cigarette hanging from his mouth and dressed in a boiler suit and baseball cap. They pulled up and he waved them into the compound. He grunted, "Hi!", unlocked a side door and went inside. The large roller doors gave a sudden bang then lifted.

"Sociable prick," Clinker commented.

Joe's attention was on the vehicles inside. One vehicle in particular was under a dust cover, which the boy removed, revealing a customised Range Rover. They walked around, inspecting everything, and the boy opened the bonnet. The engine was a six-cylinder diesel and looked like new.

Another Range Rover was close by but covered in dust. Joe looked at it and the boy spoke for the first time.

"That's the one Grandad was workin' on, when the battery exploded. It's nearly finished." He bent over in his baggy overalls and blew away some dust. "Other two, are spares," he said, adjusting his baseball cap and pointing at two vehicles in the gloom.

Joe looked around, this was a fully functioning garage and by the look of things, no work had been done here since the owner had his accident.

"You worked here long?" he asked the boy.

"Since I left school, six years." *He didn't look old enough,* Joe thought.

"So, what's the situation with the business?" Clinker asked; his observations were the same as Joe's.

"They won't let me work here myself, so everything's on hold till his eyesight gets better," he answered. "You want to buy this or rent it?" he asked them, pointing to the finished machine.

"Don't know yet, let's fire it up and see what we've got," Joe answered.

The boy leapt into the driver's seat and fired up the engine. "There's not much diesel left so if you want to go for a spin, jump in," the boy invited them.

He pulled out of the gate but headed straight across the road and drove headlong into the scrub.

"Fuck me!" Joe yelled in alarm.

"What's wrong with you? Any piece of shit can go up and down the road. Mike reckons if the bloody thing's going to break, break it here!" the boy yelled and took off at speed. He didn't go far and stopped.

"You next," he said and jumped out. Joe moved into the driver's seat and the boy came in next to Clinker. There was plenty of room for three people in the front and the back had been fitted out to carry anything except passengers. Joe threw them around and Clinker became very uneasy; this boy was brushing up against him and there was a smell to him that just occasionally hit Clinker's nostrils. He pushed him away several times with his knee and was glad when they returned to the garage. He felt very uneasy around this boy.

"Brilliant! How many mechanics were working here?" Joe enquired.

"Me and Mike, we had an old geezer working for a little while but he buggered off after the accident. His voice was getting louder as he continued. It was his bloody fault. He put the welder clamp onto the battery lead, when Mike was under the fuckin' engine – the stupid prick. then he buggered off." His voice tailed off and he drew a dirty glove across his eyes, obviously very upset by the memory.

"Dinky! How the hell did you get a name like that?" Clinker suddenly remembered what Mike had called him.

A wisp of a smile appeared at the corner of his mouth but he didn't answer.

"OK, Dinky, we're going to see Mike. You OK here, or do you want us to drop you off someplace?" Joe asked him.

"No problem, I'll lock up and put the dog back. That's my house next door."

He came around to the passenger's side as they went out the gate and winked at Clinker, who jumped in response.

"Get the hell out of here, that little bastard's bent," Clinker hissed.

"Who's bent?" Joe asked.

"That bloody Dinky, you didn't get a whiff of perfume off him. Kept rubbing his leg against mine all the time you were driving; the little shit just winked at me just now." Clinker shuddered his shoulders in a repelling motion.

"I never smelt anything – you need to take a cold shower?" Joe asked.

"Fuck off," was the reply.

Mike came to the door and invited them inside. "Coffee, Martha!" he shouted through to the kitchen.

"Well, was she in a good mood or being a bitch?" he asked.

"No! Great. We took her for a drive, and everything is fine," Joe replied.

"I'm not speaking about the bloody Rover, I'm speaking about Dinky!" Mike said.

"*She!*" Clinker blurted.

"Don't tell me she was a *boy* again – Martha, Dinky's pulled it off!" Mike shouted to his wife.

The two looked at one another, wondering if they were in a mad house.

"She's a good mechanic but she won't go and work anywhere else. She's been doing stage parts with her mother and loves it, especially fooling people in real life. Good on her!" Mike smiled.

"She'll pay for that," Clinker whispered to Joe.

"Mike, we need to speak with my brother on this but would you be interested in leasing the garage for a couple of months and leasing the Range Rover? The other one, the one you were working on, how much needs to be done to it?"

"Electrics mainly. Dinky doesn't know how to do that, but the rest I reckon she could finish in a week. You want to take both of them?" Mike asked.

Joe took his coffee from Martha and pondered for a moment.

"You work out a good price for a two month hire of both vehicles and the use of the garage for as much time as it takes to get our expedition ready to leave. And we will pay Dinky's wages. Get me a cost and I will see what Ian thinks, OK? Ian's in West Lakes," Joe added as an afterthought.

"OK, I can do that. Is that all you are looking for or is there anything else?" Mike asked.

"I'm sure there will be. Mike, we will go. We should be back soon and I'll try and get Ian here. See what you can do about costs."

"She only put that advert in yesterday and you're the first that came. What if somebody else comes?" Mike asked.

"Well, if they want all three things and a mechanic, I suppose you won't have much choice but to show them the goods. We'll be back shortly — come on, bloodhound!" he shouted at Clinker.

The house was a tip. Wilson and Dick had a table full of maps. They were spreading them out over the floor, making one large map out of many. Linda and the girls were in the kitchen but Ian and Dan were nowhere to be seen.

"Where the hell is Ian?" Joe asked.

"What's up?" Dick enquired from the floor.

Joe explained the situation quickly and Dick rose to his feet.

"Bloody hell, Wilson, we're getting too old for this shit! Never mind Ian! Let's go!" he said, rubbing his knees.

Mike welcomed them back and recognised Dick.

"You've been in the garage a few times," he said.

Dick looked into the black glasses and just agreed. He hadn't a clue who he was looking at.

"I reckon eight thousand for both vehicles — and the use of the garage for two months. You pay Dinky's wages, fuel and everything else on top of that. I'll pay the electricity. What you reckon?" he concluded.

"Sounds like a deal to me. Anything else we need, we can rely on your help to get it?" Dick asked.

"Like what?" Mike replied.

"Trailers, bowsers and so on, any other vehicles we need," Dick prompted.

"Anything for going bush I can get no problem. Twelve percent uplift, OK with you?" Mike responded.

"It's a deal." Dick held out his hand and took Mike's, they shook on it.

"That was simple. Make decisions, you two. Don't rely on anybody else," he commanded Clinker and Joe. They headed back to West Lakes and Clinker filled Dick in on the encounter with Dinky.

"I tell you, Dick, when I got a whiff of that perfume; it scared the hell out of me. That bastard is nose blind." He whacked Joe on the head.

Ian and Dan had gone to the dealers. Dan was advised what he was looking for they didn't have; however, the assistant knew who had. He advised it was illegal to have a remote-control drone, which flew more than five hundred metres horizontally and one hundred and fifty metres vertically. The assistant wanted to know exactly where they intended to fly. Anywhere near Adelaide was out of the question as they would need a licence and he could get one for a fee.

"I have a licence, ask your boss," Dan informed him, puffing his chest out.

"And your name, sir?" the assistant wanted to know.

"Dan Gordon," Dan replied.

"One moment, sir, and I will confirm that." He scampered off to phone his boss. "OK, Dan, you're good to go!" He sounded like he had won the jackpot.

"I'll call Charles. I'm afraid he's in Wild Horse Plains – do you want to go there, or will he come here?" he asked.

Dan looked at Ian. Wild Horse Plains was a good hour's drive away to the north.

"We'll go there," Ian decided.

The journey was worth making but ate up the entire day. He longed to phone Lada but he had made the rules and had to stick to them.

What they were looking for, Charles certainly had. It transpired Charles had also a few convictions for breach of privacy and had lost his licence for that reason; he was also unlikely to get it back any time soon.

His machine wasn't an off the shelf purchase; he had a customised version and had built most of it himself. He had also increased the flying time to one hour from thirty minutes by adding extra batteries. It had a maximum transmission range of two thousand metres, monitor and all accessories.

He gave them a demonstration and Dan took the controls. Ian refused; he wasn't going to screw the thing up now they had it.

Charles surprised him with the price also.

"By the time I get my licence back, this model will be defunct and I will need another one so I will let you have it for what it cost. One thousand Australian dollars."

"OK! How long will it take you to make up another model the same as this one and how much for both?" Ian enquired.

"Another one!" Charles exclaimed. "Now, let me think? Exactly the same is easy; parts are easy, time is something else. How about… three thousand for two. And give me a week to get the other one ready?" he said, finally.

"Excellent! Do you need cash now or wait until it's all together?" Ian enquired.

"No! We can get things put together if you like, I don't expect you to carry that much cash around. You need to leave this one here, it will make things much easier for me," Charles requested.

To add to things, they hit the rush hour traffic all the way to West Lakes but they had a great sense of achievement. Ian had never expected such a result in the first day. Dan was over the moon and Ian was glad he was involved. Ian had no knowledge of drones or legislation governing their use. They arrived at the house and he embraced Lada, taking in the scene around him and grinning.

"Wilson! There is no need to grovel on the floor when I come in. You can just bow," he advised.

"I wasn't grovelling, I was looking for vermin. Somebody said you were missing," Wilson replied without looking up.

Linda and the other women were cooking food which was screaming to be eaten. Everybody was starving.

After dinner, they piled in to clear the dishes and retreated to the living room.

"Right. Dick, Wilson, where are we with maps?" Ian asked.

"All in order," Dick replied.

"Joe! How did you two get on?" Ian didn't expect the answer.

Five minutes later amidst laughter at Clinker's interpretation of Dinky, Ian was elated.

"Debbie, have you a list prepared?"

"Yep! Medical and food. For one month. Christ knows how you are going to carry it and that's without water," she answered for all.

Ian shook his head. "I don't believe this! I had allowed a week to get this put together and you've done it in the first day. Brilliant!" Ian exclaimed.

"What about you two; where have you been all day?" Joe asked.

"That's top secret but I can tell you it was a very successful day and if Dan tells any of you where we were or why we were there he's not coming with us. Got that Dan?" He raised his voice in meaning and Dan's eyes enlarged at the threat.

"One more thing: from now on Dick and Wilson will be calling the shots. I am taking a back seat on this because they are the navigators. I'll give them coordinates, and they'll get us there. Then it's a search, that has to be coordinated by people who know what they're doing or it will turn into a shambles. We need to pull everything together from here, and from what Joe's saying we start at the garage first thing in the morning. If it's as good as he says we can make that our base. And if Clinker's fancy man pulls her weight we can look at where she can fit in, if required. Any beer around, Dick?"

"Thought you'd never bloody ask!" Dick snorted and headed into the kitchen. Ian followed and slipped a piece of paper into Dick's hand. Dick looked at the coordinates, then at Ian.

"The starting post, get us there! Any vodka?" Ian asked.

They scooped until Maria decided she wanted to go home, taking Joe and Clinker with her. Lada and Ian made it to the veranda. It was still warm outside; the day had gone as the days before, cold start then hot.

Dick had poured her a vodka fit for a Tsar, against her protests, and she had finished half of it. Ian knew he had a lot of explaining to do. He knew she couldn't possibly understand exactly what was going on but she wasn't complaining, she had sat politely and let them get on with it.

"You don't say much," he said, releasing his lips from hers.

"Ah! My grandfather's advice is follow the teachings of Ghandi – you know Ghandi?" she asked.

"Not personally," Ian replied and got a poke in the ribs for his effort.

"Ghandi said that, if you cannot improve the silence then stay quiet." She threw her hair over her back and pulled him hard against her chest. "It's beautiful here; I like it and I don't want to leave Australia. I love your family. I have a sister and a brother and a husband. That is good enough reason to stay quiet, don't you think?" she purred.

Ian looked at her with renewed admiration; there was more to this girl than met the eye. They kissed and cuddled, sipped their drinks and stayed there until the chill forced them to the bedroom.

CHAPTER SEVEN

The garage was more than Ian had expected; it put a new perspective on what they could achieve and how quickly it could be achieved.

His silence over the use of the drones was good in theory but not in practice. He had been collared by Dick and Wilson and had been told in no uncertain terms they had to know what tools they had to conduct a search with, before they could formulate a strategy. Any equipment required to follow that strategy could be identified. They needed to know. So he had to tell them.

"Prick! We never thought of that!" was Dick's response.

"You got all the back-up gear organised, spares and everything else needed?" Wilson asked.

"Dan is on it and he will train everybody how to fly the thing on-site. He'll use a cheap model in case some dickhead crashes it." He smiled at Dick.

"So, we're good to go to the starting line. Apart from the fact we have no bloody idea where we're going after that. What kind of terrain, it looks like the bloody moon on the map and a few other minor details. We're good to go?" Dick fished for more.

"You can piss off. Weather changes and you adapt at sea, so you can bloody well adapt there. Good try," Ian answered.

"Be gone!" Wilson instructed him and he left for the garage.

They were into the second vehicle's guts on the second day. Mike had drawn up a wiring diagram for Clinker, who understood what still had to be done. The second encounter with Dinky was something else. This time she appeared dressed to the kill in high heels, a mini skirt, a blouse which bordered on see-through, make-up which must have been put on by an expert and her hair styled. She looked divine.

Clinker ignored her, didn't even acknowledge her presence and she came closer and closer.

"You see that bloody Dinky!" Joe shouted at Clinker when she was in range.

"I'll kick him in the balls when he gets here," Clinker replied and lunged at her.

"Got you, you little bugger," he whispered into her ear.

"Not before I got you," she replied, laughing.

"You sure it's what it looks like this time?" Joe shouted.

"You reckon I should use the Bowling Ball Grip to find out?" Clinker yelled back.

"You try, and I'll kick you in the balls!" she yelled, struggling.

"OK, Kinky! Get your arse into your work clothes and get back here. You're on wages, and we have work to do." He slapped her hard on the arse and she squealed.

"Arsehole!" she shouted over her shoulder and ran, as fast as her heels would allow, next door.

From then on, the two of them were slinging shit at one another constantly but the work was getting done quickly. Clinker had to admire her skills. She was good and knew exactly what she was doing. She had fitted out vehicles for the bush many times but always to the owner's specifications.

"Make your own specifications," Joe advised and she was thrilled.

Ian arrived to find them engrossed in sandwiches and coffee which Kinky, as they now called her, had fetched from her house.

"Got another boiler suit?" Ian asked, pouring himself one.

Over the next two days they had the second Rover's electrics and mechanical repairs done. Ian and Joe worked on what they were directed to do by Kinky and listened to her great adventures with Mike, shooting pigs up the river and the two of them had even taken part in the Trans-Australian Overland Race. Ian noted she didn't stop work to speak. He was impressed with her and she was infectious. Full of mischief and incentive.

"Two ain't gonna cut it," was Dick's welcome.

"Two what?" Ian enquired.

"Vehicles! We need three at least – here! That's the search strategy. You can go through it but we've looked at all options. To implement a sustainable strategy over the long term will require what's on that plan." He tossed the sheet of paper to Ian.

"Nothing to do with me, Captain!" he said and tossed it back.

"Joe! Pick out of that list everything you think Mike *may* be able to lay his hands on and write them down. Take it to him tonight and let him work on it," Dick growled at Ian who smiled back.

"Jesus Christ, it'll be Christmas before we get going!" Joe exclaimed.

Dick took no notice. "Here, do you want to see the safe manning complement or is that our problem as well?" he shouted at Ian.

"All yours," Ian answered and headed for the kitchen to join the females.

"One is developing very sloping shoulders," he heard Wilson comment, and raised two fingers above his head.

Mike was not exaggerating when he told Dick anything he needed he could arrange. The only thing outstanding by close of play the next day was a split Bowser for fuel and water and that he located the following day in an army surplus sale.

The drones Dan had tested and paid for out on the plains and under Ian's instruction they were to be kept in the house, not in the garage like the rest of the equipment, which was growing by the day.

"I reckon Tam Pax would be proud of this," Dick suggested.

"*Who?*" Ian asked, bemused.

"That guy in the bush with all them weirdos and bikes," Dick replied.

"Mad Max. You bloody idiot – bugger off!" Ian scoffed.

"You are aware, young man, that not a man amongst us has any experience of desert dwelling?" Wilson pointed out.

"We're not exactly going unprepared," Ian replied.

"There is one female, I am led to believe, who will accompany us," Wilson told him.

Ian looked at Dick, who gave him an 'if you dare stare'. They were braced for conflict.

"Dinky! OK, if you insist. It's your call," Ian said, matter of fact.

"OK! That finalises our crew and we have a POB (persons on board) of ten," Wilson confirmed.

"In *three* vehicles, I hope you know what you're doing?" Ian answered curiously.

"Trust us! We will leave as soon as everything is checked and packed; checklists for trailers, here! Checklist for vehicles here! Dan has a checklist for everything he needs, I presume?" Wilson looked at Ian for an answer.

"Yeh! He has everything he needs plus," Ian assured them.

"Right then, our schedule is to finalise everything tomorrow, departing for parts unknown the next day at four a.m. That will allow us to get well clear of the city before daylight. You had better go and inform Dinky her services are required. Be off with you," Wilson snapped.

"Yes, Your Majesty!" Ian replied and went to get Lada.

He went to Mike's first to see if he had any objections about his granddaughter going with them. He was delighted they were going to ask her, and her grandmother was even more delighted to see Lada, whom she described in fine detail to her husband, much to Lada's embarrassment.

"I suppose to confirm all that by touch would be a no no! I've gotta get my sight back," Mike laughed.

Dinky threw her arms around Clinker and Joe. She was covered in grease, as they were, and she danced around demented. "Bloody beauty!" she kept repeating.

"I think she wants to go or she's having a fit," Clinker advised.

The following morning Joe and Clinker were approaching the garage. Dinky came running towards them in an obvious state of distress waving her hands. Joe braked and Clinker grabbed hold of her, she was crying uncontrollably. He shook her, shouting, "What's the matter?"

"The dog, the dog!" She looked at Clinker with tears streaming down her face. "I think the dog's dead!" she choked.

Clinker ran into the compound and saw the dog. It was inside the fence but its head was out through a hole in the mesh. He ran around to the outside and looked at its mouth. Its tongue was hanging out and its eyes were half closed. The dog was dead all right. He went to Dinky and ushered her into her house.

"Stay here, I'll come back." He gave her a comforting hug and left.

Joe was already by the dog's body.

"He's dead all right, looks like his neck's broken. Tongue's hanging out," he gasped.

"Fuck me, why the hell was he trying to get out a little hole like that? It's the same size as his bloody head," Joe observed.

"Poor bastard, yesterday she was as happy as hell, today, she is heartbroken." Clinker was speaking about Dinky.

"Well, nothing we can do about it now. Get the bloody thing out of there and go bury it I suppose," Joe concluded.

That wasn't easy; the dog's head was jammed into the hole tightly. Using a bar, they prised the wire away enough to free it. The dog's collar was thick and broad; it should have protected his neck, even if he had to stay stuck all night, but it didn't. Joe looked out through the fence to see if anything was there which might have triggered the dog to force his head through but there was nothing.

"We'll bury it before she sees it again." They agreed and carried the dog across the road into the scrub. Well away from the road they dug a hole and put the dog to rest.

"Now the worst part," Clinker said quietly. Joe nodded.

"We will take her to Dick's. She's shattered, the women can take care of her."

Ian was confused when they arrived until Joe explained what had happened. Lada and Debbie comforted Dinky, drying her tears and hugging her. Linda made her a drink and they were in another world.

"Let's go back," Ian ordered the two and jumped into the car with them.

"Did you lock the gate?" he asked.

"Don't be bloody stupid. Fuck the gate," Joe retorted.

Ian said nothing. He looked at the hole where the dog had died and looked around the compound. One vehicle was outside and had been all night.

"Open her up," he asked Joe, pointing to the roller door.

It was, as he thought, packed to the door. There was no room inside; one vehicle had to be left outside.

"I'll take the car back and get some help; we need to stick to the schedule," he informed them.

Ian left and headed back but his thoughts were in Vietnam. He had seen this before and this dog wasn't a trained watchdog. Get its head out through the hole with food and hit it across the neck with a spade. That's how the Vietnamese robbers dealt with such an inconvenience. But for what reason would this dog be killed? "No doubt we will find out," he said aloud.

"I thought I heard him barking but he does that if he sees a fox or a rabbit around the fence and then he went quiet. I should have checked on him." Dinky was close to tears again.

"Are you two going to sit on your arse here all day or are you going to do some work?" Ian shouted at Wilson and Dick.

"Lead the way, young man," Wilson replied.

"Look after her," Ian said and they left.

"Well! What's going through that head of yours?" Dick asked as soon as they cleared the driveway.

"No hiding place, you should know that; with the technology around anybody can track you from his bed. I expected something, but not this. I reckon there might be a tracking device attached to the vehicle we left outside. I might be wrong but it's possible," he said.

"So, we find it or don't find it?" Wilson asked.

"Your call, but if it was me I would leave the finding till we were out in the bush. At least we know which vehicle was exposed. Could be used to our advantage in the future if somebody is sure we haven't found it. If indeed it exists."

There was silence.

At length Wilson piped up, "OK. No fuss. Carry on as planned, as if nothing has happened, except a dead dog," he announced.

They reached the garage. Clinker was anxious to hear how Dinky was faring. Joe was more concerned about a soft tyre on one of the trailers.

Dan and Debbie joined them at lunch time. They stayed until the last trailer and compartment was packed, Dan taking great care with the drones and ancillary equipment. Lada and Linda had taken Dinky shopping, which was a godsend.

"Take that one home with us tonight and put everything else inside and lock up," Dick ordered. Ian got his drift. *If it moves, somebody, somewhere will be very happy*, he thought.

They took Dinky home after dark, to pick up her things. She didn't want to go near the garage and was still shaken by events. She had commented that her mother was away to Sydney with her partner and she didn't want to stay in the house herself any more.

"You want us to help?" Clinker volunteered.

"No problem, everything I need to go bush is already packed," she replied and went into the house. They waited a few minutes and she appeared cradling a long bundle. She opened the hatch at the back and put it inside.

"Right, I'll get my things!" she shouted and scarpered back inside.

"What the hell was that she put in there?" Joe asked. Clinker leaned over the seat and had a look.

"Buggered if I know, mate, just a big bag," he concluded.

Dinky came out, locked the door and put another bag into the back. She pushed Clinker into the centre seat and whistled.

"Does that mean go?" Joe asked.

"Yep!" she scoffed.

She stayed at Dick's, spoiled for most of the night by her two mentors, and she was slowly returning to herself. She sipped a vodka and coke on Lada's advice, and the world became a better place.

Suddenly she uttered, "Oh shit! We're not going into the Northern Territory, are we?" It was sudden and nobody spoke. Dick looked at Ian.

"No! We're not going to the Northern Territory – why?" Ian replied.

"Ah! That's OK then, the two, four, three is OK," she sighed.

"What the hell is the two, four, three?" Ian said, curiously.

"My rifle. It's not allowed into the NT because it's too high velocity," Dinky explained.

"You have a rifle with you?" Dick asked.

"Bloody right, two rifles! You can't go into the bush without *that*!" It was a statement not to question.

"I knew it – lions!" Wilson yelled.

They roared with laughter and the conversation drifted away from the subject but Ian had thought about bringing some weapons with them. He dismissed the idea as it would have alarmed everybody. Not essential, he had concluded, but he was glad they had appeared and were not associated with him. He felt as if something missing had just been found.

"Let go fore and aft – pimba or bust," were Dick's instructions as the convoy departed.

They cleared the city by six a.m., ahead of the rush hour traffic, and were well on their way to the first stop for fuel after a five-hour drive. The day was uneventful; the drive became boring after a few hours and most slept between taking turns driving. Lada was still as bewitching as ever and never stopped looking at the surroundings. They had the sliding roofs open and stayed below fifty mph. Eventually, when they arrived at Port Pirie services, they had a great hunger, aching limbs and an urgent desire for toilets.

The plan was to leave there by one thirty p.m.; they had plenty of time. They took fuel and filled the water bags hanging in front of each vehicle, suspended from the Roo Bars. The air rushing against the canvas bags cooled the water significantly; this was normal procedure.

They left for the next stop at Port Augusta another hundred miles to the north. Just outside the town they pulled into a lay-by, following Ian in the lead vehicle.

"What's up?" Joe enquired.

"Here, stick this on your doors." He handed Joe two medium sized stickers.

Mooka Hunters inc, emblazoned in red letters, stared back at Joe.

"You must be fuckin' kidding?" Joe exclaimed but Ian went to Debbie in the third vehicle. Her reaction was similar.

"Where we're going is a national park, police permission and all that bullshit required, because they race on the lake. We're not racing and if they see that they should die laughing." He smiled.

"And if they don't?" Debbie asked worriedly.

"Well! We'll just have to get permission."

They drove on and followed the signs to the campsite. It wasn't busy. The attendant was glad to see somebody, he informed them, and after explaining they were going to Lake Gairdner he asked if they had permission and permits.

"No! We're going hunting for them, we're not racing or driving on the lake." Ian slapped the sticker on the door.

The attendant gave a little laugh. "Good luck with that one, mate. You're on the wrong track, you should head for the Flinders or Andamooka; you might have more luck there. OK, let me contact the cops; do you have VHF?" he asked.

"Yeh! Three of them, one in each truck." Ian informed him.

"How many of you?"

"Ten."

"How many years are you going to be searching?" He tried to keep a straight face but failed.

"There's no need to be so negative," Ian said sternly.

"OK! OK! Mate, go and park over by the caravans and I'll see you in a minute." He left, chuckling to himself, and disappeared into his hut.

"We'll stay here for the night, get fuel in the morning and get going so, tents up if you please; we can eat in the town."

The attendant wasn't long in returning and he was jovial.

"Right; I explained your mission to the constable, this is your call sign. He wants a radio check when you go out, and if he doesn't reply you get back here! This is your permission. How long do you estimate you're gonna be out there?" he asked, handing two sheets to Ian, who hesitated with an answer.

"I'll put it this way then: how long can you stay out there before we have a search party looking for you? Does that make it easier?" he asked, grinning.

"We could stay for a month. Hopefully it won't take that long." Ian looked at him for encouragement.

The attendant looked at him with more than a little pity.

"I'll log you out for one month but report every day to make sure you're alive! You miss three days we come looking for you." He turned on his heel and walked back to the hut.

"You're a devious bastard," Dick said.

"*That* was easy." Ian was ecstatic and relieved; he looked at the call sign "Cheeky bastard!" he said and handed the note to Wilson.

"Wildgoose one, how dare he insinuate we are on a wild goose chase? You must try politics. Kindly explain why you revealed our mission which has been conducted in strict secrecy until now!" Wilson demanded, and Dick stifled the same question.

"Yeh! We have two choices, either go in from here, or from Ceduna, which would mean a back track, no way can you get in from here undetected either at this end or the other end of the track. It would take days to back track and a lot of fuel. So it was take a chance in going in from here and get turned back, or get

138

permission here. The mookas are a joke! A Nessie hunt, just a harmless quest and nobody is going to stop anybody from looking for either. You get their sympathy, Wilson! They think we're drongoes. If the subject of telling the cops comes up, we already did, and they just laughed," he explained and waited for reaction.

"Clever; how long did it take to think this shit up?" Dick threw at Ian.

"Research, something you two didn't do. If you had, you would have known the track up to the lake was policed and you need all kinds of permits. It's a good job you two have a baby sitter," Ian replied.

"Fuck you too," Dick responded.

The track was rough and Ian was glad they hadn't tried this in the dark. The added weight of fuel and water was evident and they made steady but slow progress north. The last supper, as Joe had described the evening meal, had meant light breakfasts at the same restaurant but by noon they were all starving again. It was also getting hotter as the day wore on and the land offered no respite from the sun. Farmland had given way to scrub and in turn that had petered out to semi-desert: deep brown rocks and sand dunes. Yakka bushes and small Malley trees were predominant and wildlife didn't seem to exist. They had sixty miles to traverse before reaching the lake, then another thirty-five before they reached the coordinates Ian had given to Dick and Wilson.

They didn't get stuck, but nearly did on several occasions, the Ranger towing the bowser being the main concern. Dinky had insisted she would drive it. She did well and had the admiration of the men who followed behind. Only Linda was with the men. Lada and Debbie were standing on the seat with their upper bodies out through the roof. Their tits jumping up and down were a good source of entertainment and all were in good spirits. They passed the junction which branched right to St Ive Station thirty miles away and kept going.

It was two p.m. before they caught glimpses of the shimmering spectacle ahead, a fine haze hanging over glittering crystals of salt.

They were silent as they surveyed the scene. It became apparent by the dozens of vehicle tracks out on the salt lake that this was a busy place in the right season. They couldn't make out any movement on the lake but old tracks and new tracks just looked the same.

They decided, on Dick's command, that they would take the vehicles onto the lake before stopping for something to eat. Chisellers were already swarming on their backs and Ian decided to hand round the Soffell he had taken with him from Vietnam. That pissed them off and they stayed away from people's eyes which was the most annoying place. They had plenty other sources of moisture; everybody was dripping with sweat and there wasn't a breath of wind. To their right, they could just make out some structures which must be the campsite. Ian had resisted the temptation to stop there.

"I'm on the Moooon," Wilson said, elated, and spread the map out over the bonnet. The men gathered around. Dick had a hand-held GPS; he read out the position and Wilson confirmed the readings as their present position. He entered that as a way point, entered the coordinates Ian had given them and read out the compass bearing to that position. Wilson checked the bearing and it was exact.

"Well! The navigation systems are A1. You want to test communications here or wait until we are on the other side?" he asked Dick.

"Other side," Dick replied.

The women had rustled up a snack as instructed and were already into it; they seemed to stay together more than mix but the same could be said about the men. The one thing which dawned on all of them was that the ancient tide-line marked the end of one world and the beginning of another. What lay out there beyond the horizon was uncertain and a little disturbing.

"Shake a leg. Thirty-five miles to go," Dick announced.

Dinky set the pace and it wasn't slow. She did slow a little when she ran out of tracks but never went below thirty. They drove on as if they were floating on air, a featureless white sea stretching into the sky. When the far shore came into view it was no more than a dark blotch on the horizon but, as directed, Dinky slowed allowing the two vehicles behind to come either side of hers. They went ahead at twenty miles an hour and, from nothing, suddenly the features of a shoreline encrusted in salt stretching to the high tide line became apparent. The thin line of brown was ten feet higher and they were close before the haze allowed them to focus clearly.

Ian sat on the roof staring north and south searching for something, as it was obvious to him that where they had made land-fall was not what he was looking for. There was higher ground to the north and he directed them to stay on the salt and head there.

It was much higher than the bank and it stretched away into the haze; a rock ledge of weathered sandstone serrated along the softer layers by wind and water.

He called a halt and they went to look closely. They left the vehicles on the salt and walked to the ledge. All eyes were on Ian

"OK," he said at length. "What we are looking for is a small cairn of stones on one of these ledges, about shoulder height. We will have to walk the ledge, so one vehicle drive on and two of us will walk. The rest of you can stay here. Take the trailer that has the metal detector and shovels in it."

Lada joined Ian and asked, "What are you looking for?"

"A pile of stones on a ledge. Sorry, you wouldn't know what a cairn was," he apologised.

"Ah! I understand. I will walk with you," she insisted and he turned to face her.

The bra had long since been removed, and she stood there, her shirt open to the point of erotica, hair over one shoulder windswept into volume, her face blushed with the sun and a pair of tight shorts on. All soaked with sweat.

"You look slippery!" he whispered to her.

"I feel slippery," she replied, gazing into his eyes.

"Will you two move your bloody arse and stop fuckin' by sight!" Dick yelled at them from the vehicle. Ian grinned and yelled at Joe to find a way up the bank with the other vehicles and make camp, then they started searching along the ledge.

Fifty metres from the end of the ledge there was a vertical crack in the rock face. It was deep and Ian was tempted to look further inside. Such a defined feature would have been noted but there was no mention of this in his father's directions; low, deep, shallow and non-existent, the ledges were erratic along the rock face and they walked quite a distance seeing nothing that looked like a cairn. Ian was recalling the instructions from his father; these positions are not accurate but near enough. They went on for over a mile before he saw a mound of stones appear, set in from the edge of a ledge. His heart pounded as he pointed them out to Lada.

"Is this what we are looking for?" she asked curiously.

"I don't know but we'll find out in a minute," he answered.

Ian pushed the smaller stones off the larger one at the bottom.

"This is the moment of truth," he said.

He stared in silence at the coin below. Tarnished and green it was a beautiful sight and his heart leapt with delight. Lada reached under the slab and took the coin out, staring at it in bewilderment.

Ian snapped out of it. He'd been thinking, the last one to see that coin was his father and God knows the state of panic he was in when he put it there.

He grabbed Lada in a bear hug and danced around with her feet off the ground, whooping.

"Put her down, stop groping, what did you find?" Wilson demanded and Lada showed him the coin.

"Well, we're one Australian penny richer!" he concluded and looked for an explanation.

Get the metal detector," Ian instructed anybody, and started pacing fifty paces from the ledge at ninety degrees.

Dick arrived and switched the detector on. There was nothing where Ian had stopped but Dick swept all around working his way out and at about ten metres back in the direction Ian had come he got a distinct echo, a big one.

In silence, Ian started to dig away the salt; it was rock hard and he had to use the spade as a pick to make any impression. Slowly, something red appeared through the crystals. It was a lamp. Below it they could see another and recovered it also. Ian was exhausted.

"Right! That's enough. Dick, take these coordinates and let's go!" he panted.

"Now one is enlightened!" Wilson commented, shaking his head in confusion.

They returned to where the vehicles had left the lake, close to the southern tip of the ancient sea cliff. On close inspection it was about forty feet high and leaning to the south. It must have cracked at the split, Ian observed. He was a geologist and read strata instinctively. They followed the tracks for a short distance around the south end and saw the camp immediately; it was taking shape. Curious eyes met them and they cheered when Ian gave the thumbs up.

Lada jumped down and immediately went to show the women what they had found. Joe, Clinker and Dan crowded Ian for information. He was going to do this later but decided now was the time before he drove the captains crazy. Ian took the penny and held it up.

"This is the proof that the mookas exist – my father put this coin under the cairn when he came back to look for Lacey. These lights were buried by Lacey. So was the fuel can in a pre-dug hole and covered up. When Lacey failed to turn up on schedule my father had to check back to where his last position was and this was his last position."

Everybody was listening intently.

"The reason they got away with the robbery was because they went west and nobody thought that was possible. How they managed to go west was even more ingenious; they used a microlight aircraft. These lights were Lacey's landing signal in the dark and they worked. He landed, took fuel, buried the evidence and took off again.

"Dick and Wilson will know where Lacey was heading so they can start a search pattern. They are the only ones who need to know. Don't get too excited; we have something like a ten thousand square miles of desert to search, because he never arrived at the next fuel stop. What we can celebrate is that we now know for sure the gems came in this direction and we know where they were going to. That's something nobody in the world knows. So any doubts you had before you shouldn't have any doubts now!"

There was a buzz of excitement and Ian spoke to Dick and Wilson.

"I know this is a dry ship, Captains, but where have you hidden the whiskey?" he asked.

The two looked at one another in denial.

"I'm insulted! How dare you think we would break our own rules?" Wilson retorted.

"Never mind the bullshit, I know you two," Ian said, turning to Joe and Clinker, "and you two must have beer stacked somewhere so piss off and get some," he ordered and left to join the women.

"One will endeavour to find hidden sustenance in this desert!" Wilson shouted at him.

Dinky had taken the reins in setting up the camp. When Ian informed her they would stay there for at least three days, maybe longer, trailers were parked and unhooked, freeing up the Rovers. Two large tents erected and a third smaller canopy for cooking, once she had things moving she instructed the men to gather driftwood from the beach.

"I'm not cold, dear," Wilson had informed her.

"It's for snakes, not you," she pointed out.

"I didn't know snakes ate wood?" he teased her.

"Bloody Hell, we're doomed!" she shouted and whacked Wilson on the arse.

They had a series of fires lit around the camp before dark and Dinky had smoked along the rock face for fifty metres dislodging several large centipedes and a few spiders, which she duly dispatched with the heel of her boot. She noticed a crack barely wide enough to slide through and the smoke was heading into it. Curious she followed and discovered it went completely through the rock in a dog-leg and opened out overlooking the salt on the east side some twenty metres distant. It was the same crack Ian had seen from the opposite side, a fracture from top to bottom. Her curiosity satisfied she retraced her steps and emerged again on the west side. Linda called her to help with food and she scrambled back to the tarp.

"That was better than the bloody restaurant," was Dick's verdict and all agreed.

Sunset was spectacular; however, darkness descended quickly. Joe had insisted Tilly lamps had to go with them. They had a small Honda generator but he insisted they had to have another source of light. He won and the results were brilliant.

"Doesn't just attract bugs, it fries them as well," he pointed out.

It came in bulk, in a billy can, but looked like Black Label. Southwark beer also appeared and not to be outdone a bottle of vodka mysteriously landed on the table when nobody was looking.

"Brilliant, I'm glad I didn't have to use mine! Dick, you had better report in before we forget," Ian said, amidst much abuse about the drink.

"Port control – Oh shit!" Dick started. "Port Augusta control, this is Wild Goose One, radio check, over."

"Wild Goose One, this is Port Augusta control receiving you loud and clear, over," came the reply.

"Port Augusta control, all well with Wild Goose One, we will report in tomorrow as instructed. Over."

"Wild Goose One, that's affirmative. Port Augusta out."

"Right, that's that shit over with; any bloody music around here?" Dick demanded.

CHAPTER EIGHT

They were into drone training after a quick breakfast. The drone was small and, after explaining and demonstrating the controls, Dan decided to let Debbie go first as she had already used the one he lost.

It was serious but hilarious; she had to fly the thing around and land on the top of a Rover, take off and land on another, and repeat the procedure without crashing it. Dan gave a demo, and they were all impressed. He was good, very good, not just at flying but also on instructing.

The women were delegated to learn first. The men sat under a tarpaulin attached to the rock face at one end and two guyed poles at the other. They had a map spread over a pile of boxes neatly placed to form a table. What they were looking at was formidable. It looked rugged enough on the map, but in reality, it was worse. Wilson had plotted the coordinates for the third fuel stop and marked it with a small stone. A crescent of pebbles marked the maximum range of the microlight to the north.

It was obvious to all; the intended route Lacey was supposed to take was from where they were positioned at the end of the ledge. He would fly west by north following a broad flat region which ran between large hills to the north and smaller ones to the south. This area was marked on the map as the arid zone. Following the arid zone would take him directly to number three where Russell was waiting to guide him in.

One thing for sure was that just to reach number two, Lacey knew what he was doing. He should have timed the latter part of the flight to correspond with daylight. When he arrived at number two and when he left was a mystery.

"We need to get inside his head," Dick instructed.

They retraced Lacey's journey from Andamooka south down the length of Lake Torrens to the first fuel stop.

"Dark at six p.m., he would have taken off then not before. It's one hundred and thirty miles to site at full speed, he wouldn't be holding back, that makes it approximately two hours. Land, re-fuel, bury the evidence and take off. An hour, we can surmise. Then he headed west across the main road and landed here; that's another one hundred and fifty miles, so he could have landed here around midnight or prior to midnight. Daylight was at six thirty a.m. so he had six hours of darkness between him and number three. Did he wait or did he go? He wasn't flying along flat lakes which would allow him to fly as low as he liked yet he could ease back on the speed and take height. What would you do?" Dick asked.

"I can't understand why they didn't go straight across here to the north of Woomera and follow this lake south," Joe expressed.

Dick looked at him with what could only be described as pity, and then chuckled, "Joe, that *is* the way to go, but in the seventies, this was an active rocket range. The Brits were firing bloody blue streak bloody missiles, and all kinds of shit, into space from Woomera. The radars at Woomera would pick up anything crossing the exclusion zone and, in theory, anything moving within a hundred miles of the place. They didn't pick up anything suspicious because of the southern way they took and the height he could fly at kept detection to the minimum: it worked. They couldn't go that way, it would have been suicide. The fact Woomera had no radar sightings focused the search on the ground. Don't you young fellas know any bloody history?" Dick yelped.

"I say, this was planned to the finest detail. The lights, which obviously did the job. The machine and Lacey's ability to navigate. There wasn't much left to chance, so why take a chance here? By all accounts he had escaped. No reason to risk anything from this position but – he would have been tired, pumped up with adrenaline. and probably starving. We should address these factors," Wilson advised and they all agreed.

"Work it back. He was due to land in daylight, say around six thirty; he had six hours to fly one hundred and thirty miles. He knew that and surely he wouldn't take off knowing he would arrive before daylight – unless he was confident enough that he could land the thing in the dark at number three regardless of the hazards on this stretch. The bottom linc is, could he land in the dark there?" Ian pointed to the small stone.

"Well, we would need to look at that to make a judgement, but it's not anything like number one or two—" Dick was interrupted by Clinker.

"I reckon we've jumped the gun here. You reckon there was more stuff in that hole out there. If there's more in it we need to get it out to see how much fuel he was supposed to take. They wouldn't leave ten gallons if he could only take five." Clinker looked for support.

"Come on, you two. Leave the fossils to fuck with this!" Ian shouted at Joe and Clinker.

They stole a light from the females amidst yells of complaint and headed back to the fuel dump.

"You dig," Ian insisted and Joe knew why immediately. He went through a crust and hit the light below. The going was softer and moisture was welling into the hole. A rusted jerry can was at the bottom and they couldn't detect anything else.

"Sweep all around here and make sure there's nothing else," Ian instructed, putting the rusted can and the light into the

Rover. Joe filled in the hole and they joined Clinker with the detector.

Nothing else was found and they returned to the camp making sure they parked the Rover where it was before. Dinky was at the drone controls and Clinker didn't like the look she gave him; he ducked under the tarp quickly.

"Five gallons, that's it, and another light. A white one this time."

"I figured it might be! Let's see your guts," Dick spoke to the lamp.

They prised open the top and took out the guts. The battery had all but disintegrated but the bulb was still intact. Clinker inspected the bulb.

"That's a strobe light!" he concluded.

"That would make sense; Lacey would see that miles away and home in on the red ones for landing, all three light-sensitive they would last for days on one battery – clever," Dick concluded.

"So, we have five gallons of fuel, that's not a lot. But would he have another fuel tank in reserve? I checked on these things online and the info I could get was around fifty miles an hour full speed and two-point-five gallons hour consumption. That doesn't conform. He still had another one hundred and thirty miles to go unless he had extra fuel he was going to be thirty miles short, at least! Buggered if I know," Ian concluded.

"That's the problem, we haven't a clue what was onboard. Fuel, instruments, cargo, even his weight; everything would come into play and there's no way of finding out other than find the bloody thing," said Dick.

"We will brainstorm a little longer," Wilson ordered. "Your father mentioned the full moon. Obviously, there were no weather or visibility issues. But what if the weather changed when he arrived here?" Wilson asked.

"Well, the old man never mentioned anything about weather but he was over a hundred miles away so we can put that into unknown as well," Ian said.

Their concentration was broken by cheers from outside. Linda had landed the drone on top of Dan's head on instruction and they all looked fascinated as she lifted off and landed it back on the bonnet of a Rover to much applause.

Dan came into the tarp and announced they were all ready to go out on the lake with the big one.

"I want to see them controlling it when we're moving," he explained.

"OK, I think we can safely conclude we've found more mysteries than we've solved. Let's get up there and see what we're up against," Dick said, pointing to the ranges to the west.

The men might as well have been on the moon; the women were having a ball and left the camp in great excitement bound for the salt.

It was worse to see in reality than it was on a map. The ridges were running north-south each about fifty miles long. They ran west for sixty miles and there were twenty ridges plus marked on their map. The first bluff was five miles from camp; nothing could be seen beyond it.

The drive wasn't bad along the flat stony surface. Obstacles in the form of large boulders were everywhere as were many sandhills and sparse vegetation. As they neared the bluff got higher and higher.

"Three or four hundred feet I reckon," was Ian's guess.

"Yeh, and we've got ten thousand square bloody miles of that to cover, Jesus Christ," Dick pointed out unceremoniously.

"One has a task ahead, I believe," Wilson agreed.

"See if we can follow along the base for a few miles," Ian told Dick at the wheel.

It was similar to what they had experienced heading west but hotter; the sun seemed to radiate off the barren rock and they were dripping with sweat in a very short time.

"I reckon the drone will melt," Dick mused.

"You'll lose some fat now, Wilson," Ian sniggered.

"Yeh, you bring your scales with you, Wilson?" Dick put in.

"I have truly arrived in hell and it's affecting my hearing," Wilson replied.

His weight was a standard joke in Vung Tau. He had lost five stone in a month and panicked. Flew to Singapore to see his doctor of thirty years who weighed him again and his weight was the same as it always was. 'Your scales are broken' was the verdict. However, Ian insisted he had used the weight thing as a guise. The real reason was he went to get carbon dated. Thus he had gone deaf.

"My lord, look at that poor cow, it can hardly walk!" Wilson yelled suddenly.

Ian looked at the large red kangaroo that had just appeared from behind a large boulder and was about to reprimand Wilson but remained quiet.

"You want my bucket and stool, Wilson? I fancy some milk," Dick asked.

The roo hopped away, not overly concerned with the intruders. Further on they could see a herd of them standing upright, staring at the truck as it approached, then they scattered in a frenzy bounding in all directions before settling on north. Wilson's cow followed.

"These upside-down things walk very strangely," Wilson voiced his observation.

"You can go to hell, Wilson!" Dick shouted at him, and Wilson grinned.

A twisted mile further on, Dick suggested they should go back. There were no objections and he cleared the bluff by half a mile and stopped facing it. The heat was distinctly less.

"Out of the fire into the frying pan," he said and they surveyed the challenge ahead.

"There is one head we haven't been into yet – your father's." Wilson broke the silence.

Ian got the cue.

"He reckoned he stayed at number three for two days then came here. He searched for about a week and left because he had run out of water and was low on fuel. That's it, that's all I can tell you, I wish to hell he had told us about this! When he was alive. I reckon we could be flogging a dead horse."

Dick looked out the corner of his eye at him.

"Thank Christ we're not adrift and this bastard is looking for us, Wilson," he said.

"Negative thinking has been banned since you found that penny," was Wilson's reply, and he continued, "Your father would have been very distressed when he came here. Low on fuel, and water. Knowing his mate might die if he didn't find him quickly or he was already dead." Wilson thought out loud, "He had to conserve enough fuel to get out himself. That's for sure, so driving all over the place was out of the question. No way could he access the tops of the bluffs, that's out. Lacey is coming east to west so he can't hit the west side of the ridge; he can only hit the top or east face. I would consider searching from here and working west, searching on foot. Were I in his position," Wilson concluded.

"A week. I reckon he could have done one ridge a day. Walking we can only guess how far in he could get. He would have no more idea where to look than we have. I can see why he reckoned Lacey was dead. Nobody could survive in there for more than three days even if he wasn't injured. And that's unlikely," Dick concluded.

"What you got in mind?" Ian asked.

"Two teams, one in each valley searching the top and east face of each ridge on the way in and west face on the way out.

Make a penetration of around ten miles to begin with and see how we go. We can increase the penetration as we work our way west. Deviation to the north will increase as we move west. Right, Wilson?" Dick finished.

"Absolutely, and I believe we are banned from the ladies' tent," Wilson pointed out.

"Eh?" Ian responded.

"Yes! A total ban on penetration has been imposed. So you can look forward to your work every day because it's the only penetration you're going to get." Wilson chuckled.

"We'll see about that," Ian argued.

"Normal times for me then. We better get back and see how the aviators are getting on," Dick decided and headed the Rover towards the camp.

"Two hundred miles from civilisation at the back of the Black Stump," Dick mumbled.

"I say, two hundred miles! I thought we were further from Britain than that," Wilson quipped.

"You gonna slap him or me?" Dick asked Ian.

They arrived to a deserted camp and decided to walk to the beach. The team were still out on the salt, engrossed in drones. They headed back to camp after collecting some driftwood, Dinky's orders being 'anybody sees any wood, bring it back'. They noted on their return a substantial pile of wood was stacked against the rock face. Joe and Clinker must have collected it before joining the others.

They relieved their thirst and planned the search strategy for the next day. Crack of dawn start. They had to get into those hell hole valleys before the sun scorched the east face. Wilson made a vector with stones heading northwest and noted the coordinates for three valleys along the line.

"It's all guesswork, Dick, but we have to start somewhere! You know, there are sixty people registered as missing in the Scottish Highlands. There's a population of six million all around, and tens of thousands go into the Highlands regularly. Hundreds of searches haven't found any of the sixty. If a hundred people have visited this area in history I would be surprised, but nobody was looking for Lacey or a microlight. The odds are greatly in our favour that Lacey is still in there somewhere. We just have to find him – simple!" Wilson deduced.

The sound of the Rover returning got louder and mingled with the engine noise whoops of laughter were evident. They looked in expectation as the vehicle rounded the cliff and came into sight.

"Looks like an Indian train," was Dick's observation; they were hanging on around the outside of the vehicle whooping like idiots at every bump.

They all crowded under the tarp and quenched their thirst with great gulps. They were saturated with sweat. Lada was glowing like a small fire and the others weren't much better but they were in fine fettle regardless of the sunburn. Ian only realised how exposed they had been when they took off their sunglasses and they all looked like pandas but with white eyes instead of black.

"A bloody zoo," Dick concluded.

They all wanted to speak at once and from the mix things had gone better than expected. It had cooled slightly but was still hot. Dan explained, taking a notebook from his belt, that he had marked each pupil's ability over a set course and awarded points for each discipline. He pondered over the figures under the expectant stare of the participants and finally said:

"Debbie, you have the most points. Dinky, the second, Lada and Linda have the same. And you two are banned!" he said decisively to Joe and Clinker, who moaned.

"No bloody sense of humour, that bastard!" But before a post mortem could commence Dick raised his voice above them.

"Right, listen up! Wilson will show you where we start at daybreak tomorrow," he stipulated.

Wilson went through the strategy for the first three valleys quickly, adding, "Anything you see out of the normal you must investigate or, if there is no access, get the drone close enough to check beyond doubt. Any obstacles we will deal with as we find them. All communications between vehicles must be tested tonight, water and food put into the Rovers. Dan has a list of drone requirements and remember these drones can't be transported in the vehicle under any circumstance if they are not in their protective packing, not even for a short distance. There will be three persons in each vehicle and we are taking two vehicles only. Four of you will remain here. Set up the camp properly and get more training on flying the drone. If you have time, take a look up along the flat ground to the south but, if you do, make sure you contact us by radio to let us know where you are and go no more than ten miles. That's your limit, understand! And, finally, this strategy must be sustainable over a long period. Drivers and operators will be changed regularly and every third day will be a day off. There's a lot of things that need to be done at camp. Cooking, charging batteries, fetching wood etc. but the main point is to maintain your concentration during operations. We can't afford a lapse of concentration for one minute and, believe me, you will be glad of the break when it comes," Wilson concluded and there was silence.

"I feel sticky – Linda! come and lick me clean!" Dick shattered their thoughts.

"Go lick your arse, come on, girls, cooking time," Linda scoffed.

Ian managed to get Lada away from the others; she was looking burnt and beautiful. Her shirt tied in a knot under her breasts, the neck open, only the sunglasses spoiled her looks by hiding these beautiful eyes, but he was worried about her. Everybody was used to the heat but she wasn't. She seemed to

156

take it in her stride and wasn't complaining but he needed to break her in and going into the inferno the next day wasn't realistic.

They kissed and he held her against him, beckoning to a flat rock overlooking the salt.

There she started speaking about her day.

"I am excited about what we are doing. I am learning new things. I like the drone driving, I have never done anything like that except in games. This is a great experience for me. I never expected to come to a place like this, it's wild and I think frightening, but I love it. And the other girls are so kind; I love them all but especially Debbie, your sister. She looks after me like my mother would." She laughed.

"Brilliant, but are you feeling all right? I told you to take a lot of water and keep the suntan cream on, especially your face. You got a bit burnt today so be careful. Tomorrow, I don't want you out in the sun, you must stay under shade. If you're practising with the drone stand under the tarp and operate it; don't go into direct sunlight and keep your hat on."

He stroked her hair which looked and felt like straw and she knew it but she just smiled.

"Do you like my bush woman look?" she asked and he answered with another long kiss.

There was a limited amount of water for washing but not much and it had to be used last thing at night or the benefits would be lost.

"I would like a white wedding. I think there it's white. I wonder what it was like here when the sea and fishes were here and plants along the shore and everything, it must have been a lot different. When did the sea go away?" she asked.

"A few million years ago. It still floods sometimes but it can stay dry for a long long time. That driftwood could be a hundred years old, dried out, and salted like pretzels," he said, picking up a small branch.

"In Siberia they find things and animals frozen in time. Do you think there is anything here preserved in the salt?" she quizzed him.

"I reckon so but ice melts, salt doesn't so we're not likely to see something sticking out of the salt like they see in Siberia. Still, that's a good question. I don't know," Ian confessed.

"Tomorrow, I will fly the thing and make no mistakes. Debbie is very good and so is Dinky but me and Linda we were the worst. It's not easy, have you ever tried it?" she asked.

"No! I never had the chance but by the look of you lot it seems like fun. When you learn properly you can teach me!" He buried his face into her open blouse, she wriggled and giggled and got it out.

"Let's go! Before you get me excited," she ordered, pulling him to his feet, grumbling.

The others were grouped around the tarp apart from Dan, who was busy setting up a solar array for charging batteries.

Wilson and Dick were going over the map again further to the west and Ian joined them. Debbie insisted Lada went with her to their tent.

"Man, it's a harsh place, a tortured land," Wilson said.

"Not as bloody tortured as we are," Joe spoke and whacked Ian on the shoulder. Ian looked at him quizzically.

"Can't you get that bloody woman of yours to look ugly? How the hell are we supposed to concentrate with her around?" Joe demanded.

"Dream on brother. She's your sister-in-law, look, but don't touch. By the way she has a black belt in martial arts. A swift kick in the balls is what you have to worry about, not her looks."

"One has a way with words. Dick, we better call in and report," Wilson suggested. He turned to Ian and pointed to the map.

"Looks like this East Well area is in the vicinity of where we will have to move camp to in the next four days. How about taking the Bowser there and off-loading fuel and water into the storage bags? Joe reckons he and Clinker can return to Mount Ive and fill them up again, then join us for the move. I mean in good time before we have to move, either way it will mean a trip there and back. What are your thoughts?" he asked.

"Yeh! We don't want to jump the gun but as soon as the distance back here gets too great we can do that. What you reckon, Joe; two days, one there and one back?" he asked.

"Bugger off! We can do that in a day. Early start, late return, no problem from here." He was adamant.

"You can bring back a good-looking sheep as well or some bromide," Ian suggested.

"Ask Linda for bromide, she's got a five-gallon bucket of it somewhere. Right, I'll get the wild bloody duck reported," Dick sighed.

Ian bade Joe and Clinker to follow him and, once clear of the others, he instructed.

"After we leave in the morning take that Rover out somewhere and search it from top to bottom and everywhere in between. If you see anything you're not sure of don't touch it, leave it where it is," he said. They looked at him blankly. "There's a chance it might have a locator beacon attached. If there's nothing, check the other two when you have an excuse to get under them. Make an excuse."

Joe looked at him puzzled.

"You reckon the dog was killed in the compound?" Clinker asked.

"Might be, but if it wasn't an accident it had to be for a reason," Ian answered.

"Well, the whole bloody world knows we're here since you stuck them bloody stickers on, so what the hell would anybody want to track us for?" Joe asked.

"Track us on the way out!" Clinker stipulated before Ian could answer.

They were interrupted by Dinky swivelling her little arse in authority.

"Captain Wilson says to tell you that if you require sustenance report to the galley immediately. Whatever the hell that means? What's a galley?" she quizzed. The three of them looked at one another, wondering how they could wind her up.

"An old Roman ship," leapt from Ian's lips.

"Ahh," she said and headed back going into the ladies' tent.

Ian went towards the women's tent to get Lada but was stopped in his tracks by Linda's shout.

"Don't even think about it!" she yelled at him. "Men are banned. Bugger off, she'll be here. When she's ready!" He beat a retreat and Dick grinned at him.

Ian's curiosity was getting the better of him, made worse by the occasional fit of laughter coming from the tent.

At last she appeared with Debbie and Dinky.

Ian panicked. "What the hell!" he shrieked.

"Keep your hair on, brother, she has!" Debbie shouted at him and lifted the hat from Lada's head. She looked stunning; her hair was braided across the crown and all of it fitted under the hat.

"Thank Christ you never cut it," Ian hissed at Debbie.

"Yeh! And she better keep it under a hat, or she'll have split ends like drovers' whips if she doesn't," Debbie announced.

Lada sat beside Ian and he had a close look at Debbie's work; it was impressive. It had been a long time since she had abandoned hairdressing for nursing but it looked like she didn't forget much. It looked intricate and stylish, just the thing for sitting around in the desert eating stew. For that assessment he got a clip along the side of his head.

"A sleeping bag would have worked better," Joe commented and Ian gave him the finger.

Dawn broke to reveal a flurry of activity; most of them had been awake half the night with the heat. The men had breakfast cooked before the females emerged, the smell of bacon extracting them from oblivion. Chisellers were spoiled for choice.

Dan was running the show getting the drones and monitors as he wanted and by the time they could see clearly they were moving. Three in each vehicle, four left behind as arranged.

The only change Dick had suggested was that Debbie should scour the west side of the valley first, which meant the drone would not have to go high. She could then scan the high side on the return; that would give her more practice and made sense.

Radios were checked and the first bluff saw Dick turn north.

The other vehicle carried on for quarter of a mile and turned north along the west side of the same ridge.

Dan managed to get a drone into the air and the monitor set up within minutes. He sent it high above the ridge to check along the top. "Altitude one hundred and fifteen metres," he said. "I'll take her up to one hundred and fifty metres and see what result we get."

They watched, fascinated, as the picture came onto the monitor; it was a panorama of rounded humps, dark brown and black in still shaded places.

"Drive on," Dick commanded and Ian put the vehicle slow ahead.

The other team were not so fast but they were in the shade. Debbie was glad she didn't have to fly the thing up high and gingerly nursed it along the face of the cliff. They had good reception and, satisfied, Wilson requested Dinky to drive carefully, watch where she was going, and look out for wild beasts.

They only had a maximum of forty minutes' flight time on each bank of batteries and Dan had set the alarm on each monitor to go off five minutes before the batteries would start to run down. This gave them a flight time of only thirty-five minutes between battery changes.

When the first alarm went off on Dan's monitor he muttered, "Thank Christ for that," as he landed the drone.

"I see what you mean by sustainability, Dick. This takes some concentration. We need to get two trained in each vehicle. Take turn-about, that's for sure," he suggested.

"You should try keeping a three-thousand-ton ship in position under an oil rig for twenty-four hours, in all weathers, without DP," Dick replied.

Dan didn't know what DP was so said nothing. He changed the batteries and set the drone high again and they continued heading north. Ian could feel the heat starting to increase on the side of his face.

The others were in the shade mostly and Debbie was growing in confidence; however, she had reached the same conclusion as Dan: this was indeed intense concentration and she too was glad to hear the alarm.

"Dinky, if you think you can manage, my dear, you can have a practice. Whilst we are only doing the lower levels. Just go slowly, there's no hurry. What do you think, Debbie?" Wilson asked.

"Be my guest, this takes some concentration," Debbie agreed.

"I screwed up a landing," Dinky informed Wilson and bit her lip.

"Try again and just be careful," he encouraged, "One has to walk before one can run," he concluded as she switched places with Debbie.

Dinky was speaking to the drone all the time for the first five minutes but her nerves were settling. Soon enough she was flying just as well as Debbie. They came to a clear patch of sand and Wilson instructed her to land the drone on the sand. This she did without incident and followed his instructions to take off and land again.

"Good! Now, carry on, only practice will make perfect," Wilson encouraged and she was elated.

Dick announced they had reached the coordinates they had agreed and Dan put the drone high to look as far north along the top as possible. The view was the same and he landed it. Once it was packed in its box they headed back to the bluff. They had only taken one and a half hours and the day was young.

Debbie was on her second mission when Wilson called a halt as they had also reached their coordinates. The east face was around half a mile away and the temptation was great to just carry the thing over there but they stuck to plan and also boxed it. The heat hit them when they cleared the shade and Wilson knew from the experience of the day before it was going to be blistering before they traversed the east side. Unlike what they had just left, the east side was like the teeth of a saw: jagged and brutal.

Dinky somewhat reluctantly flew the drone high until they observed the strata on top. She was quiet now and watched the monitor intently. Wilson noted there were huge overhangs in the rock formation and deep ledges, running horizontally along the upper level. He instructed her to stay fifty metres out from the face and go along looking at the ledges rather than concentrate on the top.

This she was glad to do and by the end of her shift she, too, was glad to hand over to Debbie.

"Shall we carry on to the end or stop for a break?" Wilson asked.

"Carry on!" both shouted simultaneously. He smiled.

Joe and Clinker had the Rover a few miles out into the flat and stopped over a small depression which allowed them easy access under the vehicle. There weren't many places anybody could conceal anything, only the exhaust braces or behind the wheel trims; they checked everywhere and found nothing. Under the bonnet was a different proposition, a hundred hiding places, and Joe stood back. Clinker had the mechanical know how to detect anything suspicious and he drew a blank also.

"I reckon he's flipped his lid," Joe commented, slamming the bonnet down hard.

Clinker frowned and thought for a minute.

"Could be, but if he's right. This was the only Rover left outside. The others were inside and the alarm never went off. If somebody is tracking this vehicle only it would be a piece of piss to put them on a bum steer. I think he wants this vehicle to have a tracker on it; he's not bloody stupid," Clinker stated.

"Well, he's out of bloody luck," Joe concluded and they headed west along the flats as requested.

It was a full two hours and four battery changes later, before Wilson and his team managed to reach the bluff. They were exhausted and about cooked. The heat radiating off the cliff face was burning to the point of painful and he knew they would have to change strategy before somebody got heatstroke. Wilson called Dick on the radio several times but it was Joe who answered him.

"You all OK?" Joe asked.

"Yes, we're fine but I can't raise Dick," Wilson replied.

"That's an age thing, Captain, you should try Viagra," came the reply, to which Debbie and Dinky roared with laughter.

"Tell him to bugger off, Wilson," Dick's voice cut in.

"Ah! You're alive at last, Dick! We have completed our sweep without incident and are awaiting further orders. Where exactly are you?" Wilson asked.

Dick read out their coordinates and Wilson checked the map.

"There!" he pointed it out to the girls. "About two miles in that direction, we will join them." He directed Dinky to drive on. They spotted the drone before they saw the Rover. There was no shade now; the sun was overhead and baking everything in sight.

"A change of course is in order, Wilson, to avoid a collision with a pine box," Dick greeted them with.

"My thoughts exactly," Wilson replied.

"Batten down, get the AC on and get the hell out of here. Well catch you up," Dick ordered.

They closed the sliding roof and all the windows and put the AC on. The result was instant and was to be used only in emergency. This was as close to an emergency as they wanted to get.

"Call Joe and find out where they are please," Wilson asked Debbie.

"Hey! Bait balls, sandwiches, where the hell are you?" she yelled into the mike.

"My God, woman, you can't speak over the radio like that." Wilson recoiled in horror.

"We're cutting across towards you," Joe replied.

"What you want them to do?" Debbie asked.

"Kindly stay where they are and we will rendezvous with them." But Dick got in first.

"Anchor where we can see you. Use the mirror," Dick instructed.

"Exactly! Just what I was going to say," Wilson lied.

They saw the flash a long distance from the Rover. Clinker was standing on the roof watching their dust approach with some satisfaction. He used the mirror like a heliograph and was highly impressed with the result.

"Bullseye!" Ian commented when they stopped.

"Right, a pow wow!" Dick shouted and they gathered together. "We're not gonna get in there without the AC running and that screws up our fuel consumption. We would need to run it on full with the roof open. Low if the roof was shut. We need to find a way to get that sorted out but, in the meantime, we can search along the flat. There's too much daylight left to waste. So spread out and we can head west another ten miles. Go about half a mile apart and slowly so the drones can be flown. Joe, you stay in the middle which is here! OK. Let's go; when you see the drones move, you move," he instructed.

Ian drove north, Dinky drove south. The drones were quickly in the air and Joe spotted both. They started to sweep west. It wasn't as hot there as it had been inside the valley. Ian had explained the iron oxide in the rock was acting like a radiator; it retained a lot of heat during darkness and heated up quickly when the sun returned. It was still in the high thirties out there but it was over forty inside and that's in the shade. They were in the sun.

"Make a plan and change it!" Ian remarked to Dick.

"That's the name of the game, mate. We're here to look, and as long as we're looking we're going ahead. Work out some strategy for tomorrow morning; we need to get back into them valleys somehow," Dick replied.

"If we could isolate the drone operator we can have the AC on at low," Dan advised.

"We have a drill with us?" Ian asked him.

"Dinky has a workshop, never mind a drill," Dick scoffed.

"OK! We've plenty of bungee so how about we rig up something like a kayak and keep the module inside? We can use some tarp to seal off the roof if we can fasten it to the sides," Ian suggested.

"OK, we'll brainstorm this when we get back. We need something in position before daylight." Dick dropped the subject.

The terrain was easy to traverse, vegetation was sparse and stunted. Erosion, in places where run-off from the bluffs had gouged the land, was the only obstacle. They went west slowly for another hour and saw nothing. Dick called for a sweep back towards the camp and they went north before turning east again.

Dinky was totally relaxed flying the drone and Dan wished he had somebody to give him a break also. The captain's sustainability prophecy wasn't wrong.

They searched all the way back to the camp and arrived there at three p.m., exhausted. In contrast, Lada and Linda were in high spirits, eager to know if they had seen anything and demanding Dan get the large drone out and complete their training, to which he reluctantly agreed.

"We have been flying the little one for hours." Lada spoke excitedly when she pulled her lips from Ian's. "We can go tomorrow?" she pleaded, pouting her lip.

"That's for sure. The quicker you two get the all clear, the better." He slapped her bum as she scarpered after Dan and Linda.

Dinky and the bait balls were busy getting tarp arranged across the open roof. They had to remove the sliding glass and drill along the lip. They had a box of welding rods and made small hooks from the rods. Within half an hour they had a prototype in position but the hole which the operator could get through presented the biggest problem.

Joe started saying, "It looks like a big c—" He got a whack from Dinky before he could finish.

Clinker stuck his head through and shouted, "It's like getting reborn." He got a whack too.

They screwed around with the bungee around the hole and no matter how they arranged it getting in from the bottom was easy, getting back was impossible.

"And that's without tits," Clinker advised and got another whack.

"Will it keep the air inside, that's what matters?" Dick yelled at them.

"Dinky, get into that hole! You, start the bloody thing up AC on low, and see what we get," Dick snapped.

They waited five minutes without anybody saying anything.

"How long we doing this! My bloody arse is frozen!" Dinky yelled at them.

Clinker stroked her leg and she leapt out of the hole yelling merry hell.

"Emergency escape as well, brilliant. Fix up the other one the same," Dick instructed Joe.

It was still light when the three came back from the lake and Dan gave the thumbs up. "OK!" he added.

Ian had a sudden thought. "Lada, can you drive?" he asked her.

"Yes! But I have only done it on the right side, I have never driven on the left," she replied innocently.

"OK, if you can find the left side you can drive there," he chuckled.

Linda and Lada had food prepared and after watching the spectacular sun set again, they all ate heartily.

They had re-fuelled the vehicles when the cracks as they had named them (much to Dinky's disgust) were being finished.

"We go straight to the east facing cliffs first thing in the morning, get them done and try and get back along the west facing side while there's still shade. If we get caught like we were today, shut the crack and put the AC on low. We might have to run all day like that and we will decide where we will search after we do the next two valleys. We might go for another two or go for the flat.

Joe, you and Clinker take the other vehicle with the Bowser to East Well. Find a good campsite and leave the Bowser there. Start searching all around that area and keep in contact," Dick finished.

"I will report," Wilson announced, getting up stiffly.

The morning saw a repeat of the day before, only now they knew what was ahead of them they set off before it was fully daylight. They were at the mouth of the valley which caused so much grief by the time they could see without the headlights.

Dick turned into the next valley and Dinky carried on under Wilson's directions past the bluff and towards the next one. It was glowing a soft red by the time they turned right and stopped to get the drone in the air. It was a daunting place. More brutalised, more ravaged, but with a raw, wild beauty it was hard to ignore.

"OK. You drive," Dinky said and made way for Lada, who yelped in alarm, she was so engrossed in the view.

She was dodgy with the gears to begin with and crunched a few times but soon fathomed out what she had to do with her left hand as opposed to her right. She improved as Dinky flew the drone expertly along the rugged face. Wilson had the monitor and saw nothing which stood out as not natural. Likewise, Dan was doing the same, with Dick on the monitor and Ian driving.

It was Joe who noted the sudden drop in temperature out on the flats. The wind had picked up a little from the south but the sky was still cloudless so he said nothing. Contrary to being the odd ones out the bait balls were well aware they, not the others, were on Lacey's intended flight path and their visible swathe of search was much less but it was undertaken intently. They made their way to the area marked as East Well in the map, a large roundish pool about ten miles in diameter which looked as salty as the lake. They aimed for the north edge, to go into it was not a good idea with no knowledge of what exactly it was comprised of.

Both drones reached their respective coordinates and headed for the shade. It was hot but not hellish as it had been the day before. Again, they found nothing of any interest all the way back to the bluffs.

They rendezvoused at Wilson's end and decided to go into the next two valleys; they too were aware of the drop in temperature and still the sky was cloudless.

Their vigilance didn't falter. Even towing the heavy bowser, they were making good progress. The change in temperature made Joe search the sky to the south. There were no clouds and the wind was slight but he knew the weather was going to change; he hoped not before they got back to the camp. Bleached bones were not uncommon, mostly kangaroo and fox.

The swathe of their search wasn't much more than fifty metres either side of the vehicle but the distance covered meant they were searching a serious amount of territory. They opted to head for the north side of the well and didn't fancy driving anywhere near it until they had company. They were almost sixty miles from camp, and thirty from the other Rovers. He called Dick on the radio to make sure they had contact. Just a radio check; he didn't tell Dick where they were and he didn't ask. All he said was get back before dark, which was their intention from the start.

Gullahs, the pink breasted parrots native to the area, appeared in masses above some taller trees, shrieking their annoyance at being disturbed and several kangaroos were spotted bounding through the scrub. *Signs of life; there may be drinkable water here after all,* Joe thought, but wasn't optimistic. They pulled in beside a ridge and followed it north. It wasn't high, about twenty feet; they followed it around to the north and were confronted with what Clinker described as a safe anchorage. Joe agreed there was a substantial overhang on the north west tip. The overhang was enough to keep direct sunlight away for most of the day.

They unloaded the bags from the top of the bowser. They were specifically for fuel and water. They decanted the bowser into the respective bags and covered them with a tarp. They pinned it down with rocks and headed back towards the other Rovers, searching all the way for the illusive Lacey but noting the cloud formation now visible far to the south.

Taking advantage of the drop in temperature, the other two Rovers had completed four more valleys before Joe and Clinker saw them, and they were not as far away as he had thought.

The wind had increased to a gentle breeze but not enough to blow away the chisellers. They were in force and made them act quickly. Dick insisted they head back immediately. They would sweep east like yesterday along the flats all the way back.

"Get away from these bloody things!" he yelled.

They made it back to camp without seeing anything of interest but the sky had clouded over and the temperature had plunged.

"Bloody Adelaide weather now," Linda acknowledged.

"Long johns tonight, I think." Wilson puffed on his pipe and relaxed under the tarp.

Their wash-up meeting about the day's coverage and plans for tomorrow was interrupted by rain. Not a lot, just a brief drizzle which barely wetted the tarp top and fizzled out. The plan was for the bait balls to head for Mt Ive Station at first light and try to get back. Ian reckoned one day was out of the question and Dick agreed, so as a compromise they would leave a shelter at their present location. If they managed to get back here they must stay until daylight before heading to the East Well location, taking the shelter with them.

This arrangement seemed logical and they agreed to move camp at first light to the new location sixty miles away. The tracks they had already covered seemed to split the nearer they got to East Well and Ian explained that was not a concern as from East Well they would conduct a rigorous search all around and towards the number three fuel site some fifty miles to the west. The eyes in the sky, everybody agreed, were brilliant; so too was the array Dan had configured for charging batteries.

They ate and started packing as much as was not required into the trailers. The drones would be operational all the way to East Well and cover gaps in the areas already covered. Dick and

Wilson agreed the next day was moving house, as Wilson put it. "So, let's just get there fully operational, that's the priority."

They reported in to Port Augusta and mentioned two persons heading for Mt Ive Station departing six thirty a.m. ETA at Mt Ive approximately ten a.m. for fuel and water.

"Acknowledged, we will contact the station and make sure there is somebody to meet them," came the reply.

There was no brilliant sunset. The light just faded into darkness and sleeping bags were the order of the night; the temperature had dropped to below twenty and it was getting colder.

The bait balls were away at first light as planned and the dawn revealed an overcast sky but the clouds were high and not threatening so they packed as planned, left the tarp rigged for shelter and were heading for East Well by eight thirty a.m.

The going out on the flats was steady, there were very few obstacles, low sand dunes linked by rock strewn terrain; the rocks fortunately were small and rounded, obviously some long-dead sea-bed. It was hard ground and allowed steady progress. Dick called a halt at what he determined was the halfway mark and the time taken was two hours.

They saw nothing before or after the break which was of any interest. They were going fast enough to keep the chisellers away but as soon as they slowed down the attack resumed, spurring them on again. The women were ecstatic, they had the drones all the way and, as the bait balls had found, the wildlife increased the further west they went.

Dinky couldn't get the wills of herself chasing kangaroos after she explained to Wilson they were not deformed cows; he got somebody to bite at last. She homed in on a herd of big reds and one stood on his hind legs pawing the air in defiance at what must have sounded to him like the biggest mosquito in the world. She didn't go too close, she didn't know how high the bloody thing could jump.

"Me and Mike's gotta get one of these things. Jesus, you can see everything, the bloody pigs won't hide now." She spoke to herself up through the crack; the monitor was inside with Linda who was shouting at her, "Don't go near that bloody roo, it'll tear the thing to bits."

They startled several red foxes and she chased them as well like a fighter pilot yelling merrily to herself but not interrupting the task at hand. Lada was performing similarly, also up through the crack. Ian licked her bronzed thigh and Dick went mental.

"Gimme a lick, you prick. You drive this bloody thing!" he shouted from behind the wheel.

She was also homing in on whatever jumped out ahead and had been even more excited than Dinky, but what appeared next took them all by surprise. Camels, a small herd galloping across their path, several large ones and about eight smaller ones. What she was saying about them was anybody's guess as she was yelling loudly in Russian and shrieking wildly.

"She likes the hump. I reckon women would last longer than men out here," Dick announced and Ian waited. "They have the humps on the other side but the result would be the same, I reckon," he concluded.

"Yeh! That's the reason they don't ride women across the desert because the humps are on the wrong way. Is that what you are trying to say?" Ian enquired.

"Exactly," Dick replied, getting a clip along the ear from Debbie, who was lying in the back listening.

Dick might have been eccentric on the water carry capability but he was spot on with Joe's arrival at Mt Ive. They pulled in at nine forty-five a.m. and were warmly greeted by an old geezer wearing a slouch hat.

"G'day, mate! We're expectin' ya. Bang on time like the cops said. Good trip?" he asked.

173

"Fair to middlin', mate. You got plenty diesel?" Joe asked.

"After tha mookas, are ya? Man, you'll need plenty before ye find them, mate!" he replied.

"You got five hundred gallons?" Joe asked.

"Five hundred, you not gonna fill it?" he said, looking at the bowser.

"Half water," Joe explained.

"No problem, mate, when those races are on out there we go through five hundred a morning. You need a swim?"

That was an invitation not to be missed.

"Where?" Joe asked.

"The back of the shed," he answered, pointing to their right.

"You go and dunk, mate! I'll get the thing loaded; wash the dust off, there's a shower beside the tank," he instructed.

The bait balls dived headlong into the cool water and dived again and again until they were breathless, their white arses flashing in the sun which had just reappeared. Side to side underwater somersaults and twists, they were reborn. They came out and washed under the shower; there was soap there and they made the best of it, beards and hair were matted with dust. They went into the pool again and relaxed but as soon as they stopped moving the chisellers were into them. Half an hour later, the old fella came to tell them they were fuelled up and watered up and ready to go hunt.

"You fellas are onto a good thing. Ya can tell them tourists anything. Be good business for us too if ya keep comin' this way. See ya next time, mate. Make sure ya don't find them," were his parting words and he laughed loudly, gripping his belly.

They swung out of the station and the weight of the bowser was immediately evident.

"You thinking what I'm thinking?" Clinker said, looking at his watch.

"Go for it! This bloody thing won't bounce as much now," Joe answered.

Clinker had tracks to follow and headed back much faster than when they came south. The Rover handled the bowser on the flat as if it wasn't there but they both knew if they had to stop quickly it could jack-knife, accordingly he didn't go as fast as he could have. At a steady fifty they reached the campsite at one p.m., tore down the tarp quickly and threw everything that had been left for them onto the bowser rack. With more than three hours of daylight left, they headed west.

Dinky spotted them first, she was doing her security thing, looking for undesirables. She was on top of the rock.

"The bait balls are coming back!" she yelled excitedly, pointing east and scarpering down from the rock. The setting sun cast long shadows and the terrain in the shafts of sunlight glowed deep red.

"The bastards, they had to prove they were right," Ian said to Dick.

"Yep! They were," Dick confirmed.

"That's beside the bloody point," Ian said angrily.

"Drop it! As long as they managed to get what they were sent for, and no problems? They're good! I ordered them to make decisions," Dick said sternly.

Joe drove the Rover alongside the other two while the last rays of the sun were still visible.

"Made it in daylight!" he shouted, and took a bow.

"Where the hell did you get clean?" Debbie screamed at them.

"Went for a swim. Brilliant, you should have come," Clinker suggested.

"We're bloody starving, any grub left?" Joe asked.

After Ian insisted on calling them all the stupid bastards under the sun, things settled down. They gave a full account of the day's activity and the old geezer's request that they keep taking these tourists their way. "And we can't find the mookas, it will ruin our business."

Brilliant, Ian thought, *the bush telegraph was working overtime.* He wondered how long it would take before somebody set up another mooka hunting operation; it certainly had potential for a couple of hundred years.

The job at hand, Wilson laid out the map and while the two heroes downed their tucker he explained the principles of a sector search. They could cover around one mile by ten miles. Swing back and do the same, using the edge of the East Well at the fulcrum. Depending on what terrain they encountered, he estimated they could make at least four sweeps per day, arriving back at East Well on the return of the fourth.

The remaining valleys, they decided, would be looked at as soon as the temperature dropped. This camp was far superior to the first. The overhanging rock offered shelter and must have been used before as Wilson had discovered a condom at the back.

"Must have been a breeding ground. An ancient brothel, I'm shocked," he said holding his trophy out for inspection. Ian and Dick looked at him, smiled and said nothing.

"That's a bloody snake skin, drongo! They cast them off like that. What a Dick!" Dinky blurted out.

"Don't bring me into it. He might be right. I say, darling, I'm feeling randy; I'll just go kill a snake and we can hump. Snakes don't go backwards. Wonder how they solved that problem. Never mind about the condom, what about the bastard thing that was wearing it?" Dick insisted.

"Yeh! It's old, there's nothing around the rock. I checked," Dinky replied with authority.

CHAPTER NINE

On the third day of searching around East Well, Linda nearly gave Wilson a heart attack.

"Stop! Stop!" she screamed at the top of her voice. She was through the crack and nobody could see what the hell she was screaming about. The drone she was operating came close to the vehicle low and going full speed from left to right. Wilson's ears popped and suddenly a willy-willie came into view a mere hundred feet in front of the windscreen.

"I say! A tornado!" Wilson spluttered, transfixed with the antics of the whirlwind ahead. It wasn't big but the power was evident, spinning violently and meandering slowly, dust and dry material sucked high into the air. It lasted for about one minute and died as quickly as it had been born.

"Bloody hell, that was close. It nearly got the drone!" Linda shouted through the crack.

"And what does one call that animal?" Wilson asked Dinky who was driving.

"It's a willy-willy! That was a little one. You should see a big one, they're great!" she informed him.

"Yes! I dare say," Wilson said thoughtfully.

They spotted many more during that day. Some small, some big; whatever had triggered them was finding conditions ideal for doing so. They were high on the agenda that night. Wilson asked the question which had been bugging him all day.

"Does the willy, Large or Small, come out at night?" he threw into the fire for discussion. There was a roar of laughter and Linda sniggered.

"All willies come out at night except his!" she gestured towards Dick, who bent his elbow in response. There was a flurry of Australian local knowledge batted about. Some adamant, some theories shot down in flames but the conclusion was final.

"Who the hell is going to see them in the dark? It's the temperature that triggers them and if the temperature is right what the hell has dark or light got to do with it?" The argument went on for a long time, they agreed to disagree. Even Willie that came out at night in Vung Tau got a mention.

"So! The bloody things would knock the hell out of a drone. What the hell would they do to a Microlight?" Dick asked, getting Wilson's drift spot on.

"Willy-willies produce an electrical discharge and a magnetic field; we learned that at uni but nobody discussed if they appeared at night. If a microlight hit one or it hit the microlight the vortex would spin it. Might even turn it upside down, but even without damage the magnetic field would spin a compass. Bloody hell, we could be looking at what happened to Lacey if he run into a willy; his compass would be buggered," Ian assessed.

"Certainly food for thought? So, until proven otherwise we must conclude this is what happened. It seems the sector we just searched is the most active but we did observe many further west. I think we should concentrate on Tornado Alley for a couple of days. What ya reckon?" Dick asked.

"Linda had a close call today; if that thing had hit the drone it would have crashed it. So, in future if one is close to the drone fly it up high, then fly it clear. Don't take any rash decisions no matter how close it is; up then clear, OK?" were Dan's instructions.

After breakfast, they headed for the coordinates they had stopped searching at yesterday, and picked up where they had left off. The heat steadily increased but the search was fruitless all that morning and it was mid-afternoon when Lada slammed the brakes on and nearly put Ian's head through the windscreen.

"I see something!" she yelled in explanation, jumping out of the driver's seat. He followed her curiously, rubbing his forehead. She was bent over what looked like an old tin, rusted through and half buried.

"How the hell did you see that?" he asked, putting his arm around her shoulder.

"I thought it was something good but it's just rubbish," she said, disappointed. Ian scraped the sand away from the side which was covered and saw the remnants of red paint. It was an unusual shape, he thought, and cleared all the sand away. On the down side there was a small perished rubber hose protruding from what appeared to be the top of the tin; it was slightly rounded, the bottom was flat. One corner was collapsed; it looked a mess of rust. Something was ringing bells in Ian's head but he couldn't put his finger on what it was. He decided to call the other two Rovers across on the VHF.

"What up?" Wilson asked on arrival and Ian was showing him the tin when the bait balls arrived.

"What the hell! An outboard motor fuel tank." Joe identified the tank on sight and Ian slapped his own leg for not doing so. They lifted it carefully and set it on the bonnet of the Rover.

"This thing has a good dent in: it must have been hit with something," Joe pointed out.

"Yeh or *it* hit something!" Ian added.

"This fuel line, what's left of it has come off the other end. Still attached to the tank top but from there to what?" Clinker asked.

"I reckon the microlight. This could be a spare tank. If it fell out, that would account for the damage when it hit the ground.

But why would it fall out and rip off the fuel line unless the craft was way over or suddenly dropped?"

"Speak to me, you bastard." Joe stroked the tank.

"Get the metal detector and search this entire area, see if there's anything else that might have fallen here if this was Lacey's," Ian instructed. He was excited and hugged Lada tightly, explaining to her what they thought she had found and the excitement was transferred to her.

The brains trust was isolated from the rest for what seemed an eternity. Wilson and Dick pondered their findings and discussed all aspects related inside one of the Rovers. They had unceremoniously told everybody to bugger off and leave them alone. Nobody minded; they were elated that they had found something.

When at last the two captains appeared they were straight faced and summoned everybody around.

"Whatever happened here we don't know and probably we will never know," Dick started, pointing to the coordinates where the can was found. "However, we are of the opinion the loss of the fuel tank or if it was jettisoned would make no difference in Lacey's ability to get to number three. He could still have had enough fuel. It's not cut and dry that he would run out of fuel. So, if he was hit by a willy in the dark the only thing which would be affected would be his compass." He paused.

They all stared intently, hanging on Dick's every word and nodding agreement with him. He went on.

"We conclude the compass would have been severely impacted by the magnetic field. However, if the sky was clear he would have stars to follow and he would have been focused on these stars for over an hour. He would only check the compass periodically, not continuously; he had to see what was directly ahead and also watch his height. That's two reasons not to rely entirely on a compass. If he had a fuel shortage there was nothing to stop him from landing. According to Ian, the machines can still fly at just over twenty miles an hour even in the dark; his chances were good to bring it down with minimum risk of injury to himself. The machine, on the other hand, wasn't a concern; it had done what they wanted and if it was out of fuel, or if it was damaged, so what? On the flight path he would be found.

"We reckon there was more than a willy-willy he had to deal with. If the sky was overcast he would have lost the stars. And then the compass becomes all important. If it didn't settle down quickly, and remember he is flying at around fifty miles an hour, he could have been ten miles off course before it did settle. Until then he's flying blind into the dark. Five minutes at fifty is enough to take him from where we found the can into the region of the three valleys we haven't searched – here!" Dick pointed to the map.

"We go back to the coordinates in the morning, spread out and go all the way to the East Bluff, then we will search each valley thoroughly all the way to the end no matter how hot it is or how long it takes – agreed?"

There were whoops of agreement from the women. Lada clung to Ian and Dinky had a stranglehold on Clinker.

"You use perfumed soap or something?" Dinky enquired, pushing him on the ground.

He rubbed sand from his beard and grabbed her leg. They rolled around in the dust and eventually, she sat on top of his belly laughing hysterically; Ian had noted they were in one another's company at every excuse. A far cry from the queer boy she first appeared as.

The morning was not kind. The sun was burning and by the time they reached the coordinates it was brutal. They spread out and headed for the bluff to the north, taking their time and searching carefully. The willies were few and far between but they were getting more frequent as the day went on. They had found nothing by the time they closed in on the bluff and Dick decided to send the bait balls back towards the coordinates and to continue searching the flats until they were told otherwise.

The first valley was wide, over five miles wide, and Dick decided they would persevere and search the east facing side of the cliff regardless of the intense heat radiating from it; air con on low and operators through the crack they began, one Rover in each valley.

Wilson had Dinky and Debbie with him. Dick had Lada and Linda with him. Ian and Dan had been stood down, protesting like hell but to no avail. "Day off!" Dick had insisted. "No bloody argument."

"Linda! Make sure that bastard doesn't lick her leg!" Ian shouted to her.

"He'll be licking his wounds if he does," she retorted, and slapped Dick across the back of his head.

They stayed at the camp and moaned until Dan suggested they rig up some lights using the solar charger, a spare car battery and some spare headlight bulbs. This kept them busy but they kept looking north towards the bluffs.

The day wore on and the heat increased to torturous. Over forty in the valleys, they had reduced operating time on the drones to twenty minutes each. This improved their chances of completing the assignment, but there was still a long way to go.

The radio crackled in Wilson's Rover and Dick's voice came through loud and clear.

"Looks like a bum steer, Wilson," was all Dick said.

"Quite!" replied Wilson.

The radio clicked twice in reply and Wilson pulled out his pipe.

Dinky looked at him curiously. He lit his pipe and switched off the monitor. Tugging at the bottom of Debbie's shorts he shouted to her, "Bring the drone back, dear, we must return to base."

"Eh! what ya mean? We're OK, we can carry on no problem!" Dinky shouted back in protest. Wilson puffed his pipe, his eyes closed, and gave a big sigh.

"What did Dick just say?" he asked Dinky.

"They're on a bum steer he reckons. But we're not there! We can still search here," she answered, agitated.

"It can have your interpretation or it can have another," Wilson informed her. "The other is steer by the bum!" he elaborated.

"Drive in reverse, are you mental?" she exploded.

"Not quite. You don't have to go back in reverse, just go back the way you came," he instructed her.

"Why the hell didn't he just say that?" she asked, irritated.

"Because, my dear, they have found something and they don't want to broadcast it to the world. We go back to camp to find out what they have discovered, rather than on the radio," he replied grabbing her hand as she reached for the mic. "No!" he warned her.

Dinky stopped the Rover and jumped out screaming at Debbie, "Get that thing down. They found something. We have to get back to the camp. Hurry up! Hurry!" she instructed the bemused Debbie, who was concentrating on landing and trying to listen to her at the same time.

"Keep your bloody hair on!" Debbie retorted.

Ian saw the dust from first two, then three, vehicles approaching. They were still several miles away and he looked at his watch. They seemed to stop for some reason then came on. He wasn't surprised they were coming back early, the sun had been relentless all day and the camp was becoming unbearable also. He dreaded to think what it was like in the valleys. He was concerned; this exposure was dangerous regardless of precautions, so it was with apprehension he watched their approach.

They pulled up in front of the overhang and got out. They were all haggard, even the newly scrubbed bait balls looked red with dust. Dick instructed Linda to take the monitor with her and they came under the overhang.

"Right, children, cast your pork pies over this!" Dick instructed.

Ian was intrigued and had to push his way in to get a view. The monitor flickered into life and they watched as the film traversed the cliff then went up. It filmed along the top and descended back to the bottom.

"Stop! Did anybody see anything just now?" he asked and nobody spoke. "I take it you didn't then? But she did, Linda saw something. Now replay slowly," he directed Linda.

The playback was enacted and slowly the film climbed back up the cliff face. It was just like all the others, deep ledges gouged out for millennia.

"Stop!" Dick shouted. Ian peered at the screen; he couldn't see anything but Dick's voice cut into his observation. "Look closely at the dark area; you see that thin line," he said, pointing out the anomaly with his finger. Ian could make it out but wasn't stunned by it. He shrugged, as did Dan.

"OK, play the rest," Dick instructed Linda. They watched as the film descended again then started rising slowly back up to the ledge. Again, the thin line came into view but the drone went closer and slightly higher to see clearly inside the ledge. A straight piece of tubing could be seen running parallel to the ledge and another bent at an angle was the support for what now looked like a thin shiny wire. There was silence.

"I reckon it's either a whirligig, for drying clothes… or a microlight wing," Ian said softly.

"Yeh! It's probably a whirligig," Dick agreed.

"No! It's the microlight, it's the microlight!" Dinky screamed, dancing around like she was demented; her efforts were infectious and they all danced around

"Yes! Yes! We found it. We found it."

Their joy lasted a long time and was only interrupted by Wilson, who insisted they should drink a toast to Linda for being so alert. Whiskey. Ian had another idea and kissed her hand to the cheers of all.

"How the hell did you see that?" they marvelled and she laughed.

"I have good eyes," was her only explanation. How close they had been to missing the bloody thing was what was bugging Dick and Wilson, who had ambled away to the side-lines. At length, Wilson came back and addressed them,

"Ladies, can I have your attention please!" he shouted, holding his hands aloft until he had their attention. "Tomorrow, we will endeavour to reach the target. Exposure to what we might find there must be considered carefully. Our opinion is that none of the women should go up there, because it's likely there is a body there and we feel it may have a detrimental effect on you to be confronted with such a hideous scene and it can be avoided." He stopped, waiting for a reaction.

Only Debbie spoke, "Yeh! I know where you're coming from, Wilson. Not a problem for me. I see plenty, but you're right!" She looked at the other women and continued, "That's good advice. I know we are all breaking our necks to see what's there, but you might regret it for the rest of your lives. Like Wilson, my advice is stay on the ground, don't go there," she finalised.

Dick had joined Wilson and he spoke.

"Remember, this is a crime scene, or we hope it is; nothing must be touched until every angle and every detail has been photographed or filmed. We can't go in there and tear the place apart. I say this because it is relevant. We haven't decided what to do yet as we still haven't found the mookas but it's in our interest to photograph everything as we found it undisturbed — for future reference, if required." There were no comments to

185

that and he continued, "Access to that ledge from the bottom is impossible, we looked closely but there is access to the top about three hundred yards from there, where the ledges have collapsed. I reckon there are only two people who should go there and that's Ian and Joe. We have rope and they can go down to the ledge rather than up to it. We'll go through the video again after we have eaten and come up with a plan for tomorrow. Your father never found him, his sons finding him should put things right!"

They all mumbled agreement to Dick's last statement. Euphoria was rife but, since it had been mentioned, food was also a desire. Linda and Debbie manned the stove; the others hung around the monitor. The chisellers were everywhere and nobody cared.

They planned and discussed their next move under the lights Ian and Dan had rigged up. It had cooled a little but was still uncomfortably hot. It was decided that Clinker should accompany Ian and Joe; he was fit and keen. The ropes they had were proper climbing ropes; they knew from the map they would encounter such terrain and came prepared. The orthodox method wasn't an option for them as none of them, except Lada, had ever abseiled before.

"I reckon take the wire off one of the winches and we'll use it for pulling and lowering, if we can rig a snatch block at the top," Dick suggested. Wilson, Joe and Clinker backed that idea as long as one of them controlled the rope.

Sleep didn't come easy. Dick lay by the fire for most of the night. He was joined by nearly all of them at some stage or another. He dozed there until Linda woke him at dawn with a kick.

"Bugger off, woman, I was just about to get my leg over," he complained.

"In your dreams. You're too old for bicycles, move your arse," she quipped.

The atmosphere was electric during breakfast and Dinky had to be subdued by Clinker to stop her heading for the bluff on her own; she was so excited, and her antics were infectious. They all piled into the Rovers and took off before they got another lecture from their leaders, much to Dick's annoyance.

When they reached the coordinates for the shelf they stopped directly underneath and a period of calm settled on them. Only then, did Dick manage to get a word in edgeways.

"OK. Ropes, spikes, hammer, knife, block and water. Inspect these ropes again. Lowering line, and safety line. Make sure that bloody knife's sharp. You three go along the base and see where you think the best place is to climb up. Not the most convenient place; the safest place, understand?" he barked.

The three chosen were accompanied by all of the women, who were intent on missing nothing. The area Dick had mentioned was inspected and dismissed as risky owing to loose rocks half way up. Further north they found a more stable area with only a small ledge jutting out which had to be negotiated. They came back to the vehicles and reported their findings as instructed.

"OK. Let's go there and get you lot on top," Dick decided.

The climb was steep and hard going but they made it safely and Ian yelled at them to put a drone in the air and mark exactly where they had to lower themselves. Dan had already anticipated this and was ready to oblige. The top was hot to the touch even now but it was smooth and with no obstacles between them and where they could see the drone. Cracks were everywhere so the anchor point wasn't a problem; they drove the spikes into cracks ninety degrees from their line of descent and secured the block. Joe ran the rope through the sheave and threw the loose end down to the Rover about sixty feet below.

"When you're ready!" Ian shouted.

"OK. Lower away," Clinker replied, pushing his legs away from the edge. The winch had the lowering line, Joe had the safety line and they lowered together. They couldn't see anything and followed shouted instructions from Dan, who had them and their target on the monitor. Clinker saw the shelf below, and prepared to haul himself inside, the slight overhang making that difficult. He managed to get his legs in and reckoned he could pull the rest of his body into the gap. He needn't have worried; there was a section of tubing along the entire length of the shelf only a few feet inside and he managed to grasp it. He let out a yell as the tubing burnt his hand. He grabbed his hat and used it as a glove for the second attempt and managed to get a firm grip on the tube. It held firm and he told them to lower him slowly until the weight came off the ropes.

He rolled inside; his elbow was cut and his knee. He lay there exhausted, staring at the roof only a foot above him, then slowly looked around.

"It's here!" he yelled at the top of his voice and heard the yelps of excitement from above and below.

He unclipped himself from the harness and let the ropes swing out. They were raised skywards quickly.

"Ready?" he heard Joe call from above.

"Ready!" he replied and waited for Ian's legs to appear. His legs appeared and Clinker grabbed his foot. He signalled to the drone to lower then held the flat of his hand to it as the signal to stop.

"Bloody hell, mate, how'd you manage to get in there for Christ sake?" Ian challenged Clinker.

"You have to slide in sideways. Stretch your legs out and lie back," Clinker gasped, turning Ian's legs into the ledge and shouting for the winch to lower gently. The only way was to drag Ian onto the shelf between himself and the wreckage. Like Clinker his knees were cut as he cleared the overhang and his arm grazed as he wormed his way inside. They lay side by side, exhausted but elated. At length, Ian released the ropes and harness. He wiped the sweat from his eyes, leaving a streak of blood from his knee across his face, and he stared at the wreckage inches from his face

"Mother of Christ," he gasped when he saw what confronted them. They both stared at the tangled wreckage of the microlight squashed into the wedged angle of the ledge. Crumpled, it looked as if a hydraulic ram had pushed it into the ledge, or a pile driver.

"There's no bloody way this got in here at fifty miles an hour," Ian grunted.

"Poor bastard, he never had a chance," Clinker uttered, looking at the dust covered pile squashed into the wedge. They could see no sign of bones or a skeleton as they had expected; there was nothing but wreckage visible. And the tube they were lying on was burning their legs.

Ian slid on his belly to the edge of the ledge and looked down. They were all staring up at him expectantly.

"The camera, a bag and water!" Ian yelled down. The camera was one from the second drone; Dan had fixed it up with a battery and tuned it into the second monitor. His request came up; hanging some thirty feet below the drone, the rope was long enough to allow the drone to hover above the top. Ian caught it easily and untied the package.

He and Clinker drank eagerly from the water bag and turned their attention to the job at hand.

"OK, MR Lacey, a fine fucking mess you got yourself into," Clinker said and started filming. Ian was too close to film he could hardly move as it was.

There were gasps below as the extent of the damage became apparent. Everybody was glued to the monitor, except Joe, who was freaking out on the top.

"OK. That's about all we can film, there's nothing we can do until we get some of this wreckage removed," Ian informed everybody.

That wasn't going to be easy; it was painful on their elbows. There wasn't enough height to sit up straight and it was painful after a few minutes. They decided lying down was their only alternative. Some material from the wings was still attached and screened most of the left side from view. They found out why when they pulled it; the wing had hit solid rock and folded back so there was no left side. The tube they had was the right-wing strut and it still had the stainless-steel stay on it that Linda had seen. If it had broken off they would never have found this thing; it would have been impossible.

"There wasn't a hell of a lot your father could have done here, mate!" Clinker said quietly, as Ian pulled more loose bits aside.

"Bloody hell. The engine frame's jammed under the ledge and squashed everything up in front of it. How the hell can we shift that?" Ian pondered aloud.

"I'll try and work my way around to where Lacey should be," Clinker added and crawled into the low end of the wedge. "I see bones. broken bones. plenty." Clinker spoke quietly and came out again.

"Looks like the fan unit engine and frame are one mass. I reckon it'll take the winch to pull this clear," Clinker concluded.

"We need the winch.!" Ian yelled to those below and had an immediate response.

"Take the rope out of the snatch block and lower it to them!" Dick shouted to Joe. Clinker reached out and grabbed the harness, took it off the clip and handed the tail of the rope to Ian, who made it fast to the top of the engine frame.

"If this thing comes clear with a bang it will kill somebody down there, so take it easy!" he shouted and joined Clinker at the tip of the right wing as far away as they could get. "OK, watch the monitor and take the strain," he yelled, and switched on the camera.

The rope tightened and they expected the worst, but the top came clear with a squealing sound and Ian screamed for them to stop the winch. That was easier than it looked, they both agreed, and disconnected the rope.

"OK, rig the rope for lowering again!" Ian shouted, letting the tail go. They took stock of the situation. As Clinker had said, there were plenty of bones; the front of the craft had bent upwards and Lacey was sandwiched between the front and the back, literally minced between them. His skull was smashed and it looked like every bone in his body was broken. Clinker filmed everything that had been revealed and turned the camera off again.

"You reckon he was killed outright?" Clinker joked.

"Yeh! I'm surprised this thing didn't burst into flames," Ian voiced.

"Well, if we find the black box that would explain a few things," Clinker suggested.

"Never mind the bloody black box; it's the other box we have to find. This isn't gonna work, we'll have to start from the top and work our way down," Ian said curtly.

"Meaning?" Clinker asked.

"Pass me that bag; we'll have to put Lacey in it or we'll end up with him piled on top of us," he explained. That got Clinker's attention no end. "You hold the bag open, I'll put the bones into it," Ian suggested and Clinker didn't argue.

Ian's head and back were hurting but one by one he managed to clear the bones away from the wreckage. Clinker held the bag open as best he could and grimaced in pain also.

The skull was bad enough handling with bare hands but the rest was purgatory. A landing wheel underneath the frame allowing everything touched to fall into the gap it had created, Ian felt blindly for anything that moved; he couldn't see for sweat and his eyes were stinging. Dust billowed around them at every move. What felt like a tank or something was under the frame but his fingers couldn't grasp it enough to pull it clear. Glass and debris hard to identify were put into the bag. Their backs were breaking it was so tight. Direct sunlight seemed to be pounding them and the temperature was soaring. Claustrophobic was an understatement and a corpse to boot made life hell. The fine dust was red hot and hurting their throats. Only Lacey would have changed places with them.

"Where the hell would you put the mookas?" Ian grunted aloud.

"Hit a willy-willy, lost my fuel tank, jam anything valuable between my legs," Clinker hissed.

"Where anything valuable should be," Ian agreed.

He scraped more debris away from the location he estimated was between Lacey's legs but saw nothing, however, there was a gap likely created by the undercarriage between the chassis and the rock. He stuck his hand through the gap and could feel something underneath. It moved but was too large to get out.

"What the hell are you two doing in there?" Joe yelled from above, obviously agitated; they had been in there for nearly an hour and he was getting cooked on the top of the bluff.

"That's about all of Lacey in the bag; if we send it down we can screw the wreckage round towards us and see if we can get whatever is under it out," Ian panted; he was starting to feel sick and it wasn't because of handling the bones.

"Lacey's in the bag!" Clinker's shout ended in a croak.

Gritting his teeth in pain, Ian reached as far as he could towards the front of the wreckage and grabbed a tube; he pulled, the exertion grimacing his face. It moved and, once clear of the low side, he managed to lever it up. The object underneath was indeed a case or something resembling a case. His fingers slipped off it many times but it came out a little. He was in serious pain before he managed to get his hand around the back of it and pull it clear. Only then did he see the handle. A briefcase type, but solid. He grabbed the handle and squeezed the case across his chest to Clinker.

"Tie this on and send it down," he gasped, and started dry retching violently. Clinker grabbed the case and tied the rope to the handle.

"I think I'm gonna throw up," he announced, accompanied by a violent bout of dry retching.

"The mookas! – I feel like a bloody tomb robber." Ian grimaced with cramp and all he wanted to do was to get out of there, mookas or no bloody mookas. Clinker fumbled with the rope and pushed the case over the ledge. He tried to shout but clutched his throat immediately. He collapsed on his chest and turned his face to Ian. Below they untied the case, oblivious to the drama unfolding above.

Lada took a photograph with her old phone and pressed save. The women were excited.

"We're getting cooked," Clinker croaked.

Ian grinned and it hurt; Clinker's face was covered in a mix of blood and dust; it looked like he had war paint on.

"Geronimo! Get the hell out of here. You cramp?" Ian gasped.

"Yeh, bad." he said and held his hand up, fingers hanging limp; there was no sweat dripping from them now.

"Bugger it," Ian said, taking the camera, but collapsed on his side exhausted. He was light headed and things were starting to spin in front of his eyes.

Both of them were dry retching uncontrollably and fighting to breathe. Panic started to rise in Clinker but Ian grunted, "Lie on your side… take it easy… we get out…" He cringed as a spasm seared across his stomach and he screamed.

"Get me down there, quick!" Joe shouted at Dick and hooked on the safety harness. They took his weight and he went downwards, kicking himself off the face as he went. He stared into the void and swore, "Bastards!" He grabbed Clinker.

Getting his arms around Clinker's chest, he pulled him out as far as his legs could stretch. He rolled him out and held his limp body tightly. "Lower away!" he shouted to Dick, who slackened back quickly.

The descent took time; he had to keep himself off the rock face with his feet and slammed into it several times. His arms ached with the weight of Clinker and he realised he had made a big mistake in his rush to get down. Clinker was in serious danger of slipping from his grip. He squeezed him tight between his knees and struggled to stop his hands from sliding out from below his armpits. The result of this was that Joe's head came in contact with the rock face more often than his feet. Blood started running into his eyes and soon he couldn't see. It seemed like an eternity before he reached the outstretched hands below.

Lada and Debbie grabbed Clinker and Joe hung like a dried fish from the rope. Dick lowered him still in the sling onto the ground and rushed over to him. One look was enough for Dick; there was no way Joe could go back up, there he couldn't even stand.

"We gotta get Ian outta that bloody hole – fast!" Dick screamed at Debbie. Dan and Lada were with her, sponging down Clinker with towels and water. The AC was on full; they had laid Clinker out across the front seats. He dry retched violently and threw up what water Debbie had managed to get into his throat.

Joe tried to get up and collapsed on his knees. He was dry retching also and Debbie went wild.

"Somebody get up there and get him before he dies!" she screamed at Dick.

He knew that but how? They couldn't pull a man up that distance; they were all too big and it would take too long for anybody to climb up the long way. The winch on the Rover was for pulling the vehicle out of difficulty. It was a sealed drum with guide-on gear and they couldn't use it. It was too dangerous; if they got a riding turn, they would have to slack back until it was cleared and it could take forever. But that wasn't his main concern. It might fail. And that was.

Lada hastily untangled Joe from the harness and started to put it on.

"What the hell are you doing? You'll never haul him out!" Dick yelled at her.

"Pull me up!" Lada ordered, taking no notice of Dick.

He looked at Dan and decided there was no option, it was either her or Dinky and she was a climber. Dick cut three metres of rope from the main line and tied one end tightly above the harness.

"Get this under him and we'll heave him out. Get it under his arms. Tie it securely and kick out from the rock." He demonstrated his desires as he spoke and she nodded her understanding.

"Quickly!" was all she said and stared upwards.

"Bring that other Rover close. Straight here, face the cliff!" he shouted at Dinky.

She did as he instructed and Dick tied the end of the rope to the Roo-bar on the front of the vehicle.

"Back off and watch her," Dick instructed and Dinky put the Rover into reverse.

"Quickly!" Lada encouraged as the Rover took the weight and Lada went skyward. "Faster! go faster!" she yelled frantically and Dinky responded. Dick walked backwards, his hand on the door window, and spoke quietly to Dinky.

"Take it easy, just get her up there safely," he instructed. Dinky was leaning over the wheel, her eyes at the top of her head, but she could see Lada clearly as the angle increased. She could also see the hole in the cliff face and as Lada approached it she slowed to a crawl, watching Lada's arm signalling. The last metre was critical; if she pulled her up too high she wouldn't get hold of Ian, if she was too low she still wouldn't get hold of him. She bit her lip and didn't blink.

Lada suddenly stretched both arms out from her side and Dinky put the brake on, then the hand brake. She took the vehicle out of gear and looked at Dick.

"Well done!" he said, without taking his eyes off Lada. He could see her struggling, trying to reach inside and feared the worst. The ledge seemed to be about her waist level and he knew if she couldn't move Ian from this position, he didn't know what she could do.

Lada looked into the ledge and her heart sank; Ian was lying on his side and vomit still trickled from his mouth. His eyes rolled in his head and he was incoherent. She feared he would roll over onto his back or face and it would be impossible for her to get the rope around his chest. She remained silent and managed to grasp the thin hot tube, which was painful but she hung on. She managed to insert the end of the rope under his arm and pushed it until she saw it appear behind him. She was dripping with sweat and it was running into her eyes, stinging her. She shook her head and sweat flew everywhere. Ian was groaning and trying to move, but he didn't move. She managed to reach behind him and grabbed the tail of the rope. That done she still had to get it under his left arm and tie it or he would slip out. She tried several times; his skin was strangely sticky. Eventually, she managed to hook the bight of the rope over his left hand and pulled it below his wrist carefully until it stuck. She rived it and it came free, Ian's watch falling onto the dust as the strap broke.

She was now in a race for his life and pulled with all her might to tighten the rope around his chest. She tied the end beside the one Dick had tied as he had instructed her and waved frantically for the Rover to pull again.

"OK, girl, put it into gear and let the clutch bite. take off your brake and go astern — backwards dead slow!" Dick instructed Dinky.

The added weight on the rope was obvious as Dinky took the weight. Lada had both feet firmly planted sole first against the rock and they could see her jerking frantically at the rope around Ian.

"Keep going dead slow. If we take his weight she can pull him out," Dick advised.

Ian appeared close to her and she pushed away from the rock until he dropped over the edge of the ledge. The rope twanged and the snatch block clanged against the rock. Dick's heart was in his mouth; he feared the anchors would come out from the top, but Ian stopped swinging and Lada signalled to lower. He was hanging between her legs, one arm over her leg the other she couldn't see but the rope was digging into her. She gritted her teeth as they descended; Dinky was driving ahead slowly and Lada knew she couldn't risk going any faster. Ian was on an open loop and she squeezed both sides of the rope together to make it tighter. The descent seemed to last a long time and her hands were sore squeezing the rope by the time they hit the ground. The way Ian was hanging had allowed her feet to keep them away from the rock and, unlike Joe, she wasn't cut to bits.

Dick and Wilson helped Dan and Debbie carry Ian into the cool of the Rover and lay him out like Clinker. She checked his pupils and knew they were just in time. They were contracted to pin pricks and she knew unless she got water into him he would die, but there was no panic from either Debbie or Dan; they were both experienced paramedics and they knew what they were doing.

They had to get his temperature down quickly and get water into him. The AC was on full and wet towels were cooled quickly by the blast of cold air. Debbie left that to Dan; she concentrated on getting water into him. He choked several times and they placed him on his side quickly, Debbie thumping his back several times before he stopped. Slowly, she observed him swallow as she dribbled water into his open mouth from a drenched towel. He was cold to the touch but his core temperature was falling more slowly than his skin temperature. She cursed; the thermometer was with her first aid kit at the camp. In their excitement they had forgotten to take it with them, but there was nothing else they could do even if they had it. This was a time issue and they knew they had to keep going.

Dinky had taken over Clinker's care and Wilson was looking after Joe. Lada sat on the ground and Dick put his hand on her head. She looked up and he handed her the water bottle.

He said nothing and she said nothing.

Clinker came-to first and vomited. Dinky screamed for Dan to come. He wiped him clean and poured some water into his mouth. Clinker vomited again and Dan repeated the process until he managed to keep some water down. Ian had a similar reaction but it took a lot longer for him to start coming around.

"I'm blind!" Ian screeched.

"No, you're not!" Lada said and lifted the towel off his face. She kissed him on the forehead and he smiled weakly. She replaced the towel and tended to his knee. It was still bleeding, as was his elbow; she hadn't been fussy how she got him out over the edge.

Dinky had managed to get between Dan and Clinker; she was following instructions and cleaning the blood from his face. Dan attended to his forearm, which was badly grazed. He stirred and opened his eyes. He tried to say something but Dinky planted a kiss on his lips and he stayed quiet. She smiled nervously and looked at Dan, expecting a reprimand, but he just smiled at her and said nothing. He took Clinker's pulse and looked at his watch. He and Debbie monitored both, going in and out of consciousness for an hour, changing cool towels and getting water into them at every opportunity. Their core temperatures were nearly back to normal, they guessed, but pulse rates were still high. Debbie left Ian to Lada and went to where Dick and Wilson were cooling in the third Rover.

"That was a close-run thing," she said, relieved.

"We were just discussing that. Close run is correct. But why is the concern. You have any idea why they passed out like that? It isn't exactly a confined space," Wilson asked.

"We'll have more idea when they can tell us but my guess is they disturbed enough dust in there that their oxygen levels started to drop. If they had dust masks on that might have made a difference. It's over forty here; it could be as high as fifty inside there. Might have been a combination of both but what I do know is if they were in there any longer, they would be dead."

"They going to be OK?" Dick enquired.

"Yep, they'll throw up for a while and cough like hell but they should be OK in a few days. We just have to watch now that we don't freeze them to death. Out of the frying pan, into the fridge." She grinned and returned to see Ian and Lada.

"Thank God we have two professionals with us," Wilson pointed out.

The case lay where it had landed. Nobody was focused on it. Joe had mustered the strength to climb back onto the top and was hammering out the pins; they couldn't leave with everything still attached and he worked quickly. He was worried to death about both of them and the flying doctor had been foremost on his mind. He had concluded they would take four or five hours to get back to the lake, the only place they could land. He was frantic when he got back to the Rovers but Dick quickly put him at ease. He went to see Ian's and Clinker's progress first hand. His relief was compounded by Debbie's reassurance that they were out of any danger, but they would need time to recover.

"Bloody mookas," he said, throwing the case into the front of the Rover.

They headed for the camp slowly but no more than half a mile into the journey all hell broke loose. Joe came up screaming in the Rover and they stopped.

"What the hell are you shouting about?" Dick yelled across.

"I forgot the bloody camera!" Joe yelled, and thumped the side of the Rover in disgust.

"Christ," Dick sighed.

"Come on, we have to get it. Who's coming with me?" Joe insisted.

Reluctantly, they decided that Dick and Wilson should accompany him back. They swapped vehicles.

The routine was the same as before but slower this time; they were all exhausted. Eventually Joe peered into the ledge and the hairs on the back of his neck stood on end as he looked at the wreckage. He could reach the camera where Clinker had dropped it and Ian's watch was even closer. Both were hot to the touch. He grabbed the tube but let go instantly cursing the hot metal. A sudden fear gripped Joe and all he wanted to do was get away from this place quickly. He grabbed the camera and watch and screamed out to be lowered. Dick lowered him and Wilson took the camera from him.

"Take a rest and get some water into you," Dick ordered.

Joe rested but he needed water more than rest. He then climbed back to the top; it was more of a very steep walk than a climb but loose stones hampered him and he was totally exhausted by the time he pulled the anchors and returned to the Rover. He was dizzy and also felt sick. They had the AC on full waiting for his return and water cooling on the blowers; they were ready this time.

It was late afternoon before the three of them arrived back at the camp and were met by Linda and Dan.

"We thought you lot had double crossed us," Linda shouted at Dick, who looked at her, confused.

"You took the mookas with you," she elaborated.

"For safety reasons, woman! You think we would leave them with you lot?" Dick retorted and looked blankly at Joe. Joe recovered the case from the back and handed it to Linda; Dick didn't even know the case was there.

"You reckon there's enough there for a promise?" Dick jibed.

"Dream on! Get your brain above waist level Romeo and go eat." Linda pouted.

The sun went down in a fireball and the heat persisted. It was a steady forty degrees after dark and the wind had shifted to the north; there was no relief. Dan's lights were fine but a fan would have been more appreciated. With people missing, Dick decided they would discuss what they were going to do when everybody was present, Debbie having decided the best place for the two invalids to sleep was in the Rovers. They had more than enough fuel so leaving them idling with the AC on low wasn't a problem; it was better they heated themselves up under covers than try and cool them down. The sleeping bags were put to use and the two would-be nurses were on duty.

Joe suggested they have a look in the case and he was shot down in flames by Dick.

"We break the seal on that bloody case who's going to believe you when you tell them what's in it?" Dick yelled at him.

"What you mean?" Joe was confused.

"Let me elaborate; if you open the case, young man, you or should I say we have to prove what was inside it, whereas if we leave it closed we don't have to prove anything!" Wilson pointed to the seal.

"When Ian's here, we'll decide what to do. Wait till morning," Dick ordered, "I think a drink is called for –Wilson!" he concluded.

"My thoughts precisely; I need rehydration," Wilson agreed.

CHAPTER TEN

The Leper had heard nothing since he had ordered the three who were working on the fence to go, threatening them loudly that if they didn't go he would shoot the bloody lot of them when they protested. Whatever Ian was doing he considered justified and there was little else he could do except keep an eye on Korena until somebody came back. He could contact Maria but there was no point. As his father had said when his mother asked him when he would be back, he always answered 'I'll be back when I return, lassie'. There was nothing else to do but get on with life.

He had prepped the bike and buggy for another leaf gathering session but had decided to feed the pigs before going into the scrub again. He gathered grain from the bin in the shed and was about to go outside when he heard a loud engine noise above.

"By the lord harry," he said and peered out round the door.

A plane was touching down in the back paddock of Korena. A small Cessna, it taxied towards his boundary fence and stopped. The Leper stared in disbelief; what the hell would anybody be doing landing an aeroplane here? he wondered. *They must be in trouble*, he thought. Alarm bells started ringing as two men jumped out and vaulted his fence. They started running towards him at speed. He knew from experience that somebody holding a gun runs differently from somebody not holding one.

His eyes focused on their right hands and they were each holding something

He grabbed the rifle from the cabinet and slammed in a full magazine. He made for the entrance to the old shearing pens, hearing the dog barking as he slipped outside, and disappeared into the scrub. He stopped where he knew he could best observe the house.

The dog stopped barking suddenly and the two men came into sight, running towards the Leper's veranda, then he could see clearly, they were armed. He watched as they threw his door open and disappeared inside. He gently worked the bolt action and slid a round into the chamber of the rifle. There was the sound of smashing from inside and a chair came out through the window.

"Bastards," he muttered, his heart heavy, thinking about the dog.

They appeared suddenly, standing side by side on the veranda, and looked around, pointing with their guns for areas to search.

The bullet struck the upright of the veranda, sending splinters into their faces. The Leper had another round in the chamber instantly and the second bullet ripped into the same upright. They both flattened on the floor and froze. The third bullet hit the paving along the front of the veranda and ricocheted into the wood with splintering fury. They didn't wait for the fourth and made a headlong dash for the cover of the shed.

The Leper slipped away further into the scrub and waited.

Several minutes later, he heard the plane engine rev up and it taxied back down to the far end of the paddock. He retraced his path and watched as the plane became airborne, standing on its wing tip to stay well away from his property, but it was still well in range of the rifle. He took a bead on the underbelly of the plane and followed it as he had done many times, but he didn't pull the trigger. He lowered the rifle. If he wanted to kill somebody he could have done that already. It disappeared from sight and hurriedly he ran back to the shed to see if the dog was OK. It wasn't but it wasn't dead, either; it was stumbling around as if it was drunk.

He ran inside and was immediately boiling with rage. His plaid lay on the floor and his busby was run-through with the sword from the fireplace, its point was stuck hard into the floorboards His good chair was broken and the other was out through the window.

"You bloody bastards, I'll put a bullet through your brains if you come back here!" he yelled, shaking the rifle above his head.

He tended the dog; it had a lump on its head but was coming round slowly. It looked at him as if he had hit it, and whined each time he touched it. He managed to get it inside and gave it some water, never taking the rifle out of his hand. He was seething and ready to do battle with anybody but he slowly regained control of himself and went to finish what he had started; the pigs were squealing in protest. He eventually put the gun down but not back into the cabinet.

It was getting late and he had to put something over his broken window. He wondered what the hell that was all about. He remembered saying to Ian 'I won't go easy'. Perhaps he had just proved the point. He thought about Maria but as quickly discarded the notion; she was in the city and had plenty of people around her; better not to alarm anybody. He was OK and they hadn't got what they came for. Whatever that was.

Maria's thoughts had been with them since they had left, but she had a business to run and that was keeping her busy. She knew there was no way they would contact her even if they had the opportunity, which she doubted. The revelations about Russell's behaviour had meant the world to her. For years, she had blamed herself for the break-up of the family, yet she could never figure out what exactly she had done wrong. Now she knew she hadn't done anything. Her anger at Russell had subsided but she still despaired about not being able to help him. Too late now and life goes on.

The restaurant was popular amongst the Italian community and they were numerous in Adelaide. She employed three waitresses and a cook but *she* ran the kitchen. After a lifetime of cooking she couldn't stand by and see somebody else do it all. She assisted the two cooks; it was her nature.

The waitresses were all Australian and Maria had to laugh at their interpretation of the menu.

Clair arrived in the kitchen and ordered one spag van galle

"You mean one Spaghetti Alle Vongole," Maria teased her.

"Yeh! That's what I said. I'll get the drink. Table four." She skittled off, giggling.

Maria loved this dish and cooked it herself. She decided to serve it herself as the restaurant was getting busy.

Table four was in an alcove and sitting there was a beautiful young woman who smiled as she served her. She was very attractive and, being Italian, Maria observed her style, which was not Australian. She also had a suitcase beside the chair.

Maria set the dish in front of her and she smiled her thanks.

"Enjoy!" Maria said and returned to the kitchen.

"That woman at table four, Maria, she wants to speak to you," Clair announced ten minutes later.

"Anything wrong?" Maria frowned.

"No idea; she finished her meal and asked to see you," Clair said.

Maria removed her apron and went to the table a little apprehensively. The woman stood up as she approached and held out her hand, much to Maria's surprise. She looked curiously at the young woman but shook her hand as invited.

"Hello, madam, are you Maria Ingle?" she asked.

"Yes, I'm Maria; who are you?" Maria asked curiously.

"I am Hanna, I am a friend of Lada. I can't get in touch with her, can you help me please?"

Maria's eyes widened in surprise and she hugged the young woman.

"Welcome! Welcome! Hanna come, come with me, take your bag, follow me. This is a big surprise," Maria said excitedly.

Maria led her through the kitchen and out the back door; the stairs to the upper floor were separate from the building for fire reasons. They climbed the stairs to the balcony through the sliding glass doors and into a large spacious living room.

"Leave your bags here," Maria insisted and went to prepare a drink for her guest. It was early evening so she offered Hanna vodka. "I will have a small grappa," she informed her and they sat down together.

"Lada gave me your address because she said Ian lives here when he is in Australia, but I can't get her on the phone. I don't know what to do," Hanna explained.

Maria looked at her luggage and concluded she hadn't booked in anywhere.

"You must stay here until they come back," Maria insisted.

"Are they far away?" Hanna asked.

Maria had to think quickly to come up with an answer that didn't keep her to a time schedule.

"Hanna!" she started, then stopped. "Did Lada know you were coming here?" she continued.

"No! It was a surprise for her, I thought it would make her happy because she is here alone and she has never been on her own before," she said in perfect English.

"That was nice of you. They went away over a week ago to the bush, that's why you can't phone her. I'm sorry but they didn't tell me when they were coming back. They could be out there for several weeks. They are so in love, and she is beautiful. She is so kind, I love her as much as Ian. But this must be a great

206

disappointment for you coming all this way. Can you wait until they return or have you to go back soon?"

"No! I can wait. If I find somewhere to wait. It doesn't matter how long they stay away, I am free and I have all the time in the world. I don't have to go back until my visa expires," Hanna explained.

"You must stay here; you will be company for me and if you like you can do something in the restaurant to pass the time away," Maria said, delighted and put the TV on. "Have you met Ian yet?" Maria enquired.

"Yes, I met him in Vietnam but he preferred Lada to me," she laughed.

"That must have been a difficult choice; you are very beautiful, just as beautiful as Lada," Maria consoled her.

"I think it was the hair, she is very lucky," Hanna suggested and toasted the pair with her vodka. Maria did likewise and opted for another grappa.

"What is that you are drinking?" Hanna asked curiously.

"Ah! You can taste it." Maria offered Hanna a sip.

She recoiled in horror at the taste; it was revolting to her and she wanted to spit it out but forced herself to swallow.

"Ehhh! That's very strong," she stammered. "What is it?"

"This is grappa. A spirit from the grape. Not wine, a spirit. My father made me and my sisters drink this sometimes because he had no son. If you can drink this, he used to say, that's good enough. I nearly died the first time I tried it. But you get used to it, as you say it's very strong, I find your vodka is just as strong," Maria pointed out and continued, "I don't drink usually, but things have been a little bit, eh what it is in English? – Yes! As Ian would say screwed up, so now I have somebody to drink with, why not?" she surrendered.

"I will make up your bed. You go and shower, then we can have another one," Maria suggested, after they had both finished their second drink.

Maria walked in on her getting out of the shower and stopped dead; she had a body to die for and was standing completely naked and dripping. She handed Hanna the towel she had brought and apologised but quipped, "I have another son the same as Ian, you know!" as she left the room.

She came out as if she could have stepped onto the catwalk anywhere in the world. She was dressed in Lycra-like jeans which showed every curve below the waist. Her top did likewise and the open cleavage was adorned with a gold pendant; she was stunning and in bare feet.

"Hanna! Are you a model?" Maria asked. Hanna smiled and cocked her head to the side; she gave Maria a look which would have melted men of marble.

"Do you think I should be?" she replied.

"If I had your looks I would be," Maria said, adamantly. They watched the TV and chatted for a long time. Maria phoned down and pepperoni pizza was delivered by Clair, who looked approvingly at the guest.

"We starting a model agency?" she asked Maria. Maria laughed.

"That's what I was saying, she should be a model. Hanna will be staying here for a while so I might want you to take her out on the town if she gets bored," Maria added.

"No problem!" Clair replied, and smiled at Hanna. Clair herself was pleasing to the eye and much sought after by the bucks.

They talked about Lada, about Russia, about Australia, food, clothes and global warming. Maria liked to get people's opinions and give her own. The grappa challenge had been met and Maria opted for a red wine. The time had passed quickly; the staff called Maria to tell her all the alarms were set and they were leaving.

"Hanna! Thank you for coming; I really enjoy your company. I needed this but I have had enough," Maria said, her voice slightly slurred and held up her empty glass. Hanna insisted they have one for the road. Maria protested, but to no avail.

"Only a little one," Hanna insisted, pouring a small wine. She poured a small glass of water for herself; unknown to Maria, something she had been doing since she started getting the drinks.

"They say in English, one for the road. Is that correct?" Hanna asked, handing Maria her drink.

"Yes! One for the road. I am really tired, I will sleep well tonight. You can stay and watch TV if you like but I have to go to bed. I'm not as young as you," Maria laughed.

Maria finished her drink and Hanna helped her to her feet; she was wobbling a little but insisted she could make it to bed unassisted.

"Bona note, Hanna!" she said, and closed the bedroom door.

The screens along the length of the French doors were Venetian vertical and offered no line of sight directly into the living room, but Hanna closed them completely and checked her watch; it was 10.24 p.m. She sat and watched the TV with the lights on full and shortly afterwards heard the distinct sound of snoring coming from the bedroom, not loud but steady. Maria was out for the count. At 11 p.m. she opened her bedroom door slightly and by the dim light entering she changed her top to a black polo neck long sleeve sweater. From her case she took out a black balaclava and black gloves. She sat on the bed and put on a pair of black trainers. Lastly, she removed a pistol from the zipped section of her case, checked the magazine and, satisfied, tucked the gun into the top of her jeans.

She waited another hour before turning the TV and the living room light off. She took the towel Maria had given her and in the dark she slid the glass apart silently as she went out onto the veranda. There were several deckchairs there which she had taken note of when she climbed the stairs with Maria.

Closing the door she stooped low and arranged one slightly to the right of the landing. She hung the towel over the handrail on the other side making sure it only went halfway to the floor and settled into the chair she had positioned, keeping her head below the level of the back and the gun on her thigh.

An hour passed and there was no movement to be seen, only her eyes moved as she scanned the terrain below. It was dark, no moon and only a fleeting glimpse of stars, sparkling between clouds which, by the carry in the sky, indicated strong winds were not far away, but only a gentle breeze was present, sometimes rippling along the towel. The traffic noise was audible and occasionally a car horn would sound. There was access to the restaurant, and subsequently, to Maria's flat, through which supplies were taken in to avoid blocking the busy road at the front; however, the access was narrow and any vehicle other than a motorbike had to stop on the back street some twenty metres distant. The gate leading to the alley was shut, but she had no idea if it was locked.

She saw nothing moving in any direction; her eyes were used to the dark and she estimated the time to be around two a.m. but looking at her watch to check wasn't an option. She noticed a slight movement of the gate and a shadowy figure appeared silently checking around, and making its way to the stairs. It climbed and slashed a knife below the towel in a sweeping movement. Hanna grinned but didn't show her teeth. Satisfied there was nothing behind the towel, the figure came onto the landing. She could make out the knife in his hand as he took a step towards the glass doors and silently inserted it between them.

He froze as the barrel of her pistol was pressed into the side of his head

"Da Nyet Viktor Manin – ZUB," Hanna whispered into his ear and pressed the gun harder into his head.

"What tha fuck?"-he uttered as the muzzle pressed harder

"Drop the knife," Hanna whispered and the knife clattered to the balcony deck.

Hanna smashed the side of the weapon into his temple and he crumpled to the floor.

"Australian!" she announced as another shadow emerged from the far end of the compound and climbed the stairs. Hanna pulled the man's hands behind his back and the figure cable-tied them. Her accomplice stuck a syringe into his arm and together they dragged the unconscious intruder down the stairs laying him on the ground. Hanna shot out of the open gate and sprinted silently along the alley. A dark car was there with the engine idling but no lights on. She surveyed the scene for a brief moment. There was no sign of a driver, then she suddenly realised the driver would be on the right, not the left.

The windows were closed and the driver was sitting with the AC on. Keeping low she slowly approached, hoping the passenger's door was open. If it wasn't she would have to go street side quickly or fire through the glass. She grabbed the handle and gave the slightest tug on the door; it moved but clicked. The driver looked at the passenger's door and trained a gun on it rather hesitantly; he could see nothing to fire at and his left hand returned to his face. Small wood splinters were annoying him. With a shout of alarm, he whipped his head around quickly as the side window shattered all over him and Hanna thrust the barrel of the gun into his startled teeth.

"Da nyet, the gun!" she said in English. He handed it to her; it was still pointing away from her and he was holding it against the steering wheel in his right hand.

"Turn off the engine and throw out the keys," she ordered; he complied, wild eyed.

The passenger's door flew open and a figure entered the car. Hanna still had the gun against his teeth. "Move and you will die," she reminded him quietly as the figure frisked him. Another gun emerged from behind his back and was duly thrust into his side forcing him to move towards Hanna. She opened the door to let him out. As soon as his head cleared the roof she smashed the butt of the pistol into his temple and he too crumpled to the ground.

"Australian!" Hanna announced.

They moved quickly; the figure injected and cable-tied the driver. They bundled him into the back seat. They ran inside and returned with the first intruder. With both in the back seat the figure removed the thin balaclava, allowing a cascade of blonde hair to fall over her shoulders. She remained silent and drove the car away slowly. Hanna walked back along the alley dusting off glass fragments from her clothes as she went. She closed the doors and locked them, then changed her clothes back to what she was wearing previously. She opened Maria's door quietly and satisfied herself Maria was still in the land of nod. She phoned Victoria.

It was the middle of the night but Victoria answered immediately.

Two Australians, Elvis has taken them to the house," Hanna said.

"OK. Get to Lada as quickly as you can; here are her coordinates."

Victoria read off the coordinates for the camp site at East Well and Hanna pressed record.

"We think they have found what they're looking for. She's out of range and I will get music to her. Go as quickly as you can," Victoria ordered.

Hanna agreed and poured herself large vodka. She would have to wait for Elvis to return and they would collect their transport to the bush.

She wrote a note for Maria: *Back soon, Hanna* and waited.

212

CHAPTER ELEVEN

The others had gone in their own directions and left Wilson and Dick sitting on their own sipping whiskey and sweating it out as fast as it was going in. Wilson lit his pipe and wiped his brow. It was after midnight but it was so hot there was no point in lying down; they could doze where they were with the help of the nightcap, they decided.

"There's something in the wind, Wilson, I can feel it," Dick said quietly.

"I can see it," Wilson replied, tracing the smoke from his pipe in a downward spiral. Dick understood and looked at the sky. It was clear all around; the horizon was clear also as far as he could tell.

"I wish we had a barometer, this heat's not letting up," he informed Wilson.

"It's very hot here, Dick, I had no idea. It's hotter than up the Gulf," was Wilson's claim.

"The Gulf, Wilson! This is one of the hottest, driest, places on the bloody planet. Didn't Ian tell you that?" Dick queried.

"Really! I only came along to be a bridesmaid, you know. There was no mention of exploring Mars. I must have a word with him about this!" Wilson replied, and again noted the descent of the smoke, as did Dick.

"Whatever is coming, can't be far away. We better make a plan. If it's wind, wouldn't want to lose the tents and all the sleeping gear. You reckon we should take that tarp down and stash it?" Dick suggested.

"Better safe than sorry. Wait until I finish my smoke." Wilson agreed and both of them scanned the sky for a sign.

"Might as well finish the drinks as well; how's the stock?" Dick asked.

Wilson grinned. "He still hasn't found it. He keeps looking, it's fine. Another week, we will start to get worried," Wilson assured him.

They both set to work. The light was dim but adequate to dismantle the stays of the tarp. They folded it up and put it into one of the three trailers, sweating profusely as they did so; even that exertion was too much. They were startled by Joe's voice behind them.

"What the hell are you two up to?" he asked curiously.

"Battening down. Can't you sleep?" Dick replied.

"No, I reckon we're in for something," Joe stated.

"We know we're in for something. Ask Wilson's pipe," Dick replied.

That went over Joe's head and they instructed him to lash all three trailers together and put everything loose into them. They had another idea and recovered the tarp; they spread it over all three trailers and lashed it in position with the climbing ropes. Everything except the seats.

They were exhausted but satisfied when at last they returned and collapsed on the seats.

"Only the tents," Dick said.

"We can flap them quickly and drive the vehicles on top if we have to," Wilson proposed.

"Yeh, as long as we don't break the poles," Joe added.

Wilson fetched another billy and they resumed their drinking. Joe decided to join them but declined the whiskey.

"Drink all night and sleep all day. Brilliant!" Dick declared, when Joe joined them with a beer.

"Drink till midnight, piss till dawn," Joe added. By the end of the billy they were all fast asleep on the chairs. Wilson stirred and looked at his watch; he was soaked in sweat but wasn't hot. He felt the gentle breeze on his face and it was cool. He yawned and put his glasses on. Joe and Dick were beside him and both were snoring contently. A bolt of lightning suddenly illuminated the entire world and Wilson yelled in alarm at what it revealed. Before the thunder reached them, he had grabbed Dick by the leg and shaken him awake.

"Bugger off, Wil—!" was drowned by the crash of thunder and Dick sat bolt upright, as did Joe.

"What the fuck was that?" he shouted.

"Move! Get the tents down get everybody into the Rovers!" Wilson screamed as another bolt of lightning shot across the sky.

"Bloody hell, a dust storm!" Dick gasped, on seeing what was approaching. They herded Linda, Debbie and Dan out of the tents and screamed at them to get into the Rovers. Joe unceremoniously flapped each tent and retrieved the poles from inside.

"Anything breakable in there?" Dick yelled at him but didn't wait for an answer; he jumped into the Rover with Ian in it and put it into gear, drove it on top of the tent and stopped. Ignoring the barrage of questions, he did the same with the Rover Clinker was in, telling Dinky to get dressed in the process. Joe scarpered into the Rover with Debbie and Linda, who were the most bloody annoyed.

"Dust storm coming!" he blurted out breathless. Wilson squeezed in beside Dick, Lada and Ian.

"My God, sir! What kind of animal is attacking us now?" he said to Dick.

"Dust storm!" Dick answered.

"Lightning and thunder from dust? Strange!" Wilson exclaimed.

"Wind first. Then hail. Then heavy rain. Then dust. Better switch this bloody engine off before the dust does," Dick replied, checking Joe had done likewise. He had.

Ian looked at Lada in the light of the next lightning bolt and she smiled.

"You not scared?" he asked, as the thunder clap vibrated the vehicle.

"No! I have never been in a dust storm and I am more curious than afraid." She crawled over him to get a look out of the windscreen and suddenly his attention was on what he had in his face but it was short lived.

The first gust hit the vehicles, violently rocking them from side to side and the wind was screaming. A loud bang followed, then a deafening roar as hail pounded them for half a minute; it was followed by driving rain which was as loud as the hail, it was so heavy. There seemed to be a lull for several seconds then the vehicles rocked violently again as the dust front hit. Instantly the windows went black. Lightning shimmered in the gloom and thunder, almost deafening, roared through every bone in their bodies. The turmoil lasted five minutes, and then slowly, the vehicles stopped rocking. It went quiet suddenly.

"That's it! Bloody hell did you see that!" Dick shouted, switching the interior light on. He glanced over his shoulder and stared.

"Get some bloody clothes on, woman!" he ordered Lada and switched the light off again. She giggled and retreated into the back.

"What happened? I was stuck in a valley," Ian pleaded.

"Freak! You respectable yet?" Dick yelled at Lada. No reply, he switched the light back on again. All glass was red with dust they couldn't see through it even when he switched the headlights on.

"Wait a couple a minutes. Give it time to settle. I reckon we should get sunstroke like that bastard in the back, Wilson," Dick suggested.

"Such a valley is a safe place to hide, apparently," Wilson deduced.

Dick gingerly opened the door and was immediately confronted by a red hell, made even more unworldly by rays of sunlight arching through dust from the departing turbulence. Dinky shouted to him before he could get out.

"Don't get out, Dick. We have to drive the vehicles away and blow the dust off them. The sun will dry this lot up in a couple of hours. If we walk about it'll spread everywhere. Just your wipers, nothing else," she ordered with authority.

"Well, that's you told," Wilson acknowledged.

"Probably right," Dick agreed, switching the engine on. The wiper was slow to respond but it managed to remove enough dust for him to see. Dinky led the way and they followed, Joe coming behind. Within a few minutes, dust started to blow off all the windows and he could see it coming off Dinky's vehicle like a red spray.

"She knows what she's doing. You stay out of that bloody valley, arsehole," Dick threw over his shoulder.

As Dinky had predicted, the ground soaked up the moisture quickly and what didn't go down, went up. Within an hour the dust was back to being dust, not a quagmire. Hail and rain underneath caused slurry to form across everything in sight except where the rain had run off.

"Just wait! It has to dry!" Dinky insisted.

"Well, at least she was dressed," Dick thought aloud, and decided to doze off, as was Wilson's choice; it had been a long night.

The radio crackling woke them up and besides being stiff as hell, they were also very hungry. To their surprise the camp had been returned to near normal. Joe and Ian were in deep discussion, sitting at the side of the overhang. The women were in their reddish tent and Clinker was screwing around with a radio mike.

"Any tucker?" Dick called out and Linda's face appeared at the tent opening.

"On the stove!" she yelled, ducking back into the tent.

"About bloody time you two woke up!" Ian greeted.

"It was better when the bastard was dying, Wilson," Dick commented. They both grabbed a plate of mash and beans, then opened a small tin of ham and split the contents between them. They ambled over to join Ian and Joe.

"So! how the hell did you know that was coming?" Ian demanded.

"Wilson's pipe!" Dick replied and sat down beside them.

"I told him that but he reckons bullshit!" Joe exclaimed.

"OK, smart arse, explain!" Ian insisted.

"Smoke rises, my dear boy, but in low pressure and with calm conditions it will fall. We were in such a deep depression and it was calm. The pipe never lies you know. Not like people who pretend to be dying," Wilson said pointedly.

"I'll believe it when I see it. Anyway, that thing puts a new slant on what Lacey hit. And it did come just before daylight. What you reckon?" Ian asked.

"We'll never know what Lacey hit *or* hit *him*; you reckoned that microlight looked like it was hammered into the ledge by a pile driver. Must have been travelling a hell of a lot faster than fifty klicks… I reckon that wind was seventy or eighty knots or more. That up his arse, he could have been doing well over a hundred, and he had no way to get clear. He couldn't land. It would just have blown the thing back into the air with or without him in it. If he ran before it and it came from the south it would have pushed him into the bluffs in three or four minutes from where we found the tank. Fighting to go west along the weather front to see if he could come clear of it would face the thing in

218

the direction you found it. Who knows? It's a prime suspect and explains the velocity. A willy can't. We'll fart like hell after this lot, Wilson!" Dick declared, through a mouthful of beans.

"Wilson! Rent out your pipe to the met office. Yeh! Makes more sense. He must have been going like a bat out of hell when he hit that ledge. That would account for anything torn off on impact having disappeared, not sitting below the crash site. He must have been terrified," Ian added quietly.

"Yes, at least he died quickly. We do tend to forget the human aspect of this," Wilson agreed thoughtfully.

"Yep! His arsehole would have gone up around his neck like a jumper," Dick consoled them.

Their sympathy was interrupted by laughter from the women's tent. They came out still laughing and Dinky was carrying a rifle with telescopic sights. Lada had another scope across her belly.

The men looked questioningly at them as they approached.

"Competition, you lot. Man against his superiors. We'll set up the targets. Dinky, teach this lot what end the bullet comes out of," Debbie said cheerfully waiting for a reaction.

"You beauty! I'll be in on that!" Joe shouted.

"Me too," Clinker said, coming towards Dinky.

"We shall seek cover immediately," Wilson added.

"Right, you lot. Two of you. Who's gonna fire?" Dinky demanded.

Joe and Clinker won the argument that followed and Dinky ran through the safety aspects of the Winchester .243. "Telescopic sights and can bring down a big pig at two hundred yards," Dinky boasted with Lada looking over her shoulder.

"You gonna fire that bloody thing?" Ian queried the latter.

"Yes, I can shoot – a little. Debbie and Linda no, so I will support Dinky," Lada announced.

"No chance! We're tops," Joe declared.

Dinky smiled and nursed the weapon. It gleamed in contrast to its surroundings, oozing quality.

"Right! When they get back, we have one practice each at whatever you want to fire at except the targets. Then we have two bean tins and two ham tins at two hundred yards." They looked at one another in silence. Dinky waited silently

"That could be too far away for men," she said. sarcastically to Lada.

"You can see it, we can hit it," Joe declared.

They moved to the first Rover and waited for Debbie and Linda to set the tins up. They were far away and immediately Dick was sceptical.

"Not a hope in hell," was his conclusion.

Lada lowered the scope she was looking through and handed it to Dick. "Look through this," she instructed him.

"Now that's a sight if I ever saw one – Linda's got huge bloody ti…" Dinky kicked him.

"Look at the targets!" she hissed.

Debbie and Linda came back and Dick followed them with the telescope until it was thrust into Linda's chest. She leaned over and looked through the lens.

"I can see a pervert," she announced.

"Joe first! Take a practice shot." Dinky handed him the rifle.

He leaned across the bonnet and took aim on something they couldn't see. He fired. The noise was deafening, taking all by surprise. This was a powerful weapon. They saw a puff of dust far away and he handed the rifle to Clinker. He did likewise and Lada followed suit. Everybody was holding their ears when Dinky fired the last practice shot.

"OK, target time! No excuses! Bait balls first, any target two shots each. We check the results," she said, taking the second scope from Dick. Joe took careful aim. And repositioned his legs. He aimed again and, satisfied, he fired.

"Missed!" shouted Dinky. He aimed again at the same target and fired.

"Missed!" she repeated, as Joe pushed the rifle into Clinker's hands in disgust.

"Missed!" she danced excitedly. "Missed again! Bloody hell, they couldn't hit a cow in the arse with an orange!" she bellowed, and handed the scope to Joe.

"Yeh, let's see what the Sheilas can do then! You want a hand to lift the rifle?" he quipped. Dinky slid the bolt closed and didn't lean on the bonnet. She took aim and fired.

Before Joe called hit she had the second bullet into the chamber.

"Hit!" he yelled as the second shot roared from the rifle. "Hit! Lucky bloody hit," he repeated, staring at Dinky.

Lada wasn't so confident; she took position across the bonnet and fired.

"Hit again! Christ!" Joe exclaimed. "Again, tarry bastards!" Joe yelled above the clapping.

"One is thinking one has done this before, young lady?" Wilson queried Dinky.

"She's done this before too," she answered, pointing to Lada, who blushed.

"Superior sex, four, bait balls, zero – official result!" Debbie shouted excitedly. Dick had the telescope pointed at Lada. He didn't hear a thing. Ian put the cap on it and he handed it to Dinky.

"No wonder Nelson had one of these things, Wilson – brilliant! I'll have to get one, I'll get two," he decided. Dinky cleaned the guns methodically and placed both of them in their respective cases. She filled the belt where she had extracted the bullets they had fired and put everything into the large bag, which looked like a golf bag.

"How the hell can you shoot like that?" Clinker wanted to know.

"Practice! Snap shots are all you're going to get when the pigs are on the move. Lada's pretty good too," she answered.

"Bloody right! That's some scope," Clinker pointed out.

"Yeh! It should be. It cost more than the rifle and Mike paid over a thousand bucks for it," she said proudly. Debbie and Dan were at the stove brewing tea; the others were deep in conversation about the challenge and the amazing shooting of both Dinky and Lada.

"Good thinking; a psychological diversion, as it says in the book," Dan said.

"Yeh! That should hold their attention for a while. Better make a big brew," Debbie suggested and gave him a hug.

The temperature was hot but the humidity had vanished, the air was clear and a joy to breathe. The noise of the Gullahs had increased and several small herds of kangaroos were seen close by. Despite Ian's assessment he and Clinker had relapsed several times, feeling dizzy on occasions and a little sick, but steadily they improved. Dick had laid the law down. "Today, we take the day off. Tomorrow, we decide what we are going to do and the following day, we leave."

He put the case with the mookas in it beside the stove, where everybody could see and touch it.

"Have a good think because tomorrow *you* must decide." He called Port Augusta and they made no mention of the dust storm. He just reported in as usual; all was well. It looked to Dick as if the beast had blown itself out before it hit the coast. Even before it hit Mt Ive. They would have reported it and the cops would have told him. It was how the bush telephone worked, it never changed. It might have been localised, not as big as it seemed. They were forty miles from number three and Ian's father didn't mention any weather concerns according to Ian.

"At least the bloody chisellers have buggered off," Joe pointed out to everybody.

"That's what you think, bait ball. They're digging their way up through the dust right now! Ya aint gonna get rid of them that easy," Dinky assured everybody, to moans of despair.

CHAPTER TWELVE

The Winger checked every anchor point on each van with a kick against the wire. The dust storm had taken him by surprise. Two anchor points had ripped out and the van affected had flipped but the other two anchors had held, preventing it from getting airborne and smashing into the rest. Everything was covered in red dust. He cursed but not with any venom; he had seen this a hundred times before and a hell of a lot worse. The damage shouldn't be too bad but he would only find out once it was righted. On the positive side he had something to do.

He decided to get the tractor, rig up the forks and up-end the van. He made his way to the longhouse, as they called it. To him it was the big shed. All the windows had been boarded up for the close season and he was glad of that. The racers wouldn't return for several months. This time of year, the chances of getting top speed out of their bikes and racing cars was fifty-fifty. That was OK if you lived close by but nobody lived close by and nobody was going to chance hundreds, sometimes thousands, of miles driving here only to find water on the lake. Unlike the earth, which soaked it up and cooked to evaporate it, the salt acted differently and a thin film of water could stay there for many days. Too dangerous for racing, too dangerous for speed of any kind and aquaplaning had already claimed several lives.

There were motorbikes of all descriptions in the longhouse, mostly under expensive covers, from Harley Davidsons to

Hondas. Trail bikes, racing bikes, four wheel and three wheels; even a land yacht had appeared the previous season and it was a big hit. Rumours were some more might be purchased; the Winger hoped not or his tractor would be pushed out of the shed. He opened the large doors at the end.

The fiat started first time and he fitted the forks easily, considering he only had one arm. The vans were staggered so each could view across the lake, so access to the overturned one was simple. He carefully inserted the forks under it and lifted slowly. He made sure the tips of the forks stayed on the rim and had to move ahead very slowly as he lifted. It went well and the van reached its tipping point. It went over with a crash and he gritted his teeth. One window came out and landed beside the tractor.

He returned the tractor to the longhouse, locked it up and returned to survey the damage, the dogs glad to see him on the ground. Inside was a shambles of broken glass, upturned furniture and bedding but nothing had ripped away from the structure and the frame wasn't bent; he opened and closed the door several times to check and it was OK. He cast his eyes out into the lake and hoped the bloody idiots out there that Whitey had told him about weren't running around in the desert trying to get their tents back. He reckoned it wouldn't be long before he had a visit from somebody. He looked at the interior and decided his first priority was to reset the anchors before he forgot to. The storms could and had, hit from any direction. Another one was inevitable. It could arrive in days or weeks, but it would come; it was the season.

There were other things to check and the Winger climbed into his small Jeep to drive the short distance east to where the well was. The wind driven pump was in storage position as not a lot of water was needed but the tanks were nearing low and he would need water to clean the vans and buildings. He set off with the dogs beside him; he couldn't escape them, it was bred into them to go where their master went and to work to silent commands. If the vehicle pointed right they went to the right of the sheep; to the left, similarly and straight ahead they fell in behind the sheep and drove them straight ahead. It was only the humans who thought they were too old; they didn't.

He reached the well and broke out the blades on the windmill, filled the grease cap with grease and screwed it down. There was a little wind but not much. The pump piston started to go up and down and dust, falling from the blades as they turned, made him exit quickly. He drove to the generator shed on his way back. Again, routine maintenance was called for; he shut it down and checked the air filter; a small amount of dust but nothing to worry about. He filled the diesel tank and dipped the sump. Satisfied, he started the generator again and headed back towards the vans on foot. He decided to make a brew before starting on the damaged van and he had plenty of time; there was no hurry with the Winger.

He heard the vehicle's approach before he saw it and his immediate thoughts were the idiots out in the bush, but the noise was coming from the wrong direction. Somebody was coming north along the track. He watched intently, wondering if somebody from the station was coming but he didn't recognise the vehicle when it finally came into view. A big Toyota land cruiser with tyres on it fit for a tank; *no problem going bush with that thing*, he concluded.

It came to a halt beside him and the dogs gave their usual greeting. A woman accompanied by two men came out and stretched themselves; she wasn't bad looking but he didn't like the look of her companions.

"G'day, it's a long way to here!" she called to him.

The Winger smiled. "Yep! What can I do for you?" he enquired.

The woman took another long stretch with her arms out and head back. The men were doing the same, but Winger was focused on the female. Not bad, he reckoned.

"Hi! I'm Veronica; are you in charge here?" she asked.

"My name's Bruce but they call me the Winger. Yep I'm in charge during the close season," he replied. Veronica glanced at his stump and shifted her gaze to the dogs.

"They bite?" she asked.

"No! They ain't got any teeth," the Winger replied.

"Ah! This is Alex, and this is Viktor. They're new Australians. They don't speak much English, they come from Estonia."

"Hi! I don't speak much myself, there's usually nobody here to speak to," the Winger grinned.

"Oh! Are you here yourself? That's terrible," Veronica said, sympathetically.

"No problem. Would you all like a brew?" the Winger invited.

"That would be brilliant," Veronica agreed and they followed the Winger into his end of the longhouse.

"Hope ya never came here to race, Veronica?" Winger stated.

"No! We came to see our friends; they're out in the desert, I believe," she said, matter of fact. Winger looked at her and laughed.

"I know who you are then. You're the opposition. They reckoned the opposition would arrive trying to muzzle in on their business, eh!" Winger smiled accusingly and Veronica's face hardened.

"What do you mean?" she asked, puzzled.

"Yeh. Yi can't fool me. Whitey at the station told me. They come up with the idea of taking all a them idiots out back looking for mookas, and you're trying to grab their business, is that right?" Winger asked with a big smile.

Veronica frowned and looked at Alex; he nodded.

"My! There's no fooling you, Bruce. You saw through us straight away. I'd no idea you knew about us. I suppose they reckoned you shouldn't help us then?" she enquired in a low voice.

"Yeh! Something like that, but we need business in the closed season. Two operations would be better than one. What you reckon? Ya want cow juice?" he asked, opening the fridge.

Veronica took the milk and strolled to the window. She looked out across the lake and her mind was working overtime; she needed to think quickly. Cooperation had never entered her head. She was conscious of the Winger's attention to her body, especially her buxom bosom.

"About two operations, Bruce. They want to set up a base in the bush. We want to operate from here! If possible?" she said, softly. He looked at her and thought out loud.

"I reckon this search could go on forever. Different tourists who haven't a clue where the last tourists looked. Bloody hell, it's a doddle; why didn't we think of that? Too simple, I suppose. But, if you were to base here we could hardly start up a third operation, could we?" He smiled at Veronica.

The two men were sitting facing one another and looking questioningly at the Winger; they didn't know what to make of things, it wasn't what was planned but they left the issue to Veronica. They sipped their tea without cow juice.

"Yeh! I reckon setting up here would benefit this operation more than a bush set-up, so how can I help?" the Winger asked.

"We need a caravan. Is that possible?" she replied.

"You report into the cops before you came here or the Station?" Winger asked bluntly.

Veronica stared at Alex and asked, "Were we supposed to?"

"Standard procedure coming all the way out here but not compulsory. Did you report in?" he insisted.

"No! We're not racing so I didn't see the point." She saw Alex put his hand into his pocket.

"That's great! Nobody knows you're here; I can do whatever you like. Cash!" the Winger made clear.

"Cash is OK with us," she replied and Alex took his hand out of his pocket.

"One van or two?" the Winger asked, looking at the two men and back to her.

"Better we have two. It's hard to negotiate with an audience, wouldn't you agree?" she replied, and bent down to pick something imaginary from the floor, her blouse falling away from her breasts as she did so in full view of the Winger, whose second arm gave a jerk.

"I'll get the power and water on and get them ready. You can stay here, I'll give you a shout," the Winger gulped and, grabbing a ring of keys from a peg, he made for the door.

"I'll come with you, if that's OK?" Veronica suggested.

The Winger was in a flat spin; he rasped at the dogs and they slunk away. Veronica took in his build; regardless of one arm missing he was prime roughage and she was partial to a bit of that.

"It's lovely, not like the outside," she commented as she entered the first van.

"Yeh, the first rain'll clean them off. You were bloody lucky coming here in the dark. That dust storm had hit ya you'd still be on the track, stuck! Without them fat tyres on you wouldn't have made it now. There's linen in the wardrobes, towels and everything. I'll get the water and power on under here; this is their van, yours is next door," he said. She followed him to the next caravan; it was bigger and when he opened the door she stared in disbelief.

"It's beautiful; what kind of people do you get here?" she exclaimed, taking in the lavish furnishings.

"All kinds. Millionaires, celebrities, bikers, all racers and some would-be racers this is a hot spot," the Winger boasted. He put the power and water on and located the linen.

"You'll have to make your own bed, it's kinda hard for me to do that," he explained.

"No problem, I'll get my things and tell them to move in next door. I'll be glad of a shower, I'm all sticky." She giggled and went outside.

Veronica made her way to the Winger's quarters quickly.

"Change of plan. We stay here and get this idiot working with us. Move into the caravan, get set up and get some sleep. I have some negotiations to take care of," she instructed them quietly. They smiled, and nodded their admiration. This girl could adapt.

The Winger was on the hook and she would play him until she had everything she wanted before he got what he wanted. She made her way back inside the deluxe van and he had already started putting a sheet on the large, kingsize bed. She said nothing and set about on the other side to complete the task, making sure she had to maximise the view under her shirt.

"What happened to your arm," she asked with concern in her voice.

"Combine ripped it off when I was young. Playing silly buggers," he explained.

They finished the task with the pillowcases. The air conditioning was on full bore and she asked him to turn it down a little so he left the bedroom. It was en-suite and she hurriedly stripped off naked. She went into the shower and closed the opaque blue glass doors. The water was not clean but she ran it for several minutes and it became clearer.

"Bruce! Can you give me the shampoo, I left it on the bed?" she called to the Winger and watched his movements. The glass steamed inside. She leaned her back against the glass revealing all to the Winger who gave two raps on the sliding door.

She opened it fractionally and accepted the shampoo with a little giggle, closed the door again and, knowing he was still watching, went through motions which ensured as much contact with the glass as possible. The Winger shot through, he bolted out the door desperate to hide his desire and that was hard.

She looked cute when she came into his quarters, her hair in two small plaits and the freckles on her face made her look like a Swiss maiden.

"You didn't wait, Bruce?" she scolded.

"No, I had to feed the dogs," was all he could think of. She came close and he could smell the perfume from her. Every nerve in his body was tense as she sat opposite him at the table.

"Our opposition, as you rightly call them, are slightly strapped for money. We're not! So, Bruce, it's like this. We would set up our operation from here but the drive here is a nightmare. So we would fly our clients here and leave all our vehicles here permanently; would that be a problem, do you think?"

"Sounds bloody good to me. We get a lot of flights here for the racing so there's no problem with that. But the problem is, in the closed season you can't get out on the lake when there's water laying on it, like now," the Winger replied, glad of the diversion.

"Why?" she asked curiously.

He explained the dangers but emphasised the fact that any damage to the surface of the lake would be unacceptable under any circumstance. Absolutely no driving on the lake when water was present.

"What about the aeroplane; can it land if there is water?" she asked anxiously.

"Yeh! No problem with the plane, they don't dig into the salt and aquaplaning they don't give a shit about, even skids. A thousand miles of runway to play on. The trouble is when they're here and you can only go overland. If the water is on the lake, conditions overland won't be perfect either and sometimes it can take a few days before we can even go down the track."

"Oh, I never thought about that, Bruce. By the way, call me Ronnie. Everybody else does," she invited.

The Winger looked ruffled, then banged his hand on the table.

"Right; come with me. I'll show you what we got," he invited.

They went into the longhouse and she was stunned by the amount of bikes there. All kinds, some she had never imagined could exist they were so big, but her eyes fell on the quads.

"What about these? Can they go into the bush?" she asked.

"Yeh! Bloody right, they can go anywhere in any conditions; they're in top nick but they don't carry much. It's them I was thinking about if the overland is dodgy; these babes are the alternative for like, day trips, or overnight, but no longer. They would do till the ground dried."

"Bruce, you're a wonder," she said and held his arm against her.

"What about the other facilities, can you show me?" she purred.

The Winger was delighted and excited, showing her through the workshop, the gym, into the restaurant and even a small swimming pool, which was empty... which Ronnie declared was a disaster, she would have loved a swim.

"I think we will go to my caravan, Bruce, I have something to show you!" she said, on leaving the longhouse.

"Wait there," she instructed at the door and went into the bedroom.

"Come in!" she shouted almost immediately.

The Winger opened the door and his jaw dropped. She was lying on her side, naked and smiling.

"Fuck me drunk," he whispered, and closed the door behind him.

Alex and Viktor wasted no time in returning to the Winger's quarters. Ronnie would keep him out of the way for quite a while, they both knew that from experience. The phone was their main concern; had the Winger reached for it when he mentioned reporting to the cops, he would have been in a hole but not one to enjoy. They had a dilemma; the station would call unless the Winger called them but, if he didn't report everything was all right, they would send somebody to check. The dogs were wary of them but stayed away far enough for their own safety.

Viktor had an idea and he grabbed two stones from outside. He put the cable between both and rubbed it through carefully, explaining in Russian to Alex that if the cable was chewed it could fail at any time. Satisfied the cable looked as if a rat had been at it and leaving only several unbroken strands he lifted the receiver. The phone was still live and he replaced the receiver, satisfied with his work.

They returned to the caravan and showered; they were both exhausted after driving all night, the last twenty miles were slow and slippery. At one stage they were stuck, but they let some air out and managed to get clear. Looked like Ronnie had everything in hand. They were hungry but food could wait.

The Winger was like a spent Snook when he emerged an hour later. She wanted to sleep and he was glad of that. Glad also that she wanted him to cook some tucker and let them rest until five p.m. If she wanted a take-away from Adelaide he would have obliged; he was on cloud nine and whistled merrily as he made his way to the storage area.

"Quads! Hope to hell *she* doesn't have quads," he voiced to the dogs.

He started three, and drove them into the yard beside the fuel tanks. Each had two jerry cans strapped to the roll bar frame, diesel not petrol; they had been customised. Petrol was a pain in the arse in the bush. The only vehicles likely to be encountered were all diesel so if you ran out of petrol you were also out of luck.

He filled all the tanks and jerry cans, checked tyres, oil and integrity of each vehicle. It wasn't easy for him to drive the quad bikes. Going slowly, he could manoeuvre them but that was about it; he parked all three close to his end of the longhouse.

He recovered a selection of steaks from the restaurant freezer and took them home. The leftovers from the racing season were plentiful and high quality. Whitey could eat mutton, he grinned, wondering what the old man would make of his latest conquest. But now he had to feed her and keep her happy; there was still a long night ahead and his batteries were on super charge. Steak, egg and chips with beans, he settled for and prepared everything throwing in some mushrooms and fried onion for variety.

He called Ronnie at five p.m. as instructed. She pulled him back onto the bed but when he started to respond she slid out the other side completely naked and hissed, "Go call the other two, we have all night!"

The Winger flew to the second van and rapped on the locked door, calling them to come and eat. Slapping the palm of his hand hard against the van he got a response. Hearing sounds of discontent from inside and a shout in some language or another, he sprinted back to his quarters.

The three of them arrived at the same time; Ronnie was delighted with just the smell but they were over the moon with the meal and praised the Winger in two languages. He was chuffed to bits. Alex and Viktor going with him to inspect the quads, they took all three on a trial around the yard and were delighted with the performance.

"Now me!" Ronnie said, as they were about to go inside.

She straddled the quad and took off across the yard like a professional. The Winger was impressed; she could ride anything, he reckoned.

They returned to the kitchen; she had cleaned up, which was a surprise, and across the kitchen table she had spread a map of the area.

"East Well – Bruce – here." She pointed to the map.

"Yeh! What about it?" the Winger asked, curiously.

"Can we go there on the quads?" Ronnie asked.

"Bloody hell – East Well, that's a long way from here!" the Winger exclaimed.

"If we went straight across, is that possible?" Ronnie traced her finger along her suggested route.

"Not a hope in hell! The only way is across the lake onto the track and head west along the bowl, as we call it here. That's the old shoreline. If you don't follow it, it'll take a week to get across. It's about sixty miles – you wouldn't save anything by going straight there!" the Winger insisted.

"We want to spy on them and see what exactly they're doing, Bruce. You understand, but what would you suggest we do?" Ronnie sighed.

"Ahh! Well, here's East Well. On quads. Let's have a look." He traced his finger along several options and they remained silent; Alex stared intently at every option.

"Yeh. I reckon cross the lake here, follow the salt north to here, cut inland, hit the track, follow it to here then straight through the bowl they call the arid zone to East Well. That's about the best way and the quads will be OK on the salt even with the water, their tyres are broad enough not to damage the surface if you go about thirty. Any faster you could get trouble and you might have to go slower depending on the depth of the water, it's not the same everywhere."

"How long do you think that would take, Bruce?" Ronnie asked.

"Eight to ten hours, I reckon, no way could you get there and back in one day and it's too dangerous at night," the Winger estimated.

If we leave first thing in the morning and stay overnight, we can get back the next day?" she suggested.

"Yeh, I reckon, but you need to take camping gear and spare fuel. There's not enough to do the round trip on the bikes but we've plenty of tanks and I can get some camping gear organised easily if you like. How come you know they're at East Well?" the Winger queried.

"They radio in to the cops every day and we have a direction finder to pinpoint the signal and it's come from around East Well for about a week, so we reckon that's their choice of campsite or why would they stay in one place for so long?"

"Cunning, very cunning." The Winger gave her a squeeze. "You know what you're doing OK. They must a got pissed off chasing a myth and decided the best thing to do was set up their base. Mind you, it's bloody hot where they are and the dust storm would have rattled them a bit coming in the dark. Yeh, it would be interesting to see what they were up to but I can't go. You're on your own." He looked at Ronnie hoping she would insist he went, but she didn't.

"We'll be Ok, we have GPS and if you trace out our route we can get there and back no problem," she announced. "Alex and Viktor will help you put everything together, Bruce, and when everything is together could you visit me in my van, as we have some more negotiations to take care of?"

The Winger was about to answer her when Viktor pulled his shirt and pointed at the floor.

Winger followed the pointed finger and cursed.

"Bastard, the bloody rats have chewed the bloody cable," he seethed and kneeled down to inspect the damage. "Shit," he fumed. "I'd better give Whitey a call if this bloody thing's still working." He lifted the receiver and dialled number two.

A broad smile flashed across his face and he spoke, "Whitey, the bloody rats have chewed the phone cable Eh! Can you hear me? No! The bloody rats have chewed the cable, it's near through. Yeh, yeh, that's right. No problem, mate, a couple of days will be OK. I'll try and fix it but if you can't get through don't worry about it. I said don't worry, OK." He replaced the receiver and looked at all of them. "That's Whitey at the station, he'll bring a new cable in a couple of days no problem. Bloody rats," he fumed, and cast his eyes over the waiting reward. "Right, let's go!" he shouted at Alex and Viktor.

Elvis and Hanna started north along the track; they could clearly see the fresh tracks ahead of them and were concerned. The Rover they drove was making good progress but the track didn't allow for speed, it was a long, slow struggle. They stopped and changed drivers several times before they reached the fork. They both got out and followed the tracks which kept going north, they didn't turn right into the station. Hanna got the map out and they spread it over the bonnet.

It was another thirty miles north to the campsite or twenty to the station. That meant if they went to the station they would have to cover fifty miles to get to the campsite in the morning, but their options were limited. They were exhausted and didn't fancy sleeping in the Rover all night but they couldn't reach the campsite before dark. Whoever was ahead of them were there by now, and if it was who they suspected, they would have to close in at daylight, and getting close undetected other than on foot was a risk not worth taking.

They turned right and headed for the station. It was dark when they arrived and the barking dogs started well before that. Whitey came out to have a look and waited until the Rover pulled up before going to meet them wondering who the bloody hell this would be.

Hanna came out first, followed by Elvis. Whitey thought he was dreaming as he took in what was before him in the headlights.

"You lookin' for the Miss World competition? It ain't here! What the hell are two ladies knocking around these parts for in the dark?" he asked, greatly concerned.

"We're sorry to arrive like this, we're looking for somewhere to sleep for the night; can you help us?" Elvis said, shaking her mane clear of dust.

"My God," Whitey marvelled. "Come on into the house where I can see you." He invited them and shouted at the dogs to shut up.

The house was cosy and cool. Whitey put a brew on and seated his guests in the living room. He had a Gallah squawking in one corner, sitting on a perch, and another appeared around the corner of the sideboard shouting 'Hello! Hello!'

The women both laughed and answered it accordingly.

"That one barks," Whitey said, pointing to the one on the perch. "Woo! Woo! Woo!" he shouted at the Gallah.

"Woo! Woo! Woo!" it replied, lifting the comb on its head high and giving a bloodcurdling shriek.

"I'm Whitey; glad to make your acquaintance, ladies." He introduced himself as eloquently as he could remember and wished he had shaved.

"Hello, Whitey; I'm Hanna and this is Elvis," Hanna introduced them.

"Elvis never looked like her." Whitey smiled and Elvis blushed.

"We've come from Adelaide to see our friends but we're too tired to keep going," Hanna explained before she was asked.

"All the way without a stopover?" Whitey said, alarm in his voice.

"Was that not a good idea?" Elvis asked, pouting her lips and turning her deep blue eyes on him. Whitey was in a dither but decided a lecture in safety was not in order.

"Well! You made it here in one bit. You'll know better next time. Don't try that again. You got a radio?" he asked.

"Yes, we have VHF to make contact with our friends," Hanna explained.

"A VHF ain't gonna get you out of trouble. Range is too short. OK if you're within ten miles but useless for a hundred; it's a good job you didn't need it." Whitey whistled softly. "I see you drive the same vehicle as them mooka jokers; they the friends your lookin' for?" he asked.

"Yes, have you seen them?" Hanna put in.

"Saw two about a week ago, came here for fuel but they radio in every night and they're OK. I reckon if you're with them they can report in for all of you. What's your move from here?" Whitey said, leaving them to switch off the whistling kettle. They looked at each other and Elvis whispered to Hanna not to mention the caravan park.

"Come here. Get something to drink and a bit of tucker," Whitey called from the kitchen. The tea was strong and black. A piece of lemon would have made it complete but that was unlikely; they settled for what they had and Whitey was impressed.

"We get some beautiful Sheilas here in the racing season but none as beautiful as you two. They're all cow juice and sugar. Not a real brew like this!" Whitey declared.

"What do you do here?" Elvis asked.

"Here's the station; we run twenty thousand sheep, but this time of year the shearing's all over, the sheep are back in the bush and everybody has buggered off, before the racing starts. There's only me here, and the Winger at the campsite. Feed the dogs, feed the milk cows for cow juice, there ain't so many horses now; they use them quad bikes so that makes life easier, give out fuel to whoever wants it and keep the place up to scratch. That's about it, for the next two months. Then, we'll get a break for a month. Good life!" Whitey concluded.

"What do you call the other man?" Hanna asked, frowning.

"The Winger, he's only got one arm. Chopped off here. He manages OK, I just spoke to him on the phone; he's got mice trouble, he reckons rats, but no way they chewed through his phone cable and it's just working and no more. He reckons he'll have to fix it but God knows how he's gonna tape two wires right with one hand. A pain in the arse, I'll have to… Hang on, if you two are going up there in the morning you can take a spare cable with you, that'll save me going up there. Can you do that?" he begged.

"Of course we can. We'll be glad to help, but we might leave early in the morning; can you get it ready tonight?" Hanna suggested.

"Brilliant! Finish your brew and I'll show you the shearers' quarters; you'll have to doss down there for the night. The showers are workin' and I'll put the AC on. Now! Where the hell did I put that bloody cable?" Whitey wondered.

The shearers' quarters were modern and clean. Whitey giggled to himself, looking at the two beauties carrying their bags and wondering what a bunch of hairy-arsed shearers would think about two beauty queens sleeping in their beds. They would go mental. Whitey had to get a photograph to wind them up next time they came back.

"You two make yourself at home. The showers through there; when you're done, come back to the house. I hope you like mutton cause that's what you're gonna get." He departed, shaking his head in disbelief and cursing his age. Mama bloody mia, he kept repeating all the way to the kitchen.

Hanna and Elvis stripped off and went into the shower; it was communal and powerful. The waterfall soon had their skin stinging; it was delightful and woke them up. They put the same clothes back on they had arrived in after making sure all the dust was shaken off. There was a strange smell in the quarters but apart from that it was better than some places they had slept. An hour later they headed back to Whitey's and were met by a smell which made their hunger intense.

"Roast sheep, spuds and tinned veg," Whitey said proudly, seeing the effect his cooking had on what was now staggering beauty. He could hardly keep his eyes on the stove as they volunteered to set the table and cleaned around where he had made a mess.

"You ain't Australian?" he asked eventually.

"We're from Russia," Elvis said, smiling.

"You speak good English for Russians. No offence," Whitey replied.

"Yes! We're English teachers, we're on vocation and we wanted to see the wilder side of Australia, not the tourist side," Hanna explained.

"You come to the right place for that, then, but you'd better be careful out here, it can be deadly. Snakes and all sorts. How long them mooka fellas likely to be in the Bush? You payin' to go with them?" Whitey enquired cautiously.

"No! We're not paying; we're friends, we just want the experience. Do you think they will find what they are looking for?" Hanna threw at him.

Whitey laughed heartily, "If you'd bin payin' I would have said yes, but seein' as you're not there's not a hope in hell they'll find the mookas on this side of the lake, everybody knows that. Impossible they came this way. But I take my hat off to them, could be big business for eternity," Whitey declared.

He served dinner and both women were surprised by the quality of the meal; it was delicious. Whitey further surprised them with the choice of a sweet.

"You like ice cream or fruit or both?" he queried.

They both opted for fruit; he had both. Whitey insisted he should clean up but was outnumbered and told to go look for his cable, which he had forgotten about, his concentration being on impressing his guests.

They cleaned up and he found the cable. Pulling an old camera from a drawer he approached them quite timidly.

"Girls, the bunks you're gonna sleep in are usually used by the toughest, roughest bunch of he-men in Australia. They'll never believe me you two were here, never mind sleeping in their beds. Do you think I could take your photograph in their quarters? It has to be in their quarters, it'll drive them nuts," he giggled.

"Come!" Hanna said, putting her arm over Whitey's shoulder and winking at Elvis. They made their way to the quarters.

Elvis lay on the bunk and posed temptingly with her lips pouted and her hair hanging across her eyes she slithered around and Whitey clicked away merrily. Hanna did likewise and he managed to get both bunks into one shot – there was no mistaking where the photographs were taken. "Brilliant!" Whitey kept shouting, "Bloody brilliant, this'll drive them mental."

"I'd better leave you ladies before I get a heart attack. You be here for breakfast?" he asked.

"No, we will leave early; we have a long way to go. Thank you very much; Mr Whitey," Elvis said; they both had a fondness for this old man.

They wished him well and he departed with, "My pleasure, I hope you come back." He smiled and returned to his quarters on cloud nine.

CHAPTER THIRTEEN

Dinky was right, the chisellers were back with a vengeance at first light, but more concerning was the cloud formation Joe spotted to the south; another shower of rain would effectively strand them at East Well for a little bit longer, but at least the clouds were white, and not red, he pointed out at breakfast. They were well slept and the temperature was down to twenty-six, according to the Rover's thermometer.

"Another day in paradise," Dick greeted everybody, coming back from the dunny they had erected around the far side of the rock.

"Wash your bloody hands," Linda ordered him.

"I did, I pissed on them," he replied and scooped up a plate of tucker.

"Horrible creature," she shuddered. Wilson grinned into his pipe and marvelled at these two. He had known Dick for over twenty years but never suspected there was a female version. She gave as good as she got.

"Where's the other two?" Dick asked Ian, referring to Debbie and Lada.

"Your bucket's in there again. Wash down!" Ian replied.

"Bugger! I better go and wash my hands," Dick exclaimed.

"In your bloody dreams! Go if you like. You'll come back like Ned Kelly with a bucket over your head," Linda dared him.

"One cannot carry out basic hygiene without threats of violence," Wilson announced.

Dan had already eaten, so had Joe, and they were busy cleaning one of the drones. Joe had changed his mind about the things; he reckoned he could use one to spot teeth when they were diving if Clinker could land it back on the boat. That was the problem he discussed with Dan; landing on land was one thing but a boat was another.

"What about fitting floats like a float plane, would that work?" he asked and Dan laughed.

"You'll never know till you try," he advised.

Dinky and Clinker were eating and staying close; he was OK but she insisted he should take it easy, just in case was her concern.

All eyes turned to the woman's tent when Dick gave a wolf whistle. Lada appeared with her hair returned to her hips and gleaming in the rising sun. She looked like a million dollars and Debbie took a bow.

"I bloody heard you. The buckets all yours," she snapped at Dick.

"Naw, I don't know where it's been," he returned. Ian took Lada in his arms and squeezed her tightly. He never spoke, just held her.

"She'll die of starvation. Let go of her," Linda ordered him and she slithered free.

They finished their breakfast, Wilson and Dick headed away for a stroll on their own and the others gathered around the tarp; the mooka box was there and the subject was superstition.

Dinky was scared to hell of the box, she reckoned it was cursed; a belief which Ian objected to as belonging to the Dark Ages. She didn't know what the Dark Ages were until he explained it was before electricity came to Adelaide. Then she understood – kind of.

Lada had no opinion when asked by Linda, she just smiled. She had her old phone on and she was listening to music through the earpiece. The music was terrible according to

Debbie, who stuck the earpiece into her ear and took it out quickly.

"What the hell is that?" she asked.

"Opera – Russian opera; it is very classical. Don't you like it?" Lada said, sulkily.

"It's right up my street. In the middle of a bloody desert, getting hounded by chisellers and waiting to get cooked, listening to opera in Russian. That's cool. I *love* it!" Debbie shouted joyfully. Lada gave her a look of disdain.

"Where's the brains' trust away to now? The ancient mariners?" Linda wondered aloud.

The rest were engrossed in the marine application of drones. "If yours had floats on it that bloody magpie throwing it into the river wouldn't have been a problem," Joe pointed out to Dan, who couldn't deny the fact.

"See any chickens?" Ian greeted Wilson and Dick on their return.

"Yes, there was a huge chicken out by the edge of the salt. Running like the wind; no wonder they never end up in the shops," Wilson declared.

Dinky jumped to her feet instantly. "Did he see an emu? I'll get the rifle!" she asked, excitedly.

Dick grabbed her. "We ain't gonna eat a whole emu in a day, leave it be," he instructed, quietly.

The tone of Wilson's voice changed to serious as he spoke, ending the plight of the emu.

"Right, people, listen up, this is important – Dick!" he said, waving his hand towards the bag with Lacey in it.

Under everybody's gaze, Dick took out the shattered remnants of Lacey's skull and rested it on top of the mooka box. The women were transfixed; they knew it was there but nobody wanted to look. Lada took the earpiece out and listened.

"Just to recap on what we discussed last night," Wilson began. "This adventure is coming to a close. Tomorrow, we are scheduled to depart but there is still the matter of what to do about that! He pointed at the box but everybody looked at the skull, except Dinky who had her head buried in Clinker's shirt.

"To date, I believe this adventure has cost Ian around thirty thousand dollars. That's a lot of money and it has to come back… This is a reality check, that's the reason Mr Lacey is present. This is not a game, it's for real – ask him!" he suggested and they got the point.

"One dead. Two near deaths, and a probable cause of another still unproven. How serious can you get?

"Stealing by finding is just that. You find something stolen, you know it's stolen but you don't give it back. It's found in your possession intact you're likely to get a severe reprimand, little else. It's discovered you have sold it and no longer are you in possession you have effectively continued the robbery Lacey started, and you will be sentenced for the crime in its entirety. Until proven otherwise.

"That's the reality of what you have to decide. Take a chance on selling off what's in that box and take the consequences or try and negotiate for a larger reward. Do you all understand?" Wilson asked. They were silent. This subject had been high on their informal discussions. They slept on it all night, and this was crunch time.

"There are three people present who will ultimately make the final decision if there is a need. Ian, Joe and Debbie.

"So! Kindly raise your hand for keeping the mookas and selling them." Wilson looked at each and smiled. Nobody had raised their hand.

"That's it, then. We put them in safekeeping, renegotiate the reward and see how things develop. Dick will put them into his safety deposit box in the bank. I have no idea what we are going to do with Mr Lacey but I'm sure he's not in a hurry to find out. May I thank you all. I think your decision is a wise one but bear in mind if the reward doesn't increase the other option still exists; however, that will depend on your total silence. We did not find the mookas and we were never expected to find them so everybody should be happy. Dick!" Wilson finished.

"Yeh! There's something else we have to consider. You know, in this day and age there's no hiding place. Radios, GPS, satellite imaging; they can see a fish hiding behind a stone now so if you think we're not being watched think again. We know, and only we know, what we have done. But we must assume that where we are is no secret. If anybody thinks we have the mookas they will go for them on our way back. Don't be worried – be alert! We'll put the drones up regularly to check we don't have company and tomorrow morning at first light we head south. The chance of us being robbed is much greater in the desert. We won't be out of danger all the way to the highway, so, people, our great adventure ain't quite over yet!" Dick declared, and Linda tapped him on the shoulder.

"Put that in its bag now!" she ordered him, pointing to Lacey's skull.

"If it was a roo's head, she wouldn't give a shit! Bloodthirsty little bugger," Dick retorted but did as requested.

Clinker whacked his guest on the arse and Dinky yelped, pulling her head out of his shirt angrily.

"Arsehole! What was that for?" she demanded.

"Don't be a wimp, Lacey's teeth just started grinding – have a look!" he wrestled her body around but she broke free and kicked him on the leg.

"Bastard! It's not there!" she lashed out again with her foot and missed.

Ian and Lada assembled one drone, Dan and Debbie the other. Her hair kept tickling Ian's back as she swished her head deliberately from side to side. He grabbed her by the waist and crushed her against him. She laughed and they resumed their task.

"I'll have to leave the solar charger going all day," Dan advised Debbie. "Should be easy enough to spot vehicles, they have to come up the peninsula or cross the salt and I don't think anybody trying to sneak up here would be that bloody stupid," he concluded.

"Yeh! Here's pretty safe. I think it's when we get underway Dick's on about, but you never know. We better keep a lookout here as well. You OK? You seem to be nearly back to yourself." She had wanted to say that for days.

"Me? I'm fine, never felt better in my life. Never enjoyed myself so much and Ian reckons when this is over we can have the drones, so we can start our own business." If Dan expected an argument he didn't get one, she just smiled and started the drone.

"This one first!" she called to Lada and launched it skywards.

"We're in kind of a bind, Wilson," Dick voiced.

"Yes!" Wilson agreed.

"We get visitors, we can't call the cops on the radio. We could, but that would be a last resort. You any ideas yet?" Dick asked. Wilson sucked his pipe thoughtfully and sighed.

"Apart from keeping them at a distance I can't think of any other way. If they're armed, and there's no reason to think otherwise, *that* could turn into something nasty, and we don't want that. We have to stick together, no splitting up," he acknowledged.

"You learn that from *Rawhide*?" Ian butted in.

"Aw – the greenhorn has arrived. I'm sure he will have a dastardly plan," Wilson jibed.

"Dastardly, my arse. If they come anywhere near us we keep the bastards away. It's a good job Dinky took her rifles. The way she and Lada shoot, I don't think we have anything to worry about. They can use you two to rest the rifles on if they return fire. What you think?" He laughed and strode back to Lada.

"One is now a sandbag," Wilson advised.

"Yeh! But that option's the only one we got. Dinky, come here!" Dick called to her and she ambled over. "Get both them rifles fixed up and ammunition. Make sure the scope you took off is zeroed in and keep them rifles in your sight at all times," he ordered her.

"Yes! Yes!" she said excitedly, shouting at Clinker to move his arse and help her.

"She won the lottery?" Linda asked, joining Dick and Wilson.

"Her skills might be called upon but we hope not," Wilson replied.

Ian and Lada joined the brigade of rifles and Dinky explained in detail how to zero in the scope but she had to fire the rifle to do so and she only had fourteen bullets left.

"It's not bad as it is. But it's not spot on." She looked to Ian for advice.

"That one's spot on. That should scare somebody away. If it comes to the crunch I don't think you'll need telescopic sights. Remember, you'll be trying to miss people, not hit them," he emphasised.

"I never tried to miss things before, that's difficult!" she retorted, looking at Lada. She just smiled and stuck her earpiece into her ear. It was going to be a long day.

Joe watched the sky to the south; the cloud formation was going west to east slowly. He concluded it would stay dry until the wind changed; he hoped it wouldn't.

Hanna and Elvis moved out from the station before daylight. The track didn't allow for speed; Elvis drove as fast as she dared but they were anxious to get to the campsite as soon as they could. It was fifty kilometres away and at top speed they estimated at least two hours before they were near. Hanna

248

checked their progress on the GPS, conscious of the increasing shafts of daylight to the east.

Their location was slowly getting revealed and they marvelled at the scene unfolding before them. Several kangaroos had bounded out in front of the Rover but none hit it. Looking behind in the mirror, Elvis drew Hanna's attention to the plume of dust they were kicking up and they decided to slow down; their approach to the campsite undetected wasn't going to be easy but they had no choice. Ten kilometres from the station they slowed, steadily watching the dust get less and less until Hanna was satisfied it was acceptable. Fifteen miles an hour, she read out from the speedometer and cursed silently.

They stopped two kilometres from the campsite and drove the Rover into the sand dunes. It was hot and nearly nine a.m. when they set off, following the track. They ran and walked until they sighted the buildings, then went east along the sand dunes to get a view into the compound.

Hanna scanned the place from the chalets to the longhouse and everywhere in between. They spotted the Toyota parked beside the longhouse and two dogs were lying on the ground beside it but there was nothing else moving. They decided to go further east and come back using the longhouse as cover, but they had no chance of getting anywhere without the dogs barking. When they reached the gable end of the longhouse they were confronted with large, open doors. They looked at one another and reached the same conclusion. They were too late!

Throwing caution to the wind they walked directly towards where the dogs were lying and were immediately spotted. The dogs went mad, barking loudly, but they didn't appear ready to attack them; they kept walking, eyes locked on the door they were approaching. Nothing moved and the dogs just followed them, still barking but offering no threat.

Elvis opened the door, quickly stepping to the side as it thumped against the wall. Guns at the ready they both darted through the entrance.

The Winger was slumped over the kitchen table. He didn't move. Hanna shoved the barrel of the gun against the back of his head and Elvis checked the adjacent rooms.

She returned quickly and felt the Winger's pulse at his neck. She pulled his head back and checked his pupils. Dilated. Hanna saw the phone cable separated as Whitey had explained, but the rat was nowhere to be seen.

"He's been injected," Elvis said, pointing to the right side of the Winger's neck.

"Get the Rover!" Hanna ordered and Elvis sprinted quickly towards the entrance to the compound.

The dogs had lost interest and watched as Hanna made her way back to the large doors at the opposite side of the longhouse. She blinked into the darkness and looked in disbelief at the array of vehicles inside. She ran outside and checked the tyre tracks. It was immediately clear the tyres were comparable to the ones on the quad bike just inside the door but how many quad bikes was hard to establish. She ran quickly, following the tyre tracks to a space between the chalets where they descended to the lakeside.

Hanna gave a big sigh and returned to the Winger. There was nothing she could do for him; this was the call sign of Viktor Manin. The Winger would suffer brain damage and wouldn't even know his own name when he woke.

Elvis arrived at the front of the door and they went to the Toyota. The door was open; they searched quickly for anything they could find but there was nothing.

"There not coming back!" Hanna exclaimed in alarm, pointing to the broken key in the ignition.

"Lada!" she ran to the Rover and snatched up her mobile phone. It was the same as Lada's. Hanna pressed *save* four times and looked at Elvis apprehensively. Her phone gave a low whine and she relaxed.

"We better move quickly, they've gone out into the lake. Quad bikes, two or three. There's one quad left and some scramblers. This is not good; we can't follow on the lake and it's a long way round to go by track; whatever, we will need transport."

Elvis ran to the fuel tanks and Hanna went inside the longhouse. She started the remaining quad and drove it outside. She returned and selected a Yamaha scrambler from the array of machines. She took that outside and went back to the quad. Diesel, she established, looking at the injectors. Elvis came running back from the fuel tanks.

"We need diesel and petrol?" Hanna enquired.

"Yes!" Elvis replied and mounted the scrambler. She drove it to the fuel tanks and Hanna followed on the quad.

Leaving Elvis to get on with fuel, Hanna returned to the longhouse and snatched up two empty jerry cans. She ran back and Elvis filled one with diesel, the other with petrol. It was getting hot and both were sweating badly but there was no time for respite. They went to the first chalet; it was locked as were the next five. The sixth was open and obviously recently used by the jumble of bedding. The AC was still on and they were glad of that. Elvis grabbed two white sheets from the beds. Hanna searched for anything left behind but found nothing. The next chalet was an eye opener and cold; it was beautiful and again the bedding was used. Hanna spotted several stain triangles on the sheet and Elvis peered over her shoulder.

"Somebody has had a good time!" Elvis suggested.

"Fletcher is here!" Hanna looked at Elvis, somewhat puzzled.

"OK! That's one and Manin makes two. You don't think Alex would come here, do you?" Elvis queried.

"Would you trust Manin and Fletcher? They would have taken a quad each and there were four, three is best guess, Hanna concluded.

They switched off the AC in both vans and headed back to the Winger's quarters. He was still unconscious and they didn't waste time on him. They grabbed some tins of beans and ham, a water bottle and a flashlight they noticed hanging beside the phone. Hanna looked at the cable and remembered Whitey had given them a replacement. It was broken completely where it had been supposedly chewed. They returned to their Rover and hauled out their sleeping gear, more water bottles, GPS and map; they returned to the Winger's abode and laid the map out on the table in front of him.

East Well was where they knew Lada was. To get there was straight across the lake, then following the shoreline north. Elvis traced the route and it was simple but they couldn't go that way for fear of being seen. Alternative routes were horrendous. Impossible in the dark and completely out of the question; they must follow the tracks ahead and be vigilant. The one good thing was they had a better chance of seeing what was ahead of them before anybody saw what was behind them.

Elvis hunted around the longhouse and came back with an array of bungee rope; they lashed as much as they could onto the quad, then the scrambler. Both sheepdogs jumped up onto the quad and sat there waiting for instructions; they were ready to go and wagging their tails. Sadly, they were chased off and the women mounted the bikes.

They followed the very distinctive tracks on the salt for miles heading west, and Elvis stayed behind Hanna on the quad. At least there was no dust to worry about but they became aware of the thin film of water on the salt, the scrambler throwing slurry skyward. Its deep treads were tearing into the surface. They stopped and checked the GPS two miles from the old shoreline and scanned the terrain for any movement. They could see none and continued more slowly.

The tracks turned north half a mile from the shore but Hanna kept going straight ahead towards solid ground. They reached the ancient beach and stopped. Chisellers were everywhere and settled on their backs instantly. The salt was stinging their eyes and the chisellers were delighted with the resultant flow of tears.

"We must follow the coastline carefully and stay very close to the edge. We can use some sheet to break up the silhouette," Hanna suggested, and they set about shredding one sheet and wrapping bandage wide lengths around the frame of the quad. They split the second sheet and cut holes for their heads like ponchos. That upset the chisellers but now, they could blend in with the salt. They started north, slowly.

After several miles Hanna waved her left arm in the air and turned towards the beach; Elvis followed, thinking something was wrong. She stopped beside Hanna.

"Is anything wrong?" she asked, switching off the trail bike's engine.

"This isn't going to work," Hanna exclaimed lifting both hands and banging them back on the handlebars. "We need to get ahead of them; we need to get to Lada before they do. Have another look at the map," she suggested to Elvis.

They laid the map out on the ground and Elvis checked their position.

"We're here," she pointed out.

Hanna looked at her watch. "We have about five hours of daylight left and the distance to the East Well from here is forty miles direct through that!" She pointed to the rough topography. "If we follow them we are sure to catch up with them, but if we go direct we're not sure whether we can cut them off. If we don't we're in no position to stop their return to the lake. We won't be able to assist Lada and we won't be able to intercept Manin."

"We split?" Elvis asked, frowning.

Hanna smiled and put her arm around her. "No! Together we have a chance of getting through but alone I doubt it. We go to here – Kittles Dam, we can go as fast as the terrain will allow without fear of anybody seeing the dust. I think we should try." She looked at Elvis.

"Let's go!" Elvis started the scrambler; pointing it west, she opened the throttle.

Their fears were soon realised; rock outcrops were predominantly running north and south; each one had to be rounded and there was no alternative. However, it soon became evident that animal tracks were undulating between the formations, some also heading west. They locked on to such a track and started to make good progress. Within an hour, they reached the main track to Jumpuppy Dam and stopped to take another GPS reading. They checked their position and they were only twenty miles from Kittles Dam. They wasted no time in continuing west towards Kittles Dam; the track was arduous and they had to keep their speed down, which meant Elvis had to struggle with the trail bike.

An hour later, Elvis signalled to stop; she was completely exhausted keeping the high suspension bike upright. They swapped bikes and kept going; no matter what they tried there always seemed to be one in front one behind; they couldn't run side by side for very long. The track weaved its way through the maze of boulders and outcrops. Dust was minimal; they weren't going fast enough to stir up much but what the lead bike stirred up landed on the one behind. They were both red with dust and so were the bikes.

They saw the bunds of Kittles Dam in the distance just because it was a straight line and the only straight line in sight. They approached with caution, not knowing what to expect; they didn't know if there was water in there or not. They stopped several hundred metres away and went forward on foot.

They peered over the bund and froze; Elvis held her finger to her lips and grabbed Hanna.

"Wild pigs just below us," she whispered and they both slunk backwards.

They ran back to the bikes and came at speed around the bund; there was a track on the west side and they knew if the pigs were there nobody else was there. They came into the bund entrance and surveyed the scene. The herd of pigs were staring at them from the far bank. Some were huge. They snorted their menace and jostled one another, holding their ground for several minutes before all hell went loose in screeching, squealing turmoil as they fled over the top of the bund and disappeared.

Without speaking, they both stripped their clothes off and raced for the water. Hanna, laying her gun on the bank, before running up to her waist and diving under. The water was cool, beautiful and every other compliment they could give. Reflection on the water from the clear blue sky was hiding the reality of the light brown liquid, so desirable for a wallow.

They filled their petrol tanks and water bottles and decided to dry on route. Naked! They mounted the hot seats which were slippery instantly. They headed west again in great spirits and laughing loudly at one another's bouncing body parts. They hoped to reach the edge of the salt at East Well before dark. They were refreshed, loose and determined. Also they had only another fourteen miles to go. Another twenty on the salt and they would be opposite the end of the peninsula where they hoped Lada was.

They made it before the sun went down and got dressed in shirts and shorts. They decided venturing out on the salt was not a good idea and decided to wait until the sun set. They spread a sheet between the two bikes; it kept the sun off but not the chisellers. There was plenty of light inside their shelter and Hanna opened the back of her phone. Printed circuits were evident; the board she reversed and put back. She turned the volume to full and withdrew a thin aerial from the side of the case. She scanned in front of her in an arc.

"I don't think so. Twenty miles is too far," Elvis commented.

"Vladivostok's not a problem. But we can't pick her signal up from twenty miles away. Our people are good – sometimes!" Hanna sighed.

They had the torch and looked at the small area of the map which was relevant.

"We need to get into Manin's head. If he hasn't made a move yet, they will when the sun sets," Hanna advised.

They traced Manin's options but, not knowing Lada's position exactly, they could only guess her party were camped at the outer end of the peninsula. They had little choice on their approach; it had to be across the salt and the distance from the nearest island to the peninsula was only two miles. They had to keep to the south. Manin had to come from the north across land or northeast across the salt and that distance was similar, only about two miles. However, they were twenty miles away and Manin, they were certain, would be a lot closer.

"Come, we must go around the south end of the island and follow it north. I think we should leave the trail bike here; it's too noisy," Hanna suggested.

They set about changing their steed. Fuel was OK for the quad and also the trail bike had half a tank of petrol still in the tank, plus the reserve they took with them. They left everything with the bike and mounted the quad. Elvis drove slowly, heading west towards the setting sun. A red orb in a red sky, set in a base of silver, it was mystic. Hanna, looking over her shoulder, stared at the horizon with mixed feelings.

It was dark when the sliver of land came into view several hundred metres ahead. It had taken them half an hour to reach it and they headed south to go around to the west side. Their navigation wasn't far out and within minutes they could see the salt on the other side of the ancient island. They rounded the south point and headed north, going a little faster as they now had land between them and their quarry. They soon discovered speed was dangerous; several large rocks were clear of the island and not easy to see. Elvis swerved violently to avoid one but went over another smaller one, nearly tipping the quad over. Reluctantly, Elvis throttled back and they proceeded with caution.

Ronnie, Alex and Viktor left one quad at the first campsite the mooka hunters had used. There was no point in taking all three any further and a spare ready fuelled was a good reserve. They had followed the Rover's tracks all the way, keeping their speed down to prevent a dust cloud. They stopped and took GPS positions. This revealed they were only ten miles from the inside end of the peninsula. Viktor was suspicious of why they camped at such an easily defended position. Was this by accident or did they suspect they might have visitors? He opted for the latter so, if they were expecting visitors, what was the best way to approach them? Up the peninsula, or across the salt? He knew they reported in to the police every evening so they would report in again. He decided to move closer at walking speed; another five miles, then they would wait until the police report was made before deciding their strategy.

Ronnie was pressed into Alex's back and half asleep; it had been a long day and it looked like it was going to be a long night as well. She wasn't keen on Viktor. Alex, she liked but Viktor was worth watching; she didn't trust him after what he did to the Winger. She didn't see the need to harm him; she had him by the balls and he was so naive he would never tell anybody anything, in her view. Viktor had insisted she inject him with some kind of drug which he insisted would only make him sleep for a long time.

The Winger's phone was an extension from the main switchboard. Peter, the pilot of the Cessna, had been tasked with getting the Leper as a hostage and failing that to get Maria. He would also pick them up from the lake. She called his land line. The hostage hadn't appeared and neither had the men who went to get her. He told her about the run in with the Leper and he dismissed that as unfortunate. He must have seen they were armed when they went to his house and he did what anybody would do. He didn't fire on the plane so they decided to go for Maria instead. That was all he knew. Why they hadn't arrived with her he had no idea. "You'll just have to do without a hostage or take one there. I'll land at first light at quadrant six. Relax! Even if they've been picked up, they have no idea what's going on. A debt collecting business, they're under the impression if you can't get the father get the daughter. They think Maria is the old man's daughter. They're used to that," Peter assured her and hung up.

"We have no hostage!" she advised Viktor.

"We can get another. Is Peter on track?" he asked, unperturbed.

"Yep! Here at first light, quadrant six," she replied.

"Good!" was all he said.

They stopped behind a large sand dune as the sun was low in the west and waited for the radio report to go in to the police in Port Augusta. They ate and refreshed themselves. They discussed the implications of the two men who went to get Maria being picked up but, as Peter had said, they knew nothing about this operation; as far as they were concerned, the mafia wanted to recover money and that was that. The Leper scaring them to hell was more of an incentive to get his daughter; Peter had told them Maria was the Leper's daughter. Failure there would be a huge dent in their ego and further revelations were out of the question if they ever wanted to work again; they had no reason to divulge anything. At worst it would be a robbery gone wrong.

"Forget them! Concentrate on what we have to do now!" Viktor snapped.

He never left anything to chance. These people were amateurs. He was a professional. He assessed their perspective. They were unlikely to radio for help but that wasn't guaranteed. Their radios had to be neutralised. He could find no reason to harm anybody, provided they cooperated. If they had to inject somebody, he had to inject all of them. That was a problem, as he didn't have enough serum for all of them. If they didn't report, a search would soon find them. By that time, he and Alex would be in Sydney so that wasn't a problem. The white stubble around his face was annoying him and these flies were torture. He hated this place and was having a hard time keeping his temper in check; however, the rewards of doing so outweighed the alternative. He had to restrain Alex; fifteen years in prison in Luanda had had savage consequences. Now he knew who was responsible for his life in hell he might need to be restrained.

The trackers they had planted on both Rovers had worked well. They had no problem getting into the garage, by-passing the alarm and setting the trackers inside the radios. The dog was easy also and the fact one vehicle was outside served as a decoy. These people had nothing to base suspicion on. The property they had searched with Ronnie on the island had revealed nothing, but they knew it was only a matter of time before the boy returned. His rapid departure had taken them by surprise, but only served to strengthen their belief that the old man wouldn't take his secret to the grave. They waited and they were right.

He had the information they lacked and they had no choice but to leave him to find the mookas. Now, they were certain they had found something. They had tracked the Rovers three times over thirty miles, from and to the exact same coordinates.

There could only be one reason for that. Even if they were wrong they would get the information they wanted and find the mookas themselves. Either way they would gain. So far all they had left behind was a vegetable at the campsite and a stolen vehicle.

Ronnie was convinced if the worst was revealed and they hadn't found the mookas she could persuade them to work with her. That was why she was here. If they had the mookas she was of no value. She had served her purpose arranging everything in Australia, as her father had done for Alex.

The sun went down in its fireball glory and Alex came close. He wet his finger and held it aloft; the slight breeze was from the south and in their favour. They would drive slowly until they reached the end of the peninsula. Leave the bike there with Ronnie and both of them would follow the salt line on foot to the coordinates which must be their camp, a distance of two miles. They would make no plan of action; they would assess the situation when they got there. They moved out and headed west at slow speed in the half light. With both quads they would have a passenger on their return journey.

Debbie replaced the batteries in the drone, the other one taking its place. She was about to say something to Lada when she saw her physically jump.

"You OK?" she enquired, concerned and looking at Lada, who was wide eyed.

"Yes! I got a fright. Is this music that you like?" Lada asked, taking the earpiece out and handing it to Debbie. She took the phone from her pouch and pressed *Save* four times; Debbie took no notice.

"Yes! That's more like it; 'Honky Tonk Woman'. Brilliant, you're too young to be listening to bloody opera anyway," Debbie declared.

"I'll put it away unless you want to listen to it?" Lada enquired.

"Bloody right I'll listen to it. I'm getting bored flying that damned thing looking for nothing," Debbie replied and took the phone from Lada.

This was not good; she had been warned of imminent danger and she knew Hanna and Elvis wouldn't have sent that unless they were in trouble or unable to act. She walked over to Ian, who was speaking to Joe and nipped his rump, leaning her breast into his back as she did so. He winced but grabbed her around her buttock with his free hand.

She looked over his shoulder and pressed her chin into it. He could smell the scent of her and could have stayed there all day.

"I want to go up there!" she purred in his ear, and pointed to the top of the rock shelf.

"You'll cook up there, it's too hot," Ian declared.

"No problem if you're Russian but I understand if you're Australian you must stay out of the heat," she whispered temptingly. He looked at her and immediately headed for the rock.

"Wait! Wait! We must take the gun with us, we need the telescope." She dug her heels in.

"Yeh! Right, go get it and I'll race you to the top, Russian!" He slapped her arse and she ran to Dinky.

There was no way he was going to race her to the top, she was there with the rifle before he was halfway. It wasn't high, no more than twenty feet, but the face demanded attention to detail and several zigzags. She took his hand and hauled him up over the last obstacle, her hair covering his entire head.

They looked around; the top was indeed hot but not much worse than where they had left. It was also rough, not like the Bluffs. Red dust was everywhere and they were both covered in it. They settled on a rock outcrop and winced on first contact with the hot stone.

"So, madam, what do you expect to see from here that the drones can't see from up there?" Ian asked, pointing at the drone high above them.

"They're looking for dust. There's no dust out there," she answered, pointing the rifle towards the salt.

"Nobody in their right mind would approach from there!" Ian argued.

"Somebody *not* in their right mind, might?" she answered, slowly sweeping the scope along the expanse of salt.

The shelf afforded them a view of the entire peninsula. Ian imagined what it must have been like when it was a real peninsula in a real sea instead of something sticking out into the salt like a tonsil; nevertheless, their position was defensive and they could only be approached by land in one direction. Surely anybody coming across the salt would be seen miles away unless it was dark! As Lada had pointed out.

"I reckon our imaginations are running wild. No proof anybody's likely to try and get the mookas. The Leper's theory, the dog, but nothing else. Anyway, it's more likely somebody might try something on our return, there's only one road south," Ian voiced. Lada looked at him but remained silent.

"What the hell, you two doin' up there?" Dick's voice reached them.

"Somebody else's imagination running wild," Lada said.

"Makin' babies!" Ian shouted back.

"Lucky bastard!" came the reply and some undecipherable yell from Linda.

Lada grinned and viewed the salt to the south through the scope. She could see the evaporation shimmers coming from the surface as it slowly released its water. The clouds Joe had seen in the morning had disappeared and she concluded Dinky had been right about waiting a day before setting off; it would be good to travel in the morning. It was the night that concerned her.

All day they kept the aerial surveillance going until everybody except Joe and Clinker started complaining. Dinky had opted for the top of the rock with the .243, which Lada insisted she must keep there. It didn't make sense taking it up and down and they would do thirty minutes each. Reluctantly, she agreed. The men had managed to pack the trailers with everything except what they would need until morning. Jerry cans were filled at Ian's insistence, as he intended taking the bowser with the remaining fuel back to the station. The mookas were packed into the back of one Rover and covered with Laccy as a gesture. He would accompany them on their last journey.

"How bloody sentimental, I'm overcome with emotion!" Dick yelled at Linda for that suggestion.

"Heartless animal! You were in the bag, we would make soup," she replied.

"I'm thinking one could stand watch tonight, Dick?" Wilson suggested.

"Good thinking. Sleep all the way back. What we got left?" Dick asked.

"Sufficient to see the light of day if one sips," Wilson concluded.

Ian joined them after coupling up the bowser. He was sweating badly and grabbed a water bag. He glanced at Lada, who had just been relieved by Dinky and was making her way down the rock.

"She's been as jumpy as hell all day," he said.

"I noticed," Wilson replied.

"Time of the month?" Dick suggested.

"Buggered if I know! She's looking for something, can't sit on her arse for a minute," Ian stated.

"Maybe it's too tender to sit on? I'll massage it if you like?" Dick volunteered, flexing his fingers as she approached.

She looked at the gesture and read his mind. Stretching her entire body in front of Dick, she gazed into his face and said, "Ahh, I would like a massage. Ian! Can you give me a massage?" She purred and pouted her lips at Dick.

"My dear, why are you so nervous?" Wilson asked bluntly and to his surprise she came and sat on his knee.

She put her arm around his neck and confessed, "I have a sixth sense, Captain. One which tells me we are going to get visitors. And tells me you two are going to stay up all night drinking whiskey. Am I wrong?" she asked.

"Young lady! How could you possibly jump to such a conclusion? One doesn't drink whiskey when on watch! One sips whiskey," Wilson corrected her.

"Get off his knee! Come and sit on mine!" Dick suggested; Linda obliged and he moaned in protest.

Dan had the drones packed into their travelling cases while there was still daylight. He decided they would fly them in the morning just to please Lada, who insisted they should not be put into the trailers yet. The chisellers had vanished again and it was getting cooler by the minute; the breeze from the south was light but welcome and they were tired despite doing very little all day. Ian had stuck close to Lada; all day she had changed from happy-go-lucky to edgy but he wondered if it was his imagination. She had taken turns with Dinky on top of the rock all day and both of them were still up there when the sun went down. Lada had put Dinky's hair into a short ponytail and was giving her instructions in self-defence because she claimed every time she had a ponytail somebody would grab hold of it, so she had stopped wearing one.

Dick suggested they should prepare a fire as he and Wilson would stand watch all night so as the younger generation could get some sleep. If it turned cold during the night they would light it. Lada wanted to object but declined. The small lights Dan had rigged up were also of concern to her but she said nothing. If

Hanna and Elvis were close, they would have no trouble finding her. Neither would Manin and she knew he was close. She also knew Manin had no idea she was anything other than Ian's girlfriend.

"Take the rifle down but leave it beside the rock," she instructed Dinky.

"Keep the other one inside our tent? Or leave it with the night watch?" Dinky enquired.

"They can't see in daylight, never mind in the dark and they will be drinking." Lada sniggered and added, "It wouldn't be safe to powder your nose if they had a gun."

"What a way to go! Shot off the dunny by friendly fire." Dinky laughed and they descended the rock.

The meals were filling but more of a ritual despite efforts by Linda. Variety was restricted to a three-day cycle; there wasn't much she could do without fresh supplies. The novelty of camp tucker was wearing off and they were all looking forward to a good meal of anything that didn't come out of a tin.

"Right, people, listen up!" Dick shouted when the meal was finished. "Tonight, we'll stay awake. At first light, we'll pack up and head for the station with the bowser. Take a break there, then head for Port Augusta. We can take stock when we get there and decide whether to carry on or stay the night. Any questions?" he asked.

"What about visitors?" Joe asked.

Dick looked at him with a little sympathy.

"Yep! Visitors, well, we owe them for entertaining us all day, otherwise we would have been bored to death sitting around… OK! OK! I get your point," he continued, holding his hand up in surrender at the objections to his analysis. "We'll keep watch all night, me and Wilson – for your peace of mind – but in the unlikely event of somebody coming here, for Christ sake, no heroics. No bloody bravado. Don't do anything that will endanger anybody."

"You reckon we should just hand over the mookas?" Ian cut in.

"If somebody has a gun at somebody's head, what would you suggest?" Dick threw back at him.

"What would they do in *Rawhide*, Wilson?" Ian asked, sarcastically. Wilson threw him a look of disdain and exhaled some smoke.

"Does one know what time the moon comes up?" he queried and there was silence; they looked at one another for an answer but none came. "Observant!" Wilson continued, "What there is left of the moon will appear around two thirty a.m. so effectively, we will be in the dark all night. When you don't know who is in the shadows, as Dick said, you do nothing! Even in *Rawhide*," he added.

"OK! Resistance isn't an option. No heroics, no risks, they're right. But nobody knows we have the mookas except us, so I take it denial that we found them isn't an option either?" Ian threw at Dick.

"Depends what's at stake. If somebody's life is at stake there's no choice. Go and get some sleep, the lot of you, the chances of anything happening here are a million to one. Bend with the wind, no resistance, and have a good sleep." Dick dismissed all of them with a sweep of his arm. Only Lada hesitated but Ian ushered her around the rock out of the dim lights.

Wilson had exposed a lapse in her observations and she wondered if there was anything else she had failed to notice, but she tried to act normal.

They kissed long and hard; Ian wanted to keep her there longer but he had seen a change in her also and decided not to insist.

"Don't worry, woman, you're just superstitious. We'll be OK! We're in the middle of an Australian desert, not the bloody Sahara. No Bedouins. The most we can expect is a kangaroo or maybe a brumby. Go and get some sleep, we have to start early tomorrow." Ian soothed her and took her to the entrance of the women's tent.

"I could sleep here if you like?" he offered.

"YOU can bugger off!" came Debbie's voice from inside.

Sipping was in hand at the tarp. They hadn't settled on any particular subject yet but they would and it was cooling down steadily.

Viktor felt the need to speak to Alex once they were away from Ronnie. They walked fast along the edge of the salt, both of them dressed fully in black body-hugging suits and helmets. The suits covered their feet and they wore no shoes.

"Remember! When we get close, you stay in the shadows. Don't come near me. I'll come to you. Don't kill anybody unless there is no choice. Do you understand?" Alex didn't reply and Viktor grabbed his shoulder. "Do you understand? No killing!" he repeated forcefully.

"I understand," Alex replied in a deep voice which sent shivers down Viktor's spine. He wasn't an easy man to give orders to and he was the boss of this operation. Viktor knew then that if anybody resisted Alex would kill them without hesitation. He had paid a heavy price for this prize and he wasn't going to let anybody deprive him of it, not even Viktor.

They made steady progress; it was easy to follow the edge on foot and they could make out obstacles sticking out from the bank easily. Several animals moved to their right in the bush and they froze momentarily, both of them guns in hand. They went on until they could make out a small glow in the darkness, then slowed their pace.

Stealthily they approached the lights, which became more distinctive. They made out the dark shapes of the Rovers silhouetted against the dim light. They were lined up next to each

267

other and offered good cover. They both headed for the Rovers silently. Crawling underneath they lay there in wait.

Two people were drinking and speaking quietly under a tarpaulin. An occasional gruff was heard and the occasional muffled laughter. Snores were coming from somewhere and they focused on the two tents beside the tarp. There were so many of them, Viktor was annoyed; why did they have to get so many people involved? He would have two. No more, unless getting rid of the surplus was built into the plan.

They lay there for an hour and waited. The last thing on their mind was the temperature; they were in adrenalin mode and were surprised when the fire suddenly illuminated the immediate area. They slunk back under the Rover into the shadows.

Somebody came out of the closest tent to the fire and disappeared to the left without saying anything to the men; it was a girl and Viktor immediately slid out from under the Rover. He made his way in the general direction of where the girl had faded into the dark. He smiled as he heard the sound of water and saw a white shape looming out of the darkness; he moved closer.

Dinky had just pulled her shorts up when his hand went over her mouth tightly.

"Make a sound and I will kill you," Viktor whispered, pressing the revolver against her temple.

Dinky was shaking, her knees trembled and she thought she was going to collapse. Her eyes bulged and she twisted her lower body with no purpose. Viktor let her settle down. She stopped moving and he allowed her to breathe through his fingers.

"Make a noise, you die. So does everybody else," he whispered for the second time. "I am going to take my hand from your mouth. You will go ahead of me and if you make one sound this gun will tear your head in half. When you are ready nod your head and we will go. You are in no danger if you do as

I ask," he assured her. Dinky was breathing deeply and her mind was blank but his words were somehow helping her. She responded as if she was hypnotised; nodding her head, she started walking where he guided her.

They reached the Rovers and Alex came out from underneath. He smiled in the dark. Manin was the best, the very best, that was why he had hired him. She was the key to his prize and he took hold of her hair instinctively.

"What is your name?" Viktor asked quietly.

"Di-Di- Dinky," she whispered softly.

"Dinky," Viktor repeated and she nodded.

"Remember what I said, Dinky. One sound and you are dead," Viktor whispered into her ear. She was tugged down without resisting and Alex hauled her under the Rover. Viktor slunk away into the darkness.

"Good evening, gentlemen!" the voice came from behind Dick and Wilson, very soft and very clear. They whirled around to look at the source and Viktor stood behind them with the revolver pointing at each alternately. He had his finger across his lips and they just stared at him, drinks in hand.

He came close and whispered, "I have a girl called Dinky. She will be killed if you make a sound. So will all of you so think carefully before you say anything and when you do say it in a whisper. You may finish your drink." He gestured with the gun to drink up.

Dick and Wilson looked at one another and gulped the whiskey down. They remained silent.

Viktor whispered into Dick's ear so low Wilson couldn't make out what he said. Dick rose to his feet and gestured Wilson to follow. They walked to the Rover and opened the boot quietly as instructed. Dick grabbed the mookas by the handle and pulled the box out.

"We will keep the girl until it is safe to release her. If you follow before daylight we will kill her, do you understand?"

Viktor poked the gun into Wilson's belly.

"We understand," Wilson whispered.

"We can hear you on the radio, Wild Goose, so you know what will happen if you use it. Go back to the fire and carry on drinking," Viktor ordered the two of them and they obeyed. Dick went to say something but the gun swung in his direction and he stayed quiet. They turned their backs on Viktor and went to the fire. There was silence behind them and they were distraught with anger.

Dinky was herded onto the salt between her captors and they walked quickly north. The entire operation had taken two hours; they had the mookas and a hostage, it was a good night's work and nobody had been killed which was important to Viktor.

"One has the distinct feeling one has just been shafted," Wilson confided in Dick.

"Bloody hell, Wilson, you wouldn't read about it. How the hell do we tell them what just happened?" Dick seethed quietly.

"In a controlled manner, I'm thinking, lest we let loose something out of control," Wilson whispered in reply.

They sat down and looked at one another, Dinky foremost on their minds. Her safety was paramount and they knew by the tone of their instructions any attempt at following the robbers would result in her death. Wilson handed Dick a drink.

"We better do as instructed."

Dick didn't object; he didn't sip either, downing the lot in one gulp. He stared into the fire, deep in thought, as did Wilson.

The voice coming from behind them made them jump, startled.

"Where is Lada?" Hanna asked.

The captains turned around so fast Wilson lost his balance and fell on his arse.

They stared in disbelief at the two haggard panting spectacles. Soaked, covered in salt, and one was bleeding from her knee.

"Who the hell are you?" Dick blurted out, but looked on in silence as Lada came out of the tent and embraced the two women heartily.

"It's OK! OK! Now." Lada led the two towards Dick and Wilson. Ian appeared and squinted into the light.

"What's going on?" he enquired, throwing looks at the two strangers and Lada.

"My friends are here, Ian, we are OK now," she blurted out,

"Eh! Your friends, who the hell are your friends?" he asked suspiciously, coming near. He stared at Hanna and Elvis; they were a mess but his sights were on the revolvers they were both holding, despite their appearance. He stared again at Hanna; he had seen her before but where?

"So what the hell is going on? How did they get here and what are they doing here?" Ian demanded, hearing the others come to life in the commotion.

"We are Russian police," Lada said quietly.

Ian looked at her and started laughing. "Bullshit! Russian police, you expect me to believe that? Come on! You mean they've come to steal the mookas and they're the ones you've been looking for all bloody day."

"No! You're wrong, the mookas have already been stolen," Dick said, louder than intended. Ian whirled on him.

"What the hell now?" he demanded

"Everybody get yourselves under control! This crap is exactly what we were trying to prevent. Now, sit on your bloody arses and listen to me!" Dick screamed at them.

They fell silent reluctantly.

"They have Dinky." There were yells of alarm and everybody looked around to see if she was present; she wasn't. Dick sighed and lowered his voice.

"They came here, grabbed Dinky and confronted us with 'If you don't give us what we want she will be killed'. We gave them what they wanted and they buggered off. If we follow them before daylight they will kill her. That's the situation – now, for Christ sake keep the panic down and come up with a plan of action – now!" Dick demanded.

"How the hell did they come here?" Joe asked.

"They have three quad bikes from the campsite," Elvis answered.

Ian was thinking quickly.

"You reckon no more than half an hour ago?" he asked Wilson.

"About!" he replied.

"Lada, get up on your perch and see if there are any lights to the north. They won't travel in the dark without lights. Move!" he commanded her.

"How the hell did you get here?" Ian fired at Elvis.

"Quad bike but we had to leave it at the end of the island, we ran the rest," she answered.

"Show me! Get the map," he instructed Dick.

"It's *there* and the scrambler bike is *here*. About twenty miles away," Elvis pointed out.

Ian had the bull by the horns; he hadn't had a gun in his belly and was thinking clearly.

"Get these two fed and watered and clean them up. Joe! Let's go get that quad." The two of them took off around the rock and onto the salt.

"Two sets of lights heading east!" Lada shouted from the top of the rock as Ian was leaving.

"Bastards!" he shouted back.

"Sit down, you two, you look like you were dragged here under a tractor!" Linda booted Dick and Wilson away from the fire and Debbie came with a bucket of water. "I'll get the stove fired up," Linda said.

"The man you spoke with, tell me about him?" Hanna asked Dick.

"Bloody hell, woman, there's not much to tell. He made his demands and we complied and he buggered off," Dick confessed.

"Was he polite? What did he call himself?" she drilled Dick.

"Well, he didn't exactly leave his business card but yep, he was polite. A perfect gentleman," Wilson added.

"Manin! His name is Viktor Manin; he won't kill the girl, what he will do is worse than death." Hanna explained what Manin's calling card was and they fell silent, except Clinker.

"I'll kill the bastard if he touches her," he seethed.

Debbie set about cleaning up Elvis and marvelled at what lay under the scum.

"My God, are all you Russian police beauty queens?" she commented. Elvis smiled and she turned her attention to Hanna. Likewise, the transformation from tramp to beauty queen was a mere wipe with a wet cloth. Her shirt was torn across the back and Debbie fetched her a replacement.

"Don't bloody look you two – four!" she yelled, as Hanna stripped off at the fire and changed her shirt. Linda brought food for them and they ate heartily; they were starving. Lada came down from the rock, holding Dinky's rifle.

"Two bikes heading east, they're not going fast," she announced and laid her hands on each of her friends' shoulders.

"I'm sorry we're late on getting here," Elvis apologised.

"He is always a jump ahead of us," Hanna voiced.

"You know this man?" Wilson enquired.

"No! He's our most wanted but we don't know him. We don't even know what he looks like. We know what he does and we know the trail of victims he leaves behind. Nobody who ever encounters him is fit to testify or give evidence. He strikes and disappears then strikes again."

"Alex! He's the man Manin is working for. We know all about him. We had him released from prison in Angola so he would link up with Manin. One would lead us to the other, and a loose end from the Soviet era would be cleared up." Elvis threw her a look and she changed the subject.

Debbie cleaned and bandaged Hanna's knee; it wasn't badly cut but it hurt with the salt in the wound. Dick took the map and laid it out on the ground where they could see it.

"Now, ladies, tell me where they came from. And where you came from."

Elvis leaned over the map and drew with her finger the route they thought Manin had taken, then the route they took to try and cut him off.

"You came through that?" Dick exclaimed.

"Yes! That's how we came," she answered, looking at Lada for support.

You're a pair of bloody heroes. It's a wonder you didn't kill yourselves. The way they came is the way we came and you reckon they had three bikes. Now it looks like they have only two. So, either they left one somewhere or it's broken down. And you reckon they left their vehicle at the campsite with a broken key in the lock. Strange move unless they didn't break it. That quad Ian and Joe have gone to get, is it petrol or diesel?" Dick fired at them.

"Diesel," Elvis replied.

"Thank Christ for that. We're short of petrol. Where exactly did you leave it? Will they find it easy?" he asked rapidly.

"There and it's still on the salt, they should see it easily." Hanna pointed to the north edge of the island.

"OK. Before they come back get diesel ready – Clinker – move! Lada, get that rifle sling back on so it can be carried on your back. Dan! Put a drone and batteries into a Rover. Start it up, check everything and keep the lights off. You two look buggered; take a rest and think. Wilson a minute." He grabbed the map and Wilson joined him at the light. "How the hell can we follow them without being seen in the dark? Any ideas?" Dick asked.

"Convoy style, I'm thinking. Slow but moving. I think we can move with the quad in front with the rear lights on and no headlights. The Rover can follow the rear lights. We've been through the area several times and if we follow the tracks it should be possible." Wilson traced the track back to the lake. "I'm impressed with those young ladies but I find it hard to believe they're Russian police," Wilson stated.

"You and me both, let's see what they do when we take the guns off them," Dick suggested and they went back to the fire.

"Can I have your guns?" Dick asked and Lada looked at him, surprised.

Hanna lifted the revolver from her feet and handed it to Dick. Elvis handed hers to Wilson. Both captains looked at each other and shrugged. Wilson looked over the weapon, blew on it several times and handed it back to Elvis. Dick did likewise with Hanna.

"Just checking they were clean," Wilson explained and Lada laughed as she clipped the rifle sling to the butt plate, but Hanna eyed the rifle for the first time and jumped to her feet.

"We didn't know you had any firearms. Not like this!" she said to Lada, stroking the barrel of the .243.

"We have two. The other rifle doesn't have a sling but we can take it with us in the Rover." Lada smiled.

"Dan! Is there any duct tape, or anything around to cover headlights?" Dick asked, seeing Dan return from the Rover.

"Yeh, in Dinky's tool box," he replied and went to get it. Clinker was back with two jerry cans of diesel and a drum of water. He put the water into the Rover and sat on the diesel cans, staring at the ground. Debbie came and put her arm around him and gave him a squeeze. "We'll get her back!" she comforted him.

Dinky was barefoot and both her legs were lashed at the ankles by thick cable ties to the footrest of the quad. She knew the strength of her bonds; she had used enough of them. Trying to break them was useless and she resigned herself to captivity. She could barely remember what had happened at the camp, it had happened so quickly. The forced march across the salt she could remember and the occasional push on her back from the one they called Alex. He and the woman were coming behind on the other quad and she was conscious that Alex would put a bullet into her back if she tried to escape.

Their headlights were on and they followed the tracks ahead of them at no more than ten miles an hour. The one driving her quad they called Viktor. He was much kinder than Alex, who was an animal. Viktor had calmed her down, assuring her she was in no danger provided she didn't upset Alex. She could travel with him so he could protect her. She tried travelling with her arms down her sides but gave up after getting thrown violently against Viktor's back. She rubbed her chest and put a hand on each of Viktor's shoulders to steady herself. He stiffened briefly, then a grin etched his face.

Alex had the mookas between him and Ronnie. He had one hand on the box handle and one on her shoulder. He was ecstatic; they had checked the seal and it was obvious the box had never been opened. He continuously rubbed his thumb along the handle and squeezed it tightly. It had been twenty-five years and he thought he would never experience this moment. The hell the Angolans had inflicted on him, the life in filth and deprivation, hunger, thirst, torture and humiliation; he had endured all and his hatred for them was what had kept him alive. He would go back and he would kill his mentors; there was nothing surer, they would pay. When this was over he would arrange for Viktor to take a trip to Luanda. He knew the generals; some were dead but had families alive. Some others were living the life of kings with oil money stolen from the state. They and all the families would soon pay the price. Revenge at any price, now! He could afford that and a lot more.

He leaned forward and started playing with Ronnie's breast. She didn't object and one hand started to wander, the other stayed firmly on the handle. They were in no hurry and Alex wouldn't let a chance go by. The girl ahead was the one he would have preferred and he soon felt himself getting worked up over the idea. If he wanted her, he would have her. Viktor worked for him, and he could go to hell. He would have her first, and then Viktor could do his thing with her. He stared at the strip of bronzed skin between her bright yellow shirt and small tight shorts flickering in and out of the lights. Life was good.

Ronnie concentrated on the bike in front. She noticed Dinky put her hands on Viktor's shoulder and she smiled; he had a way with women. Alex played with her as she expected he would but her thoughts were not on sex; her thoughts were on what he had in his other hand.

She had a good thing going running drugs interstate and stolen goods. She worked with the Russian mafia and also made big money trafficking prostitutes. Lisa, her mother, was Ukrainian and had her own escort service; there was no shortage of escorts from that source. Ronnie had never known anything but the good life; Lisa had. After the robbery, Fletcher had been removed from Andamooka under a cloud of suspicion. The media's insistence the robbery could be nothing other than an inside job had raised hell. Bankers were transferred and everybody connected to the robbery was under suspicion. Fletcher was relieved and was taken back to Adelaide despite his protests. Lisa's income had dried up to a police salary, then to a pension. Fletcher had been a pawn in a deadly game. Lisa was planted on him by Alex. He was a lot older than she was and if she didn't have an accident a year before the robbery she would have left him. That accident she named Veronica. Alex disappeared, her source of income dried up and she was stuck with Fletcher, but only until things improved. It was Fletcher's conviction that Lacey and Ingles were the ones who carried out the robbery, but she wasn't totally convinced. She had Fletcher disappear and set about rebuilding the trust he had lost. He was of no use to her now.

It wasn't until five years after the robbery that she was in a position to put pressure on Ingles. She had him beaten up and his fingers removed to see if he would reveal where Lacey was, but he didn't. He didn't report the incident to the police, which only served to strengthen her resolve, but what would break him? She had him watched and he soon turned to drink and domestic violence. He was cracking inside, that was obvious, but she was convinced he would die rather than reveal where Lacey was. Lisa backed off and concentrated on making money the easy way. Ingles, however, continued to spiral downwards for another ten years until Ronnie latched on to what had been her mother's quest.

She started sending 'Where is Lacey?' cards every month. His family had long since left. Even his elderly neighbour had abandoned him. She considered getting his children but decided that might backfire if he went to the cops. He was in debt up to his eyes and still he wouldn't contact her. The uncertainty of whether or not he knew anything was what restrained Ronnie. Unlike Lisa, she wasn't totally convinced about Ingles' involvement. She knew nothing about Alex or Viktor until Viktor arrived in Australia shortly after her mother came back from a holiday in Vladivostok. Viktor had immediately gone to ground and insisted nothing was to be done until Alex arrived.

They had a new strategy. Get Ingles to pass the information to somebody else or take it to the grave with him; it was that simple and it worked. Not as they had planned; the son had disappeared off the island before they could get hold of him, but, as Viktor put it, 'Now we wait', the result of which was pressing into her back. Viktor was cunning and professional; she had better watch his every move, despite his friendship with her mother. Alex tired of playing with her and rested his head on her shoulder; she hoped he wouldn't fall asleep.

Lada, Hanna and Elvis had the map Hanna used and they were deep in thought when the sound of the quad approaching from the south became louder. Ian and Joe came into sight; they were both as covered in salt as the women were and dying of thirst.

"Now I know how they feel," Joe stammered, looking at Elvis and Hanna.

Clinker set about putting fuel into the quad and Dan started blanking off the headlights with duct tape.

"Keep enough to do two Rovers," Dick instructed him.

"We have a plan?" Ian asked, seeing the decisive instructions. Dick waved him over to the map.

"They're heading back towards the lake, going slowly. How long till daylight, Wilson?" Dick asked.

"Eight hours – approximately," Wilson replied, checking his watch.

"Forty-five miles, from there to the lake. Even at ten an hour they'll only take maximum five to get there. Three hours before daylight. They don't seem bothered about our vehicles. Apart from the danger to Dinky we could still cut them off from the campsite. These two just went overland direct and there's the two tracks, the main one to the campsite and the other here that joins it…"

"What are you getting at?" Ian interrupted.

"They reckon they're not going back to the campsite. I reckon the same. They don't give a shit about our transport because they are only heading for the lake and you know what that means," Dick threw at Ian.

"What?" he blurted, agitated.

"They're getting picked up by plane. They must be. There's no another way out." He looked at Ian with alarm.

"Bloody hell, if they get onto the salt before daylight we can't get near them, if they—" He was interrupted by Lada's voice behind him,

"That's what we think, they'll get picked up by plane. We have to get ahead of them somehow so let's move, we don't have time." She sped away towards the quad and her two companions followed.

"You go in the Rover," she directed Hanna, who was limping. Her knee had seized up when she stopped running.

Dan and Clinker had finished one set of headlights and started on the other. As soon as it was finished they jumped into the vehicles and started the engines.

"Turn them west before you put the lights on!" Ian shouted at them. Lada had already started taking the quad down onto the salt.

"You bloody pair stay here. Linda! Babysit!" Ian shouted, and jumped into the cab of the nearest Rover.

The three left behind watched the rear lights disappear into the distance and returned to the tarp.

"I think we have lost our command, Captain," Dick said.

"Yes, one has been demoted but one can't help wondering if we were bad? Or they were good," Wilson replied, filling his pipe.

"They were good, the only one who screwed up was Lada. She knew they were here. Why the hell didn't she tell us, or keep watch herself?" Linda quipped, angrily.

"She reckoned she intended to get some shut-eye for a couple of hours then join us. She never got that chance. She couldn't stay up all day and all night. She was on watch with Dinky all day up there, but she should have said something. She might have been worried her friends had been caught or whatever, but bugger all we can do about it now," Dick expressed with resignation.

"What I can't understand is what the hell Russian cops have to do with Australian opals or Russian mafia for that matter; there's something weird going on here. Bloody weird," Linda stated.

"One will partake of a small one and we can brainstorm. Did you notice how dim the tail lights went at about a mile?" Wilson asked.

"Yeh! And we have a Rover left. What you reckon? Give them an hour? Two hours? Follow with the headlights on dip?" Dick added.

"I need one. More than you bloody, blind people," Linda stormed, handing the billy to Dick.

"You can't drink and drive, woman," he objected.

"Follow their tail lights," Ian had shouted at Dan, then realised he was sitting next to Hanna. She was clutching her map and GPS.

Elvis was taking no prisoners going across the salt, she was going hell for leather. Her eyes were more accustomed to the terrain than Lada's and she insisted she drive. She pulled up before Lada saw the bank ahead and slowly climbed up the ancient shoreline. They looked behind and the first Rover was close. They went on slowly, heading north until they found the tracks of the quads a few hundred metres away. Elvis turned east and they began to undulate through the terrain. There were no lights to be seen ahead and Elvis pushed their speed to the limit of her vision. Lada clung to her to prevent being thrown into the air and came close to telling her to slow down several times, but she knew it was a matter of life and death for Dinky and she clamped her thighs into the side of the seat. That didn't stop the rifle smashing into her back.

The Rover passengers weren't faring much better; they were getting thrown around but managed to put seat belts on and tighten them. That made staying on the seat easier. They were in four-wheel drive and making good progress but it was becoming more and more dangerous trying to keep up with Elvis. Several times they nearly tipped the Rover on its side and it became clear to Ian that they couldn't continue at this speed without having an accident. In daylight it would have been different but following tail lights blindly was a recipe for disaster at this speed.

"Sound the horn, get her to stop!" Ian shouted at Dan, who did just that.

Elvis heard the horn and stopped. Lada looked back to see Ian coming with Hanna behind him.

"We can't keep up with you. We're going to crash if we don't slow down!" he shouted at Lada.

"We can't slow down, we have to get there before they do," she replied.

"OK, you go on ahead. We will follow as best we can in the dark but for God sake don't crash the quad, it's all we've got. I'll come with you," he offered.

"No room for a big one. Hanna!" she said, taking the rifle off her shoulder and handing it to her. Hanna slung the weapon across her shoulder and straddled the bike behind Lada. Elvis switched the lights off and the tail lights died; they headed into the darkness.

Ian was aware of somebody behind him. It was Joe.

"We're getting battered to death back there," Joe stressed.

"Yeh! We can't keep up with them. We can't slow them down, so they're away on their own," Ian replied and went back to the Rover. "What the hell! Shit!" he exclaimed, pulling material he had sat on from under him. "She's left the GPS, map and torch. If they go off the track they won't have a bloody clue where they are," he moaned.

"The moon won't rise for another five hours; we can't sit here till then. We'll just have to try and rig something over the headlights that points the beam down. Any suggestions?" he fired at Dan and Joe, who had his head inside the window. There was a ruckus coming from the other Rover and Joe ran back.

Debbie was screaming at Clinker. He had gone mental and grabbed the wheel. He wanted to go now and started shouting at Joe, about Dinky and she needed help and they had to move. Joe switched off the engine and took the keys with him.

"Just bloody wait!" he ordered Clinker and returned to speak to Ian. "I reckon we should switch all the lights off like they have, maybe we can see better in the dark without reflection. Like we do at sea in the dark, we don't have lights."

"Worth a try but for Christ sake don't run into the back of us. I reckon we should separate and go side by side," Ian suggested.

"OK, I'll go on your left side and I'll keep away from you," Joe replied and returned to the Rover. "All lights off, we're gonna try in the dark." Joe pushed Clinker out of the seat and took his place. He started the vehicle and moved to the left. He stopped and switched the lights off. Slowly, his eyes started to pick up the topography around him. He was even more surprised when he stuck his head out the side window.

"Clinker, get your fuckin' arse out there. Jam yourself into the Roo Bar. One thump right! Two left. Three stop! OK?"

"OK!" yelled Clinker, and climbed onto the front of the Rover. He stuck his legs between the Roo Bar and the bonnet. Leaning back towards the windscreen he yelled, "OK," and Joe moved forward. Joe had his head out of the side window and yelled at Ian to get somebody onto the Roo Bar. He twigged and went there himself. Like everybody, he was surprised at the detail he could pick out in the dark without any lights and no reflection. They couldn't go fast but they could go and that was what mattered.

The terrain fluctuated between sand dunes and shale laced flats. Occasional Yakka and scrub but the vegetation was sparse in the Arid Zone. They knew this terrain; they had been over it for days. They also knew the obstacles ahead of them could be deadly if they ran into either the deep wash or rock outcrops. Ian looked at his watch; they would go for one hour and stop to take GPS positions, they could work out their speed from there.

He cursed the fact the women ahead had no way to navigate. Only what twinkled above them, and his heart sank when he thought about Dinky.

Viktor stopped abruptly and Ronnie pulled up alongside.

"Take a position, then switch the lights off," he ordered Ronnie.

She got off the quad stiffly. They had driven for two hours and the weight of Alex on her shoulder was getting annoying. He moved aside to let her get off the quad but made no effort to get off himself. Ronnie took the GPS position and traced them on the map. She measured the distance to the lake at twenty miles direct but more like twenty-five following the contours of the land. She switched the headlights off and glanced back in the direction they had come. There was nothing moving there; she knew they couldn't take the Rovers in this terrain without lights. And even if they were stupid enough to follow without lights they would never catch up with the quads.

"Water!" He thrust a water bag at Dinky and she took it eagerly. Ronnie smiled and stared at the girl. She was better than the old man on the island or the woman they had intended; they would have more fun with her. Alex dismounted and moved towards Dinky.

Dinky was stiff and sore. Her legs were chafed inside her thighs and she wanted to ask the woman to help her but declined, anger rising to replace self-pity. Viktor and Alex spoke in a language she couldn't understand and she heard them chuckle. Alex came to her side and put his hand in her thigh. He gave it a squeeze and pushed his finger up under her shorts. He spoke to the woman in the same language. She laughed, making the hairs on the back of Dinky's neck stand on end. She pushed his hand away and he laughed again. She was terrified of this man, terrified of all of them. She was shaking when Viktor climbed back onto the quad.

"Relax! We just have twenty miles to go then you will be free," he said. She put her hands on his shoulders and he drove on towards the lake.

Dinky's mind was in turmoil. As long as they were moving she was safe. The dread of stopping was taking root, and panic after Alex touching her. She didn't understand what they had said but his hand stroking her thigh left her in no doubt about his desire. She pulled tightly on the cable ties and they remained firmly locked in position. She lowered her arms and stretched them as she had done many times but she felt around her shorts this time. She had a belt on and suddenly she felt the slight swell of the tobacco pouch in her back pocket. It dawned on her that she had a lighter. It was there in her left pocket. If she could get the flame onto the cable tie it would make short work of it but no way would the lighter work when they were moving. Her thumb came in contact with something else and she realised her hair band was also in her pocket; she had taken it off to sleep. She recovered it and gathering her hair into a ponytail she put the hair band on; at least her hair wasn't across her eyes now but that was of little comfort.

Elvis had gunned the quad at every opportunity but still they could see no lights ahead of them. She stopped briefly and it was then they realised Hanna had left the GPS and the map in the Rover. Elvis had been following the stars until then and they were sure they were on the right track but they had no way of verifying that.

"We have no choice, we must go on." Lada changed places with Elvis and continued.

She had been across this area before. In the dark there was nothing to recognise and no way of checking their position. That was a major impediment but she knew they could not stray off the track to the north for very far before they ran into the bluffs. Straying to the south was more undetectable. They could go for miles off course as the terrain was the same as they were driving on. Stars move and she was not acquainted with those in the southern hemisphere; the only hope they had was to catch sight of Manin's lights. If the worst came to the worst, they would hit the lake and they could only hit it to the south.

They bounced along, sometimes violently and sometimes comfortably, on the flats. The rifle sling buckle had torn a hole in the back of Lada's shirt. She was glad to feel the softness of Elvis against her back; now it could stick into Hanna instead. Manin had no idea they had a quad. He had no idea they were on his tail and he had no idea they were armed. They had to get into position before he reached his objective, and get close enough to use the rifle. Lada was confident she could kill them from a distance before they could harm Dinky; however, if they managed to get out onto the salt for any distance, that option would be impossible.

It was three hours after Ian had left before Dick proclaimed they were ready to sail. The headlights were on low beam and the light was hitting the ground only two Rover lengths in front; distinct beams, with minimum spread to the side.

The Rover would have to stand on the back axle to lift the beams above the horizon. Linda had done a good job. It had taken her to point out that they had a bucket and if the bottom was cut out and the cylinder cut across from the top on one side to the bottom on the other side they would have two scoops, one for each headlight. That worked, but securing them to the light mounts was difficult; they tried several ways with what tape was left in Dinky's tool box and bungee rope but it was useless.

"That bloody thing I'll fall off at the first bump. If they're not secure we go nowhere," Dick insisted.

Wilson was scrummaging in the box and found a handful of self-tapping screws. Using them and the drill they managed to secure the eyebrows to Dick's satisfaction.

"Mike will go mental when he sees the damage," Linda commented.

"He'll go even more mental if we don't get his granddaughter back," Dick scolded and they set sail.

"As fast as you can, woman, follow their tracks and give it hell – wait! Wait a bloody minute. There's another rifle here, isn't there?" Dick jumped from the Rover.

"It was in our tent!" Linda shouted after him. He emerged with the rifle and shoved it into the back.

"There's only half a dozen bullets. We better take the bloody thing. You a good shot, Wilson?" he asked.

"Windage and elevation, squeeze the trigger don't pull it and remember to take the safety catch off. Which is just sublime, if you can see the target? I must see if there's a book on shooting by Braille," Wilson replied.

Linda tore across the salt. The tracks were clear and within minutes she climbed the Rover up the beach and into the flats. Things slowed down then but still she managed to keep the Rover moving steadily east. It was in four-wheel drive and low ratio, she found a speed which was not critical and looked at the speedometer: fifteen miles an hour. If she could keep that up they would make good time. They were strapped in with seatbelts tightened, all eyes were on the terrain and little was said. They were thinking a lot but there was no point in speculation. What was ahead of them was out of their hands. They could provide back-up; whether required or not would remain to be seen.

Lada climbed the quad up a sand-hill and stopped on top. They scoured the horizon for any sign of lights but saw nothing, she cursed, and drove on. Suddenly, she had a feeling something had changed and she slowed the quad down.

"What's wrong?" Elvis asked.

"I don't know, something's not right!" she replied.

She drove on and it was Hanna who shouted for her to stop.

"The sky is very black there," she shouted, pointing to their left side. The line of black ran through the stars and descended directly in front of them.

"The bluff! One of them. We must head more south," Lada explained briefly as she headed south, watching the stars reappear from behind the buttress. She took a bead on a group of stars to the east and headed towards them; she knew they had to get at least three miles south before they were back on track and she cursed the delay. On the positive side she now had a better idea of where they were.

They drove on relentlessly; she was sore but she shuddered to think what the other two were going through. They had just done this journey the opposite way but they didn't complain so neither could she.

"A light! I saw a light!" Elvis shouted half an hour later.

Lada stopped and they searched the horizon in the direction Elvis was pointing, slightly to their right There was a flash of red then another then it vanished. They were ecstatic; at last they were in sight of their quarry, spirits rising as adrenalin started to flow. They realised instantly they had to be extremely cautious. It was impossible to guess how far ahead Manin was. As long as the lights moved there was no problem but if they stopped they might hear what they couldn't see. The lights appeared again as before, only briefly, and Lada increased their speed as much as it was safe to increase. No point in wrecking everything now; they had to get close to them undetected. She toyed with their options and there seemed no other choice than to go straight for them. If she went south and cut east onto the lake they would never cut them off before they reached the shore. Of that, she was convinced.

Lada stopped and they agreed the only thing they could do was to go straight after Manin. They would follow them until they stopped and hope they didn't go straight out into the salt lake. It was still five hours before daylight and they could see no reason for them to continue out into the lake in the dark, unless the plane was going to land in the dark and that was not likely, or they were getting picked up somewhere else and would drive on the salt to their pick-up point. Whatever, they must retain visual contact, that was the most important factor, and pray they didn't harm Dinky before daylight. They knew what would happen to Dinky before Manin and his accomplice were picked up and her chances of getting away from Manin were slim; with Alex there, her chances were zero.

The Rovers which Ian and Joe were nursing along the flats were not faring well. It was slow and difficult to navigate. The spotters on the Roo Bars were cursing at every jarring drop and their calves and shins were in agony. They wrapped seat covers around their legs and that improved things but it was still hard work trying to stop being thrown sideways. They persevered but Ian knew they were flogging a dead horse. Nonetheless, they were still on track to get to the salt before daylight and if the moon came up that would help also. He had taken several GPS readings and they were spot on for the old campsite. He wondered how Lada was faring without the navigation aids and he cursed Hanna for being so forgetful. He had to admit they were half dead when they arrived, both she and Elvis. God knows how they were feeling now.

This could be a setup if they were all working together. Lada seemed to know somebody was near but she didn't say anything. She might have guided them. The other two appearing in the middle of nowhere; it didn't make sense. He threw all these theories around until he was more confused when he stopped than when he started.

"Bugger it. The only thing that matters now is to get Dinky. The rest can go to hell," he concluded.

Dinky's mind was in turmoil. She looked back many times but the only lights were those on the quad behind, and that woman leering at her was giving her the creeps. She was helpless and she knew there was no chance of getting rescued. The fact her feet were tied down on either side of the bike was a comfort. She knew they couldn't interfere with her; they had to release her legs, no matter what they had in mind both legs would have to be freed. The lighter she could try if she got the chance but if not, she had to come up with something else, even cooperation. The fact she was a virgin didn't lend any experience in cooperation. She considered herself a good actress and she may have to act for her life, no matter what it took.

They kept a steady pace heading east and soon the smell of the salt was distinguishable. Alex passed the time away playing with Ronnie and drooling at the body illuminated in front of him. As far as Ronnie was concerned he might as well have been on the moon. Her thoughts were on what was between his legs that was true, but encased in steel not material. The pretty one ahead would satisfy them; she kept looking back at Ronnie and it became a source of entertainment watching her upper half bouncing around just like hers.

Viktor saw a reflection in the headlights and slowed down. He went ahead slowly taking the gun out of his bag. The third quad came into sight, lying where they had left it beside the rock face. He put the gun back into his bag and, giving a sigh of satisfaction, pulled up beside it. He was relieved the journey was over; like everybody else he was sore all over and glad to reach the edge of the lake. Dinky let her hands drop from his shoulders; she was sore all over and her legs hurt. Despite her discomfort the sight of the gun had made her alert and she surveyed the scene around her; she had no idea where they were going but now she realised they were at the first campsite. She knew where she was and a glimmer of hope began to take shape. The lights on the quads were kept on, shining towards the lake.

Alex came towards them, holding the box with the mookas. He was walking with difficulty and stopped several times to get the circulation back into his legs. Dinky didn't miss the opportunity to voice her own discomfort and wailed at Viktor to let her get off the bike as she had cramp. She gritted her teeth and let out a suppressed scream. It was Ronnie who reacted. She came beside her and put one hand on her thigh.

"Girl, I am going to let you go. If you run you will be shot. Do you understand?" she said coldly.

"Yes, yes, I can't run, I have cramp. Ahhh, it's agony!" Dinky replied.

Viktor and Alex were looking at them and Alex handed Ronnie his knife. She cut the cable ties on Dinky's right leg then went around to the left side. She sliced through the other cable tie and Dinky tried to lift her leg up and over the bike to dismount. She failed and asked Ronnie to pull her off the bike.

Alex answered the call and grabbed her by the shirt front. The buttons popped off and she threw herself towards Ronnie, who grabbed her by the hair. She struggled out of the shirt and Alex laughed loudly. He stood there with the box in one hand and her shirt in the other.

Ronnie spun her around by the hair and Dinky's elbow smashed into her face. She screamed and let go, dropping the knife. Dinky crouched and bolted for the crack she knew was only fifty metres away, expecting a bullet to smash into her back at any moment. They were yelling loudly behind her but she presented as small a target as possible. She ran blind along the black rock and stumbled on pieces of wood they had gathered from the shore. Suddenly, the lights of the quad illuminated all before her and her heart sank. The engine revved up and she knew they would be on top of her in seconds. The crack opened to her right and she entered it in full flight hitting her shoulder as she went but she knew she had to get past the dog leg to avoid being shot.

She held her chest with one hand and put the other out in front of her. Just as the light penetrated the crack she saw the wall in front of her and veered left into the blackness.

There were screams of anger behind her that only served to drive her faster. She emerged through the crack and the silver sheen of the salt was before her. She ran onto the salt and headed north. They would have to follow her on foot or if they discovered the crack ran through to the lake they would have to get the quads onto the salt and she would head up and over the rock. She was breathing heavily but her focus was on distance and she ran several hundred metres along the salt before stopping to get breath. It suddenly dawned on her that she was dressed in shorts only. That was put to the back of her mind as she scanned the rock face for a way to get on top. She had to go where they could not; she was young and they were old, adrenalin was pumping through her and she was oblivious to the pain in her feet and elbow.

She managed to find a steep slope littered with broken rock and scrambled up. The ridge wasn't high but the effort left her gasping for breath. From here, she caught a glimpse of the quads' tail lights heading away from her. The engine noise was not from one quad and she soon saw all three round the bluff and descend onto the salt. They didn't come her way, they headed straight out into the lake and she headed inland as quickly as she could, fearful that she might run off the inside edge of the rock. She had to go slowly, her bare feet were bleeding and her elbow felt as if it was broken. The lights on the quads suddenly went off and everything was quiet. She knew all three of them were out on the salt and unless they came back on foot she was safe. However, she kept going, gritting her teeth in agony at every step.

Lada saw the flash of a quad's headlight ahead and stopped. It wasn't close but it wasn't far away either. They had to wait where they were and assess the situation before going any further. Hanna looked through the scope in the direction they had seen the light and cursed.

"There are three quads now; they must be back at the lake if they left the other one there," she spoke, still holding the rifle at her shoulder.

"Hanna gave a running commentary until the weight of the rifle made her hand it to Elvis They are moving... I have lost them... now I see them – they must be on the lake, I can see the white... Shit! the lights have disappeared." She lowered the rifle and sat back on the quad.

"What do we do now?" she asked, with resignation.

"We must go ahead on foot," Lada answered, and switched off the engine.

They dismounted and suddenly realised how sore they were. Grunts of agony coming from all three eventually ended in light laughter as they had a group hug.

Water was shared equally and they knew there would be no more. Lada looked at Hanna; she was suffering badly. She didn't complain but it was obvious she was in distress. She limped forward but Lada grabbed her by the shoulder.

"You stay with this quad. We will go ahead. Wait a half hour and come to us. If there is a need to stop you we will come back," she suggested.

Hanna didn't answer; she handed Lada her weapon and hugged her. The two set off towards the lake, Elvis leading and carrying the rifle. It was impossible to judge how far they had to go but they estimated over a kilometre at least. A fast walk soon settled down to a more sustainable pace and they resigned themselves to the fact they would never again see Dinky as she was. If Manin was out on the salt, there was no way of getting close enough to use the rifle. What they would do to Dinky before he injected her they dreaded to think. Alex was renowned for cruelty; torture, rape and murder were all his specialities whereas Viktor would not kill anybody, it was against his religion. 'Thou shalt not kill' was engrained into him. He didn't mind somebody else killing somebody but not him. He did not consider brain dead as murder; they could still breathe and were alive so he had killed nobody.

Lada was torn between trying to get close on foot and having the quad to go out onto the salt if they had to. She concluded they had little option. She wondered how far behind Ian and the others were and if they would be close before daylight. If there was a plane involved and it landed at first light they would have few options open to them which would prevent it taking off again. If they couldn't get in range with the rifle there was nothing they could do. The ones out on the salt might have a rifle with them as well as hand guns, or there might be one in the plane; it was impossible to estimate distance in a featureless environment such as the salt lake. They would have to get close enough to be certain; they had little ammunition and certainly not enough to exchange fire from a distance. They had both Hanna's and Elvis's hand guns but they were only of use in close quarter situations. She concluded they had to get close. They had to get Manin and Alex at any cost.

CHAPTER FOURTEEN

Joe was furious with Clinker's moans and groans, shouting to speed up and shouting to slow down, when he got thrown against the Roo Bar.

"Shut the fuck up!" he screamed at him but it was Ian's voice that came back in the darkness.

"Stop here!" he yelled across the divide.

They stopped both Rovers; Joe, Debbie and Dan got out. Ian climbed out of his forward position and Clinker did likewise; they were both black and blue from constant battering against the Roo Bars. Even with the seat covers wrapped around their legs they were in serious pain. The others were stiff, sore and agitated. Progress seemed agonisingly slow. Ian checked the GPS and Debbie stretched the map out over the bonnet.

"You! Settle down. One more bloody complaint you're staying here!" Joe snapped at Clinker.

"We're getting there, fifteen miles to go and four hours before daylight," Ian said quietly, trying to defuse the situation. Clinker went to say something but Debbie jumped on his case.

"Your bloody moaning won't help Dinky! And won't make us go any faster. Shut up, or stay here, as Ian just told you. Now get a drink, wrap your legs up and get on with the bloody thing," she snapped, scathingly.

The Arid Zone was taking its toll; between the dust, the heat, tiredness and discomfort, all that was missing was the chisellers. Ian felt worse than he had ever felt in his life and couldn't get the dread of facing Mike out of his head. He blamed himself for everything; he couldn't even find reason to blame his father or Lacey. They were both dead and it was he who had fucked up leaving the two fossils to keep watch, thinking nothing could go wrong. Even Lada; he could understand why she went to sleep but she should have alerted them that they were in danger, that was the least she could have done. There again, she did that and nobody took her seriously. Until Hanna and Elvis showed up nobody would have believed her no matter what she said. They had Dinky and the mookas; he would gladly give one for the other but Lada was adamant they would not release her unharmed. He felt sick and helpless, the adrenalin rush was wearing off and reality was setting in as they went forward. A cluster fuck, was his conclusion.

Behind them, the third Rover was moving along at a reasonable speed. The eyebrows were still in position, restricting their visible distance ahead. Several times they were forced to reverse and go around obstacles but they still maintained a speed which would get them to the lake before daylight. Unlike the group ahead, they were more positive, perhaps because they had finished a billy before they left. Wilson had dozed off and, when he woke, Dick fell asleep. Linda was more alert, having to drive, and she, like Ian, was worried to death about Dinky. She was also furious at Lada for not telling them they were in mortal danger and for not telling them she was Russian police. This she couldn't get her head around and kept returning to the same question. What the hell has the Russian police got to do with an Australian opal robbery? She couldn't understand but was bloody determined she would find out if she had to drive to Moscow for answers.

Dick woke up and demanded she stop for a piss, to which Wilson lent his support.

"Check where we are, woman!" Dick shouted at Linda. She cursed the two of them and got the map out. She spread it out on the bonnet and Dick took the GPS coordinates.

"Bloody hell, woman, we are making good time. We're here, that's – eh, let's see, three finger widths that's fifteen miles. Christ, what's the time?" he demanded.

"Two forty-five a.m. Another half an hour and what's left of the moon should appear," Wilson replied.

"You want to sleep, woman?" Dick enquired.

"Can you see to drive?" Linda threw back at him.

"Ya ain't askin' for much, seein' as we can only see ten metres in front of us, are ya?" Dick quipped and climbed into the driver's seat.

"I'll take the window, that'll keep his mind on the road," Linda announced, and let Wilson in next to Dick.

"What the hell am I supposed to do with this hand now, when I'm not changing gear?" Dick asked.

"You can play with bloody Wilson," Linda retorted.

"One has been sacrificed," Wilson observed with disdain.

He wasn't as good as Linda. In the first minute the Rover plunged down a wash and bounced violently before crawling up the opposite bank to screaming gears.

"She set a trap for me," Dick commented, suppressing criticism.

The Rover and, more prominently the driver, settled down after the mishap and within ten minutes Linda was sound asleep.

"I reckon we should stop about five miles from the lake," Wilson advised.

"Yeh, I reckon so. We can wait till we can see where we're going without lights," Dick agreed.

For the next hour they went on slowly, turning and twisting around many obstacles, unable to relax for a second. The lights were hitting the ground little more than a length of the vehicle ahead and concentration was intense. It was Wilson who noted the change in the visibility and the reason wasn't obvious.

"What ya mean, fog?" Dick asked.

"There! In the beam. Little particles, you see them?" Wilson queried.

"I can't see bugger all," Dick replied.

"They come and go; next time I will point them out to you," Wilson promised, and filled his pipe.

"I see them! That's dust!" Dick exclaimed, and stopped the vehicle. He switched the engine off and turned the lights out. He stuck his head out of the driver's window and listened.

"What's happening?" Linda enquired, waking from a deep sleep.

"Shush, woman, listen!" Dick commanded.

The faint sound of an engine could be heard in the distance. All three of them heard it and there was no mistake; it was the sound of a Rover or Rovers.

"Bloody hell, we've caught up with them buggers already!" Dick shouted, and started the engine up. "That's their dust we've been seeing in the headlights!" Dick said excitedly.

"How the hell are we going to get them to stop?" Linda queried.

"Might not stop. Might go straight past, and jump them when they come past us," Dick joked.

It was Clinker who noticed the lights coming behind them. He had such a reprimand he wasn't sure whether to shout out or not but eventually he hammered on the bonnet for Joe to stop.

"What the hell now?" Joe shouted.

"Somebody coming behind us!" Clinker yelled in alarm.

Ian heard him and spun around, he was alarmed also. The vehicle was close, only several hundred yards away at most.

"Switch off the engines! Get out and hide!" he called to everybody. They scrambled out of both Rovers and shot into the darkness. The vehicle came on steadily and Ian's heart leapt as he realised it had to be the third Rover, it couldn't be anything else.

"How the hell did they manage this?" he questioned, as the vehicle came to a standstill behind the other two.

"Want a lift?" Dick's voice boomed out into the night.

They all descended on the Rover at the same time and all wanted to know how the hell they had managed to catch up with them. Ian made straight for the headlights and shook his head as he identified the remains of the bucket.

"Christ! This bastard has a thing about buckets," he mumbled to himself.

"Right! Never mind the bullshit, get into the vehicles and follow their tail lights – move!" Ian yelled and they scattered. "Lead the way, arsehole!" he shouted at Dick and headed for the Rover.

"One suspects they are glad to see us," Wilson declared.

"Yep! He's following an arsehole. What does that make him? The little shit." Dick sniggered and drove between the two Rovers.

Each Rover fell in behind the lead, not side by side as they were previously. Clinker and Ian were nursing their wounds and relishing the comfort of a seat. They were in agony and Ian had to admit they could not have gone on for much further.

Ronnie was in agony; her nose was broken and her teeth had gone through her bottom lip. She would kill that bitch when she got hold of her, she would cut her throat. She had moved so quickly they were all taken by surprise. Alex had fumbled for his gun, handicapped by her shirt in one hand and the mookas in the other. Viktor made haste to grab the gun from his bag but he had zipped it shut to prevent the gun being removed by Dinky. By the time they were armed she had disappeared into the darkness. They only caught a glimpse of her going through the crack then she vanished. Viktor had followed, thinking she was cornered, and cursed when he found out the crack ran all the way through the outcrop and onto the lake side. Both Alex and Ronnie wanted to hunt her down and kill her but Viktor decided otherwise.

"We must get out onto the salt. Put her shirt on," he ordered Ronnie, throwing the shirt at her.

She took off her own shirt and used it to stem the flow of blood from her nose. She couldn't button up Dinky's; it had no buttons so she tied the tails together across her middle.

"I'll take care of you when we get out into the lake," Viktor assured her.

They drove onto the lake, using the headlights to clear the boulders and reached the salt. Viktor estimated they were at least five hundred metres from the shore when he switched off the lights and they stopped. They were safe here and there was no way anybody could approach them without being seen. He noted a loom of light appearing on the horizon to the east. The moon would illuminate the salt in a silver sheen and, when daylight came, Peter would soon appear. They were in good shape and there was no reason to go after the girl. She had served her purpose; they wouldn't dare come after them in the dark and by the time daylight appeared they would be too late. He set about cleaning up Ronnie's face, which was now badly swollen.

"I want to go back and get her," Ronnie seethed.

"We don't go back, we stay here. The girl did well. She must have known the escape route wasn't far away; we didn't. It's our fault she escaped. Your face will get better and we have what we came for," Viktor assured her.

Alex laid down the mooka box for the first time; stretching his legs and arms, he sat on the side of the quad and watched the moon appear across the salt lake. Even he was impressed by the serenity of what was evolving, the tranquillity and mystical beauty which enveloped the lake, calming his temper. Viktor was right; the girl had done well and there was nothing to gain by going after her. He would have liked to strip her and satisfy his lust on her but she was a mere toy; she had served her purpose. His eyes fell on Ronnie and a rare smile etched his face.

Viktor washed Ronnie's face clean of blood and used her shirt as a towel to dry her and his hands. Both her eyes were nearly closed but her nose had stopped bleeding. He gave her a painkiller from his bag; she looked frightened as he rummaged in it until he found them. She knew what was in that bag and she would gladly ram the needle into that girl if she got the chance, this time with a full dose. The silvery shaft of light allowed her a look in the rear vision mirror and she was horrified at what was looking back at her. She would never grab anybody by the ponytail again.

Dinky could make out the dark shape out on the salt; the reflection of the moon was directly in line with her. She could wait where she was or she could move further west. She knew she could never outrun them if they came looking for her on foot and now the moon was casting some light on the terrain she felt extremely exposed. If she watched from her present position she would see if they moved, but they could get to her position in minutes and she wouldn't be able to outrun them. On the other hand, if she moved she would lose sight of them and she wouldn't know if they were after her or not. The sunrise would spell her end if they were looking for her. She was on her own. She gritted her teeth and started moving west; cut feet or not, she had to move.

She managed to get down from the ridge on the west side, sliding most of the way on her bum and using her heels as brakes. It was painful but she felt sand below her feet instead of stones and her spirits lifted. She headed west; she was at least half a mile to the north of the old campsite and able to move faster. The only problem she had now was her footprints; they were easy to follow on the sand and spending any effort or time to try and hide them was not an option. She kept going as fast as she could.

Mallee bushes appeared ahead of her and she sought refuge behind them. She rested there for several minutes, breathing heavily. She had no water and thirst was starting to agitate her. She had forgotten all about being topless, it didn't matter; her aches and pains overshadowed modesty and she felt like screaming defiance. The comfort she got was from the pain in her elbow; she knew whatever part of Ronnie had been on the receiving end of it would be feeling a lot worse than her elbow was. She sat for a while and assessed her situation. She was well north of the track to East Well and she knew the only help she could expect at daylight would come from there. Should she risk heading more south or keep going west? She would cook if she was exposed to the sun; she looked at the white of her breasts and her mind was made up. She was in enough pain without looking for more; she headed southwest.

The going was good; her body had accepted the pain and it became bearable. She jarred her feet against several stones and cursed but kept going. Her ears were her best sense; she couldn't see very well in the dim light but she could hear and that was a comfort. The deathly silence was shattered by the sound of an engine starting up not far ahead of her; it was a quad and panic froze her to the spot, her heart was thumping and she was shaking uncontrollably. She fell to the ground and wept. She had walked right into them and she was dead. She waited for the lights to shine on her and the fate awaiting her in total resignation. But the quad moved east slowly without lights on. They hadn't seen her; she could still escape. She tried frantically to get up, her legs refused to support the effort and she stumbled several times before crawling herself upright. She headed north away from them as fast as she could.

Lada and Elvis had made their way towards the old camp as quickly as they could. The moon coming into view was helpful but they were heading towards it and had to shade their eyes to make out the obstacles in their path. The bluff was now very visible and they had a good sense of distance as Lada knew how high it was. They slowed to stalking speed several hundred metres from the bluff and went forward cautiously. Lada decided to scan the area with the rifle scope. She could see nothing in the shade of the bluff and searched out onto the salt where she had seen the quads go. She could see nothing there either and they continued cutting north and putting the bluff between them and the lake. They were now in the darkness and waited several minutes before going on.

"They're not here," Lada whispered.

Elvis sighed; she was pumped up, alert and ready for anything except another disappointment. They went ahead slowly and came in contact with the rock face beside the crack which was where Lada had intended. She confirmed her position and entered the crack. Elvis followed curiously behind her. They reached the dog leg and headed out towards the edge of the lake. Lada raised the rifle again and viewed the scene through the scope. A small black obstacle was visible hundreds of metres out in the salt. She cursed silently and they headed back through the crack.

"Stay here, I will get Hanna," Lada said, handing Elvis the rifle.

She headed west, back towards where they had left Hanna. She had only travelled half a mile when she heard the quad's engine ahead to her right. She sprinted north and soon the sound was coming towards her. She waited, unsure how to attract Hanna's attention. She was glad she had Hanna's revolver; at least she wouldn't shoot her if she suddenly appeared out of the gloom. She had nothing white on, her clothes were covered in red dust and she was bronzed all over except her breasts and bum and she couldn't wave that around in any convincing fashion. Not the bottom half at any rate. She peeled off her shirt quickly and started jumping up and down waving the shirt above her head. She didn't want to shout but was forced to as Hanna threatened to bypass her.

The quad stopped and Hanna peered into the gloom. It was Lada's voice she could hear but she couldn't see her at first. Then she made out the white strip hurtling towards her and smiled at what appeared beside her.

"Topless in starlight, that's new!" she greeted Lada.

Hurriedly Lada put her shirt back on and jumped onto the quad.

"Keep going left, then straight ahead. Give me some water," Lada panted.

They came into the lee of the bluff and stopped the quad. Elvis came out of the shadows and joined them.

There were still two hours until daylight and Lada knew she had to get on top of the bluff before that. She didn't fancy crawling along the top and she knew the only way up was several hundred yards away on the lake side.

"I will go up there with the rifle and get as close to the end of the rock as I can. We can't see yet what's going on out there or if they are out there. There is something, but it could be a decoy; it's impossible to tell. They could have gone on with two quads. You say they had three; they could have left one out there as a decoy and we need to find out as soon as there is light enough to see. We have two hours to wait so I will go now and get on top," Lada outlined her thinking.

"I will go with you. We need two on top; there is nothing we can do from down here," Elvis announced.

She was right and Lada's objection was curtailed by Hanna.

"You fall, we're finished and I think I had better head back," Hanna added.

"Back where?" Elvis said, alarmed at the thought.

"Back to intercept the ones coming behind us. There's nothing I can do here, is there?" she stressed.

"You could sleep!" Lada suggested.

"If I go to sleep I will never wake up. Take the water with you, it could get hot up there," she said, and mounted the quad.

The two of them headed through the crack, taking care not to scratch themselves this time. They had boots on and were able to negotiate the foreshore easily. They decided not to venture onto the salt; that would invite detection as the moonlight was shining at them. They had plenty of time and made their way to the slope in a leisurely fashion. As Lada had expected, it was steep and loose. She had no idea Dinky had climbed the same slope several hours before. Reaching the top, they headed back in the direction they had come. Now they had to be careful and they knew the crack was ahead of them; they had to cross it to get to the end of the bluff. From memory, Lada knew there was a narrow part on the dog leg and she advised Elvis crossing there would allow them to stay in the middle of the rock rather than risking the edge.

They reached their target in good time and crossed without trouble. The top of the ridge was shelved like the sides and they headed as far out towards the end as possible before squatting down in a depression between two shelves. Lada made herself comfortable sitting with her back against the rock and her legs outstretched. Elvis lay down and rested her head on Lada's thigh. Lada stroked her forehead. Elvis was exhausted and she fell asleep quickly. Lada stared out across the salt and focused on the area where she had seen the dark object; she would not sleep. She was thinking about Dinky and she was saddened by their failure to intercept Manin before he went onto the salt. What could they do now? She had no idea.

Hanna left them and headed west; she could see more detail with the moon behind her and after travelling a mile inside the shelter of the bluff she headed more south and increased her speed. She felt fine when she was moving but even the short stop had allowed her fatigue to catch up with her brain. It had since been kicked into touch and her focus was entirely on what was ahead of her. The two Rovers would be far behind, she knew that, but she had to stop them from coming into sight from the lake. Lada had knowledge of this area, all of them had been here before and she was confident she could get them to the bluff as Lada had guided her.

At about five miles she stopped and waited, straining her senses trying to detect anything, visual or audio. Several kangaroos had leapt around in front of her and disappeared into the bush but there was silence when she switched off the engine. She would walk around, determined not to sit down as she knew she would be asleep in minutes. After running around the quad, sitting on top of the roll bar and doing press-ups against the seat, she suddenly saw a flicker of light to the west. She jumped onto the quad excitedly and started the engine. She headed west slowly, looking through squinted eyes for another flicker of light and she saw another shortly afterwards. It was as well she had come back; these idiots had their lights on! How bloody stupid could they get? she seethed, stopping to listen for engine noise. They were far enough away she couldn't hear them and she decided to head towards them instead of waiting; the sooner they switched the lights off the better.

Hanna was taken by surprise when she suddenly realised they were nearly on top of her. She stopped facing them and flashed her headlights on and off once. There was a yell from ahead of her and the vehicles stopped. She went ahead into the light and was greeted with a resounding cheer from the Rovers.

"Thank God it's you! Look at you!" Debbie yelled at her as she grabbed her around the waist.

Hanna was a sight, covered in red dust and matted blood around her knee. She didn't realise how weak she was until she tried to act normal. Ian grabbed her and carried her to the Rover.

He put her into the passenger's seat and handed her the water bag. They all stared at her as she quenched her thirst.

"Dinky?" Clinker spoke quietly.

Hanna looked at him and shook her head.

"We don't know, they are out on the lake. Lada and Elvis are on top of the rock with the rifle but they are a long way out. We don't know if the three quads are there or if they left a decoy. You must go to the old campsite; Lada told me you know it well but you must keep the rock between you and the lake. You can't use the lights, it's too much of a risk," she said, definitively.

Ian's mind was in turmoil; he had to get there before daylight.

"How far is it? I mean how long to get there on the quad?" he asked.

"Half hour, no more," Hanna replied.

Ian turned to Dick who was leaning out of the Rover window.

"Take them north, get the bluff between you and the lake and don't make too much noise. You can't use the lights now so go easy. I'll take Dan with me and get there on the quad. You sleep!" He patted Hanna on the shoulder and left.

She didn't object and Debbie washed her face; she was again impressed by the beauty of what lay below the dust.

Ian and Dan headed towards the old camp, both of them dreading what lay ahead.

"If these bastards are out on the salt? There's no way of getting near them without being seen and Dinky wouldn't stand a chance, they would kill her," Dan voiced what Ian was thinking. The situation seemed hopeless but Ian knew the Rovers were fast, faster than any quad; if they could arrive in time they would have another asset, another three assets. Getting to the mafia wasn't a problem; they had two rifles and two hand guns. Four vehicles, they could come at them from four different directions and kill all of them, but at what cost?

Dinky, and nothing was worth her life, not even killing her killers.

Ian headed towards the bluff; it was much easier to see from the quad and the moonlight was reflecting from the salt like a giant, silver mushroom, the bluff cutting into it black and distinct. The reflection indicated there was still a fine layer of water on the salt. If the object out there was a decoy they would have to follow the tracks of the other quads with the Rovers at full speed, as they could be many miles away.

He stopped where he estimated the crack to be and Dan followed him into the opening.

"I'm going up. You stay here and wait for the others," he instructed Dan and made his way to the dog leg. The climb wasn't as difficult as he had envisaged; however, he was acutely aware that any slip could spell disaster. The walls were close enough to brace against and he made his way to the top quickly, feeling around the top for a good handhold before committing himself to his arms only. He heaved himself onto the top and lay there gasping. Despite his efforts he opened the wounds he had suffered two days before and blood ran down his forearms. He called out to Lada and she answered 'Here!' Unsure whether to stand up or not, he made his way to where her voice had come from crouched.

He saw the two of them laying in the depression and immediately realised Elvis was asleep. He kissed Lada on the cheek and sat beside her. She handed him the rifle and indicated he look out onto the lake.

The view from the elevated position was fantastic, moonlight turning the lake into a silver cauldron of sparkling crystal. Ian held the rifle in firing position and scanned the terrain slowly. He stopped on the black dot far out in the lake and his heart sank.

"What do we do now?" he whispered to Lada.

"Wake me as soon as daylight appears, or if they move," she answered, also in a whisper.

Ian watched as her head sank slowly forward; she was exhausted. He looked at his watch and estimated another hour and a half until daylight. Any sleep would rejuvenate both of them and at the moment there was little else they could do. He rested the rifle on the rock in front of him and fixed his sights on the target. He had no idea whether the quads were in range of the rifle. He started going through every scenario he could think of and could see no way they could get Dinky before they harmed her; it was impossible to get near them without being seen.

Dan lay down beside the rock face; there was nothing he could do either. Wait until the Rovers arrived, wait for daylight; he dozed off. Hanna had estimated they were five hundred metres out on the salt and, like Ian, he concluded there was no practical way to get to Dinky unobserved.

Dinky was very afraid; she was terrified by the sound of the quad when she nearly walked into it. She was shocked and confused; she hadn't heard the quad until the engine started up, how it got there without her hearing it was scary. When it went east she had run north. Then she heard it coming back. This put her into blind panic and she headed further north as fast as she could. Her legs were starting to wobble below her and every bone in her body was screaming for her to stop, but she was so terrified she wept and stumbled forward. Eventually, she collapsed on a sand dune and lay there gasping, the sky was spinning above. Stars were wandering all around the moon. Then the lights went out.

Joe was leading the three Rovers along the route Ian had stipulated, keeping well to the north towards the bluffs. The going was slow but steady. Those not driving were sleeping, all except Wilson. He was deep in thought. Linda was leaning her head on his shoulder and the only sound other than the engine was an occasional curse from Dick as obstacles were met, by-passed or driven over. Wilson wasn't totally convinced these people were intending to be picked up by plane but no matter what alternatives he came up with there seemed no other way they could get safely out of the lake without exposing themselves to a very long drive. They had to get Dinky back safely; that was all that mattered. He would have loved to see the cause of all this trouble, the mookas, but whether he saw them or not, all that mattered was the girl's welfare. He felt sorry for Ian; he knew he was very distressed but this was damage limitation. The damage had been done and from experience he knew they had to read the situation as it developed; no amount of speculation would help. He knew also they must act decisively if an opportunity presented itself. They would have three Rovers and a quad in position before daylight, undetected with any luck. They were armed, something the man called Manin overlooked. However, Manin's interpretation of the situation had proven correct. Had the two Russian girls not appeared with the quad there was no way they could get near them undetected before daylight. As it was now, it looked like they would arrive at the old camp just before daylight. That was only achievable with the knowledge they had; they knew where Manin and company were.

Ahead, Joe could make out the distinct shape of the bluff where the old camp was and headed more north, making sure it was between them and the lake. He knew they would have to drift to the south to avoid the rugged terrain west of the bluff but he was confident they would make it before daylight. The shimmer of reflected moonlight was getting more pronounced by the minute and eventually the surface of the lake appeared in a thin silver line to the right of the bluff.

"Thank Christ for that," he mumbled to himself.

Clinker sat beside him and snored steadily. Joe didn't object; he would rather he snored than complained. He was glad to see he had fallen asleep before he had to strangle him. Desperate people are dangerous people and Clinker was desperate with anxiety over Dinky. He would have to watch him closely when they arrived, before he did something stupid. He would get Dick or Wilson to lay the law down. He didn't trust himself to do that without punching him and Clinker didn't take kindly to being punched.

Debbie followed up the rear of the convoy. Hanna was spread across two seats and she was out for the count. Several times Debbie had to stop her coming off the seats as the Rover bounced along; they were only going slow but some of the ruts and boulders caused violent reactions from the springs. Her mind was also on Dinky; at least they would be in a position to help her if the chance presented itself. If those two cops hadn't arrived? Without the quad their present situation would have been impossible. She was worried about Dan and Ian, but her main concern was Elvis; she must be worse than Hanna and she was dangerously exhausted. Debbie slammed the brakes on as she saw the Rover ahead stop suddenly. She waited and saw Joe speak to Dick, then approach her.

"Debs, we only have a short way to go so we will go one at a time. Switch off your engine. When I stop, Dick will go; when he stops you go, OK? Get out and listen, then, we don't have much time," he instructed, and headed back to the lead Rover.

Debbie did as requested and joined Dick, stretching himself against the Roo Bar.

"He reckons you're deaf so I have to listen for you," she baited Dick.

"My arse is deaf, give it a rub!" Dick requested.

"Massage?" she suggested, slapping him hard across the arse.

311

"Fuck me dead, woman!" he responded and jumped away from her.

"Shush! Listen and take your mind above your waist," she said, quietly. "You'll waken everybody up."

The Rover ahead disappeared and shortly after the engine went silent. Dick waited a few minutes and went ahead. When his engine was switched off, Debbie did likewise. She came under the rock face before she made out the two vehicles parked side by side ahead of her; she parked the third one beside them and switched off the engine.

The ones who were awake joined her and Joe ushered them towards the quad, which was hard alongside the cliff. Dan hadn't woken up; he was still sound asleep beside the quad and they left him sleeping. Joe was tempted to go on top of the bluff to see what was happening but Wilson objected.

"There are three people up there already, that's enough. They only have one rifle. If we're needed, we won't have time to wait for somebody to come down. Stay here and wait," Wilson insisted.

Ian had noted their arrival one by one and he was impressed with whoever decided that was the quietest way to approach. He hadn't taken the scope off the target whilst the Rovers traversed the last leg of the journey; he was looking for any movement which might indicate they had heard the engines but nothing stirred on the salt lake. He could not make out details; if all three quads were there they must be parked close together and in line. If there were any people there they were keeping the vehicles between them and the beach.

All went quiet as they returned to the Rovers and relaxed; everybody was dog-tired except Dick and Wilson, who were very much alert. Years of command had tuned their senses to overcome such temptations; they walked to the end of the bluff and looked out onto the silver world. They couldn't see anything but the walk was good.

"I wonder if they would smell my pipe," Wilson voiced his concern.

"There's no wind. Buggered if I know, light the bloody thing up and take a puff. Stay inside the Rover," Dick suggested; he knew Wilson needed his pipe when he was thinking.

They had half an hour before dawn would start to break. The sky was clear and Ian knew daylight would come quickly when it started. If a plane was going to land here at first light, as he suspected, it would be airborne by now, unless it was coming from somewhere close. He had a sudden desire to grab Lada and shake the hell out of her. Who were they? What were they? How were they involved? Why were the Russian police involved? What the hell did all this have to do with the mookas? He seethed, then calmed down quickly as he remembered the task at hand and that was to get Dinky at all costs; everything else could wait.

CHAPTER FIFTEEN

Ian tugged on Lada's shirt and her eyes opened.

"It's time," he said quietly.

She nodded her head and shook Elvis. She woke up instantly and looked at Lada. Silently, Elvis sat up and Lada moved next to Ian. She took the rifle from him and sighted the scope on the target. The quads were there grouped together and clearly all three were there. She looked at Ian and put her hand on his arm.

"They are all there," she spoke quietly.

It was still dawn, not yet fully daylight, but she could make out the quads, nothing else; no movement, no people.

"We wait," she concluded, and reached for the water.

Elvis crawled beside them and Ian found himself sandwiched between the two of them. Elvis rested her head on one shoulder, Lada on the other. Any other time he would have been in seventh heaven but he just put an arm around each and gave them a squeeze; there was nothing to be said. They waited.

Lada looked again through the scope. As Ian had thought, it was getting lighter by the minute.

She tensed and lowered the rifle.

"I can see Dinky – look." She handed the rifle to Ian.

The figure sitting on the quad was unmistakably Dinky; her brilliant yellow shirt was unmistakable.

Ian lowered the rifle and cursed silently. He looked at Lada.

"I see her. What now?" he asked.

That's good. She is there, and she is alive. If Manin had injected her she wouldn't be sitting on top of a quad. She would be lying on the ground," Lada answered.

"How far do you think they are?" Elvis asked, and Ian handed her the rifle.

"You tell me?" he answered.

"At least five hundred metres! That's not too far for this rifle," Elvis answered, definitively, and Lada agreed.

"We can't shoot three people with one shot. The instant we kill one, the others will kill Dinky, and there is no way we can be sure of hitting anything at this range. If we fire and she makes a run for it, they will shoot her. She has no cover," Lada pointed out to Ian.

"OK, that strategy would be a disaster, I agree, but we have to think of something. The Rovers can do more than a hundred miles an hour; we could get to them in no time. Getting them is easy, it's her we have to worry about, Bloody hell!" Ian smashed his knuckles into his palm in frustration.

Wilson sucked on his pipe and stared at the windscreen. He gave a grunt and climbed down from the Rover.

"We must negotiate!" he said to Dick.

Dick looked at him as if he had lost his mind.

"Negotiate with what?" Dick asked, making no attempt to hide his scepticism.

"The way I see it is, we are here in strength. I believe if we show them what strength we have, they will have no choice but to release the girl in exchange for their own escape. Just an option!" Wilson stated.

"They give us Dinky, we let them go!" Dick condensed Wilson's proposal.

"That's about it," Wilson agreed.

"And how the hell are we going to do that?" Dick was keen to know.

"With a white flag and a show of force. I can think of no other way," Wilson replied.

Dick remained silent; he didn't like the idea. They could kill Dinky as soon as they saw the Rovers going onto the salt. The threat was specific, 'follow us and she will die'. It was a hell of a risk. Dan's shout cut into his thoughts,

"Come here!" he yelled. "Look at this!" He pointed at the ground.

"Blood! And a lot of it!" he exclaimed, crouching beside the stained ground.

"Holy shit!" Dick whispered.

"This is a major bleed. It's into the sand half an inch," Dan concluded and scanned the area carefully.

"Cover it up!" Dick commanded and scraped sand over the blood with his boot. Dan assisted and the stain disappeared. Dan looked at Dick for an explanation.

"Clinker! If he sees that he will go mental," Dick said, as the others approached.

"What have you lot found?" Debbie asked.

"Only tracks, of little value now we know where they are," Dan replied.

"What do we do now?" Debbie asked.

Dick looked at the sky, then at Wilson.

"You're right, we have no choice. Get Ian down here as fast as he can and get something white we can use as a flag. Move! We don't have much time," Dick commanded.

Joe called up to attract Ian's attention and Hanna led Debbie to the sheets tied around the quad frame.

Ian heard his name and made his way to the inside edge of the Bluff. He looked over, lying on his belly; it was a long drop to the bottom.

"What's up?" he called down to Joe but it was Dick who answered him.

"We're going to negotiate and we don't have time to screw around; can you get down easy?" he asked Ian.

"No! Down's gonna be tricky," he answered.

"OK, stay up there. Me and Wilson will take one Rover out to them with a white flag. The other two Rovers will go onto the salt and stop there. We'll try and get Dinky back or we will ram the plane when it lands."

"Bloody hell! What if they take you two as well?" Ian replied in alarm.

"If I raise my hands above my head tell Lada she has to put a bullet close to whoever we are speaking to. Don't hit him, just let them know we are armed."

"They're too far away!" Ian retorted.

"Right! We'll try and get one of them to come closer. A hundred metres? Or more?" Dick queried.

"A hundred would be enough, but more would be better," Ian replied.

Debbie and Hanna came with the sheet; it looked more like the stripes of America but the spaces between the dust were white.

"This is all we've got," Debbie explained.

"It'll do, find something to tie it to. Wilson, we don't have much time. If this plane lands before we get to them, we're done. Come on! Get two drivers organised and the rest stay here."

There was a bustle of activity as those still asleep were extracted from the vehicles and the engines were started. Dan grabbed Dick's arm tightly to get his attention.

"I'm coming with you. We can take that Rover, Debbie's." Dick went to object but stopped.

There's a drone in that Rover and the controls. You know what they say about keeping drones away from aeroplanes?" Dan smiled.

Dick slapped him on the back. "Keep your bloody head down and if things go tits up we'll need all our options," Dick replied.

Debbie handed Wilson the sheet; it was tied to an old branch.

"We need to put lights on as soon as we hit the salt," Wilson advised Dick

"What about the other rifle?" Linda asked.

"I'll take it in the Rover with me and Clinker," Joe offered.

"That means Debbie will have to drive one vehicle. Linda, you go with Debbie. Just follow us onto the salt and stay there with your lights on, no more. And for Christ sake don't move, not even if you hear gunshots. Don't bloody move – you got that?"

There was no reply and they went to the Rovers. Hanna watched as they climbed into the vehicles and she came to Dick.

He looked at her and couldn't help admiring her beauty, but she was serious and he stared into her eyes.

"If the one who comes to you is the same one who took the girl? Remember one thing. He will not kill you. No matter what he threatens or does he will not shoot you. If it is another, he will kill you. All of you and the girl. Do not mention we are here. If you do even Manin may kill you. You must not say anything about Russian police." She was adamant and her advice was taken by Dick as standing orders, not advice.

"You go and rest, we won't do anything stupid," he assured her.

Viktor had tended to Ronnie's wounds as best he could. The painkillers had worked and he had a few left; they had water and they were out in the safety of the lake. She was sitting on the quad wearing Dinky's shirt as she had been ordered to, Viktor explaining she was the hostage as long as nobody found the other one. From the back she would pass but from the front she looked like a balloon with slits. Alex lay on the seat; there was a thin layer of water still on the salt which was only discovered when he sat on it in the dark. They were exhausted, elated and frustrated. They were also exposed and conscious of the fact.

Dawn had broken with the promise of extreme heat to come. Peter would leave at first light and, according to Ronnie, he would take an hour and a quarter to reach quadrant six. They had segregated the lake into landing areas and six was the closest to their exit point. Alex wondered if choosing six was wise but if they were short of fuel it was wise. However, the quad they left at the campsite had plenty of fuel and all three and the other two had been topped up. They had agreed no radio use, no communications with the plane. Radio communications could be picked up by anybody. Peter had insisted he undertook this mission in exactly the same manner as if he was on a drug run. Treetop level in and out; no detection by radar or radio communications. This strategy had served him well for years and he had no intention of changing things now. Crop sprayers flying low were a common sight throughout Australia and nobody batted an eye seeing one, the tanks which were supposed to hold crop spray being excellent for other cargo.

They had to wait, exposed or not. The girl would be hiding somewhere. Contrary to Ronnie's wish to slit her throat, Viktor had some admiration for the way she escaped. It was so fast, even he had been taken by surprise and he was seldom surprised.

Viktor spun round and stared westward, slitting his eyes in concentration, his focus on the end of the bluff where access to the lake was possible. He saw the headlights of a vehicle come clear of the rock then turn towards him.

"We have company!" he yelled at Alex and Ronnie.

Alex sprang from his rest position, revolver in hand. He ducked behind the quad and stared at the developments. Ronnie did likewise.

Two more vehicles followed the first and Alex cursed. Ronnie was cowering beside Alex and she stared in disbelief at what was developing.

"You have fucked up this time, Viktor!" Alex proclaimed.

Viktor wasn't listening; he was concentrating on how to combat this threat and indeed what threat was being presented.

The first Rover stopped and the other two came beside it and also stopped. The centre one switched on the hazard lights and started coming towards them. The two remaining stayed stationary with their headlights still on.

Alex checked his firearm and so did Viktor; they had plenty of ammunition. He scanned the horizon to the south looking for any sign of the plane but the sky was empty.

"We can rush them with the quad, they are stupid sending only one vehicle," Alex spoke out loud.

Viktor raised his hand for him to be quiet and wait. The vehicle was nearing slowly and Viktor made out the figure waving something above it. It was a flag of some kind; an occasional flash of white could be seen but only sporadically.

"These stupid Australians want to negotiate," Alex seethed.

"If they had the girl they wouldn't negotiate. Ronnie, take off that shirt and put your own one on. Alex, tear a seat free from the quad and put it into the girl's shirt. Move quickly!" Viktor ordered. "Ronnie! Does Peter have a weapon in the plane?" he asked.

"Yes, he has a rifle of some sort. I don't know what," she replied, stripping the shirt free of her head; grimacing at the pain it caused she passed it to Alex. The seat came off with a sudden crack and Alex stuffed it inside Dinky's shirt.

"No head!" he shouted at Viktor.

"Lay it down; I'll go to them and keep them at a distance, they won't be able to see anything. Keep down and out of sight. As long as they think we have the girl they won't do anything. They could stop the plane from take-off but if Peter has a rifle in it they won't get close enough to bother us; we just have to buy time until the plane gets here." Viktor mounted a quad and started the engine. He passed his revolver to Ronnie, who looked at him as if he was an idiot.

"They get me? You're on your own," he said, and started heading in the direction of the approaching Rover.

Viktor speeded up; he didn't want them too close and he only eased back when the Rover stopped about a hundred and fifty metres from his previous position. He could see clearly now that one of the old men he had approached at their camp was holding the flag and it appeared the other one was driving. Viktor slowed down and came face on to the Rover. He stopped twenty metres in front of it and waited silently.

"This bastard's got some nerve." Dick's voice filtered up to Wilson, who put the flag down and shouted to Viktor.

"The girl, sir! We have come for the girl. If you return the girl unharmed, we will leave the lake. you have my word of honour!" Wilson shouted at Viktor.

Viktor smiled; it was as he had deduced: they wouldn't try anything as long as they thought the girl was still captive. He had the bargaining chip, not them.

"Your word of honour means a lot to me. The girl is unharmed and she will be released as soon as the plane is ready for take-off, if you all remain in your present positions and do not approach us. If you do, the girl will be shot. and you, sir, have my word of honour on that!" Viktor replied.

It was a standoff and Wilson needed to say something, anything to change the subject before he demanded something else.

"You have stolen from us. but all we want is the girl back, no more!" he shouted at Viktor.

"No! you are wrong. Ingles stole from us, we have stolen back. You have no idea how much pain was suffered because of him and the other one. We are taking what we lost!" Viktor's voice was getting spiteful and Wilson wasn't keen to push the subject.

"Very well sir, we will wait here! We will allow the plane to leave as soon as the girl is seen to be safe."

"The girl is tied to the quad. She will remain there until we leave. As soon as the plane moves for take-off you can go and get her – agreed?" Viktor outlined his requirement.

"Agreed," Wilson replied, thinking that would be the end of negotiations, but he was wrong.

"One other thing! Switch off your engine, and throw the keys to me, so there is no misunderstanding – the keys will be left with the girl," Viktor instructed.

Dick cursed but Wilson persuaded him to do as instructed and hand him the keys. This he did, and Wilson threw the keys close to the quad. Viktor nodded with satisfaction and scooped the keys up without getting off the quad. He turned and headed back to the others.

"That's fucked it!" Dick exclaimed as Wilson joined him inside the cab.

"Dan! Get that thing ready to fly, don't let them see you. Keep it, and you, out of sight," Wilson instructed. "So far so good." he advised Dick.

"You trust that bastard, Wilson?" Dick enquired.

"Strangely enough, I do," Wilson replied.

"Yeh! He gets me that way as well. A good job Lada knows the other side of him or we might have invited him for coffee. He's one smooth customer that one. A dangerous bastard," Dick concluded.

Dan opened the rear door as directed and began unpacking the drone. There was little room for him to work but he quickly located everything he had removed for transportation and started fitting the rotor blades onto the eight drives. This was accomplished quickly and he inserted the batteries, switched the monitor on and tested the result. The rotors were all working, something he was worried about by all the rough terrain they had just traversed; anything could have come loose but, by all accounts, the drone was operational.

"She's ready to go," he panted, from his crouched position in the rear.

"Now we bloody wait," Dick voiced.

"As soon as the plane's engines cover the noise of the drone, send it up, but wait until they are busy," Wilson directed Dan.

Lada took her eye from the telescopic sight with mixed emotions. She had had Manin on the crosshairs for several minutes and could easily have killed him. Dick had drawn him into range but they had them by the balls, as Ian would say; there was nothing she could do that wouldn't endanger Dinky and she resigned herself to losing Manin again.

Ian put his hand on her shoulder and took the rifle from her. There was nothing to say. He scanned the sky to the south and still nothing showed. The sun had some heat in it already and he knew this was another forty degrees day, without doubt. They were already sweating just lying on the rock and the salt was starting to glare. Soon the shimmer of evaporation would make sighting through the telescopic sights difficult, although less so from the elevated position they held than from lake level. He had seen the lights go out on the Rover and the quad going back but could only guess what had transpired between Wilson and Manin. Lada had relaxed when she confirmed it was Manin and not Alex who went to negotiate. She had no idea what Manin looked like but she knew what Alex looked like and it wasn't Alex. Had it been she would have killed him before he killed the three in the Rover, because she knew he would then kill Dinky and suspected he wouldn't stop at her; if there was any objection, he would kill his associates as well, and it wouldn't be the first time.

Manin never killed, it was his belief, but God help Dinky if he got near her with his alternative to death.

They waited silently for another half hour before Elvis drew Ian's attention to movement in the south. He had to squint into the glare but finally picked up the small dot coming low and fast across the lake surface. The Cessna was so low it looked as if it had landed but the speed it approached made that impossible. It touched down three hundred metres to the south of the quads and barely reduced speed as it approached. Ian viewed the scene through the sights as one of them guided the plane in a circle around the quads and stopped it between the quads and Rover sitting silently out on the salt. All they could do was observe and it was frustrating to the point of anguish. Ian put the sights onto the back of Dick's Rover and saw the back door was open to let air flow through. He had not heard the conversations other than the ones shouted to him and had no idea Dan was with Wilson and Dick, let alone that he had a drone in the Rover, until Dan jumped out and the drone shot skyward.

Ian watched as it took height. Simultaneously, the plane's engine changed as the propeller pitch was increased. Slowly the Cessna cleared the quads and Dan immediately sent the drone down towards the abandoned quads. He saw immediately that Dinky's shirt was there and homed in on it. The plane turned to port and headed away from them, going east.

All Dan could see was the shirt; there was nobody in it, only a shirt draped over the seat.

He screamed out to Dick, who had already stepped onto the salt.

"She's not there! Dinky's not there, only her shirt!" he shouted.

"Ram that bloody thing into his propeller!" Dick yelled at Dan.

The Cessna picked up speed quickly and there was no chance the drone could catch it. The Cessna was threatening to clear the salt within several hundred metres and did so on the third jump. She was airborne and pulling steadily away from the drone heading east. Dan steered the machine back to the quads but Dick was already approaching them at a very fast walk.

The Cessna banked to port and stood on its wing. Coming around in an arc. It hadn't climbed and was only a hundred feet high. It headed directly back towards them. What was he playing at, they were away, why come back? Dan flew the drone high and set the camera on the Cessna's nose cone. Up a little, left a little; he had seconds before the craft was on top of them and didn't see the actual impact but he heard the crash as the drone smashed the propeller to pieces. The plane fell almost on top of the Rover, coming down with a resounding crash on the salt, which billowed up all around it, covering the entire structure. Black smoke poured from the wreckage and both Rovers immediately headed at full speed towards the wreck.

Dick looked on in amazement, he was stunned. He held Dinky's shirt in one hand and the keys in the other; he couldn't move and just stared.

Joe leapt from the Rover with a fire extinguisher; Hanna headed for the cockpit, her revolver cocked and ready. She opened the door and looked inside. They were either dead or unconscious; nobody stirred. She grabbed the woman closest and pulled her onto the salt. Flames were coming from the engine compartment and Joe was shouting for another fire extinguisher. Clinker climbed past Hanna and searched frantically for Dinky; she wasn't there. He wrenched Alex out of his seat and threw him out the door. He did the same with Manin and the pilot. The mooka box was on the floor and he kicked it out before hurtling himself after it. They pulled the people clear of the plane quickly; the fire was now threatening to engulf everything. Debbie insisted they had to get further away and they were exhausted before they were clear. There was no explosion; the fire took hold and engulfed the fuselage but it just burned furiously, sending flames a hundred feet into the sky and black smoke higher.

Everything had taken everybody by surprise, it had happened so quickly. Ian, Elvis and Lada were on the ground quickly and headed towards the flames at a fast run. Ian's heart was in his mouth; he had never seen anything like it. His concern for Dinky was making him sick and he threw up before they reached the scene.

Lada went straight to Manin and checked him. Hanna was at Alex. Elvis looked at the woman and Debbie was tearing the pilot's shirt off. Large red welts were appearing where his safety belt had pressed into him on impact; he was alive. So too was the woman, the other two she didn't know. Dan came beside her, he was wide eyed and in shock. She looked at him and immediately understood he had relapsed; he wasn't going to help.

Dick went hurriedly back to the Rover with the keys and they drove the short distance to the crash site. Manin was alive and so was Alex, but they had severe injuries to their spines. Alex opened his eyes first and grimaced; he tried to reach for his gun but couldn't move. Hanna had removed it from the shoulder holster immediately and Manin's bag was still in the burning plane; he wasn't armed. Lada poured water across his lips and passed the bag to Hanna who did the same with Alex. They were in a bad way but they would live. The woman, despite her appearance, seemed to come around with all her faculties; she was in the rear seats with Viktor, the other two in the front and she had a seat belt on. Viktor and Alex had no belts on. The pilot's legs were broken and his head had been in contact with something sharp, splitting his forehead open. He was groaning in pain.

"Dan! Move your bloody arse!" Dick yelled at him, and he suddenly snapped out of wherever he had been. Debbie saw the change and looked at Dick.

"That worked!" she said in appreciation. "Help me here!" she yelled at Dan and he responded.

"Looks like back injury; we must keep him still," Debbie explained, holding Alex's head between her knees.

Lada looked down at Manin and smiled. He was staring at her and he looked so humble, so trusting and so human; the animal he truly was she found hard to believe. He looked young but she knew he wasn't. She didn't trust herself to speak to him and left him in the care of Linda and Joe. She went to the woman; she was sitting up, leaning her back against the wheel of the Rover. She stared at the burning wreckage, transfixed.

Lada crouched in front of her blocking her view. Ronnie was in shock and couldn't fully comprehend what had happened. This beauty in front of her only added to her confusion. Part of the dream.

"The girl! Where is she?" Lada asked her softly.

Ronnie's eyes rolled in her head and she shrugged. Lada waited and repeated the question. The response was the same; she just shrugged and this time held her hands out palms upwards in resignation.

Lada was tempted to slap her across the face but she realised the woman was traumatised and in deep shock; any attempt at extracting information by force would only make her worse. The pilot hadn't been here long enough to know anything and the two Russians would never tell her where Dinky was or, as she feared, Dinky's body. There was other work to be done; she had to let the others deal with this situation.

CHAPTER SIXTEEN

The rising sun had fallen on Dinky's prone body, the heat causing her to squirm on the sand. It stuck to her sweat, but it was the chisellers that dragged her into consciousness. She tried to open her eyes but they were stuck shut. The chisellers were having a feast in her nose and around her eyes. Some were perched on the red sand around her right elbow, others were crawling all over her breasts and legs.

She stirred and a cloud of flies hit the air. They settled back on her immediately she lay still. With great effort she managed to prise her eyelid apart with her left hand and screamed in pain as sand entered her eye. It jolted her upright, tears welling from her left eye. She tried again to move her right arm; there was little pain, it just seemed to be stuck. She reached for it with her left hand but it wasn't there. She was sitting on top of her hand and it had gone dead. She rolled to her left and pulled her hand clear. Her arm suddenly became alive with pins and needles, adding to her discomfort. She was more careful with her right eye and prised the lids apart without any sand entering. She sat there and suffered; slowly the feeling came back into her right arm and she started to feel better all over, even cursing the chisellers.

Her mouth was dry and she could feel her lips starting to crack as slowly her senses returned, each sense making her feel worse. She lowered her head and pulled her knees up under her chin, wrapped her arms around her legs and stayed like that for several minutes. Her feet began to demand her attention and her elbow was now throbbing. She opened both eyes and stared at the terrain. Her memory returned slowly and she knew she was in trouble, without knowing exactly why. She turned her head and looked towards the sun. She squinted again and again there was something wrong with the sun, it had a big black tail hanging down from it. She followed the tail to the ground and the tail was going up not down; this was strange, her eyes were playing tricks on her. She closed both eyes and waited several minutes before she opened them. The tail would be gone. Suddenly, the heat increased and she opened her eyes. The tail had moved away from the sun and the full force of it was on her.

Dinky tried to stand up several times and the world spun around her. She fell back onto the sand, but repeated the effort until finally she was upright. Her legs responded reluctantly and she slowly made her way towards the tail; it must be smoke, it could only be smoke. As she moved, the memory of her terrifying ordeal in the darkness began to return. She tried to work out where she was but had no idea. The only thing drawing her towards it was the smoke. There must be people there but what people she didn't know. Her feet were hurting when she reached the stony ground and she started picking her way from one sand hill to the next. A cloud of chisellers accompanied her but she didn't have the strength to brush them away. She stopped and surveyed the scene ahead. She saw the bluff and instantly her fears returned. The column of smoke seemed to be coming from the end of the bluff. She knew exactly where she was and she knew she had to get there. She would not survive in this heat without protection and water, she had neither.

She came to a stunted mallee tree and it offered a little shade. As she neared it the smoke again covered the sun and it was like a godsend. She noticed the Arid Zone had transformed in places; desert roses were in abundance, the little rain they had had springing life into them. Dinky was amazed at how far she had travelled in the dark. She knew Captain Dick and the others would be looking for her at daylight if they could; she also knew if they didn't come or she missed them she was in deep trouble. Clinker would find her no matter what. He would search for her, she was sure of that. She kept going, not stopping at the tree.

Her body was getting weaker but her mind was getting stronger. Things were becoming clearer and she pushed her fears aside. She could see and that alone bucked her confidence. Her dread of hitting the stony ground soon became a reality and she slowed as she picked her way carefully through the obstacles; her feet were hurting badly and she winced at every step. She stayed close to the higher ground, following along the foot where sand had been blown into long dunes. The sand was hot but soothing to her feet and she was making good progress. The column of smoke was still hiding the sun enough to reduce the burning but it seemed to be less dense than when she first saw it.

She rounded a small outcrop and stared in horror at the quad bike parked alongside the rock face. Panic seized her – they were still here. She collapsed on her knees and sobbed but nothing happened; nobody came to her. There was nobody there. From a state of helplessness, she suddenly realised if she could get to the quad she could drive it away and get back to the others. The smoke was still coming from behind the bluff but there was nothing else moving. Satisfied, she made a quick and painful dash for the quad. It started first time and she headed west at speed, determined nobody would catch her. The smoke must be their signal to be picked up, she could find no other explanation for it and didn't care; she gunned the machine, looking behind at every opportunity to see if anybody was following her. Nobody was and the rush of air was drying her sweat.

Her eyes had been everywhere except on the machine as she stole it. Now she saw the water bag lashed to the frame and she stopped immediately. There wasn't much water in it but she gulped what there was in a frenzy of satisfaction. The frame had some cloth of some kind wrapped around it on one side; she hadn't noticed that either but hurriedly unwound it. She bit through the centre and ripped a hole big enough for her head to go through; she pulled the make-shift poncho over her head and draped it over her shoulders and arms. The relief was instant and her nudity was covered; she was heading home to East Well.

The heat out on the salt was getting intense. Debbie insisted they had to move the injured people into shade and the only shade was the Rovers but leaving them out on the salt didn't make sense. They took the three Rovers back to the bluff and emptied each in turn, folding the seats back so as the injured could be stretched out. One by one they returned and loaded their cargo carefully; only the pilot and the two Russians needed to be laid out, Ronnie could sit, but Lada had a problem. She needed one Rover and insisted the pilot and Manin share the one vehicle. She had her way and gathered Hanna and Elvis to the side. Ian strode towards them defiantly.

"OK, no more bloody secrets. What the hell are you planning?" he demanded.

"Sorry! We're only trying to work out who can drive to the campsite. We need to contact our people to get assistance."

"From Vladivostok!" Ian exclaimed.

They laughed and looked at him with a little sympathy.

"No Ian, we have people on standby, we need to get them here but we have no radio, as you are aware, and the only way is to get back to the campsite and use the phone. And that's two- or three-hours' drive."

"OK, I'm a bit confused at the moment. You have people on standby where, exactly?" he asked, his voice still raised.

"Adelaide," Hanna replied.

"And how the hell are they getting here?" Ian queried, lowering his tone.

"That's what we're discussing and the only way is by plane. We will require medical assistance as well as Australian police," Elvis added.

Ian grunted surrender; he didn't argue. All that was on his mind was Dinky and he was convinced they had killed her and buried her somewhere.

"You sort it out, we will try and find Dinky," he said and returned to Wilson and Dick.

"What's the Kremlin up to?" Dick asked.

"They're going to get help here as fast as they can. We're going to find Dinky. Better take that bloody box with us in case it gets stolen," Ian said, sarcastically.

Hanna limped towards them, Lada and Elvis headed south towards the campsite at speed.

"Come on, girl, give me your arm," Wilson offered Hanna, and supported her as they made their way towards the ancient shoreline.

"Don't know about you lot but I'm bloody starving and Wilson has all the edibles," Dick complained.

"What about the quads out there?" Wilson queried.

"Send the young bucks to get them," Dick answered.

They joined the others. Dan had come good and Debbie was satisfied they had done all they could for the injured. The Rover's AC was on low and the temperature was comfortable inside. Outside, it was becoming bloody hot and anything but comfortable. They had some water but no food and it would be at least six hours before Lada returned; it was going to be a long day.

Ian, Joe and Linda went to get the quads back. Linda was adamant she had to have a go and Clinker was kicked into touch.

On their return, Ian called the men together and they gathered at the rock face, all except Dan. Clinker hadn't spoken for hours; he was deeply distressed and didn't know what to do or what to say. He was worried sick about Dinky and had his eyes on Manin's throat several times and the woman's, but he had been dressed down by Wilson and Dick and he got the message. It was a blessing, however, that they had covered the blood before he saw it or he would have gone crazy.

"Right, here's the situation. Lada and Elvis have gone to the campsite at Mt Ive, they will phone for assistance there; apparently, there are some people who are on standby to assist but don't ask me who the hell they are. Our task is to find Dinky, nothing else. All we can get out of the woman is she doesn't know where she is and the other two can't speak. They might be more helpful later but, for now, we need to look for her around this area. OK, we have four quads; we can search along the edge of the high ground and along the shoreline, two each direction. OK, let's go," he finished and they headed for the quads.

"What's wrong with you? You look like you've been kicked in the balls," Joe voiced, looking at Clinker.

"I've no bike!" he replied.

"What ya mean, no bike? One, two, three and the other one must be here somewhere. Look for the bloody thing," Joe scolded him.

"I've bloody looked and it's not here," Clinker retorted.

"Hanna!" Joe called out and she came. "Where did you leave the quad?" he enquired.

"There!" she said, and pointed towards the rock face.

Ian and Linda were already on their bikes and Joe screamed at them to stop.

"What's up?" Linda shouted.

"There's a quad missing!" Joe yelled back.

Ian switched off his engine and Linda did likewise.

"We had four quads. Now there's only three!" Joe yelled, approaching Ian. He frowned briefly, then a broad smile lit up his face.

"She's alive! The little bugger must have stolen the quad when that shit was happening on the lake!" Ian bellowed in relief and laughed loudly.

"Bloody hell, if she has the quad she'll be heading back to East Well, that's sixty bloody miles away!" Joe exclaimed.

"Don't even think about trying to catch her on the quads. She thinks they are the only ones with quads and if she sees you coming for her she'll keep going till she runs out of fuel. You need to catch her with a Rover so move your arses and get one ready," Dick's voice cut into their haste.

"He's right!" Linda acknowledged and they dismounted.

"Get Manin out of there," Dick ordered Dan, who looked questioningly at him. "We need the Rover. Dinky is alive and she's stolen a quad. We need to catch her with this. Here, grab his legs." Dick moved behind Manin's shoulders and started dragging him out. Dan caught his legs and they laid him on the ground.

Clinker had already mounted the driver's seat and Joe hurriedly reinstated the passenger's seat. Swinging the vehicle around the others, they headed west at speed.

Ian leaned on the bonnet, exhausted but elated; a huge burden had been lifted from him and he shook his head in disbelief.

"She's a hard, little bugger, she'll be OK!" Dick assured him, knowing his concern.

"You lot get this shit sorted out!" Debbie yelled at them and shouted orders until they had Manin in beside the pilot and both of them as comfortable as they could make them.

"I still don't understand why that plane came back towards us. He was away and clear, what possessed him to turn around?" Wilson said to Dick but Debbie heard him also. She was now certain the woman had sustained her facial injuries before the crash. She suspected she had because the bruising was intense, yet there was very little blood and it was obvious her nose was broken and her lip would have bled also.

Debbie leaned beside Ronnie and whispered, "Why did the plane turn around, dear?" she said, kindly. Ronnie raised her swollen face and peered at her through the slits.

"Gloat. He wanted to gloat. Watch the stupid Australians defeated," Ronnie whispered.

"Ah! That simple. Thank you," Debbie said. "They changed direction so as they could gloat on the stupid Australians they just defeated," she announced.

"You've gotta be bloody kidding me?" Dick exclaimed.

"All that because they wanted to give us the fingers, I don't believe it!" Ian declared.

They sat on the quads but the heat was so intense they moved around and into the crack. There was shade there but no comfort, the ground was littered with stones. Hanna stayed with Debbie and Dan; not to help but to make sure none of the injured had a sudden cure. She knew Manin had played dead before and escaped. This time, however, she knew in her heart he was badly injured, as was Alex and she wished them both a long life as vegetables; now they would know what they did to others.

Dick had enough crouching in the crack and the others followed him out.

"I reckon we should open that bloody box," he said, pointing at the mooka box lying against the rock face.

Hanna came close and listened to their conversation. "They reckoned your father stole whatever's in that box from them. That's what Manin was shouting when Wilson was speaking to him. It's theirs and your father stole it from them? Buggered if I know."

Ian was more than curious about the contents of the box but, as Wilson had explained, if it remained sealed they wouldn't

335

have to explain anything about the contents regardless of what it contained.

"It must remain sealed!" Hanna announced and they looked at her.

"OK. Can you at least tell us what the connection is between Andamooka, them in the back, and the Russian police?" Ian asked her.

"Not yet! When my superior comes she will explain everything. You have waited this long, I am sure you can wait a little longer. They will request two planes; one medical and the other will contain the authorities of Australia and Russia. This box must be handed over intact to the Australian police. They will verify the contents, then it will be handed to my superior." Hanna smiled at Ian and he remembered the encounter with her in Vung Tau.

"Pity we can't go for a swim in the meantime."

She knew exactly what he was speaking about and winked.

Lada and Elvis were nearing the end of the lake and watched for tracks cutting across their path. They would lead them to where the quads had entered and the campsite. They saw the tracks; they weren't very distinctive but visible nonetheless. They headed east towards the shore line a few miles distant and soon made out the buildings ahead. Elvis had explained the state the caretaker had been left in and they expected the worst. The Rover climbed out of the lake bed and onto the road leading towards the longhouse and the Winger's quarters.

Whitey stuck his head out of the door and looked curiously at the new arrivals. He smiled when he saw Elvis and hurried out to greet them. He was surprised by the other one, he had never seen her before.

"Hello Mr Whitey," Elvis greeted him with a peck on the cheek. Whitey blushed and eyed Lada.

"Who is this young lady?" he enquired.

"Her name is Lada. We need to use the telephone, Mr Whitey; is that possible?" Elvis asked.

They were both surprised when the Winger's frame emerged from the doorway. They looked at one another, then at him. He came towards them rubbing his head, but he was walking normally. The Winger hadn't seen either of them and he was very keen to do so despite their state of neglect. Whitey introduced them and gave a spiel about the ones who slept in the shearers' beds and they went inside. Both women were dying of thirst and gulped down the cold water the Winger had put on the table in a big jug.

"The telephone, can we get through to Adelaide?" Lada enquired.

"You can get through to London if you like, but you'll have to go into the main building," the Winger replied. They followed him to the reception area; Lada insisted he show Elvis the rest of the building while she made a phone call and he accepted quickly.

The phone rang at Adelaide and a female voice answered with one word. 'Vladivostok'.

"Sea of Japan," Lada replied.

"Lada, what status?" the voice enquired.

"One hundred percent; we require medical plane and authorities as soon as possible with food and water. We are leaving the campsite heading back to those coordinates." She looked at the readings on the GPS and recited them precisely.

Everything she said was repeated and the phone went dead on her acknowledgement. She found Elvis and the Winger were coming back and looked curiously at Elvis who was holding her throat.

"I feel sick," Elvis explained and winked at Lada.

She didn't understand why but played along with her. They returned to the Winger's quarters and Whitey had bacon and eggs frying.

337

"Go and throw yourselves in the pool, this will be ready in five minutes," he instructed them.

The Winger ushered them outside and pointed towards the longhouse. "That way," he pointed and they ran towards the pool. They didn't bother to strip; they just plunged straight in, clothes and all. The water was cool, beautiful and every other compliment they could think of. The salt which was engrained in their every crevice dissolved immediately and their hair changed colour as if by magic. Whitey's voice beckoned them to come and eat; they reluctantly obeyed but their hunger was in charge by the time they reached the door, dripping wet.

"Can we eat here?" Lada enquired.

"No problem!" the Winger said, and came out with their plates to the veranda. He again rubbed his head.

"Do you have a headache?" Elvis asked sympathetically.

"Yeh, I got bit with something couple of days ago. You with the first bunch or the second bunch?" he queried.

Lada had no idea what he was speaking about but Elvis answered, "The second bunch." She smiled.

"Well I was speakin' to the two of your men and next thing I blacked out. Got a sting or something in the back of my neck. It was bad for a while but it's getting better now. Maybe a Red Back got me." He laughed and went inside.

"If he was speaking to the men the woman must have injected him. She might have saved his life," Elvis deduced.

"We must leave you. Thank you very much for your hospitality, gentlemen. Tomorrow, we will all come back with the vehicles. By the way I believe the key in that one is broken in the lock; could you possible take it out?" Elvis requested, pointing at the Toyota.

"Done already," the Winger replied. "I saw that when I tried to move it; we've got a lot of keys here, they're always losing them on the lake so no problem. Is that one of the first bunch's vehicles you're driving?" he enquired.

"Yes! They lent it to us so we could call and see how her mother was; she is very sick but getting better, like you," Elvis explained.

"I filled yer water bags!" Whitey shouted, as they climbed into the Rover.

"They could kill us with kindness. What's with the feeling sick in there?" Lada asked, as she drove towards the lake.

"You sent us exactly where I didn't want to go. We stole a motorbike and a quad from there and I don't think he realises they are gone yet. You sent him to show me the place I was trying to avoid. I don't suppose you have a comb?" Elvis asked.

"It took you only an hour and a half from the wreck to the campsite; let's see how fast I can get back," Lada replied and hit the accelerator.

Dinky shook off her tiredness and her pain; she was ecstatic, her elbow was moving freely again and her feet had nothing to do except stay on the footrest. She had covered half the distance to East Well when she noticed the small dust cloud coming behind her and her heart sank. She carried on as fast as she could for the rest of the way and reached the edge of the salt. The cloud was no closer and she gunned the machine onto the salt, heading for the campsite and the safety of her friends. It was empty; no Rovers, no people, nothing. She despaired and relapsed into panic. She ran into the women's tent looking for the rifle she had left there, but it was gone. Water, she must have water; her body was screaming at her and she gulped hot water from a container beside the stove. It did little to quench her thirst, but beside it was a large knife Linda used. Knife in hand, she looked again for the dust cloud and saw it in the distance.

Fuel! She grabbed a jerry can of diesel and poured it into the quad's tank; it took all of it and there was room for more. She decided she had enough and started the quad again. She was shaking and pouring with sweat. The cape she was wearing kept

339

catching on everything and she tore it off; there was another shirt in her bag inside the tent she remembered, and she put it on quickly. Water, she must take water with her. Two bags were there and they were empty. She cursed at the speed they filled up and hung them on the quad's roll bars. She had water and fuel; the only thing missing was somewhere to go. She slumped over the seat and tears started flowing freely; the chisellers were delighted and moved in for drinks. They were enough to get her temper up and she dismounted, leaving the engine running. She would wait till they were nearly here then make a run for it; she would be rested, they wouldn't be.

She climbed a little way up the rock and waited, watching the dust approach. There was a lot of it for a quad, perhaps two quads together, but she couldn't make out the vehicles yet; when she could she would take off again. The cause of the dust was nearing the edge of the salt when she managed to glimpse it and her heart leapt with joy; it was a Rover. She jumped onto the quad and sped towards it, waving frantically with her good arm.

Joe looked ahead; he had no sightings of anything since they went in pursuit and he was sceptical. Both of them were dehydrated and starving. Clinker saw her coming and screamed at Joe so loud he nearly had a heart attack; he got such a shock, and slammed on the brakes instinctively, throwing Clinker against the windscreen with serious force.

"Bastard!" Joe yelled at him.

Clinker never heard him. He was out of the cab in an instant and running towards Dinky. She screamed her delight and slowed enough for him to jump on behind her. She waved at Joe, and headed back to the camp at full speed. Clinker was hugging her from behind, and kissing her neck. She tasted salty and dusty. He spat repeatedly from his dry mouth and she laughed loudly.

Joe followed the quad to the campsite. He was badly dehydrated and starving, but his main concern was lack of communications. Dinky was alive and well, but he had no way of letting the others know. There wasn't a hope in hell he, or any of them, would manage to drive back to the lake.

Dinky came and threw her arm around Joe. Clinker made busy with the stove and a tin opener. They were all asleep on their feet but hunger and thirst came first. Then there was the state of Dinky; she could hardly walk and her arm was hanging limp. They had a lot to do before sleep took over and to hell with communications for now, Joe concluded.

"What's that coming across the salt?" Linda yelled, and they all looked in the direction she was pointing. Hanna snatched up the rifle and pointed the scope at the moving anomaly.

"Lada and Elvis coming back!" she yelled, unable to hide her joy. Ian frowned and took the rifle from her. That was impossible; they couldn't get to the campsite and back in this time. He focused the sights on what was getting larger by the second and stared in disbelief at the sight approaching.

"Nutcase! Look at that!" he shouted, and handed Dick the rifle.

"Hell's bells; a gunboat, by the look of the spray." Dick chuckled. They didn't need the sights now; the sight was visible with the naked eye. The Rover was sandwiched between two columns of white spray shooting out and up on either side. The headlights made it easy to appreciate the speed.

"You'd think she was on a racetrack!" Ian shouted, grinning.

"She's on a bloody racetrack!" Debbie retorted. Wilson sucked his pipe and admired the view. There was never a dull moment with this lot; you didn't know what to expect next. He leaned into the cab of the Rover and looked at the speedometer; it went to a hundred and forty miles an hour.

"One estimates she has it up to one hundred and thirty-five miles an hour." Wilson threw them the challenge.

"One thirty," from Dick.

341

"One fifteen," from Linda.

"I'll go for a hundred and twenty – Dan?" Debbie shouted. Dan was staring at the approaching spray and Debbie looked at him with a mix of apprehension and concern.

"One hundred and twenty-five!" he shouted and Debbie breathed a sigh of relief; she had feared he had retreated into himself again.

The Rover was now nearing the point where it would pass them, and it looked as if it was flying. A long white cloud trailed behind it like a comet. The sight was terrific and they all knew why people came to Lake Gairdner to race; it was unbelievably unique.

Lada slowed the vehicle and began to turn towards the end of the bluff. She looked at Elvis, fast asleep on the passenger's side, and tried not to waken her as she gently climbed the ancient beach. The applause of the spectators shattered that desire. Elvis woke wide eyed and stared around her in confusion.

"How did we get here?" she asked, as Linda opened her door and started pulling her out. Linda gave her a big hug and stopped Dick from doing the same. Ian held his hand out to Lada as she descended the driver's seat.

"How fast then, what was your top speed?" he demanded.

"One hundred and thirty-five," she announced and smiled.

"Stand aside, young man, one will collect his prize!" Wilson pushed Ian aside and gave her a full-frontal crush. She giggled uncontrollably at his actions and thought her shirt would burst.

"Enough, pervert, my turn! I came second," Dick insisted.

"Bugger off! No second prize," Ian scolded.

"Arsehole! You're a tarry bastard, Wilson. How the hell did you get that figure?" Dick questioned.

"Observation, simple observation, my dear fellow," Wilson replied and took another suck of his pipe.

Debbie and Dan rushed back to tend their duties with the injured and Hanna hugged each of her colleagues in turn.

"There's water in the back," Lada announced and Ian went to get it quickly. Lada led Hanna aside as the others quenched their savage thirst. She looked longingly at the water bags but followed.

"Vladivostok will send assistance as soon as possible. I think they will be here within a few hours or less. Have you found Dinky yet?" Lada asked, deeply concerned.

"No, not yet, but she is alive. We know that. There's a Rover trying to catch her now." Elvis smiled and Lada frowned. "She stole the quad we came here on. We were all out on the salt, watching the plane burn. They assume she will head back to your campsite at East Well. Joe and the other one are trying to catch up with her."

Lada was delighted Dinky was alive, but still concerned she hadn't actually been found.

"What about them?" she asked, jerking her thumb towards the casualties.

"If help gets here soon they will live; if not, Manin and Alex may die. The woman is OK, she will survive. What about the man at the campsite, is he dead?" Hanna questioned.

"No, thanks to the woman. He has a headache and thinks he was bitten by some insect. Apparently, he was speaking to the two men when he was injected, as you said, on the back of his neck. That makes it only her who could have done that. She must have discharged some of the syringe before the needle entered or he would have more than a headache. She must explain when she can," Lada answered. Hanna ran away, she couldn't stand watching everybody drinking any longer and she grabbed the bag from Ian, kicking him on the leg as she did so. He came towards Lada with arms outstretched.

"Well! What's the crack?" he asked.

She took his hand and they walked the short distance to the ancient beach. She kissed him and they stared out towards the remains of the Cessna.

"They will send assistance soon; I expect it here within an hour," she announced, somewhat sadly.

"You have a lot of explaining to do!" Ian insisted. She looked at him and shrugged.

"Ian, what happened is at international level. I would love to explain everything to you, but I don't know what they want you to know. What they don't want you to know. And I don't know who they want to know, what. Do you understand?" She smiled.

"No, but I get the gist of it. You're trying to tell me the authorities will decide what we're allowed to know. And what we're not allowed to know will be a cover- up. Is that right?" he replied. She looked at him and enlarged her eyes as only she could, compressed both her lips together and shook her head, sending blonde hair swinging along her back. Ian slapped her hard in the rump and she burst out laughing. They returned to the others.

"You know about Dinky?" Ian asked.

"Yes, Hanna told me, but I wish we could find out if she was all right. It's a long way from here to East Well," Lada answered.

Debbie had been tight with the water, only allowing the injured small drops from a cloth to drink so as to spread out what water they had and that wasn't very much. Now they had plenty and according to Hanna help was on its way. She managed to spoon feed Manin and Alex and could see by their reaction they were desperate for more. The pilot was also taking water; he was in extreme pain. It appeared his leg injuries were the only ones of concern but, to be sure, she and Dan had checked his head and all over his torso for any sign of trauma. He would live, he just had to suffer.

Ronnie was still in shock; her entire face was badly bruised, her eyes nearly closed, and her mouth puffed out like a fish. She squatted on the seat, a picture of pain and anguish. Debbie left the water bottle beside her and she knew it was there. She showed no interest. Debbie left and Elvis stuck her head inside the door.

"The man at the campsite, he is alive. The man with one arm, he is OK!" she informed Ronnie and left. Ronnie reached for the water bottle and took a drink. At least she wouldn't be charged with murder or attempted murder and, from what she had heard, the girl appeared to be alive. The news about the Winger stimulated her brain and she started scheming how she could pass blame. She might get out of this yet. She took another swallow of water.

Wilson and Dick had made their way to the beach and looked at the still smouldering wreckage out on the salt.

"Now the fun begins," Wilson said. Dick nodded.

"Yep! Now the fun begins. What you thinking?" he queried Wilson.

"I believe we would be wise to get a receipt for the return of the gems under seal," Wilson advised.

"Yeh, that's what's been buggin' me. We hand them over to Christ knows who? How the hell are we gonna claim anything?" Dick voiced.

"Come on, we can hide them until we have an agreement," Wilson suggested. They strolled back and waited their chance. The mookas were lying against the rock face where Ian had dropped them. They sat on the quad nearest to the box and waited.

"As soon as that plane comes, grab them. Nobody will be looking this way. We can get them hidden in the sand over there quickly," Dick suggested, pointing to the small sand hill opposite, some twenty metres distant. Ian noticed the pair and went to them.

"What are you bloody pair up to?" he demanded.

"You're a suspicious bugger," Dick barked at him.

"What the hell are we going to do with that?" Ian pointed at the mookas.

"To negotiate with *you* would be like negotiating with an electric eel, such is your finesse, young man. Resume your position as plane spotter, and make sure they all have your undivided attention," Wilson advised.

"And stuff you too," Ian said and returned to Lada.

Ian insisted those who weren't looking after the injured go to the shore and watch for the plane coming. The wreckage of the Cessna and the remaining smoke would be seen from the air miles away against the white salt, he concluded, and there was nothing to do except wait.

They spotted one, then two planes, coming so high from the south that they didn't look as if they would land on the lake. They came on, both twin engine propeller driven by the sound of them. They were at least several thousand feet high and coming one behind the other. They passed in front about a mile out and circled towards the wreckage, losing height as they went. They were still very high when they passed overhead and then headed south back the way they had come. Ian noted they were steadily losing height. Debbie and Dan came to watch and everybody was glued to developments. The first plane banked and came around in a tight turn to port. It seemed as if a big one was landing with a little one on its back, they were so lined up. The first plane hit the salt effortlessly sending spray higher than Lada had with the Rover. The second repeated the manoeuvre and both slowed steadily on approach to the crash site. They stopped several hundred yards from the Cessna and wheeled towards the shoreline. Fifty metres from the shore they turned and headed towards the onlookers, stopping only fifty metres from them.

Emblazoned on the side of each plane was RAAF - BEACHCRAFT KING AIR 350. They were impressive and much bigger than anybody had expected. The second plane halted and shut down. As soon as its engine stopped the door opened and many people scrambled out onto the salt; they were all in uniform and carried stretchers and medical bundles. Leading them was a young officer.

"I am a doctor. Where are the injured?" he asked Ian.

"In the Rovers, there are two professional nurses with them. They'll update you. We're glad to see you," Ian answered.

In addition to the doctor there were another ten people behind him. They all smiled as they hurried up the beach, but none spoke.

Dick came and stood beside Ian.

"All fixed," he announced. Wilson joined them as a third plane came low from the south. This one was smaller and was coming in low. It landed clear of the wreckage and taxied towards the two parked planes.

"Busy place!" Dick commented.

"My superior has arrived!" Lada shouted at Ian and she started moving down the beach to meet the small plane on the salt. Ian noticed there was no movement from the first plane; no door opened, nobody came out; it just sat there.

He watched as Lada approached the smaller, single engine plane. The door opened and the steps came down. Lada disappeared inside. The engine was still running and almost instantly Lada came out again. She ran towards Ian.

"You go or I go, we must see if the others are all right at East Well!" she shouted, half way up the beach.

"You go!" Ian shouted back and she left.

They watched as the plane became airborne and banked to the west.

Lada sat next to the pilot and accepted the radio muffs he handed her. She put them on and pointed ahead.

"That way," she spoke into the mike. The ground was streaming under them and the plane stayed at two hundred feet, it was exhilarating; she loved low flying but she was worried to death about Dinky. She really loved that girl and dreaded anything happening to her.

"That's East Well ahead. You can see the salt," she spoke into the mike.

"I see it; where exactly do you think they are?" the pilot asked.

"You will see a peninsula soon, they are on the south end of the peninsula," Lada instructed. The pilot saw what she described and headed straight for the end she had indicated. The Rover came into view, and then they saw the quad. Tents, trailers and everything else flashed past below them but there was no sign of life. The pilot circled around and approached much lower than his first run; this time he was barely a hundred feet high and he came over the campsite at full throttle.

The three were fed and watered; they were also in a deep sleep, all in the men's tent and all snoring loudly, especially Dinky.

Joe sat bolt upright.

"What the hell was that?" he shouted, wondering if he was dreaming but the engine sound was still audible. He crawled to the door of the tent and looked out. There was nothing but he could still hear the engine; he crawled outside and stood up. He spotted the plane lining up for another run and ran out clear of the rock, waving his arms madly.

Lada saw him but he was alone and that meant he was OK but where were the other two?

Joe dived into the tent and wrenched Clinker to his feet, he literally kicked him out the door and he scooped up Dinky in his arms. There was no way she was going to wake up.

"Move your arse!" Joe yelled at Clinker, who was totally confused. The plane made another low pass and Lada's heart sank as she saw Dinky in Joe's arms; she was distraught.

"She is injured and we can't help her," she spoke into the mike. Another voice cut into the conversation, a woman's voice, sharp and precise.

"Land the plane, pilot," it ordered and Lada smiled. The pilot circled to the south and throttled back the engine.

"The salt to the right is good; I don't know about anywhere else," Lada informed him.

"To the right of the peninsula then," he replied, and steadied the plane on the stretch they had traversed on the quad. The touchdown was smooth and professional. The plane swung around as soon as it slowed and headed back towards the figures now on the salt making their way towards the plane.

Lada felt tears welling up as she looked at the limp figure Joe was carrying and a lump grew in her throat. She jumped out of her seat and threw the door open, hardly touching the steps as she hit the salt. She ran towards Joe and the tears flowed uncontrollably the closer she got to Dinky. She smothered her with her hair and stroked her face. She looked at Joe, her lips trembling.

"What the hell's wrong with you? This little shit's fast asleep, there's nothing wrong with her!" Joe shouted in Lada's ear over the engine noise. Lada's tears switched from grief to joy and her body rocked with emotion. She smothered Dinky in hair and kisses, whispering in Russian things they could not understand. Joe smiled and so did Clinker; they had never seen such outpouring of joy. They headed for the door and the woman met them with outstretched arms. She gathered Dinky into them and headed inside.

"Get in!" Lada ordered the two of them and followed them inside. She closed the door and managed to squeeze herself forward beside the pilot. He gave her the thumbs up and she responded with the same. They were airborne within a minute and heading back to the lake at full throttle.

The woman still had Dinky across her lap and she was stroking her forehead. She looked so sweet, lying there sound asleep. Had Dinky woken up she would have thought the same of her mentor. She was stunning, slightly older than the other three but not much. She had long brown hair and blue eyes that sparkled like sun spots on the ocean. Her lips were as red as cherries. She had nothing unnatural on apart from her clothes and they were sparse. Joe and Clinker were trying not to look at her but that was difficult, and each kept turning around to check Dinky was all right. The woman smiled.

Distances which had taken them hours to traverse were eaten up in minutes. They had no sooner taken off than the pilot began to lose height and the lake came into view. His landing was perfect and he taxied the plane as close to the second one as he dared.

A stream of people piled onto the salt and ran towards the plane, Wilson and Dick amongst them. Lada opened the door and lowered the steps. Joe and Clinker jumped onto the salt just as Debbie reached them. The woman lifted the still sound-asleep Dinky carefully, handing her to Lada. Debbie's mouth dropped open and her heart leapt.

"She's asleep, nothing wrong with her," Joe whispered into his sister's ear. Debbie looked at the limp figure and stared at her feet. *Why the hell was she wearing socks?* she thought, *and in this heat?* She stopped Lada and peeled a sock off.

"Nothing wrong with her be damned! Look at her feet, they're cut to bits. Get her into the plane," Debbie ordered quietly and Lada laid Dinky gently onto the stretcher. She tried to wake up but grunted and started snoring again. They had to laugh; even in her sleep she could at least make you chuckle.

Three stretchers had already been loaded onto the second Beechcraft. The doctor looked at Dinky's feet before she also disappeared inside, the doctor following.

Debbie turned to face everybody; they were anxious to know Dinky's state of health, indeed desperate to know. She put both thumbs up and everybody visibly relaxed.

Ian joined Lada; she looked shattered and he hugged her tightly. She cast a glimpse at the door of the small plane before planting a kiss on his cheek.

Dick whistled quietly as the figure emerged from the small plane. She was medium build with long flowing brown hair which hung across her left eye and cascaded down her back to the curve at which her two legs met. A mini skirt and blouse, both matching white, highlighted her olive skin. She carried a briefcase in her left hand and walked as if she was on the catwalk. She noted Dick's and Wilson's stares and smiled. Passing the first Beechcraft she approached the second. The door opened for the first time and the steps came down. All eyes were on her, a fact which Lada noted with satisfaction. She winked at Elvis and Hanna and they knew what she meant. The boss still had it.

"Too old for me!" Dick threw at the grinning Lada.

"Too big for me," Wilson put in, slapping his chest.

Ian didn't share their light-hearted banter; Dinky was OK but this wasn't good. Too many people and too much confusion. If somebody knew what was going on here it certainly wasn't him, and he was getting pissed. He joined the fossils and they looked sympathetically at him.

"If you know what the hell's going on here, arseholes, you'd better tell me!" he scoffed.

"Patience, my dear boy, patience! All will be revealed in due course," Wilson advised, adding to Ian's frustration.

The smell of food suddenly filled the air and two men came out of the second Beechcraft holding trays of pre-packed meals. They descended on them like seagulls, everybody grabbing a carton of whatever was on offer; they weren't fussy and the trays were empty in seconds.

"KFC be damned!" Linda hissed, through a mouthful of chicken.

Another man appeared with jugs of juice and that too was hoovered up instantly. The food and drink settled Ian and he relaxed a little. Elvis and Lada were the only two who didn't eat; they explained they had had bacon and eggs at the campsite earlier and a swim to boot.

The woman appeared at the door of the Beechcraft and beckoned Lada. She went and they exchanged words; Lada returned to Ian.

"It's time! She wants you, Captain Dick and Captain Wilson to join her – when you finish eating," Lada informed him

They gulped down the last of their meal and washed it down with mouthfuls of juice. They were all conscious of their appearance but Lada looked worse than anybody and she was striding towards the plane. They fell in behind her.

"Come!" she invited, and mounted the steps.

The interior was dark and cool, the window shutters were down and bright sunlight hung in strips down each side of the shutters. Their eyes adjusted quickly and before them the plane's interior was anything except what they had expected. Five men and the woman stood before them, one dressed in RAAF uniform, the others dressed in white shirts and ties.

"This is Ian Ingles, Captain Wilson and Captain Dick," Lada introduced them and went to walk away.

"Lada! Stay here," the woman ordered. Her voice was deep, but she had no accent.

"G'day, gentlemen; I am Major Dunstan, RAAF. Let me introduce you. This good lady is Victoria. She represents Russian special operations." Victoria bowed and sat down. "These gentlemen are Australian special branch and from right to left we have Andrew, in the centre is Charles and lastly Morgan. Protocol demands we have an observer representing both governments and here we have Mr Yeltsin, representing the

Russian government, and Mr Whitlam, representing the Australian government. These two gentlemen have the power of attorney and anything agreed here must be sanctioned by them. They will observe, but may wish to question should there be a need. As you can see their names are on their shirt badges and here are yours." Dunstan handed each their respective name badge, and looked at Victoria.

"This is Lada, my team leader. She will sit in on this conversation; she may have information which is relevant. Please be seated," she invited Lada. The special branch didn't miss the beauty of her and Victoria didn't miss their interest.

The seats of the interior were set out in a crescent port and starboard towards the rear, the arrangement such that one delegation looked across the aisle at the other. They weren't far apart but far enough.

"I believe you have something for us?" Major Dunstan spoke.

"I believe you have something for us also," Wilson replied.

Dunstan frowned said nothing. He held both hands out palm up.

"A receipt!" Wilson elaborated.

Dunstan smiled his understanding and sighed. He looked at the special branch people and at Victoria. She in turn looked at the special branch.

Charles coughed several times and began to speak.

"Captains, Ian, I will get straight to the point. This incident didn't happen. The exclusion zone around Woomera has been temporarily extended. Nothing except military aircraft and personnel will be allowed anywhere within forty miles of an area extending from East Well to this position. All evidence will be removed, all equipment returned to where it belongs. All damage repaired and the injured will receive medical attention. So, you can appreciate it would be difficult for us to give you a receipt for something which doesn't exist," he said quietly.

"And you can appreciate, sir, this escapade cost a lot of money and, until there is a guarantee that the reward for what doesn't exist is paid, it will not exist," Wilson replied.

The man smiled and looked at the woman. She laughed quietly, looking at the briefcase.

"Excellent, Captain, excellent. You will not be aware that the reward for the two men, Dr Manin and so-called Alex, is as great as that for the opals. They are Russia's most wanted. Killers and robbers. Leaders of the most ruthless gangs in Russia." Victoria spoke in her deep voice but didn't look at them. She was contemplating something and they waited in silence. She lifted her gaze from her hands and looked across the aisle. "You deserve an explanation and I have a feeling you will not cooperate until you get one," she said, turning her gaze towards the government reps. They nodded and she continued, "This has been a joint Australian-Russian operation which has taken over one year to finalise. The issue is a Soviet loose end, from the era of the Soviet Union. Billions of dollars disappeared before the transition to democracy. This operation is one of many, some already undertaken, some still to be undertaken. The Keys were required to be assigned to this one, three of them." She paused and looked at Lada, who raised her eyebrows. Victoria continued, "My team are called the Keys, because they open many doors, you can see why. And *we* don't exist. The Soviets were heavily involved in the civil war in Angola. They sent millions of dollars' worth of equipment in support of the communists during the civil war. The Angolans paid for this support with diamonds. It didn't take long before the Russian mafia moved into the scene. There were plenty of gems and they had to find a means of getting onto the international market. When they did, they started smuggling diamonds in a big way.

Alex headed the mafia in Luanda. They acquired diamonds from whatever source they could find. A good smuggling strategy, which delivered hard cash with the minimum risk, was established through their Australian connections, and then on to Japan. Nobody bothered about their activity; they paid off the generals and everybody was happy. However, the diamonds the Soviets were paid in were of the highest quality and weight. Large stones with high value. They were all vetted and either accepted or rejected by Soviet diamond experts. Only the best were accepted. Only the generals knew about the transactions and the value of these Emperor Diamonds, as they called them.

The good Doctor Manin was employed at the consulate where the diamonds were stored before shipment. The generals decided they could pay off the Angolan debt. If the diamonds disappeared in the custody of the Soviets, that was their problem. They would then receive half the value of the diamonds from Alex when he managed to get them sold in Japan.

Dr Manin was Alex's insider. He injected four guards and stole the gems. Alex did the rest and they made their way to Australia by ship. There was no hurry; as with the second-class diamonds it was more important to get them safely to their destination than in any time frame. This is where my colleague here can take over." She finished and gestured towards the men on her left.

Charles spoke again.

"Yes! You do deserve an explanation, gentlemen, I agree on that, but before I can go any further, I must see that the case is intact." He looked straight at Wilson.

"The case is intact. So is the seal, and you have to take my word for that," Wilson replied defiantly.

"You are a hard man to deal with," Charles challenged.

"No! I spent forty years as a loss adjuster. I know how to adjust our loss. Good try, Charles," Wilson replied, smiling.

"Yes, very well, we will take your word, Captain. As I was saying, the corruption was in the police and only the police as far as we can tell. Fletcher, the only policeman at Andamooka, headed up a very lucrative enterprise, bearing in mind diamonds were just passing through Australia, they were not staying in Australia. They arrived by ship at Freemantle, were transported across the Nullabor by truck, picked up in Port Augusta and delivered to Fletcher in Andamooka. From there they entered the legal opal trade and were sent on to Japan legally. The system was full proof and we believe went on for several years. Hard cash on delivery to the Japanese. Plenty of ways to get cash from Japan to Vladivostok, they had it made until the robbery took place." Charles stopped and took a sip of water; he looked at Ian then at Victoria. Victoria nodded and took up the conversation.

"The result of the robbery had horrendous repercussions in Angola. Alex disappeared, and there were mass executions. Manin stayed until he was convinced investigators were on to him, then fled the country. The four guards Manin had injected were vegetables; they didn't know their own names. Manin had no support or connections, other than Alex. He embarked on a career of robbery after robbery. The same symptoms kept springing up all over the country and abroad, until somebody linked the symptoms with the robbery in Luanda. Manin had always stayed undercover, used forged documents, changed identity and plastic surgery and everything money could buy to throw investigators off his trail. We came close to getting him, but each time he escaped.

It was by chance somebody linked the symptoms of his robbery victims to the symptoms of the guards in Luanda many years before. Our investigations revealed that Manin had access to the guards. All personnel who had access could be accounted for except Manin and he had disappeared shortly after the robbery. The mafia connection was no secret regarding the smuggling of diamonds and the leader was Alex. He had also disappeared after the robbery.

Our insiders discovered Alex was still being held in Angola. The generals had held him for fourteen years, hidden away in top security, but they didn't need to hold him now. They had ordered his execution by lesser officers. They were supposed to execute him but they wanted the mafia to keep paying them for his release. The generals were now rich with oil money. Their scheme had backfired at the time, all the diamonds had to be replaced or the Soviets would remove their support. In the heat of battle this was accomplished but then they found themselves with Alex, a good source of income after the war. Alex was the link to the diamonds, and if they couldn't get them back they would ransom him instead. We sent a Key to Luanda. She opened many doors. Eventually, she managed to locate Alex. His location was leaked to the mafia and they sprang Alex from his captors and out of Angola." She lifted her hands in despair. "This is when, as *you* say, everything went tits up. We lost Alex, he disappeared into the underworld.

Australian security alerted us that a woman they were investigating for drug smuggling had gone to Vladivostok and requested that we put her under surveillance. She had old links to Alex. That was established and her phone calls were monitored day and night. The Key in Angola had discovered the diamond smuggling route, which was no longer active. This was conveyed to the Australian authorities and caused big surprise when Andamooka was mentioned and the woman we had under surveillance was the wife of the policeman in Andamooka, when the robbery took place. We started to join the dots. We now had a link. Alex, the policeman's wife, and the robbery. Our top priority was Manin. Even Alex was overshadowed; his climb back to the top was bloody and cost many lives but they were all mafia. Manin's victims weren't. A trail of human suffering stretched back from him which was beyond belief.

At this stage your father didn't exist, there was no reference to him on any police files. He had never been taken in for questioning and was not a suspect. That was discovered by listening to phone calls between the woman and somebody! She

357

insisted 'Ingles on the island knows where Lacey is, they took part in the robbery but Ingles wouldn't talk'. The only Ingles we could find on an island was your father. On the closest one, Kangaroo Island." She looked at Ian.

Ian was taken by surprise and stammered.

"That's not what my father said. He reckoned he was taken in for questioning. You mean it wasn't the police who were questioning him? Bloody hell. The same bastards must have cut off his fingers and broke his legs! But that was years ago!" Ian blurted out.

"Fletcher's wife, Lisa, tried to go it alone because she didn't trust anybody, except Alex. If she told anybody about your father they might go it alone and she had nowhere to turn. The thing is, if your father had reported the assault to the police she would have backed off. He didn't and they knew for sure he was involved. The time lapse we can only put down to improved circumstance. Drug dealing, prostitution, and everything else she was involved in was lucrative. Bearing in mind your father's connection wasn't proven and could prove costly if she was wrong."

"They didn't back off, they sent him 'Where is Lacey?' messages every month and drove him mental. He hit the bottle and everything went downhill from there," Ian added.

"Lacey was a bit of a mystery to us," Morgan's voice cut in. "We had great difficulty tracing him. He was reported missing several years later by a relative in England who was looking for him regarding the death of his mother. That's all the reference we could find. A Ronald Lacey was listed as being in the same battalion as your father and we put two and two together." He reached into his shirt pocket and pulled out a photograph. He handed it to Ian. "That's Ronald Lacey from his army records," he said.

The photograph was of a good-looking young man, well built with a square jaw and immaculate teeth. He had sandy hair, the sight of which sent a shiver up Ian's spine as he remembered scraping it into the bag. He passed the photograph to Dick.

"He doesn't look like that now. He's in a bag at East Well," Ian informed them.

Clearing her throat, Victoria spoke again.

"If your father knew exactly where Lacey was he would have found him. He didn't know but he knew where to look and that's the information nobody else had, information they were convinced he would take to his grave or pass on to his son and they were right. We had no idea how or where Alex and Manin would appear. They might not appear, they might send somebody else. We still don't know how they got into this country undetected. They were a jump ahead of us and if you hadn't returned to Vietnam when you did they would have got you. We had to get somebody close to you for your protection, somebody irresistible – a Key."

Ian looked at Lada; she remained impassive and just smiled at him, but before he could say anything Victoria spoke again.

"Before we continue, I would like you all to know one thing! Our motives were not to get the diamonds back. Our motives were to bring two mass murderers into the open. Arrest or kill them whatever was achievable—"

Andrew cut in abruptly.

"Our motives were to bring down a drug and people smuggling organisation, also responsible for the deaths of hundreds of victims," he said.

"Thank you, Andrew," Victoria said and looked again at Ian. "You may think we used you as bait?" she asked.

"The thought had crossed my mind," Ian replied.

"You're right! We did use you as bait. You were bait the moment you knew where to look for the gems, you used yourself as bait. You could have gone to the police but you didn't. They knew you wouldn't and all they had to do was wait! You had no idea who Lada was. You had no idea two Keys were looking

359

after your mother, Maria. I acknowledge this was a close-run thing, but if the Keys hadn't been present it would have been disastrous for all of you. The mafia would be very rich and very pleased."

Ian wanted to say something but was lost for words; he looked at Wilson, who just nodded his head. What she said was true, there was no disputing the fact his actions were predictable and with or without them he would have gone for the mookas.

"OK! We get the bloody point. What's next?" Dick exclaimed.

Victoria giggled quietly and opened her briefcase. She pulled out a sheet of paper and held it aloft for all to see.

"This document is for the purchase of the insurance claim to the so-called mookas or, as described in the document, the entire contents of the courier case stolen from the couriers in Andamooka bla, bla, bla; there's a lot of legal jargon which alleviates any responsibility or involvement with any items other than opals found to be present and so forth." She threw it across to Wilson. "In other words, we own the mookas, the Australian and Russian government, *not* the Japanese. They were convinced for a small fee that it would not be in their best interest to have their dirty washing hung out, in the unlikely event the gems were ever found," Victoria said, with a degree of sarcasm.

"Excellent! Now we can negotiate directly with the owners!" Wilson added quickly.

"Not yet!" Yeltsin cut in. His voice was very deep and Ian heard Dick sigh. "How did you intend to dispose of your find?" he asked.

"They were going to hand them over to the police on receipt of the reward. That was the reason for leaving the box unopened," Lada said quietly.

"Very well, you may proceed," Yeltsin said.

"All right!" Victoria said, smiling and looking at Wilson. "Captain! In this bag I have a sum of money which not only covers the reward for the gems but it also covers the reward for Manin and Alex. You can take this bag, hand over the box and everything is finalised *or* you can hand over the box. We open it and see what's inside. I am looking for six large cut diamonds; there may be more than six but we only want six. The opals were purchased by us for a very moderate amount; the Japanese were very, shall we say, understanding! We have no interest in the opals, but, sealed or not, if we open the box and it's empty, we all lose."

Wilson smiled at Victoria.

"And you think I am hard. What about the reward for them, it has nothing to do with the box!" Wilson fired at her.

"Very true," Victoria said and looked at Whitlam.

"As it stands, you will get the opals, all of them, legally and any diamonds over the six which are government property. Take a chance, Captain," Whitlam challenged.

"I'll get the bloody box!" Dick shouted and sprang to his feet. He was agitated and had been for some time, Ian had noticed, but why? He had no idea.

Dick came down the steps of the plane and made a beeline for Debbie. She was speaking to the doctor.

"Where the hell is Dinky?" he demanded.

"She's OK, what's the problem?" Debbie asked.

"Where is she?" Dick repeated.

"In the plane, where else would she be?" Debbie retorted.

"For Christ sake, woman, get her to hell out of there. She wakes up an' sees who's in there with her, she'll go through the side of the bloody plane!" Dick yelled.

"Bloody hell!" Debbie responded and flew up the steps into the Beechcraft. Dick headed up the beach and dug up the box from the sandhill. He returned to the plane and handed the box to Lada, who was waiting at the top of the steps. They all stared at the tattered box as Lada handed it to Victoria.

"Andrew, I believe this is your speciality," she said, and Andrew came towards her.

"A bit battered, looks like it's been through an ordeal. Seal's intact, now let's see the way in here…" he thought out loud.

Dick was feeling better now his concern about Dinky had been addressed. He craned his neck to see what Andrew was doing. Andrew took a ring of small keys from his pocket and started fitting one after the other into one end of the handle.

"There's a lot of dust in there. This key's the right one; we'll have to try and persuade the tumblers to cooperate," he said, quietly. They heard a dull click and Andrew smiled. He withdrew the handle upwards revealing two shining rods which kept both sides locked together. As soon as the rods were clear he handed Victoria the handle and opened the case.

Everybody was glued to the contents; the atmosphere was electric, charged with expectation and certainly not ready for a case full of red dust. They stared at it.

"That stuff would get up your arse if you stood in one place long enough. You'd better take it outside and tip it, before the whole bloody plane's covered," Dick announced, breaking the silence.

"Go ahead! We don't want a cleaning bill," Whitman drawled over his shoulder.

"One of you go with him," Victoria said, looking at Ian.

He followed Andrew out. He was holding the case so steady you would have thought it contained gelignite, but even then the fine dust was coming out; his shirt was not so white when he reached the ground. They walked around the front of the plane and he looked at Ian, then at his shirt. He said nothing but handed the case to Ian.

"Thanks, mate!" he said and Andrew stood back. Ian knew what to expect; he dumped the case on the ground upside down and lifted the case up.

There were small packages sticking out of the dust; together they started putting them, one by one, back into the case, blowing dust from each before dropping them.

"Well, at least there's something in here – not what I expected but something," Andrew voiced.

Ian wasn't impressed whatsoever. He was deeply disappointed; an anti-climax if ever there was one. He had expected sparkling gems to appear, not little paper packages. He pulled his boot through the remaining dust and, satisfied there weren't any more packages, they returned to the cabin.

There was writing on the paper and Andrew read it; "One seven five," he shouted out and Ian jolted as the numbers were repeated by Charles who was holding a pen and a piece of paper in front of him.

"That's the inventory from the dealer's records; they only stole the gems, not the inventory," Victoria explained.

"And that makes a total of thirty-four, which is correct. All the opals are here," Charles said at length.

"Any diamonds?" Dick wanted to know.

"No, Captain Dick, there are no diamonds. This was our main worry. If Ian's father or Lacey had opened the case they would have taken the opals out and disposed of the case. So would you. The diamonds are not in the case; they are in the handle – Andrew!" Victoria said, and handed him the handle.

"There is a false end covering a grub screw. This is how the locking mechanism is inserted. The screw is magnetic and has no grooves in it. It looks like a piece of plain steel. I'll show you," Andrew said. They all watched as he used a knife to prise away the outer cover, revealing, as he had described, a flush inner steel plate, round and flat. He took an instrument from his pocket and it grabbed the steel with enough force they could hear it click. Andrew twisted the instrument and the plate began to turn, making several full revolutions before it came free, stuck fast on the end of the magnet.

"Mam!" he said, handing the handle back to Victoria.

"Now we will see what Mr Alex was so desperate to get his hands on," she said, and tipped the contents into Lada's outstretched hands.

A tightly wrapped cylinder appeared, along with more fine dust, and Lada blew it away. Victoria started picking the wrapping away and there was a rush of small stones onto Lada's palm. Another section came clear and larger stones fell. The rest was removed and Ian counted eight large stones surrounded by dozens of smaller ones. All the time, Lada kept blowing the fine dust away.

Victoria picked up the largest stone and held it out for everybody to see.

"This, believe it or not, will be worth over two million dollars. When it's set and polished," she informed them. They were dumbstruck.

"Could we have some water, please?" Victoria requested and Dunstan went to get some from aft.

He came back quickly, pushing a small flight trolley. "Flight service, watch your legs!" he called out merrily.

Victoria instructed Lada to lay the diamonds on the top of the trolley. They rattled as she stooped over. Special branch was more focused on what she revealed than the diamonds. Dunstan took a container of water from the lower shelf and placed it in front of Victoria. She looked at the apprehension on their faces and spoke, "Gentlemen, now you will see the water of life in action." She dipped the large diamond into the water and rubbed it between her thumb and finger.

She removed it and held it up to catch the light. They all marvelled at the transition from a dead looking pale rock to an opaque gleaming gem. She did likewise with all six largest stones and set the rest aside. She handed the six diamonds to Yeltsin.

"Government property," she announced.

Yeltsin held the stones for the special branch to look at, and then tipped them into Whitlam's outstretched palm. He smiled and stared at the gems. He reached behind him and produced a small set of scales. He and Yeltsin busied themselves weighing the diamonds.

"The opals! Start unwrapping them, and put them on the table," Victoria requested.

Eagerly they tore off the paper wrappings and placed their contents on the table.

"Now we will see some real changes!" Victoria announced, dipping the first one into the water.

It was as if a light had been switched on. The transformation was stunning. An orb of green and blue shot through with bright red spangled pin-points of light held everyone's breath. The opal was absolutely beautiful. Lada's eyes enlarged at the sight; she had never seen anything like it. Victoria held it aloft as she had with the diamond.

"I think it's more beautiful than a diamond," she announced and everybody agreed. "OK! Put the rest in and wash them!" she ordered, and reaching into her briefcase she retrieved two small bags and put them on the table.

"Bag them as you take them out. All in one bag, please," Victoria instructed. "Now the diamonds; quick wash and into the other bag. We must weigh them!" she elaborated.

Yeltsin passed the small scales to her and she sat the small bag of diamonds gently on top.

"Wow!" she exclaimed. "Not often you see sixty-three carats of diamonds that don't exist, is it?" She flashed a smile at the three onlookers; they were numbed.

"Who is taking charge of this?" Victoria cut into their unease, holding the two bags towards them. Ian looked at Wilson and Wilson looked at Dick.

"Well, I reckon I could force myself to accept them," Dick beamed, and they laughed at his reluctance. Victoria didn't waste any time; she stood up and addressed her guests.

"Thank you, gentlemen; am I to understand our business here is finished?" She looked at the government reps in turn.

"Absolutely! And, on behalf of both the Russian government and the Australian government, we would like to thank you all for a supreme effort and a resounding result. Well done!" Whitlam said, and Yeltsin bowed.

"Ian, I want to speak to you alone. Captains, when I am through with him I want to speak to both of you together. In the other plane." Victoria headed for the door and they followed.

The heat hit them as they stepped onto the salt. The doctor approached immediately.

"Mam! We're nearly ready to take the injured out," he told Victoria.

"Whenever you're ready, doctor. Make *sure* they are sedated before you leave. Don't lose them in transit," she replied seriously. The doctor saluted her and spun on his heel; he headed for the medical plane shouting instructions to the orderlies. Ian followed Victoria under the gaze of everybody and he felt uneasy. He put the thumbs up to all and kept walking. The door of the small plane opened on their approach and the pilot lowered the steps.

"John, if you don't mind," Victoria said; the pilot came outside. Ian followed her in and sat down as directed. She put her briefcase down on the seat next to her and unbuttoned the neck of her shirt. She smiled at Ian and made him feel more uneasy.

"That's all the bullshit over. I got the best deal for you possible. I tried to get the rewards for Manin and Alex also but they wouldn't agree. Are you happy with the outcome?" she asked.

"Happy? I'm delighted!" Ian blurted out. She smiled and looked at him, then her face went very serious.

"Lada is in love with you. She has broken every rule in the book by falling in love with her target. Do you have anything to say?" Victoria asked. Ian blinked in surprise. *Where the hell did that came from*, he wondered.

"I love her more than anything in the world. What kind of question is *that*?" Ian replied, agitated. He stared at her. He had nothing to say but apparently, she had.

"How long can you wait for her?" Victoria asked.

"I would wait forever for her if I had to – what are you getting at?" Ian demanded.

"You have no choice but to wait, but it won't be forever. I promise you that," Victoria said, and placed her hand on his. "Lada must serve her time. There is no alternative. A Key can't be released until another takes her place, and there is no other to take her place. I won't lie to you; it will be at least a year before there is, and Lada must fulfil her duties. She cannot be released; she must return to Russia with me and the team."

Ian was gutted and looked aghast at Victoria. Since he found out who Lada was, he had this dread. The elation he felt about Dinky and the deal vanished in despair. Victoria understood his hurt and squeezed his hand.

"I will make a deal with you. You will ask Lada whether she wants to keep your ring or give it back to you. If she gives it back, you two are finished. If she keeps it, I will get her replaced as soon as possible. That will be as soon as possible, but it's the only choice I have," Victoria offered.

Ian knew this woman was trying to help both of them, but the thought of losing Lada for so long was unthinkable. Before he answered, Victoria spoke again,

"Go now and speak with Lada. After I have spoken with the captains I want both of you back here with an answer. Can you send them in now?" Victoria ordered. Ian looked at her. As a rule, he never made decisions when he was tired. He was exhausted but there was no choice.

"I'll go and see her. I kind of expected something like this, but it's gonna hurt," he exclaimed.

"Yes! But you have to be alive to hurt." Her words followed him out the door.

"Your turn to get reamed!" he shouted at Dick and Wilson and they made towards the plane.

"Come inside, gentlemen," Victoria invited them. Curiosity was getting the better of them both; they couldn't, for the life of them, think what she could possibly want with them.

"I think she fancies us," Dick concluded.

"Captains, let's dispense with the formal crap and get to the point," Victoria greeted them.

"I'll second that," Dick agreed.

"Both of you have been extensively vetted by our people in Vietnam. Captain Dick! You can return to your life at sea, or you can stay and hear me out; you must choose now!" Victoria looked straight at Dick and he squirmed,

"My life at sea is buggered," Dick retorted.

"Perhaps as an occupation, Captain, but people of your experience are hard to come by."

Dick grinned at her. She was something else.

"My curiosity demands I stay here and hear you out," Dick replied.

"Excellent! You two are, shall I say, getting on in years, anybody who could stand this environment for weeks has what it takes and I can assure you, it won't get any worse than this. You, more than most, are aware our captains are rather lacking in English. Those who speak English have a distinct Russian accent. All of them, we can't find *one* who speaks without an accent. You did your utmost to help some of them and you were awarded the medal for your efforts. Don't get me wrong; we all appreciate your contribution but I could hardly pass off any of our captains as anything other than Russian. Don't you agree?" Victoria asked.

"What medal?" Dick enquired, and shrugged his shoulders.

"The Russian medal of friendship… The one the Russian captains arranged in Vung," Victoria stated more than a little confused.

"Oops! Excuse me!" Wilson shouted, and raced after Ian. He caught him before he reached the beach and shouted loudly for him, "Come here!"

Ian looked at him in alarm and walked back quickly.

"The box Captain Alexi gave us to give to Dick. Where is it?" Wilson demanded to know.

"Shit! I forgot about that. It's in my case in the house. What about it?" Ian replied.

"Perhaps it's as well," Wilson muttered and headed back inside the plane. Dick stared at him in wonder and Wilson ignored him. "Please carry on, my dear," he invited Victoria.

Victoria threw Wilson a curious look

"As I was saying, to get a perfect English-speaking Russian captain would take forever. I can't assign somebody who speaks perfect English, but isn't a qualified captain. He must be both, and I don't have one – I have two – you two." She smiled and waited for their reaction.

"You are asking *us* to work with you?" Wilson queried, frowning.

"When required, and I may require you sooner than later. Do you agree?" She cocked her head sideways and she looked beautiful.

"Do I get a gun?" Dick teased her.

"How big? Captain Wilson, I would like you to return to Vung Tau. Captain Dick, you can resume your devotion to your wife for the time being. Can you say goodbye to the Keys, please? You may encounter them again and, if you do, use discretion; you have never seen them in your life?" she said.

"Blind as a bat and no memory. Bloody hell, Wilson, I'm a quick learner," Dick laughed.

"Before we go, Victoria, I want to ask your permission to give the Keys something for themselves?" Wilson asked.

"Such as?" Victoria enquired.

"'You have been very generous, my dear. Very generous indeed. We never expected anything like this. We feel the Keys deserve at least something, to show our appreciation. We would like to give them the pick of the opals… We are in command and this is our decision," Wilson advised.

Suddenly, the medical plane's engines started and drowned out Victoria's reply; she gave the thumbs up to Wilson and he went outside, leaving Dick alone with Victoria.

They were all on the bank above the salt watching the plane starting to turn. It threw spray everywhere and people ducked as the full thrust of the propellers bit into the air. The vehicles shook with the force of the wind and everybody was delighted, except the chisellers. The plane taxied well out into the lake then roared south in a wall of spray and salt.

Debbie heard a shout behind her and burst out laughing as she spotted Dinky sitting on the tail gate of a Rover rubbing her eyes, both her feet bound in large white bandages. She looked like something out of a cartoon. Debbie and Lada ran towards her, leaving Ian with Hanna and Elvis. He looked again at Elvis. She was something else and he was glad he didn't have to choose between her and anything. The anything would have lost.

Dinky was fighting off Lada and Debbie, who both wanted to cuddle her, and Clinker wasn't far away.

"Bugger off you lot, where the hell am I? What's happened to my bloody feet?" She looked around and swooned. "I know, just dreaming. You can all go to hell and let me sleep!" She laid back on the Rover and shut her eyes.

Wilson came and grabbed Ian's arm.

"We're giving the Keys the pick of the opals," he told Ian.

Ian looked at him; his mind was somewhere else. It slowly dawned on him what Wilson meant.

"Good idea, I was wondering what to do," he answered.

Dick emptied the contents of the opal bag on the seat next to Victoria and spread the gems out. She watched him silently.

"OK, Vicky, what's with the so-called Keys?" Dick asked.

"In what respect?" she replied.

"This English teacher business. Their roll in general. I'm finding it hard to believe they're even Russian and you!" Dick stated.

"I'm flattered, Captain. And I will tell you because you were awarded the Russian medal of friendship. In a rather unorthodox way, I might add. Our captains must have some powerful friends. Because of that, and the fact you may work with the Keys again, I will tell you. Keys were the brainchild of my mentor, Julia. Like all of us will, she aged out of the position to lead. I took over from her and I might have a few years left in me. Do you agree?" She smiled and Dick feasted on her beauty.

"Oh yes! Many years," he agreed.

"It's very difficult to get the most intelligent and the most beautiful girls at a young enough age. They are all fully qualified English teachers. People trust teachers. English is in demand. Every country has English teachers. To get three to the standard required is an achievement. The pass rate is not good; it's one in hundreds who are selected, and then we get the likes of Hanna. She can teach in English or Portuguese, speaks French and German fluently and some Vietnamese but the must is English; graduation in English, nothing less. Does that explain them?" she asked.

"Yeh! When everything else fails, you use them to open locked doors. Their qualifications get them to the threshold, and their looks get them through. A bit risky but simple," Dick deduced.

"They have implants that cannot be detected by X-ray; they are tracked at all times. Even here in the desert, we knew where they were. We could have mounted a rescue at any time, had they requested one; we have never had to rescue them, their pride stands in the way."

"Well, that's good to know. So, if you're gonna track us, you can stick a tracker up Wilson's…"

A giggle from the door interrupted Dick's anatomy plans and Elvis came into the cabin. She ruffled Dick's hair and looked at the opals and then at Victoria. Something flashed between them and Victoria nodded slightly.

She stared at the beautiful gems and selected a small one from the centre of the group.

"Take a bigger one than that!" Dick insisted but she ruffled his hair again and shot down the steps. Lada did likewise; she selected another of the smallest opals and thanked Dick with a peck on the cheek. Hanna came inside and repeated what the other two had done. Dick wasn't amused; he insisted she take a larger gem but she just hugged his head to her breast and left with, "Thank you very much, Captain Dick."

Victoria smiled at Dick; he was genuinely disappointed they hadn't taken the larger opals. She slapped her briefcase several times.

"Dick, the reward you refused is here. Close to quarter of a million dollars. The diamonds cover all expenses for this investigation with money to spare. The reward will go to the Keys. Their working life is short and make-up isn't an option. Does that make you happier?"

"Bloody right it does. You beauty!" Dick beamed.

Wilson came inside, panting.

"I had to assist each of those ladies up the ladder. Unfit, the young people nowadays," he announced.

"Bowling ball grip, I assume? Pervert! That's why you left me in here. The girls took small opals but Vicky here informs me they'll get the reward for the two Russians. So I'm glad about that," Dick informed him.

"Excellent, and what fate awaits the gentlemen in Russia?" Wilson enquired.

Victoria looked at him intently.

"Captain, do I have to answer that question?" she asked.

"Certainly not, my dear. One suspects they will be smothered in Russian hospitality," Wilson offered.

"The bastards will be smothered with something. What now?" Dick asked, following Wilson onto the salt.

"We wait until the soldiers arrive. I want a detailed account of where everything has been left and where it has to be returned. Everything listed and marked on the map. Vehicles, who they belong to and where they must be delivered. All equipment, everything, don't leave anything out no matter how small; everything must be removed," Victoria advised from the doorway.

"Right, we've got equipment scattered from arsehole to breakfast time. Let's go, Wilson, get that shithead and a map. What's this bloody medal she's on about?"

"How long before the army arrives?" Wilson enquired.

"About one hour," Victoria answered.

Ian had decided to wait for Wilson and Dick. He had met Lada's eyes several times from a distance and each time he had a lump in his throat. This wasn't the time, he decided.

Debbie and the others were waiting beside Dinky's Rover; they were getting a little agitated. Debbie had asked Ian what was happening but was ignored. They tried asking Wilson but he too seemed intent on other issues. When at last the three of them came towards the Rover, Debbie ranted, "What the hell's going on, what's happening?" she demanded.

Dick held out the two bags and she stared at them.

"In my right, are the mookas; they belong to us. In my left, is diamonds; they belong to us," he beamed.

"Dick! Don't be an arsehole!" Linda snapped, scathingly.

"Piss off, Dick, where the hell did diamonds come into this?" Debbie added.

"Hold out your hand and don't spill any," Dick instructed Linda. She did as asked but was ready to jump; she didn't trust Dick, it could be a spider or anything, but curiosity won.

The diamonds flooded into her cupped hands and they all stared, spellbound.

"Believe me now, woman? Sixty-three carats of diamonds, and the mookas. How's that for negotiations?" he gloated. Wilson grabbed Ian's arm.

"We need the map, quickly; we have to put the locations of all our equipment on it. The soldiers are coming and they'll take care of that," he said. Ian moved with him, reluctant to end the moment. They were so overjoyed they danced around, hugging one another, the Keys in the centre.

Ian got the map out and set it on the bonnet.

"How's your memory? Mine's gone blank," he asked Wilson.

"Get a pen or something to write with."

"Here!" they both turned sharply at the strange voice; it was Dunstan, holding a pen. "The army will arrive in the next forty minutes by Chinook. They will take care of everything. Your team will return with us to Adelaide. The Keys will leave alone in ten minutes," he advised.

Ian looked at Wilson and headed for Lada. She saw him coming and went alone to the rock face. She looked sad.

"This is the part I hate," she whispered, as he took her in his arms.

"Not as much as me," he replied, and kissed her long and hard. "Victoria has explained the situation to me. I think I understand but I need to know your feelings?" he whispered into her ear.

She was trembling in his arms and looked up at him with tears in her eyes.

"Do you have to ask?" she whispered. He stared deep into her eyes and kissed her on the forehead.

"No! I don't have to ask. Come! You can say goodbye to everybody."

Ian stepped back and took her hand; feeling the ring, he turned it slowly between his fingers. He led her to the others; there was nothing to say. She cuddled and kissed all, finally making her way to Dinky. She kissed her fingers and placed them on her head; choking back tears, she hurried towards the plane. Hanna and Elvis followed after tearing themselves away from Dick. Linda had a handful of diamonds or she would have taken a swipe at him, but her feet were unhampered and she kicked him hard.

They were all sad to see them leave, especially Lada; she was one of them but the other two were as loving as she was. Hanna and Elvis had their affection also. Debbie choked back tears and thanked God Dinky didn't have to go through this.

The pilot was aboard and Victoria pulled the steps up. She threw a kiss at them and closed the door. They were all of heavy heart as they watched the small plane taxi and take flight. They watched it until it disappeared into the haze to the south.

Their attention was immediately drawn to the large black object coming low over the salt to the south east. The Chinook had arrived.

Ian and Wilson had managed to get the coordinates of the trail bike from Hanna; they fathomed out where everything else was and Ian handed the map to Dunstan.

"Could you please board before the soldiers disembark?" Dunstan asked.

"No problem! Joe! Clinker! Get Dinky out of the Rover and into the plane. The rest of you get aboard as soon as you can.

We have to be aboard before the soldiers disembark," Ian shouted at them.

They were all inside, looking at strange faces that smiled and nodded like dogs on a car's back window. Dinky was still asleep; they laid her in the aisle on some cushions. Dunstan stayed on the beach holding the map until an officer came from the Chinook. He handed him the map and had a brief conversation. He then came back aboard and pulled the ladder up. He locked the door and went to the cockpit, slamming that door behind him. The engines fired up and the plane began to taxi out into the lake. Ian looked out the window and saw a stream of Australian soldiers coming out the back of the Chinook.

Ian was exhausted. Some day she would come back, and she had kept his ring. He looked at Dinky and smiled. Before the plane's wheels lifted off the salt, his eyes were beginning to close.

END BOOK ONE